Rupert James is a celebrity and fashion journalist. He lives in London and is married to a barrister.

He can be contacted via his website at:
www.rupert-james.com

Silk

Revenge is always in fashion...

RUPERT JAMES

CLEiS
PRESS

Published in the United States by Cleis Press Inc.,
2246 Sixth St., Berkeley, CA 94710.

Printed in the United States.
Cover design: Scott Idleman/Blink
Cover photograph: Johnny Hernandez/Getty Images
First Edition.
10 9 8 7 6 5 4 3 2 1

Trade paper ISBN: 978-1-57344-761-4
E-book ISBN: 978-1-57344-776-8

Acknowledgements

Several people, all of them experts in their field, helped me with this book. I'm particularly grateful to Marcus Soanes, Ren Pearce of Pearce Fionda, Helen Moorhouse and Stefano Beretta. I would also like to thank my agent, Sheila Crowley of Curtis Brown, and my editor, Gillian Green, for their encouragement and advice.

Getting Ready

Christine stood in front of the mirror, composing her face into a suitably serious expression, what her ex-husband called her 'legal look'. She wasn't too displeased with what she saw. Her hair was still almost entirely brown, apart from the odd grey strand, dead straight, well conditioned and cut in a long bob; so many of her fellow female barristers were strangers to the salon, and looked as if they'd been dragged through a hedge backwards. Her skin no longer had the elasticity of youth – she was forty-seven, after all, and the only way to have tight skin at her age was the have the slack chopped off. But she didn't sag or pouch, there were no double chins, no scrawny chicken neck either, just a softness and slight crinkliness that could be controlled and concealed with lotions, potions and powders. She took care with her make-up, as with every other aspect of her life. She wanted to appear subtle, high class, worth-the-money – not like some of the painted skulls that she saw rattling around the robing rooms.

Satisfied that she still looked the business, Christine put on her black legal gown – grasping it by the yoke, swinging it behind her shoulders and letting it settle – a move she'd perfected over twenty-plus years at the bar. She stepped back and surveyed the effect. It hung perfectly, accentuating her slim waist, her full bust, drawing the eye down to her legs, still her best feature, long legs encased in dark tights, disappearing up into the skirt of her well-tailored suit. It was always to her legs that men looked first – from clients to solicitors to counsel to judges. It didn't do any harm for a woman in this profession to look sexy – discreetly sexy, of course, one didn't want the clerks to gossip. But if there was one thing Christine had learnt since she graduated from law school and was called to the bar, it was that looks count. Many the promising career that had stalled, unaccountably, ten years after the call. It was easy to blame the men at the top, keeping the women in their place – but, Christine thought, bad grooming was just as much at fault.

Her career had certainly not stalled. After the children were born, she'd returned to work with one goal in mind – to ascend through the ranks of the legal profession, case by case, step by step, from knock-about work in the magistrate's court to being briefed in her own right in the county court, then up to the high court, building on her reputation to attract the lucrative private cases that now made up the bulk of her practice. And then, the final step, the ultimate goal: to become a Queen's Counsel – to 'take silk' – by the time she was fifty.

That was young for anyone, particularly a woman, but Christine was confident it was within her reach. One more big juicy divorce case, one more victory, another round of press cuttings, more credit reflected on her chambers, and she would make her application. They couldn't, in all conscience, turn her down. Her name had been associated with some of the most high-profile divorces of the last ten years. She'd freed celebrity husbands from gold-digging wives, sending the ex away with a modest settlement and a flea in her ear. She'd championed the down-trodden spouses of playboy company directors, taking those love rats so comprehensively to the cleaners that they'd be lucky if they could afford to keep the Docklands *pied-à-terre*. Crushed husbands licked their wounds with disappointed mistresses, who suddenly found that lover boy was less of a catch without endless credit. Ousted wives made a last few thousand spilling their guts to the celebrity press before returning to the hunt, a little less ambitious, a little more desperate this time. It could be an ugly business, divorce. It brought out the very worst in people: greed, spite, anger, malice.

Christine caught herself smiling in the mirror. It was true: the messier the case, the more she liked it. Crime may be more glamorous, with its robberies and shoot-outs, its murders and abductions, but family law showed human nature in all its disgusting glory. It was like having the best gossip in the world laid out in forensic detail for your own private delectation. What other people guessed between the lines of newspaper reports, she knew for a fact, had evidence, sworn testimony, photographs of the soiled sheets, the guilty holiday hideaway, the indiscreet gifts. She knew of the cabinet ministers with the second families concealed in the country, visited at weekends, the children employed as 'researchers'. She knew of the Premier League footballers who visited male escorts for a bit of discreet – in their dreams! – slap and tickle. Secrets attracted secrets. She'd heard stories in conference with her clients that would keep the libel lawyers busy for the rest of the century. It was one of the perks of the job, stories to be savoured privately, hinted at over dinner, noted and filed away for future reference. After twenty years at the family bar, Christine Fairbrother knew more secrets than anyone else in London. She could no longer look at a man in a well-cut suit, a woman in an expensive car, without guessing the worst. She was seldom wrong.

Only once had her radar let her badly down – and that was in the case of *Cissé v Cissé*. Her own divorce. Her own husband, not only having an affair under her very nose, but playing away throughout their marriage, even when the children were small, even when Christine, who always used her maiden name for practice, returned to full-time work in order to support Andy in his fledgling architectural practice. Yes, even then, when she came home exhausted from the magistrates and the county courts in far-flung corners of England to face grizzly babies, dirty nappies and sulky nannies, when Andy was allegedly burning the midnight oil over some new project that was bound to make his name, he was entertaining his girlfriends in restaurants and clubs and half-built flats all over town. Christine had been the last to know – in the time-honoured fashion. It was the gossip of the robing rooms that Christine Fairbrother could handle the hottest divorces in the world but couldn't manage her own marriage.

Well, that was all behind her now. They'd settled out of court – 'amicably' – as the euphemism has it, for Andy was far too smart to risk it all in a messy trial. They'd divided the assets, she'd held on to the family home in Highgate, and Andy moved in with his mistress. Oh, it was all such a cliché, so vulgar, so predictable. Christine would grow old alone, abandoned, wondering where it all went wrong. He'd get through one mistress after another, until his capital and his business were run into the ground and he ended up lonely and bitter in rented accommodation, scratching around for work, calling in favours, an embarrassment to his friends. She'd seen it a thousand times before. If this wasn't her and Andy, the love of her life, the father of her two children, she'd laugh.

What had gone wrong? It was easy enough, in retrospect, to blame her career. Maybe she hadn't been around enough, never had the time to be a good wife to Andy, pushed him into the arms of other women – but there was always a good reason. Mortgages had to be paid, children fed, clothed, cared for and schooled, holidays booked, bigger houses bought, cars upgraded and multiplied. She, Christine, had provided it all – at least in the early years. And when Andy's architectural practice took off, they'd been able to give the kids the best of everything. Isabelle had clothes, riding lessons, ballet lessons, skiing holidays with her friends, the best education, from nursery school right through to a fashion degree at Central St Martins. Benedict, music mad from the moment he could clap his hands and sing, had every instrument, gadget and gizmo that money could buy. He had a home studio in his bedroom. When he went to university in September, he'd be taking a small orchestra with him.

And with Ben gone, and Isabelle visiting only to ask for money and to blame her mother for the divorce, what was left for Christine? What had it all been for, this life of hard work and sacrifice? A husband who had never been faithful, children who no longer needed her, and in her daughter's case actively resented her? Well, thought Christine, standing in front of mirror, lowering the heavy horse-hair wig on to her head, there is always work. And in a couple of years' time, I'll be a QC – able to pick and choose my briefs, raking in the cash, at the top of my profession, envied, admired and feared. Loved? Well, perhaps not, but we can't have everything, can we? Work has never let me down. And if I concentrate, if I focus all my energies on this one goal, then the gown I wear will no longer be wool, but silk – the silk that's reserved for QCs, the ultimate symbol of success.

Christine adjusted her wig, shook out the folds of her gown, and turned away from the mirror, ready to deliver the *coup de grâce* to another dying marriage.

Victoria stepped out of the shower and reached for a towel. She loved this time of day – late afternoon, early evening, her skin still warm and tingling from the sun, a gentle buzz from a good lunch and a couple of cocktails, the promise of a party to come. She dabbed the water from her face, patted her hair and wrapped it up in a towel turban, then set about the long, sensuous process of 'getting ready'. Ever since she was a teenager, Victoria had loved getting ready – the anticipation, the self-indulgence, the pampering, awakening her body and mind to the possibilities of the evening. So many evenings, so many possibilities, so much pleasure to be enjoyed and given . . . And tonight, here at Le Mûrier, Massimo's 'hideaway' villa in Sainte-Maxime, she would step into her rightful place by his side, playing hostess to his friends and colleagues, more than just the mistress. Here, in France, she could be what she really wanted to be, at least for a few days: his wife.

She unscrewed the lid from a jar of subtly fragranced white cream, scooped out a good handful, rubbed it between her palms and made a start. Arms first, feeling the firmness in the muscle that she'd maintained from all those Pilates classes. Then the shoulders, still as smooth and rounded as a marble statue, up around the neck, where a few damp tresses of dark blonde hair escaped from the towel and clung to her nape, then swooping down to her breasts. Ah, her breasts, her best friends, her weapons, her nest-eggs – they deserved extra special care. She dabbed a little blob of cream on to each nipple, shuddering slightly as she worked it outwards, finally taking a breast in each hand and working the moisturiser in until they shone. Then down the gentle curve of her stomach, her thighs, calves and feet, good enough to eat.

Still naked, Victoria stepped into her slippers – all of her shoes had a heel, even these – and trotted into the bedroom. The windows were wide open, letting in a soft, pine-scented breeze, the buzz of insects, the occasional whirr of a passing bird. She could see right across the bay to Saint-Tropez – 'that vulgar resort', as Massimo called it, where they sometimes went at night to laugh at the excesses of the *nouveaux riches*. She stepped out on to the balcony and felt the heat from the last rays of the evening sun before it dipped down behind the hills. There was perhaps half an hour to go before sunset and that sudden drop still surprised and delighted her.

Massimo was down by the pool, stretched out on a lounger, naked but for a towel wrapped round his waist. The garden was shielded from the road by a thick stand of conifers, and was cleverly oriented to avoid being overlooked by the other villas that studded the hillside – and so, when there was no company, they could swim and sunbathe naked, even make love by the pool, in the pool, the sun beating down on their tanned skin, the smell of chlorine and pine resin and rosemary mingling with the animal scents of sex. Massimo loved that pool. Whenever they arrived at Le Mûrier, the first thing he did was strip off his clothes and dive straight in. It was more to him than just a swimming pool – it was a symbol of his success, the first real luxury he indulged himself in when he hit the big time. 'When I built that pool,' he told Victoria, 'I knew that nothing could stand in my way.'

It was hard to tell if he was awake or asleep. One arm was crooked behind his head, the other hanging limp over the edge of the lounger, a book barely held in his fingers. His eyes were concealed by sunglasses. His chest and stomach – firm and solid and hairy, not bad for a man in his fifties – not bad for a man of any age – rose and fell gently. A few drops of water clung to his tanned, oiled skin; Massimo laughed at Victoria's arsenal of high-factor sunblock, and used only olive oil, tanning to a shockingly deep brown, shrugging off any concerns about skin cancer with his usual bravado. 'If that bullet's got my name on it, then no overpriced crap in a bottle is going to make a difference,' he'd say, before handing Victoria the olive oil to 'do my back', which usually ended up with her straddling him and slipping and sliding her way to glory.

'Yoo-hoo!' she trilled from the balcony. Massimo stirred, scratched his stomach, looked up. She leaned forward, letting her breasts swing like bells over the railing. '*Ciao, bello,*' she said. 'Isn't it time you started getting ready?'

'Maybe I cancel everyone,' he said, his hand going down to his groin, where something was stirring under the towel.

'But darling, all the catering! All the booze!'

'We can have a party, just the two of us.' He parted the towel, giving her a bird's-eye view of his rapidly lengthening cock. She loved it like that, when it was stirring, not yet fully hard. Anticipation, for Christine, was often nine tenths of the pleasure – of a party, of a lover. 'Look,' he said, making it jump. 'There's plenty to eat. Come and get it.'

'Oh, Massimo, I just had a shower. I don't want to get all sweaty and oily again.' She knew this would drive him wild; he liked it when she played the proper English Miss. In truth, she could feel herself getting wet between the legs, and was tempted to take a flying jump from the balcony and land straight on his now-upstanding prick – if she didn't break her neck instead.

She turned around, making sure he got a good view of her white, creamy arse, and went back into the bedroom, threw the towel into a damp pile in the corner of the room – the maid would pick it up later – and started drying her hair.

'Ten.'

She knew in her head exactly how long it would take Massimo to get from the side of the pool up the stairs and into the bedroom. He was a fast mover, especially when his dick was leading the way.

'Nine.'

He was still eager, even after banging her for all these years. She was little more than a girl when he first met her – fresh out of university, struggling to make her mark as a journalist, full of ambition and dreams, with a taste for the high life that her meagre earnings could never satisfy. And then along came Massimo Rivelli, the up-and-coming name in the Italian garment industry, now the head of one of the most prestigious manufacturing companies in Milan, powerful, rich, respected – and married. That sad fact had not changed, despite her promptings. But Victoria was still there, still desired as much in her mid thirties as she was in her twenties, still – she hoped – loved.

'Eight.'

And she'd done well out of him. She had the lifestyle she'd dreamed of, the money and the leisure, the beautiful clothes, the holidays when his wife thought Massimo was on a business trip, here at Le Mûrier, or skiing in Aspen, or in the beautiful seaside cottage in the Highlands of Scotland – but never yet in Italy, which Massimo still regarded as home, for all that he'd married an English wife and settled her and his son in Surrey.

'Seven.'

Victoria had a home of her own, a gorgeous penthouse in Kensington, two floors at the top of a perfect stucco-fronted townhouse, with views across London and a key to the private gardens in the middle of the square. She had friends – good friends, she believed, however much they bitched about each other – and even, when Massimo was out of town, lovers of her own.

'Six.'

She had a job that allowed her to indulge her passion for fashion, combing the couture houses, her wardrobes bursting with samples and freebies. As an ambassador for Rivelli Srl – a cross between a talent scout and a PA – Victoria had an *entrée* to every show in London, Paris and New York. But never Milan ...

'Five.'

He would be here any minute; she could hear his footsteps on the stairs. Her hand went to her pussy and started gently stroking. He liked her to be wet and ready for him.

'Four.'

And the job that gave her a salary and a company credit card was anything but full time. She had leisure to develop her creative and cultural interests – to write the book she'd always meant to write, to practise her painting – all those things that you dream of doing when you don't have time to do them, and never get around to when you do.

'Three.'

Pound pound pound went his feet on the stairs. He must be taking them two or three at a time. She closed her eyes and imagined his huge, thick, upcurved cock bouncing between his thick, hairy thighs, slapping up on his belly, his balls swinging . . .

'Two.'

And yet, for all that he had provided, what did she really have? What could she put her hand on and say 'This is mine, I earned it, I paid for it, I deserve it'? The flat? The job? The wardrobe? The jewellery? It could all disappear tomorrow, like a feast in a fairy tale . . .

'One.'

She felt her stomach turning over, half in fear, half in anticipation. She had this strange, falling sensation more and more now – as if everything she tried to hold on to was slipping through her fingers, greasy with olive oil and expensive moisturiser and sweat and her own juices . . .

'Baby . . .'

He stood framed in the doorway, his cock harder than ever. Victoria moaned, as he liked her to, and opened her legs to let him in. Well, if that's what stood between her and penury, she'd better make it a good one – every time.

Afterwards, when she came back from the loo, there was a box on the bed that had not been there before. She squealed, rushed to open it, and from the rustling tissue paper inside pulled a brand new evening dress by Alexander McQueen, the lightest blue silk with a subtle feather print, the whole thing weighing just a few ounces.

She stepped into it, felt the silk against her breasts and hips, where it skimmed and clung. She would need no bra, perhaps not even underwear. She knew how much Massimo liked that . . .

She fixed her hair in a knot at the back of her head, and clipped in an eighteen-inch extension that cascaded down her back. A few deft touches around the eyes and lips, a quick spritz of her favourite summer scent – Gucci's *Envy* – and she was ready for whatever the night might bring.

'Isabelle!'

'What?'

'Where the fuck is she?'

'How should I know?'

'Well if she doesn't turn up . . .'

'I know. I KNOW! We're fucked.'

'So where is she?'

'Stop asking me questions I can't answer and hand me that scarf.'

Isabelle grabbed a huge silk square from Will's hand, twisted it round the model's head, tied it in a loose bow. 'Right, you'll do. Next!'

The model joined four others in a corner of the cramped backstage area. The air was thick with hairspray, deodorant and steam from the iron. Isabelle could barely make herself heard above the unnecessarily loud pre-show DJ set. She had ten models to prep, ten gowns to show, only one assistant in the shape of Will, an audience of tutors, friends, fellow students, journalists, graduates and designers waiting to judge her – and her number one model, her star attraction, who had promised promised *promised* to take her graduate collection off the catwalk and into the headlines, had not turned up.

'You'll have to go on.'

'What?'

'You . . . Oh for Christ's sake, what's this?' Will held up a dress that had a huge, dark brown cigarette burn on the front. 'Who's been smoking?'

The models shrugged and looked gormless. They had come as a

job lot from one of the lesser agencies; it was all Isabelle could afford. At least they were professionals – most of her peers were relying on their thin friends, but Isabelle had managed, after several heated conversations with her parents, to scrape together the budget for a proper show.

'It's fucking ruined.' Will threw the dress on to a chair.

'Give it here. Get that lot moving, please.' She pointed towards the remaining models, who were variously texting, gossiping or staring vacantly into space.

Isabelle picked up the ruined dress, and held it up to the light. The burn was big, about the size of a five-pence piece, right at the front, an inch above the hem.

'You.' She pointed at one of the models, a petite Oriental girl.

'It wasn't me. I don't . . .'

'Shut up and come here. Strip.'

The model pulled off her T-shirt and stepped out of her sweat-pants. She was naked underneath.

'Right. Stand still.'

Isabelle put her hands up inside the dress and dropped it over the model's head. Thank God – it fitted around the shoulders. It was a little loose around the waist, and the drop was too long.

'Scissors.'

Will handed her a huge pair of fabric shears. They whooshed through the fabric – one, two, three, and a hoop of purple satin fell around the model's ankles.

'Walk up and down. Hmmmm. You'll do. Bulldog clip.'

Will handed her a clip, and she cinched in the waist. The offcuts she fashioned into a belt, tied in a bow at the back. From the front, at least, the dress looked as if it had been modelled specifically to the girl's body – and, if it wasn't hemmed at the bottom, that could be put down to a stylistic innovation.

'Now for Christ's sake don't breathe out. You understand?'

The model nodded, giggled, and was sent off to join the 'readies'. The rest were all changed now; Will was making the final adjustments.

One dress remained – the jewel of Isabelle's collection, a violet chiffon gown split to the hip, scooped low at the bust and tightly tailored at the waist, designed specifically for Amelie Watts, the up-and-coming catwalk star who was supposed to have been Isabelle's passport to glory.

But Amelie was not there, and the gown was.

'Where the fuck is she,' moaned Isabelle, choking down a scream.

'Oh, I saw her,' said one of the models, a porcelain-skinned blonde with an unexpected Geordie accent. 'She was hanging out with Maya Rodean.'

'Shit!' The word exploded simultaneously from Isabelle's and Will's lips.

Maya Rodean – the bane of their lives, their *bête noire*, the daughter of superwealthy rock star Rocky Rodean, who had sailed through Central St Martins with little talent and a big name. Maya Rodean, who hogged the press attention for the graduate shows, who was putting her second-rate designs on the back of some of the biggest names in the modelling world, who could afford show producers who were more at home with Versace, McQueen, McCartney. Maya Rodean, who was already rumoured to be signing a deal with one of the big Paris houses before she'd shown a stitch, whose clumsiness on the cutting table had earned her the nickname The Shredder.

Well, if Amelie Watts had defected to Maya Rodean, so be it. The show was fucked. Weeks of careful planning had all gone to ratshit. Yes, she could change the dresses around, stick one of the other models in the violet chiffon, brief the tech team to change the lighting script, the music . . . And look forward to a lifetime of fashion obscurity, picking up crumbs from the great woman's cutting table, her only claim to fame being that she went to St Martin's with Maya Rodean. The Shredder.

'The bitch.'

'Well,' said Will, the violet chiffon in one hand, a hairdryer in the other. 'What are you waiting for?'

'Wha . . . Oh, come on. You can't be serious.'

'You've done it a thousand times in rehearsals.'

'I'm not a model. I'm a . . .'

'Designer. I know. And you're the best designer of our year. And this is your best piece. This little scrap of stuff is the thing that's going to get you noticed. And there's only one person who can wear it. You.'

'But I'm the wrong colour. It was designed for Amelie. She's white. She's whiter than white. I, in case you hadn't noticed it, am black.'

'It had come to my attention.' Will held the dress up against Isabelle's face. 'But you know what? I prefer it on you. Look in the mirror.'

He pushed her up to the dressing table, turned a light on her.

'See what I mean? Brown and purple. Beautiful.'

'I look like a bar of chocolate.'

'And that's a problem? Half the bitches in that audience would sell their souls for a taste of Dairy Milk.'

'Oh, Christ . . .'

'Come on, Is. You've got ten minutes.'

'But my hair! My make-up!'

'Leave it to me. Girls? You ready?'

There was a vague affirmative mumble.

'Right, then. Take your clothes off. Sit down. Let Will work his magic.'

He attacked her hair, loosening it from its rough braids, working on it with a comb and a hairdryer until it stood out from Isabelle's head in a huge, spherical halo. He put two huge crescents of black above her eyes, coloured her lips in deep plum, and dusted her with gold glitter – her forehead, her cheekbones, her neck, her chest.

'Stand up.'

She stood, and he surveyed. 'You'll do. Here.' He handed her the gown, kicked over a pair of jewelled stilettos. 'Two minutes to go. Not bad. Now get dressed.'

She stepped into the gown, the pride of her collection, felt the chiffon landing on her like cobwebs. Will zipped her up and she slipped on the shoes.

'Jesus.'

She stood before the mirror, her hands clasped in front of her legs, her shoulders high with tension.

'We're on.'

The music changed, the announcer's voice boomed over the PA, she heard the words 'Isabelle Cissé', and the first of the models strode into the glare of the lights.

'Hear them?'

There was applause, whistling even, as each new model went out.

'You're going out there a nobody, kid, and coming back a star.'

The last two models were waiting to go, bracing themselves, standing tall, smoothing their gowns. Will put his arms around Isabelle's waist, his hands on her backside, pulling her towards him, kissing her on the neck.

'For luck,' he said, but she could feel he was hard inside his pants.

'Hang on a second,' she said, breaking away. 'I thought you were gay.'

'So did I.'

She was on. She stepped on to the catwalk, blinded by light, deafened by music, puzzled by the fact that her best friend and fellow student, her assistant, her biggest supporter and, hopefully, business-partner-to-be − had just grabbed her arse, kissed her and pressed his erection against her leg.

All of this must have shown in her face. As she reached the end of the catwalk, stopped and slipped one brown, toned leg through the slit in the violet chiffon, letting the lights play on the crystal encrustations on her shoes, the applause reached a crescendo.

They like me, she thought. They really like me.

For a few seconds, she held the pose, scanning the front row for friends and family.

The seats that she'd reserved for her mother and her father were empty.

Part One

Autumn/Winter

Chapter 1

Rain rattled against the windows, mixed with grit and dry leaves swept up from the dirty London streets. It hadn't rained for weeks, but all the same it was a terrible end to a disappointing summer, the clouds marching relentlessly across the sky day after day, cold, barely a glimpse of sunshine. And now, finally, just in time for the August bank holiday, it had made up its mind to rain. The smell of wet earth wafted up from the filthy pavements, where weeks' worth of London grime was being washed away in sour, oily rivulets. The smell reached all the way to the top of the house, where Victoria stood, clutching her dressing gown around her, nursing a hangover and facing a brand new day at noon. Far below, working people hurried along with umbrellas, buffeted by the wind. The plane trees in the garden square rocked and swayed, their dark, exhausted leaves suddenly shiny with rain. It was the sort of day when she felt like going straight back to bed again. Had done so, in fact, many times.

There was nothing in particular for which to get up. Adele had suggested lunch – but Adele had been as drunk as she was last night, and was even less likely to be in shape by lunchtime. There was a Pilates class at two, and another at five, but that would mean having a bath and choosing an outfit and getting the car out and driving all the way to Chelsea . . . And in this weather, the traffic would be awful . . . She could do some work – there was the new *Vogue* to be digested, trends noted and analysed, research to be done, calls to be made. But without a deadline – Victoria never had deadlines – it was hard to get started.

Perhaps she would just open a bottle of wine, run a bath, soak for a while, shave her legs and go back to bed. After all, Massimo wasn't expected until tomorrow, at the very earliest. Plenty of time to make herself presentable, to put on the face that the world saw. But for now . . . She took one last glance out of the window, and drew the curtains. They smelt of cigarettes from too many late-night parties, too many days spent listlessly smoking on the sofa. She really should take them to the cleaners, or buy new. She was sick of green velvet, of the funereal tone it gave to the room. She wanted something light, bright, inspiring. The whole room needed freshening up. Her hands strayed over *Elle Decoration*, then drifted away again, exhausted, the magazine unopened. It would wait. She'd rather keep the money. No point in lavishing all that care and attention on a flat that wasn't really hers.

She tasted something bitter in her mouth – the taste she always got when she thought about her precarious position, her vulnerability. Nothing was in her name. She'd asked Massimo a hundred times if he would sign over the deeds of the flat to her, or at least put some serious money into a savings account, something for a rainy day – because, come what may, as the mistress of a wealthy Catholic businessman, she was going to be rained on, heavily and at length, sooner or later. And when that wealthy Catholic businessman was married to an equally Catholic wife, the mother of a disabled son who, even in his twenties, needed full-time home care, the rain would be that little bit harder. Every time Victoria raised the subject of divorce or marriage, of settlements and outright gifts, Massimo ducked and dived with his usual charm, showered her with affection and presents, stayed for a few days, making love more energetically than usual, then disappeared again, the questions unanswered, unaddressed. Occasionally, when pressed, he'd say things like 'It's all yours, baby . . . It's all for you . . .', which made Victoria hope that maybe, after all, he'd made arrangements. But at other times – on rainy days like today, for instance – she was sure that he had not. If it came to a choice, the wife would always win. Mistresses, even as loyal and beautiful as Victoria, were dispensable. A wife was for life.

If only she could do what Adele had done . . . But Adele, as she never tired of reminding Victoria, was the smart one. She'd arrived in London in the seventies, with nothing but a secretarial qualification from a college in Geneva, and supported herself with a string of temporary day jobs while concentrating on her real career in the evenings. This involved dressing up in smart clothes, sitting in expensive bars in Mayfair, trying to appear available without looking like an out-and-out prostitute, until some tired businessman offered to buy her a drink.

After several abortive affairs, Adele landed the big catch – the unmarried son of a banking family, who whisked her off to Capri and Cannes, showed her the high life and brought her back to London with a bump – in her tummy. Nine months later, she produced a son and heir to the family fortunes, and made it perfectly clear that her little bundle of joy would be willing to waive his rights as the legitimate inheritor if recompensed with a substantial trust fund which she, his poor wronged mother, would manage. The relevant pieces of paper were signed, and today Adele and her son Hugo, now a strapping twentysomething, lived in the lap of luxury, in a mortgage-free house in Notting Hill that was worth well over ten times what had been paid for it. Her name was on the deeds, her income was protected, and her wise investments (managed by one of her many subsequent lovers) guaranteed for mother and son a comfortable old age.

Adele was tied to no one, dependent on no one. She took lovers as and when she felt like it, usually managing to convert them into friends rather than dumping them outright, and assembled around herself a salon of wealthy, powerful and influential men who gathered at her regular Tuesday-night *soirées*, there to discuss business, do discreet deals, and meet Adele's ever-revolving circle of attractive female friends. It was chez Adele that Victoria had met Massimo Rivelli, and it was on Adele's advice that she had snared him. But she had broken Adele's First Law – she'd fallen in love with Massimo, and made herself vulnerable. Now, said Adele, she would never get the house, the allowance, the security that she craved. She had shown weakness in herself, and pity for her lover. She had shown her hand, and she could never win.

Adele advised a clean break while Victoria was still young enough to find a new lover, one who would treat her better, and more honestly, than Massimo. But, try as she might, Victoria couldn't do it. More than once she'd prepared herself to drop the bombshell, to deliver the ultimatum – but Massimo had a way of wrongfooting her, and before she knew it she was more hopelessly in love than ever. She took her revenge with petty infidelities, knowing full well that such things never touched him. Massimo had his wife, of course – and Victoria was too much a woman of the world not to guess that he had other girlfriends stashed away. She was pretty certain that she was Mistress Number One, but she was surely not alone.

She went to the bathroom, turned on the hot tap and emptied half a bottle of moisturising bubbles under the flowing water. If she soaked for a while, and had something to eat, she might feel up to the five o'clock class – at least it would get her out of the house. While it was running, she fixed coffee and a chicken sandwich and checked her emails. There was one from Massimo, confirming dates of their next holiday – to Sardinia this time, closer than ever to Italy (at least they spoke the same language) – to stay at the house of a friend, with a view to selling Le Mûrier – the south of France was 'too popular', he said – and buying property on the island, perhaps near Porto Cervo, the new home for the truly wealthy. Well, she would miss Provence, the vulgarity of Saint-Tropez, the peace of Le Mûrier, the shops and bars and restaurants that she had come to love – but, if it brought her nearer to the epicentre of Massimo's life, so much the better. She Googled a few images of the marina at Porto Cervo, imagined herself in one of those white houses on the hillside, looking down into the sapphire waters, sipping wine and making love through long, hot, lemon-scented afternoons. Did lemons grow on Sardinia? If not, what did? Olives? Grapes? Oranges? In any case, it looked beautiful. The perfect backdrop against which Massimo would kiss her on the back of the neck – his favourite place, after the more obvious ones – and whisper in her ear 'Darling . . . I've got something to ask you . . . Will you be my . . .'

She came to with a jolt, the sound of dripping, slopping water dashing her sundrenched dreams.

'Shit! The bath!'

It was too late. The water had overflowed the tub, and was spreading with horrible speed across the marble floor. She made a grab towards the plug, slipped and nearly brained herself on the taps, caught herself on the shower rail, which she half wrenched out of the wall, and managed to plunge her hand into the water.

The ice cold water.

She pulled the plug, watched the water drain away, then grabbed clean towels from the bathroom cupboard to mop up the spillage. Oh God, there would be complaints again, if the water had leaked to the floor below.

Cold.

Why was the water cold? Not just tepid, like a hot tap left running too long, but freezing cold.

She phoned down to the concierge. They'd have someone up within the hour, they assured her.

Victoria splashed cold water on her face and neck, made a coffee, lit a cigarette and returned to her dreams of Porto Cervo.

The door buzzer woke her; she'd dropped off, a half-smoked cigarette burnt out in the ashtray, a cup of cold coffee congealing beside it. She was in a bad mood now, her headache even worse.

'About bloody time,' she muttered as she opened the door, preparing to take her bad mood out on whatever fat bald idiot they'd sent up this time.

Then she abruptly changed her mind.

Six feet of dark blue overall stood before her. Large, spade-like hands held a toolbox and a piece of pink paper scribbled with job details. Scanning up, Victoria took in a lean, triangular torso, broad shoulders, a thick neck and – oh, my God, the cheekbones! The cropped blond hair! Was she still dreaming?

'Mrs Crabtree?' The voice was heavily accented, eastern European, obviously – well, he was a plumber – but she couldn't quite put her finger on it. Yet.

'Yes, I'm . . .' She couldn't be bothered to correct the form of address. 'Come on in. Please excuse the dressing gown. I was about to have a bath.'

He grinned, followed her to the bathroom – was that his pale blue eyes she could feel burning on her backside? – and put his toolbox down on the wet floor. Victoria's eyes darted down the front of his shirt. His chest was hairy, a few plumes coming over the neckline. That five o'clock Pilates class now seemed a rather distant prospect.

'The water is freezing cold,' she said, perching on the edge of the sink and pulling her robe around her. 'Is there a problem with the boiler?'

'I look.' Ah, a man of few words. 'Where is?'

'I'm afraid I don't really have a clue . . . Somewhere in there, I think.' She gestured vaguely towards the cupboard where she kept towels. He opened it, crouched down, stretched up, displaying his long legs, round arse and massive back to excellent advantage. Victoria feasted her eyes. It had been too long since she had seen Massimo. How long? Two weeks? More like three. And in all that time, no fun for Victoria. No fun at all.

'Is through here.' He jerked a thumb towards the hall. His hands were golden brown, the nails standing out in the palest pink. Victoria heard rummaging from the hallway, a door opening, things being moved around – the hoover, the ironing board, all the stuff she never touched but left to the cleaner – and, finally, the sound of low laughter.

'What is it?' She stood in the bathroom doorway, and saw his bum sticking out of the cupboard.

'Pilot light.' There were three loud clicks, and he emerged, red in the face, one thick vein standing out on his forehead. 'Pilot light gone out. Is light now.'

'Oh dear, was that all? I suppose I should know how to do that myself. How embarrassing.'

'Is easy. I show you?'

'Well, I don't know. Isn't it terribly complicated?'

'Come. Here. Look.'

She ducked into the cupboard, and he joined her. It was a cosy fit, particularly with his great broad shoulders. He smelt rather agreeably of soap and sweat.

'Look. See little light?' His thick fingers pointed to a porthole, where a tiny blue flicker of flame was burning.

'Oh yes . . .'

'If he is not there, you go one, two, three, boomph.' He pressed a button. 'Now you do.'

'One . . . Oh, it's stiff!'

'Harder.'

'Two . . . I can't seem to . . .'

His hand covered hers. 'Here. Like this.' He pumped her fingers down, the button engaged, the spark flew.

'Oh! How lovely!' They watched the flame burn for a moment together, as if it was the most rivetting thing in the world. 'Now may I have my hand back, please?'

'Yes. Sorry.'

They emerged, backwards and rather inelegantly, from the cupboard.

Victoria's dressing gown had worked itself open, and in rearranging it she gave him a flash. Accidentally? Of course.

He bounded ahead of her into the bathroom, turned on taps. 'Now! Hot water!'

'Thank you so much. I would never have been able to do that on my own. It's okay, leave it running.'

He was squatting down again, packing up his toolbox, filling out his form. His thighs bulged, threatening to rip the blue cotton of his overalls. He smiled up at her. God, he was handsome.

'Perhaps you would like to . . . help me test it.'

Doubt crossed his face. Perhaps his English wasn't good enough to catch her meaning − not that it was particularly ambiguous. Victoria didn't want to scare him off, but she was going to have to drop any attempt at subtlety.

She opened her dressing gown.

He understood that.

Within seconds, his hands − those huge, brown hands with golden hairs on the wrist − were all over her, on her waist, her back, her shoulders, her buttocks. He smiled, a pink flush on his cheeks, and then buried his face between her breasts, kissing and licking, sucking on each nipple, not too hard, not too gently. He knew what he was doing. He came up for air, but only long enough to kiss his way up her neck and find her mouth.

Victoria's fingers fumbled for the fastener at the top of his overalls, and then unzipped him all the way down to his crotch. The heat beat off him like a radiator. He was wearing a thin, worn t-shirt underneath, and then . . . Her hands explored. Boxer shorts. No trousers. And there was something big in there. But first . . .

She broke the kiss. 'Strip,' she said. He looked puzzled. 'Go on. I want to see you. Take your clothes off.'

Would he go all macho on her? She'd never had a Polish lover before − if he was Polish − and for all she knew they could be one of the more prudish nations. After all, they were Catholics − and even Massimo, despite all her training, was far from comfortable with being regarded as a sex object.

Plumber Boy seemed to have no such qualms. He wriggled out of the top of his overalls, revealing massive arms, dusted with golden hair.

There were damp patches in his armpits, around his chest. The overalls peeled off him, like skin from a moulting snake, hanging from his hips. He grabbed the bottom of his t-shirt and lifted it over his head. Muscled rippled under the hair on his stomach, on his chest. He pulled his head free from the t-shirt, his hair standing up, his arms hanging by his side.

Youth certainly did have its advantages. In his fifties, Massimo was a real man's man, the epitome of masculinity, strong, solid, a fabulous lover – but there was something about young skin, young muscle, the freshness, the smoothness . . . Victoria ran a hand down his chest, down his stomach. He wanted to grab her again, but she pushed him lightly away.

'Now the rest. Boots first.'

She watched him crouching, fiddling with his laces, which, naturally, knotted. He was like a schoolboy, too eager to get out of his uniform at the end of the day, in a hurry to play football, fumbling, awkward. She liked it. Finally the boots were off, and he stepped out of the overalls completely. All that was left now were his white sports socks and a very worn pair of cotton boxers, which were strained to bursting point by a very large and eager cock within.

Victoria was tempted to drop to her knees and finish the job herself, but the subject was taking orders rather nicely, and so she finished his training. She clicked her fingers. He got the message. Freed from the elastic waistband, his cock slapped up against his belly, cushioned by a light fuzz of blond hair.

'Hmmmm. Not bad.' She gestured a little circle in the air. 'Turn round.' The rear view was just as good as the front. 'Very nice. Now.' She clicked again, pointed to the floor. 'On your knees.'

He did as he was bidden – no macho hangups here, she was glad to see – and looked up at her with those ice blue eyes, his cock pointing the same way, his arse resting on the heels of his white socks.

She placed a foot on either side of his thighs.

'Now then,' she said, 'let's see if you can get this old boiler going as well.' It was lost on him, of course – but, to be honest, that was the last thing on Victoria's mind as the plumber buried his stubbly face between her legs.

*   *   *

'Ta-dah!'

Will threw open the doors – big double fire doors, with push bars, held shut with a chain and padlock that he'd just unlocked – and propelled Isabelle into the studio. It was a large, empty oblong. High ceilings, brick walls painted white, peeling, sooty. High windows, the sort that you open with a rope and pulley, reminiscent of schoolrooms. Some skanky industrial carpet on the floor, possibly once navy blue, now an indefinable grey. A metal kitchen sink was fitted to one wall, the pipes underneath exposed. It smelt stuffy, old, uninhabited. But it was big – twice as big as Isabelle was expecting – and bright, and to cap it all it was located slap bang in the middle of Hoxton, the epicentre of the London fashion world.

'But we can never afford it,' said Isabelle, hardly daring to step in and own the space. 'I mean . . . My God.' She looked up, spun around, feeling the size and the light. 'It's wonderful.'

'Do you like it?'

'Of course I like it. I love it. But come on. We'd blow everything on the first month's rent.'

'I thought the cutting table could go here.' Will gestured towards the left-hand wall.

'Yes, the light's good . . . but how could we . . .'

'And if we put some screens up at this end, we can have a couple of mattresses, you know, if we need to crash.'

'Is there a loo?'

'Outside, where we came in. It was a furniture factory. This was the main workshop. The offices were upstairs.'

'But it's huge . . .'

'Well it would need to be, wouldn't it?'

'Oh but Will . . .'

'What's wrong?'

'The money, of course.'

'Leave that to me.'

'We could never afford it.'

'We can.'

'How?'

'I've done a deal. Called in a favour. You know, friends in the right places.'

'You've shagged someone.'

'I may have done, at some stage of the negotiations, yes, and obviously I made a very good impression, because, my dear, we have got this place for virtually nothing for a year.'

'How? I can't believe it. It's too good to be true.'

'Because because because. Dreary business about leases and contracts and so on.'

'Is it legit?'

'Of course it's legit. What do you think I'm getting us into?'

'You tell me.' But it was already too late – Isabelle could see herself working in the space, modelling the fabrics on the dummies, installing a rack against the longest wall, hanging up her swatches, throwing parties, sleeping, eating and working in this one empty box which was already filled with her dreams. She took Will's hands in hers.

'Do you promise . . .'

'Shhh.' He put a finger to her lips. 'Trust me.'

Suddenly she felt euphoria bubbling up inside her. She kissed his hand, then grabbed it and pulled him around the studio, running, laughing, screaming.

'Oh my God! This is it! This is where it's going to happen! You're a genius!'

'No, Princess,' said Will, taking her in a waltz hold, 'you're the genius. I'm just the businessman. Shall we dance?'

Ben was late, and dinner was cold, but that was nothing new; Christine actually expected it these days, and simply cooked things that were equally edible hot or not. He was at home less and less, as if he was fading out of her life, for all that she wanted to relish these final months as mother and son, before he flew the nest for good and became just another adult. Oh well, she thought, his absence will be less painful when it comes. Perhaps this is his way of breaking it to me gently.

Their nights in together had never been frequent – either she was working, or dining, or undertaking some public engagement, or he was DJing at a club, doing band practice or simply 'out with mates' – which, Christine assumed, meant girlfriends, although she never asked and he never told. Could be boyfriends. Could be just friends. After encouraging her children to be independent and open minded, she could hardly complain now that they were.

It had been a hard day, like every other day – on her feet in the high court, this time acting for a woman in her sixties who had given the last forty years of her life to her husband's farming business, milking at four o'clock in the morning, raising children who now worked on the farm, taking an accountancy course so that she could do the books in her 'spare' time – and was not inclined to accept the £800,000 payout that her cheating bastard of a husband proposed. Christine had a figure much more like £1.5 million in mind, and was confident of getting it. She could hear the rustle of that silk gown getting ever nearer . . .

She put a couple of salmon fillets on a plate, a few new potatoes, a bit of salad, covered up the rest and put it in the fridge. If Ben got back hungry, it was there for him. If not, that was dinner sorted for tomorrow night. At least with one child theoretically living at home, Christine could motivate herself to cook. God knows what she'd do when Ben went to university. Probably exist on microwaved ready meals, like her other single friends – of which there seemed to be far too many these days. Marriages didn't last. Nobody could say divorce was too easy – people like Christine made damn sure of that – but that didn't put people off. She used to quip at dinner parties in the good old days that she was all in favour of the breakdown of marriage, that it had feathered her nest very nicely. Oh, they used to laugh at that one, their friends – knowing, as she now realised they must have done, the vicious irony of which Christine was blithely, smugly unaware. Well, that one certainly turned round and bit her on the arse, like a trusted family pet gone bad.

It was half past eight. Proper dinner time. Christine poured herself a glass of wine – just one, albeit a large one. She didn't want to end up like Linda, her former pupil mistress, still slogging away at the rougher end of the family bar while her *protégée* had long since leapfrogged her. Married and divorced young and childless, never got over it, Linda drank herself into maudlin misery every night, somehow functioning with a hangover – just. The clerks at her chambers didn't trust her with decent work. She fucked up too often, but wouldn't admit it. She said she preferred the rough and tumble of legal aid work, representing those who couldn't speak for themselves, an advocate for battered wives, illegal immigrants, the underprivileged.

She worshipped Polly Toynbee, with whom she claimed some kind of acquaintance ('as Pol said this morning'), and tended rather to sneer at Christine's success. The woman was a desperately lonely alcoholic, and therefore Christine couldn't quite bring herself to screen her calls – however much she wanted to.

She forced herself to eat up like a good girl, although the fish tasted of nothing, the potatoes seemed to be made of plastic and the salad was about as exciting as her love life. At least the salad was undressed – something Christine had not been for a very long time. When had a man last paid her a compliment – let alone asked her out on a date? As for sex – she could barely remember. Or, to be strictly truthful, she didn't care to remember. Sex with one's ex-husband, with whom one has just settled out of court, from whom one is now moving on and glad of it, was not to be advised. It was the sort of irrational behaviour that she looked down on in others – like dogs returning to their own vomit, she used to say of those dumped spouses who dropped their drawers at the merest sniff of interest from former partners. Well, she'd done it herself, what, a year ago? Two years? When Andy had come round to discuss the endless vexed question of Isabelle's finances and future, when they'd opened a bottle of wine and got talking about the old days, and ended up in, or rather on, what had once been the marital bed. And God, it had been so good. They fitted together so well. She knew every contour of that fine, black body, every sensitive part, every trick to bring him pleasure, just as he knew her. It had been quick, and frantic, and afterwards they both felt strange, and he left quickly, remembering a prior engagement . . .

Never again, she'd said then, little knowing that it meant never again with anyone.

Well, men were a distraction. She had other things to focus on now – like that application to become a Queen's Counsel. After this case, God and the Judge willing, she would be ready – and they would have to find some damn good reasons to turn her down. Her hands were clean, her record impeccable, there was no scandal or 'history' attached to her – and she intended to keep it that way. Work would fill the unforgiving hours at home, alone. With just herself to take care of, there would be more time to prepare her briefs, research case law, find that telling precedent that could be pulled out of the hat at the critical moment . . .

And was that it? Nights at home, swotting over papers as she had done when she was qualifying? The adrenalin rush of picking up a brief on a Monday night, with only twelve hours before your court appearance in some far-flung regional dump, no prospect of sleep, seat-of-the-pants stuff, thinking on your feet . . . And she'd still managed to fit in friends and parties and the first ecstatic months of her relationship with Andy, turning up at court still drunk, still high on sex, it must have been written all over her face, she must have smelt of him . . .

There was no point in dwelling on the past, although every avenue of thought seemed to lead there. She was forty-seven, single, starting again, the mother of two children of whom she was very proud, and very fond, although she wondered how much the feeling was reciprocated. Ben was a sweetheart, of course, big on the cuddles, always telling her (particularly since the divorce) that she was his best friend and the World's Number One Mum – but he could not have been less interested in her career if he tried. It was, for him, just a fact of life, the thing that put bread on the table. Mummy goes to work in a funny black dress and a white hat, he'd said when he was five, and never got much further than that.

As for Isabelle, her firstborn, her beautiful daughter, whom she loved and worried about far too much for both of them – Isabelle had always been a daddy's girl. Fair enough – she resembled Andy far more than she did Christine, from her skin tone onwards. Sometimes even Christine found it hard to believe that her beautiful brown baby was really her own – although she could never forget the agony of childbirth. It was always to Andy that Isabelle went first when she was in trouble (often) or short of money (always). She loved Christine with the kind of fierce, competitive love that often exists between mothers and daughters. Christine had tried, throughout Isabelle's teens, to play it cool, to ease off with the discipline, to be a friend rather than a mother – and had ended up being neither. Now, quite clearly, Isabelle saw her only as a source of finance. That she blamed her mother for driving her father away was written all over her face – that gorgeous, symmetrical, doll-like face that fell so easily into a sulk or a pout, making the smiles, when they came, even more dazzling by contrast.

She washed up, put on some music – she always worked better with some dramatic aural background, in this case Mahler's Second – and hauled her papers out of her case. Yes, the case of Farmer Giles v the Farmer's Wife was in the bag. The *coup de grâce* was prepared, the weapons primed, Mrs Giles ready to blurt out a few embarrassing facts in the witness box. Tomorrow, maybe the next day, surely by the weekend, Farmer Giles would lose the farm.

The phone rang. Assuming it was Ben with an ETA, she muted Mahler and snatched it up.

'Hello darling.' The voice was slurred, female.

'Oh! Linda.' It was only quarter past nine; she was pissed already.

'Lindy's lonely.' Christ, thought Christine, here we go again. She'd be in Daly's, or one of the other legal watering holes frequented by people a third of her age, or at home, slumped over the second bottle of wine, wanting company.

'Oh dear,' said Christine brightly. 'And Christine's working.'

'You're always working,' said Linda, running the words together. 'Come on. It's playtime.'

'Not for this little girl.'

'But I want to talk about our holiday.'

Holiday? This was news to Christine. 'What? We're not . . .'

'Yes we are. Lindy's got it all worked out.' When she was drunk, which was most of the time, Linda referred to herself almost entirely in the third person. 'We're going to the Gam – hic! – the Gambia.'

There had recently been yet another documentary about middle-aged British women going on sex holidays to that godforsaken outpost of the Commonwealth. Presumably Linda, too, had seen it, although her reaction was obviously not one of disgusted contempt.

'I am not going to Gambia.'

'But darling, the weather is so lovely, and the men, oh the men are so nice . . . And now that we're both single ladies . . .'

'It's a police state.'

'. . . and the resorts look lovely, very good security too, you wouldn't have to see anything you didn't want to see.'

'Linda, I am not, repeat not, going to Gambia with you.'

'Well where then?'

'Look, can this wait for another time?' *When you're sober*, she nearly added, but thought better of it. Linda was a pest, but for all that she was a friend, and most definitely in need. 'I have got rather a lot of work to do, and . . .'

'How's that gorgeous husband of yours?' When all else failed, Linda knew she could get response by sticking the knife in. She had been so impressed when Christine married a black man. Now she could not forgive her for letting him go.

'My ex-husband is perfectly well, as far as I know.'

'Cut the crap, Chris, you miss him like hell.'

'Sorry, Linda. Ben's home. Must run. Let's talk soon, it would be lovely to catch up. Bye!'

She put the phone down. Silence descended. Ben, of course, was nowhere to be seen.

Christine cleared her throat, took three deep breaths, picked up her sharp silver propelling pencil and set to work.

Chapter 2

'Who's next?'

'Sales agents.'

'Oh God, not more. This is doing my head in. Can't we just pick one and get on with it?'

'No. Not yet. We don't have anything for them to sell.'

'So why are we . . .'

'Because when we do, we need the best. We need them to get our clothes into the shops that matter. I don't want to be scratching around in crappy little boutiques and market stalls. I want to go straight into Selfridges, Saks, Harvey Nichols.'

'And you think we can just breeze in and get them to take our stuff?'

'No. That's why we need a good sales agent. That's why we're seeing them. We're creating a buzz. We're schmoozing.'

'And flirting, in your case.'

'Never underestimate the power of sexual attraction in this business, darling.'

'You certainly don't. God knows who you had to shag to get the lease on this place.'

Isabelle could feel herself blushing, and was grateful for a skin tone that concealed embarrassment so well. Will, on the other hand, had gone bright red. Neither could look the other in the eye. Since the 'studio-warming party' – just the two of them, and a couple of bottles of champagne, dancing around the empty studio floor, sharing the headphones of Will's iPod, finally collapsing on the futon that they'd dragged up the stairs earlier, the only piece of furniture . . . And then . . . And then . . .

'Isabelle, this is Fiona Walker, and Dan Parker, from Parker Walker.'

'Walker Parker, actually.'

'Oh.' Will looked again at the card in his hand. 'I beg your pardon. Walker Parker. Fiona. Dan. This is Isabelle Cissé, the talent in our little operation.'

Hands were shaken, seats taken; the studio now boasted four folding kitchen chairs and a rather rickety round table that Will had borrowed from a local café. As they were seeing potential business associates, there was a large piece of pink fabric draped over it, scavenged long ago from St Martins, and a vase of white lilies. Will had brought the flowers in first thing, and presented them to Isabelle with a flourish. She'd accepted them as a gift, until he said 'I always think flowers set the right tone for a meeting, don't you?'

Fiona Walker was giving Isabelle the serious once-over, taking in every detail of her hair, her clothes, her make-up. Either she was an astute judge of fashion, or a lesbian, or quite possibly both. Isabelle touched the back of her head; her hair was tied up in a blue silk scarf, another St Martins offcut, and she had big gold hoops in her ears. God, she realised, she thinks I'm some kind of chav. Fiona, for her part, was dressed for business, in a black two-piece, probably by some fabulous designer but it might just as well have come from Next, and a plain white shirt. Her red hair – dyed, Isabelle thought – was sleek and neatly cut. She looked not unlike her mother. Isabelle felt herself bristling.

'So,' said Fiona, while Dan Parker busied himself with a list of figures that Will had shoved under his nose, 'this is where it's all going to happen.'

'Yes. That's the general idea.' Little does she know, thought Isabelle, just what's happened already . . . The unexpected embrace, the kisses, and then – was it just the champagne? – the sudden flurry of passion, hands clutching, hips thrusting, before they rolled apart, silent and self conscious . . .

'Your graduation show.'

'Yes? Did you like it?'

'It was very interesting.'

Isabelle flinched. 'Interesting' usually meant 'crap'. 'Well,' she said, 'we got some great responses.'

'I loved it,' said Dan, looking up for a moment from the figures, his metal-framed glasses slipped halfway down his nose. Everyone else in Hoxton was wearing heavy frames in black plastic; only a bean-counter like this would wear metal. His blond hair was cut in what could only be described as a short back and sides – nothing asymmetrical, or spiky, and utterly devoid of product – and he was wearing a striped easy-iron shirt. And . . . well, could they be . . . slacks?

'Thank you,' said Isabelle, catching Will's eye. He was waggling his eyebrows in a way that clearly meant 'Come on, girl, follow through.' 'I'm so pleased,' she said, getting the hint, leaning towards Dan, who wasn't bad looking in a suburban kind of way. 'Good feedback from the experts means a lot.' Dan smiled, nodded, and went back to his figures. Oh God – if Mondeo Man likes our clothes, we're stuffed . . .

'So, Will was saying that you have big plans.' Fiona leaned back in her chair and folded her arms across her chest in a way that said 'Prove it.'

'Yes, we're working towards London Fashion Week in February.'

'That's a pretty tight turnaround, when you're starting from . . .' Fiona gestured around the studio. 'Well, from nothing.'

'Ah,' said Will, 'it may not look much at the moment. But you should see what's in there.' He tapped Isabelle's head. She brushed his hand away, giggled like a schoolgirl. His touch – even his presence in the room – made her feel like that. He's gay, Isabelle reminded herself. It was her mantra these days. *He's gay. He's gay. He's gay.*

'Do you have any designs to show me at this stage? Any drawings?'

'Not really . . . I've got a few sketches, but they're at a very rudimentary stage.'

'I see.'

'The thing is, Fiona,' said Will, 'we're just looking around at the moment to see who's out there, who's looking for fresh young talent, who's got the vision to support something really new.'

'Ah.' Fiona sat up straight, preparing to leave. 'So this isn't so much what you can do for us, as what we can do for you. Is that it?'

Even Will was rattled by that. 'Let's just say it's a mutual exploration.'

'Good. Well, it all sounds very promising.' Fiona couldn't wait to get out. 'I'd love to come back when you've got something to show. Some new designs at least, or even, if you can manage it, some samples.'

Oh, thought Isabelle, she will regret that sarcasm when she sees a Cissé dress on the cover of *Vogue*. When she has to live with the reputation of being 'the agent who could have represented Isabelle Cissé'.

'The business plan,' said Dan.

'Yes?'

'It's . . . quite optimistic, isn't it?'

'Sure.' Will rubbed his hands together, trying to look eager. 'I mean, you have to be, don't you?'

'I'm not quite seeing the budget for the show in here. I mean, assuming these loans come through to cover rent and materials . . .'

'Which they will.'

'And even assuming that you're not planning to pay yourselves anything for the first six months . . .'

'Well, no, we'll be living on baked beans and sleeping on the studio floor.' Will grinned, but couldn't catch Isabelle's eye.

'I still don't really see how you can put on a professional-quality show for Fashion Week.' He took off his glasses; his eyes were Wedgwood blue. 'I mean, those things cost money.'

'I'm well aware of that,' said Will, sounding snippy for the first time. He quickly checked himself. 'Obviously we're seeking additional revenue.'

'Please tell me you're not relying on the British Fashion Council,' said Fiona, with a 'heard-it-all-before' sigh.

'Among others, yes.'

'Right. Well, good luck.' She picked up her black leather mono-grammed Louis Vuitton city bag – God, how *obvious*, thought Isabelle – and put it over her shoulder, rucking up her jacket. The woman doesn't have a clue – and she's telling us how to operate? 'I'd just say, don't put all your eggs in one basket. The BFC are hard to impress, and they don't give out money to just anyone.'

'I'm not . . .' Isabelle checked the strident tone of her voice; Fiona Walker may look like her mother, but that was no excuse for picking a fight. 'I'm not just anyone, Fiona. I'm Isabelle Cissé.'

Dan laughed, and Isabelle glared at him; she couldn't help herself. 'You certainly are,' he said. 'And if it's any consolation, I'm on the BFC assessments committee for the next six months. I'll look forward to seeing a top-quality application.'

Fiona Walker raised an eyebrow, and went ahead. Dan gathered up his papers, picked up his jacket, dropped his papers, put down his jacket, tripped over the metal leg of a folding chair, and eventually made it to the door. 'Don't worry. I think you've got what it takes. Just make sure the sums add up. That's the best piece of advice I can give you. As for the rest – well, you don't need a geek like me telling you how to design clothes. Fiona always says I wouldn't know good design if it bit me on the backside.' He left.

The studio was silent; there were no more appointments until after lunch.

'Is she right?' said Isabelle, eventually.

'Of course not,' said Will. 'She's a cunt.'

'Agreed. But she happens to be a powerful and influential cunt who can get us into big stores.'

'Don't worry your pretty little head about that,' said Will, tugging on a stray lock of her hair, 'there's plenty more fish in the sea. Mind you, he liked you, didn't he? Couldn't take his eyes off you.'

'Don't be silly.' She looked down at the floor. She didn't like hearing Will talking about other men fancying her. Oh God – did this mean that she was starting to think of him as her *boyfriend*? *He's gay, he's gay, he's gay.* What happened the other night was nothing, a bit of fun, it happens in the fashion world all the time, it didn't *mean* anything, we're artists, we're bohemians, *he's gay, he's gay, he's gay . . .*

'Are you all right?'

'Of course I am.' Isabelle realised that she was standing with her mouth open, looking simple. 'It's just . . . Oh, I don't know, it's such a big hill to climb. Starting out in business, all this stuff to deal with. I'm no good at that.' She gestured at the paperwork. 'Figures. Projections. Cash flow. I don't understand it.'

'That's why you need me, Princess, and don't you forget it. Before I reinvented myself as the fabulously fashionable creature and all-round gorgeous man-about-town you see standing here, I worked for my Dad's haulage company and did a degree in business studies. How glamorous is that?'

'Not very.'

'Precisely. It's not all chiffon and bugle beads, you know. Someone in this partnership has to have his feet on the ground.'

'And that would be you, would it?'

'Come on. You need some fresh air. Let's go for lunch.'

'And where are you taking me? L'Escargot? The Ivy?'

'I thought we'd go to Al's. You know. Al Fresco. Sarnies in the square. What do you say?'

Isabelle wanted to say that she'd rather eat sandwiches sitting on the ground with Will than eat plover's eggs off solid gold plates with anyone else, but instead she said 'Oh, go on then. You certainly know how to treat a lady.'

While her daughter happily munched bacon and egg sandwiches from a Hoxton café with her gay best friend/business partner/definitely-not-boyfriend, Christine was a mile and a half to the south west, preparing to remove her clothes in the entirely unfamiliar surroundings of a gym changing room, around the corner from her chambers in Middle Temple. There were far too many full-length mirrors around for her liking, not to mention women half her age who could strip off without the slightest hesitation, just as she had done in her twenties, and well into her thirties. But now that she was in her forties, her mid forties even – she refused, at least until she was forty-nine, to consider them her late forties – she hesitated. Gravity had been kind enough to her face, and she looked good in the clothes that suited her – but naked? That was a different matter. And so she had booked herself in for an assessment with a personal trainer – something she never imagined she would do, like bungee jumping, or smoking crack.

But then again, she never imagined she'd be single again at forty-seven. What was it Linda had called her? 'A single lady.' When she surveyed the dating pool in her professional life – serial divorcers, middle-aged mummy's boys, elderly barristers with food in their beards – she realised that she was going to have to start fishing in different waters. And if she wanted to get a nibble, she needed the confidence to take her clothes off in front of a relative stranger. Exercise was indicated. And who knows? She might meet people. Nothing so crass as dating a trainer, obviously – but this gym prided itself on being the choice of professionals. She'd seen a few decidedly attractive gentlemen of roughly her vintage, thundering away on the running machines. Perhaps one of them . . .

Trying to avoid catching sight of her reflection, she stepped into a pair of black sweat pants and a white t-shirt; it was like a fitness version of court dress, she suddenly realised, and wondered how long it had been since she last wore anything colourful. She tied up her brand new trainers, bought after long deliberation with an assistant in John Lewis who blinded her with science and persuaded her that the most expensive pair would be 'an investment'. The bouncy soles felt peculiar, as if she was walking on a bed. She tied her hair back with a band, closed her locker, took a deep breath and surveyed the result.

Well, she certainly didn't look like a lawyer any more. She didn't look successful. She looked – nothing. Ordinary. Just another woman.

Her confidence crumbling with every step, she peeped out on to the gym floor, uncertain of how to proceed. Christine, who could negotiate the Byzantine complexity of courtroom etiquette without a second thought, never wrong-footed, was suddenly without a compass.

'Christine?' A male voice, an Australian accent. Not 'Miss Fairbrother' or 'my learned friend' or 'counsel'. Just 'Christine.'

'Yes.' She turned round quickly, and almost collided with a man in a tight black t-shirt, the words PERSONAL TRAINER in large white letters across his chest. 'Oh, I see. You're . . . him, then.'

He shook her hand. His forearms were thick, not massive but noticeably powerful, and covered in brown hair. 'Joel Warner. I'm going to take you through the assessment today. So if you'd just like to follow myself to the treadmill.'

Myself? Oh, young people and their use of grammar. Not to mention that irritating Antipodean upturn that made every statement into a question. That would never pass muster in court.

But she wasn't in court now. She wasn't making the rules or laying down the law. She followed Joel, and couldn't help noticing what an extraordinarily firm, round, upstanding backside he had. But he was out of bounds. She would never do anything as crass as dating a trainer.

Especially when he was so much younger than her – what, thirty-two? Thirty? Possibly – horrible thought – still in his twenties?

'Well, what about your mother?'

'Oh God, I can't ask her again. Every time I ask her for anything she gives me the third degree. She practically wants to read over the bloody contract. She's obsessed by the small print.'

'Well she's a lawyer.'

'Yeah. Tell me about it.'

'It won't do any harm to have some legal brains in the business.'

'We are not letting my mother have anything to do with this, thank you very much.'

Isabelle scrunched up her sandwich bag, brushed the crumbs from her lap, and walked over to the bin. Talk had turned to money, or rather their lack of it, and she didn't like it. Her fingers were itching for fabrics and shears and pins and needles. Business talk extinguished her creative fire.

She returned to Will, and sat cross-legged on the grass, her skirt just brushing her knees. There was a welcome blast of sunshine, but it only served to highlight her rapidly darkening mood.

'It's no good running away from this, Isabelle,' said Will, who had peeled off his sweater. 'When we decided to give this a go, we said that we'd have to be shameless when it came to raising capital. I've done everything in my power. I've got us a great deal on the lease, I'm applying for grants and sponsorship . . .'

'And you think I'm not pulling my weight, is that it?'

'Stop being so bloody prickly all the time. Christ, if you're like this now, what are you going to be like in the middle of winter when we can't afford to pay the heating bill and we've got three weeks in which to turn out a finished collection in time for London Fashion Week? Nobody said it was going to be easy. If you haven't got the guts to ask your mum for another loan, we might as well chuck in the towel now.'

Isabelle was not used to being spoken to like this, and had she not felt so confused about the whole Will situation she would have told him to fuck off. That's how she usually dealt with opposition, certainly within the family – not that it ever came from anyone but her mother. Dad always gave her what she wanted. But Dad wasn't around any more. And whose fault was that?

'I just don't want her telling me what to do all the time. You don't know what she's like.'

'Yes I do. She's a mother. She wants to feel that she's still important. Right? She doesn't want to feel that you don't need her any more.'

'I need her money. That's all.'

'That may be true, but you can't let her think that. Come on. Cut the woman some slack. From what you've told me, she's not had the easiest couple of years.'

'Don't start feeling sorry for her. She's only got herself to blame.'

'You're big on blame, aren't you, Princess? Ever considered the fact that you might not necessarily understand your mother?'

Isabelle suddenly felt like crying. This was supposed to be a good day, a great day, Day One of the business proper, the birth of the Cissé label – and she was arguing about her mother with a man who, at this point, was looking almost painfully sexually attractive, with his floppy black fringe and his funny little beard and his pale, freckly arms.

'Okay. I'll ask her.'

'Good girl. Just do exactly as I tell you and in two years' time, we'll have made it.'

'You're very confident.'

'You're very talented.'

'But there are millions of talented designers. Look!' She gestured around Hoxton Square, where she recognised at least eight recent graduates from the Central St Martins fashion course, not to mention a few former bright sparks who were now little more than fashionably dressed embers. 'What makes us so special?'

'You.'

'Look, Will, I know you think I'm great . . .'

'I do.' He put his hand over hers – the sort of gesture he'd made a thousand times before . . . before *that* . . . and it had meant nothing . . . but now . . .

'But it's not about talent, is it? I could be creating the greatest evening wear the world has ever seen . . .'

'You will.'

'And it won't make a bit of difference. This business is all about who you are, who you know, who your father is, who's paying the bills. Look at Maya Rodean. Couldn't design her way out of a paper bag, and she's already showing her own line this autumn.'

'Maya Rodean is a freak. A blip. Oh, they'll be all over her at the autumn/winter shows, she'll get great write-ups for her first collection, and if she's got any sense she'll make some bloody good deals and pocket a shitload of money before they realise that her designs are crap and that the only worthwhile thing about her is her father's famous name. In two years' time, she'll have retired.'

'Right. And we'll be the plucky underdogs who, through sheer tenacity and talent, win through to glory.'

'Why not?'

'Darling, if you weren't gay, I'd say you've been watching too much *Match of the Day*.'

'I quite like football, as it happens.'

'You like footballers. It's not quite the same thing.'

'You make too many assumptions about people, Isabelle.' They were back on dangerous territory. 'Come on. Time to go. People to see, deals to be struck, fashion history to be made.'

'Just let me *design*,' said Isabelle. 'That's all I'm good at.'

'Oh, I wouldn't say that.' Will goosed her, and walked out of the square, hands in his pockets, whistling a merry tune.

'Not bad. Not bad at all.'

Joel was holding Christine's wrist in one large paw, gently pressing two fingers on her pulse. 'Sixty percent of target heart rate after ten minutes at moderate intensity.'

'Is that good?'

'For a woman of your age, it's very good.'

'Thank you.' Christine heard the word 'age' rather than the words 'very good', and applied a sarcastic tone to match. Joel was unconcerned, if he'd even noticed. She'd reversed judgements with less, and yet he was oblivious. Thick, perhaps. But he did have very gentle hands, for all their size.

'You're fit.'

'Am I?' She took back her wrist.

'Yeah. Considering your . . .'

Christine put her hands over her ears. 'Please don't say age again.'

'I was going to say, considering your occupation. Lawyer, right? Sit at a desk all day?'

'Good lord, no. I'm on my feet, in a heavy wool gown and a horse-hair wig, and usually high heels.'

'What, like in court?'

'Very much like in court. In fact, actually in court.'

'Like on TV?'

'Usually not much like on TV, in fact, but I know what you mean.'

'You mean you're one of them that does all the "your honour this" and "your honour that" type stuff?'

Christine had never heard her years of legal training and experience thus described, but she said 'Yes. That's me. I'm a barrister.'

'Wow,' said Joel, his eyes shining. 'I'm well impressed. Beautiful and brainy.'

'Oh, I wouldn't say that.'

'No? Oh well, just beautiful then.'

Christine didn't feel very beautiful, in trackie pants and a sweat-wet t-shirt, but it was the first compliment she'd been paid for a long time, and it felt rather nice. But remember, she thought, he wants your business. Wealthy older women are bread and butter to young men like this. Dumb hunks who just have to bat their absurdly long dark eyelashes at an old biddy like me and we're handing over hundreds of pounds a month to be tortured on a mat.

Trying to remember that, she followed Joel to a piece of equipment that looked like a giant's version of the device that was used to measure one's feet in the old-fashioned shoe shops of her girlhood. A wooden box-like structure, with a graded scale of black lines marked on its angled top.

'Right, Christine, now we're going to test your flexibility.'

'Oh dear.'

'Don't worry. You look pretty supple to me.'

Did he just wink at her?

'Just sit yourself down on the mat, that's it, and put your legs straight out in front of you, your feet here.' She obeyed, and he squatted at her side, grabbed an ankle. 'Shuffle in a little bit closer. That's it.' His hand rested on her shin. 'Now, what I want you to do is lean forward, taking it gently, keeping these legs on the floor' – he pressed gently down – 'and see if you can touch my other hand with your fingertips. There you go. Breathe out and stretch . . . Great.' Christine managed, without too much difficulty, to reach Joel's hand.

'Now we're going to try a series of progressive stretches.' He stood up, positioned himself at the end of the box, feet spread, legs apart, his crotch somewhat thrust forward. 'In your own time, breathing out. That's good.' He wrote something on his clipboard. 'And again . . . Little bit further. That's great.' Scribble, tick. 'And one more time, really breathe out, keep those legs glued to the mat . . .' Christine felt the tendons behind her knees stinging, but eased herself up and forward, conscious of the fact that her face and Joel's groin were now about a foot apart. 'And hold it there for a moment, six, seven, eight, and let it go, gently, gently, and relax back on to the mat. Very good. Very good indeed. Now we're going to try some spinal rotations . . .'

The last appointment was finished, the table was littered with notes and business cards and empty takeaway coffee cups from the café two doors down.

'What happens now?' asked Isabelle, whose head was swimming.

'Onwards and upwards. We're on our way. They know we mean business. They know the Cissé name.'

'And you really think . . .'

'Listen for a moment. I'm going to tell you a story.' Will held out a seat for Isabelle, made her comfortable, and paced around the studio. 'Once upon a time, there was a beautiful princess, whose name was Isabelle Cissé. She lived in a castle with her mother, who was a wicked and very powerful queen . . .'

'I don't live with my mother, I live in an overpriced dump in Bethnal Green.'

'Don't interrupt. Where was I?'

'My bloody mother again.'

'That's right. Whose bloody mother was a wicked and very powerful queen. Her father the King had gone on a long journey, and the little Princess missed him very much indeed, because she loved her father and wanted more than anything else in the world to please him.'

'Oh shut up . . .'

'And so Princess Isabelle shut herself away in an empty tower in the castle, and there she found a sewing machine. Now, Princess Isabelle loved pretty things, because she was pretty herself, and she longed to make lovely dresses and to swan around at fabulous fashion parties wearing them, but unfortunately for the Princess she had the business sense of a small furry animal. And so she sat there, day after day, toying with her bobbins, sighing to the empty tower "Oh, how I wish that I could design a stunning autumn/winter collection that would take London Fashion Week by storm." And suddenly there was a strange flapping sound, and a fairy flew in at the window. "Hello Princess," said the fairy. "My name's Will Francis, and I'm here to make all your dreams come true."'

'You're not a fairy.'

Will ignored her. 'And he waved his special magic wand and all of a sudden the empty tower had been transformed into a fully functioning fashion studio, with really excellent north-facing windows, swatches of the finest silks from mills all over the world, and selling agents and PRs and stylists and editors queuing at the door to preview the latest Cissé designs.'

'Yes? What happened next?'

'Well, my dear, the fairy waved that very special magic wand of his again, and suddenly Princess Isabelle had a whacking great grant from the British Fashion Council, enough to put on a really good show at London Fashion Week. But she still couldn't afford to get the samples made up, because she was so frightened of asking the Wicked Queen for a bit of extra dosh so that she could employ a pattern cutter and a machinist.'

'All right. Point taken. Go on.'

'And the London Fashion Week show was a huge success, and they got licensed by a big Italian manufacturer, and got their collection taken on by Saks Fifth Avenue, and they got written up in *Vogue*, and suddenly every celebrity in London was being photographed in Cissé, and before you knew it . . .'

'Yes?'

'The most famous woman in the world was walking up the red carpet at the Oscars wearing a Cissé gown. And the little Princess became fabulously wealthy, and she and the fairy Will lived happily ever after.'

'I like that story,' she said.

'So do I.' He stopped behind her chair, and put his arms around her neck. 'I like it very much.'

Christine stepped under the hot water, her body aching and tingling as it had not done for some time. Well, that must be the benefits of the exercise, she thought. What else could it possibly be? Certainly not the feel of Joel's hands on my buttocks during the spinal rotations, or his chest pressed against my back when he was correcting my technique during the – what was it called? Bicep curl?

She had a client conference at three o'clock, so she dried her hair, dressed quickly and checked herself in the mirror. There was more colour in her cheeks than normal. For months she'd had the pallor of something living under a rock.

She was hurrying past reception when he materialised in her path.

'So, when do you want to come for your first session?'

Christine hadn't said anything about a first session; this was just a trial, she had understood, an assessment, a dry run.

'Next week would be good.' The words came without a thought.

'Monday good for you? Might as well start the week as you mean to go on. And then shall I pencil you in for Thursday?'

'Yes. Fine. Of course I'll have to check in my diary when I get back to the office. Early as possible on both days.'

'Seven?'

'Oh. Gosh. Actually, that's a bit too early.'

'Name your time, Christine. I'm entirely at your disposal.'

God, his eyes were distracting, so warmly brown, the whites so white, so wet, the eyelashes so bloody long and curly. 'Shall we say eight?'

'That's in. Eight till nine, Monday and Thursday. And we'll talk about nutrition and get you a programme that you can do on the days you don't see me.'

'What? I don't know that I'll have time for that.'

'You will. You'll be surprised what you can do, once you've taken the first step.'

He had a lazy smile, very regular white teeth, a thick neck, darkness of hair at the V of his shirt.

'Okay. You're the boss.'

'You got it. Till Monday, then.' He squeezed her hand. 'Looking forward to it already, aren't you?'

She was.

The conference with Mrs Giles the Farmer's Wife was conducted with ruthless efficiency. Even John Ferguson, her long-time instructing solicitor, who was used to seeing Christine in action, raised an eyebrow as she went in for the kill.

'The thing is,' said Mrs Giles, her hands restlessly massacring a tissue, 'my husband wants to put the farm and everything in trust for the children. If I ask for that much, he's going to have to sell the farm.' She was a homely looking creature, with fat apple cheeks, just as a farmer's wife should be.

'So?'

'Well, that means I'm robbing my own flesh and blood.'

'Are you saying, in effect, that you want us to accept your husband's original offer?' Christine sat back in her chair, pushed the file away from her, as if dismissing the case. Mrs Giles seemed to shrink.

'No, but I can't harm my children's future just to . . .'

'You do realise what he's doing, don't you?' said Christine, looking over the top of her glasses. 'This is emotional blackmail.'

John Ferguson, who was adept at the legal poker face, twitched a little.

'He's using the children to keep you from what's rightfully yours. They're a sort of human shield.'

Was that a smirk at the corner of John Ferguson's mouth?

'But if he has to sell the farm . . .'

'Look,' said Christine, leaning forward again – re-engaging with the client, offering her a lifeline – 'if you want what's rightfully yours, he's going to have to sell up. There's no way around it. But think of it this way. The farm doesn't belong to the children yet. He's threatening to put it in trust – very clever. Just what I would advise him to do myself. It's a tax efficient way of guaranteeing the children's inheritance, while allowing him to manage everything. And he'll make you, as the co-owner, a joint trustee. In other words, he's tied you up in a lot of complicated legal red tape in the hope that you'll back down. Once something is in trust, it's very hard to take it out of trust. And if it's in trust, it can't be sold. And if it can't be sold, he can't give you the money you're asking for.'

'Exactly. So what can I do?'

'Call his bluff. Refuse to co-operate, and force him to sell. The children don't own the farm yet – you do. They'll get what's coming to them when the time is right, when you and your husband pass on. I presume that you intend to leave everything to them in your will, don't you?'

'Of course I do, but . . .'

'So in what sense are you disinheriting them? They're still getting the same amount in the end, just from different sources.'

'But the farm . . . They'll lose the farm.'

'They can buy another.'

'It's everything we worked for . . . Everything we dreamed of . . .'

Christine took off her glasses, tucked her hair behind her ears. 'Do you want to divorce your husband, or don't you? It's time to make a choice.'

'Yes, of course I do, after what he did to me . . .'

'Then it's very simple,' said Christine, closing the file. 'We hold out for what we want. He sells the farm, and gives you one and a half million pounds.'

'It seems like I'm punishing him.'

Christine said nothing, but never took her eyes off her client.

'All right then.' Mrs Giles sighed. 'If you're sure.'

'I've never been in any doubt,' said Christine, putting on her jacket. 'See you in court tomorrow.'

Chapter 3

And here she was again, beside the pool at Le Mûrier, no closer to being *la seconda signora* Rivelli than before. True, there were worse things in life than reclining on a *chaise longue*, a drink in one hand, a bonkbuster in the other, a fabulous view across the bay ahead and the agreeable soreness of a post-prandial fuck between her legs – but this was not the plan. Victoria had thought, when Massimo announced that he was taking her first to Milan, then to the friends' place in Sardinia, that this marked the beginning of a new era in their relationship, that she was being 'tried out' as wife material, allowed to appear at formal and business functions, and if she acquitted herself well, proposed to in Porto Cervo. Then there would be the tiresome but fabulous business of the divorce to get through, during which she could express pity and concern for the ousted wife, and a discreet but lavish marriage under blue Italian skies . . .

Massimo was singing in the house, his voice echoing off marble floors, his favourite aria from *La Traviata*, '*Di quell'amor, quell'amor ch'è palpito, Dell'universo, dell'universo intero . . .*' Victoria put her book face down on the ground, took a vicious drag on her cigarette and flicked the butt into the pool. Let someone else tidy that up. She had thinking to do.

It started well enough, business-class flights to Milan, a nice hotel . . . But why a hotel, when Milan was the Rivelli family seat, with at least one house in Corso Magenta? Massimo had never actually itemised his properties, but occasionally he let these pieces of information drop into conversation, and Victoria assiduously followed them up on the internet, even going so far as to zoom in on Google Earth to see where she might one day be living . . . Corso Magenta was right by the church of Santa Maria delle Grazie, home of Da Vinci's *Last Supper*, a nice destination for an evening stroll . . . And there had been mention of a place in the Brera district, a penthouse in Largo Treves, where visiting designers and suppliers were put up, where Rivelli sometimes entertained (when, presumably, he didn't want details to get back to his family). Victoria would have been quite happy there; she didn't expect to be installed in the main house just yet. There was, after all, Massimo's apparently immortal mother to consider. At eighty-six, she still terrified her son, and he would go to any lengths to avoid her disapproval. And *la Mamma*, Victoria assumed, was accommodated in Corso Magenta.

But a hotel in Milan was still in Milan, and it was with high hopes that Victoria stepped into the waiting car at the airport. She had dressed carefully, in a fawn wool suit, silk stockings, black patent leather heels that could be slipped off during the flight, a Gucci bag that Massimo had brought back from a recent Milan show. Her hair was loose. She looked sexy, but businesslike.

Which was just as well, as Massimo had proceeded to treat her like a PA for the next three days. She guessed something was wrong when he mentioned – not to her, but to a business associate who asked him about the family – that everyone was out of town, on holiday in Umbria, as usual at this time of year. Victoria's heart sank; she had only been allowed into the country because Massimo knew that Mamma, and any associated aunts, cousins and nieces, would not be around to speculate and gossip. But still, chin up – she was there, she was near the holy of holies, and it was a big step forward.

What she'd hoped would be a few days of shopping, lunching and strolling arm-in-arm around Milan, listening to stories of Massimo's childhood – a surefire sign that a man had matrimonial intentions – turned out to be a packed schedule of meetings with reps, visits to mills, and tedious lunches at which Victoria was obliged to take notes. She did at least set foot inside Rivelli Srl, the mighty factory that created all the clothes for which he was famous, and the wealth that she enjoyed – and she was thrilled to see the machinists' floor, with hundreds of women hunched over sewing machines, the clackety-clack of the needles, the hum of engines, the glitter of beads and the strange mist of fibres in the air . . . But after the factory tour, Victoria was made to wait in a meeting room while Massimo went into conference with his board of directors, with only a pile of *Vogue*s for company. She saw a rather beautiful dress by Roberto Cavalli, sky blue silk, tightly ruched up the front, which she would go and get at the Cavalli store on via della Spiga, just to punish Massimo . . .

But there had not been time even for that. They had a plane to catch, back to the airport, up up and away to Cagliari . . . Well, this was more like it, thought Victoria, who had also packed resort wear, and was looking forward to some leisure time in Porto Cervo, maybe a spot of property hunting, with frequent use of the pronoun 'we' and verbs in the future tense . . .

But even Sardinia was disappointing, the friends that they were staying with a ghastly couple who drank like fish, and who seemed to be constantly on the brink of suggesting an orgy, and, worst of all, lived in the kind of house that made an English WAG's palace look like quite good taste. If these were the only friends to whom Massimo felt he could introduce her – an ageing *roué* and what looked like his ex-prostitute wife – then life on Sardinia seemed to have lost its lustre. It was with some relief that Victoria repacked her bag when Massimo announced that they would spend the last two nights of their holiday in the good old south of France, 'too popular' or not. Sardinia was not mentioned again.

And there, waiting for her on the bed at Le Mûrier, was a box bearing the Roberto Cavalli logo. Massimo was a magician. She did not ask how he'd known. She simply modelled it for him, and then, when necessary, hitched that expensive sky blue silk up around her waist and straddled her generous benefactor. If nothing else, she had a wardrobe full of expensive couture. Surely, if push came to shove, he wouldn't have the gall to ask for that back? The jewellery, maybe, but not the frocks . . .

The wind was getting up, and a shiver ran across Victoria's shoulders. At this tail-end of the summer, the weather, even in Provence, was unpredictable. Hot days could be followed by cold nights, cloud, even rain. She finished her drink and went inside to change.

Massimo was on the phone, on his laptop, didn't even turn around when she came into the bedroom, just gestured with a hand, clicked his fingers, pointed to the floor, to say 'stay', rather as you would to a dog. She ignored him, made to move away, and he grabbed her wrist. Not hard – but very firmly.

He rattled away in Italian – what little she understood seemed mostly to be figures – and moved his hand from her wrist to her waist, toying with the elastic of her bikini bottoms. She got the message, and stepped out of them. She knew that Massimo got a kick out of conducting business on the phone while eating her out. It was a little act of defiance to 'the rules' – and it was about as far as he was prepared to go, like a schoolboy wanking at the back of the class.

He concluded the call, wiped his mouth on the back of his hand and said 'Hey, baby.' He pulled her to him, and she sat on his lap; he was hard, of course. 'Put on something pretty tonight. I'm buying you dinner.'

'Where?'

'Nowhere. Here. Just the two of us. I'm having Philippe send something up from Sans Souci. You don't mind serving, do you?'

'Of course not, darling. I'd rather we were alone. I'm rather bored of company just now.'

'Me too . . .' He kissed her on the belly, caressing the back of her thighs with light, butterfly touches. Then he slapped her backside. 'Right. Get dressed. There will be plenty of time for this' – he grabbed his swollen groin – 'after dinner.'

'I'd better leave some room, then,' she said, and headed for the bathroom.

Massimo resumed his singing.

'Misterioso, misterioso altero, croce, croce e delizia, croce e delizia, delizia al cor . . .'

Joel certainly knew what he was doing. After only four sessions, Christine was feeling better, both physically and mentally, than at any time in the last ten years. She slept well, she was more alert, and her legs, stomach and backside were definitely firmer. But there was something else – an indefinable tingle that she hadn't felt since the divorce – or for a long time before that . . . When was it that she and Andy had stopped making love? When their lives together, even doing the most mundane things, were suffused with the possibility that their bodies might melt together, like they used to . . .

Now it was back, that sense of expectancy, as if some veil had been removed from the world, and everything was a little sharper, more colourful, more defined. Christine found herself smiling more often, looking at men in the street or on the tube – or even in court – with a renewed interest. Well, they certainly hadn't mentioned that in any of the articles she'd read about the benefits of exercise. But it must be so. What else could it be? It couldn't be anything to do with Joel, could it?

Could it?

She found herself looking forward to their sessions together, and had booked a six-week course, an extravagance to which she barely gave a second thought. Well, it wasn't as if she was going on holiday, despite Linda's continued urgings. And after six weeks under Joel's expert tuition, she would be a new woman – ready to begin again. That was money well spent. Hell – she would put it down on her tax return as a business expense.

But it wasn't just for professional reasons that she looked forward to seeing Joel, however convenient a cover that may have been. Of course he had to touch her, to talk about her body, to demonstrate things with his, occasionally to lift up his shirt to show her exactly what he meant when he talked about abdominals. And if she really wanted to improve her flexibility, then it was necessary for him to apply a little extra pressure to that raised leg, gently leaning into it with his torso. That particular manoeuvre seemed to bring his crotch into extremely close proximity to hers. She found that she didn't object.

Joel was flirtatious, but in an inoffensive way. He never said anything sleazy. He complimented Christine on her progress – and that quickly moved on to complimenting her on her appearance when she arrived at the gym for her morning work-out. She found herself taking a little more trouble over her dress, picking out clothes that he might like – no, that made her look better for herself – oh, sod it, who was she trying to kid? He did it all with such refreshing directness, such dazzling smiles, that instead of saying 'Oh, what, this old thing? No really, it was cheap, I've had it for ages, I normally use it as a dog blanket,' she simply said 'Thank you very much,' and felt that tingle beginning in the roots of her hair and the tips of her toes, swiftly spreading to her cheeks, her breasts, her hands.

There was no question of a relationship outside the gym – as well as being a good deal older than him, a respected barrister on her way to becoming a QC, she made it a rule never to mix business with pleasure. It was just not done. Plenty of other careers had foundered on those particular rocks. She was his client, he was providing a service, and as long as there was money changing hands, and professional standards to consider, there was absolutely no way that she would even dream of . . .

And then he asked her.

'So, Christine,' he said, in that bright Australian accent that made her think of sea breezes and wide open skies, 'how do you fancy brunch some time? You know, if you haven't got a big case on, or anything. I'm always starving after training you.'

'Me too. I mean, after you've . . . But actually, I have to . . .'

'There's a couple of nice cafés up Red Lion Street where we could grab a 'cino and a toasted ciabatta or something.'

'That doesn't sound very healthy.'

'Oh, bugger health,' he said, flashing his whiter-than-white teeth, 'sometimes you've just got to think of pleasure.'

Christine was finding it hard to think of anything else, but managed to force her mouth to say the words 'Well, that's a lovely idea, I'll have a look at my diary and see if I can fit you in.' She immediately regretted what sounded so crassly like a double entendre, and turned up the resistance on the rowing machine.

'Wow, Christine,' said Joel, leaning against the wall, 'you're on fire today!'

Victoria dressed carefully for dinner – very carefully, considering this was meant to be a cosy à deux, at home. She did not choose the sky blue Cavalli; she did not want to look as if she was over-keen on Massimo's spending power, however true that may be. She needed something that looked matrimonial. Not 'wifey' or God forbid 'mumsy', but the sort of outfit that made a man think about talking to his laywer and looking to the future. Fortunately, she had packed a calf-length chiffon dress in a black and cream abstract print, tying around the neck, the ties floating over her shoulder blades. Relaxed but elegant, sexy but soft, easy to live with . . .

Massimo was standing on the terrace, looking out across the pool to the hazy blue hills on the other side of the bay, just about to disappear into darkness. The neck of a bottle protruded from a crisp white napkin over an ice bucket. When he saw her coming, he picked up two flutes and chimed them gently together.

'*Aperitivo?*'

'*Con piacere.*' He liked it when she made a bit of an effort, although she was determined to make it look effortless. She wanted to appear low-maintenance, companionable, easy-going-but-still-majorly-hot.

He poured, drinks fizzed, they clinked.

'*Cin cin.*'

'*A te,*' she said.

'*A noi,*' he countered, which sounded promising.

He put an arm around her waist, and led her into the garden. It was still warm; the wind had dropped, and the walls of the house were giving back some of the heat of the day. They sat beneath the mulberry tree that gave the house its name, on a rustic wooden bench with an integral drinks table, where they often took their evening tipple. He stretched out his brown, muscular legs; he was wearing light blue shorts with crisp turn-ups, rather tight around the crotch, but flatteringly so. Massimo by name, she often teased him, Massimo by nature. In a drunken moment, he had once confided that his wife 'couldn't accommodate me' and had done so only for the reason of procreation. Victoria had no such trouble. Her mouth watered.

'It's beautiful, huh?' He made a large gesture, taking in the house, the garden, the mulberry tree above their heads, and beyond that the rapidly darkening sky. A cicada was singing somewhere nearby. Lights were starting to come on, like diamonds scattered carelessly across the hillside.

'Yes, it's lovely. You know how much I like it here.'

'Better than Sardinia?'

'Much better.'

'You'd like to come here more?'

'Well, of course . . .' *Put the bloody house in my name you bastard, if that's what you're driving at, let's get it down on paper.* 'But I don't really mind where we are, as long as we're together.' *The house in Milan would be a good start, and then that pile in Surrey . . .*

'*Tesoro*...' They clinked glasses again, and he kissed her. His lips tasted of champagne.

His phone rang.

'Ah! *Scusi*. The food. *Pronto*...'

He got up, walked towards the gate. Two men in immaculate white waiter's jackets relayed food from a van into the kitchen. No flatpacked pizza on the back of a moped for Signor Rivelli. It smelt delicious – rosemary, garlic, and was that prawn? Her mouth watered again.

'And then, when I've built up a chain of about five gyms around London, I'll sell the business and move back to Australia. I always said I'd come home a millionaire. Jeez, I mean money goes a lot further out there. London's a competitive city, but I can do it. I've got a good client base started. You know, I'm on the ladder. I've got a lot of passion and energy.'

Christine nodded and made appreciative noises when necessary. Usually she found this kind of speculative autobiography tedious in the extreme – she'd heard it a million times from clients, usually those with some desperate financial secrets to hide – but in this case, she was actually quite interested. God, was she falling in love? Or was Joel some kind of surrogate son – a nice young man in whose future she could take a benign interest? After all, her own children barely spoke to her these days. Isabelle just asked for money, Ben said 'hi' and 'bye' and mumbled the odd word of appreciation for meals and laundry. It made a change to be confided in, to be a receptacle for dreams and ambitions.

'You certainly have, and I'm sure you'll achieve everything you want to.'

'Really?' He put his coffee down, looked in her eyes. 'Everything?'

'Well, yes. Why not? I mean, you just have to know what you want, and go for it. It's what I've always done in my career.'

'I see. So if you want something, you should just reach out and...'

'Grab it!' She laughed. 'Why not?'

Silence fell, broken only by the hiss and gurgle of the coffee machine.

'In that case,' said Joel, looking down at his mozzarella and avocado ciabatta, 'I'd like to take you out for dinner.'

'Oh, I...'

And then he looked up, his brow furrowed, his eyes veiled by those long, curly eyelashes. 'Please?'

Under the circumstances, it would have been rude to say no.

Dinner was divine. They'd eaten on the terrace, at the mosaic-topped table, using their fingers to scoop up oily artichoke hearts, pungent slices of *pissaladière*. The *pièce de résistance* was a delicious *bourride*, miraculously still hot, the garlic sauce steaming as they poured it over white fish and *crevettes* so fresh they were practically swimming on to the fork. They washed it down with a cold, fresh Pouilly-Fumé, then mopped up the remaining *aïoli* with hunks of white bread. When they had finished, the table top was covered with crumbs of crust, shells, blobs of olive oil and pools of condensation from the wine bottle.

'Come.'

They walked into the dark garden, the only light that which spilled out from the house. They stood under the mulberry tree, kissed and lit cigarettes. The smoke curled up into the canopy of leaves, where it was swept away by a sudden gust of wind. The weather was changing, they could both feel it, as if this might be last night of summer.

'That was a beautiful evening, Massimo.'

'The night is young, baby.' He tugged at the ties at the back of her neck, loosening the top of her dress. This was not exactly a statement of matrimonial intent, but it felt good, as did his mouth on her neck. He had not shaved since morning – and Massimo was one of those men who was distinctly stubbly by the afternoon. His face scratched her, and she pressed into him, feeling the hardness in his trousers. Any minute now, he would be as big as the peppermill she'd been using on her *bourride*.

'Take it off.' His voice was low and thick with lust. Victoria fiddled with fastenings, barely able to see his face. His back was to the house. There was a glimmer of light about his eyes, perhaps the reflection of their glowing cigarettes. The dress dropped around her hips. She unfastened her bra. The evening air was cool on her breasts. Her nipples were instantly hard, aching for his lips.

The wind sprang up again, fiercer this time, swaying the branches of the mulberry tree above them.

'Oh Massimo . . .'

'Yes, baby . . .'

'I want it so much . . .'

'You got it, baby . . .'

'I mean . . .'

Another gust of wind, sharp, like a whip. Branches knocked together audibly, shedding leaves and twigs on to their heads, on to her shoulders.

At least she thought they were twigs.

She brushed the top of her head, and was horrified to feel something soft and very obviously alive between her fingers.

Another blast of wind, and they were pelting down on her, into her hair, on to her shoulders, her breasts.

She screamed. 'Oh my God! Caterpillars! Christ! How disgusting!'

She ran towards the safety of the house – and in the light she could see them, foul white larvae with blind brown eyes, stumpy legs sticking out all along their appallingly ridged bodies. She screamed again, panicking now, beating at herself as if she was on fire. Caterpillars scattered on the terracotta tiles of the terrace, on to the table, on to their plates, drowning in olive oil and the dregs of wine in their greasy glasses.

'Don't just stand there grinning like an idiot,' she shouted at Massimo, who was leaning against the pillar with an infuriating smile on his face, 'help me get rid of these disgusting maggots!'

He did nothing.

'Do you know what they are, these "disgusting maggots" of yours?'

'Yes. They're fucking . . . wa-hah-hah!' A caterpillar had just landed on her cheek. 'They're fucking horrible!'

'They're silkworms, in fact.'

'I don't care what kind of worms they are.' She flicked at herself with a napkin; the last few caterpillars dropped from her hair, and writhed on the terracotta floor.

'A wild relative, at least, of the domesticated silkmoth, *Bombyx mori*, from the Latin *morus*, the mulberry tree. A native of Asia and Africa.'

'Oh God.' She was panting in fear. 'This is a nightmare.'

'There are mulberry trees all over this part of France,' he went on, casually smoking. 'Do you know why?'

'I don't bloody care at the moment.' She sounded like a harridan, and she was furious – half naked, and bombarded with caterpillars, it was no laughing matter, certainly no time for a lecture on the cultivation of the mulberry.

'To introduce silk production into Europe, in an attempt to compete with the mills in the Far East, notably China.' He stepped up on to the terrace, and casually squashed a few writhing larvae with the toe of his expensive brown leather mocassin. 'It didn't work, of course, but the mulberries remain, and many, many of these fellows.' He picked a grub off the mosaic table top, held it up to the light. It wriggled, this way, that way, this way, that way.

'Why did they just fall on me like that?'

'Ah, as for that . . . pff!' He squashed the caterpillar between his fingers, wiped the mess on to a napkin. 'An occupational hazard of standing under mulberry trees.' He could barely contain his laughter now. 'Especially with your tits out.'

'Shut up! I hate you sometimes!'

'Ah, baby, but remember,' he said, touching her on the shoulder with the same hand that had just squished the larva, 'without your disgusting little maggots, there would be no silk. And without silk, there would be no beautiful evening dresses. No couture. And without couture, no garment manufacturing industry.'

She could see where this was going. 'All right.'

'And without a garment manufacturing industry,' he continued, the laughter no longer in his voice, 'no Rivelli. And without Rivelli, no nice flat for Victoria, no pretty clothes, no holidays in Sainte-Maxime, no skiing in Aspen. *Capisce?*'

'*Si.*'

'The world is not pretty, Victoria. The world is not a Cavalli dress, a diamond necklace, dinner for two on the terrace. It's a million million silkworms spewing stuff out their assholes and then getting dropped into huge vats of boiling water to kill them before they can turn into moths. It's about prices going up and down on the international markets. It's about cutting your competitor's throat so that you can bring in the next order just a fraction of a percent lower than the next guy. It's about crushing anyone who stands in your way – so that you can have all this.' He gestured towards the swimming pool, the blue water lit by submerged lamps. 'It's all built on death. Of one sort or another.'

Victoria shivered, and pulled up the top of her dress. 'I don't want to know about that side of things, Massimo.'

'I know you don't, baby. But I have to.'

The wind sighed around the house, blowing the crumbs off the table. Summer was definitely over. Victoria went upstairs, blowing her nose, and ran a bath.

Chapter 4

'A few days in Paris' sounded lovely to Isabelle – she had not been there for years, and never without her parents – and to go there with Will, even to work, was almost too much pleasure to contemplate. They were staying in a studio apartment that belonged to an 'old friend' of Will's, on Boulevard Rochechouart, the wide grimy street that divides the ninth arrondissement from the eighteenth between Montmartre and the Goutte d'Or. They emerged from the Métro at Barbès Rochechouart, elbowed their way through the crowds outside Tati, where Isabelle's eye was caught by a sleeveless black top for €1.99, and Will had to wait outside with the luggage while she ran inside to pay. She ran out clutching the pink gingham-checked paper bag above her head, a gleeful smile on her face.

'It's an omen,' she said. 'The perfect little black number for one ninety-nine. Dress it up with a bit of ribbon, a bit of sparkle . . .'

'Stop styling the world and give me a hand with the cases, Princess. It's not much further.' He sounded stern, but he was smiling, and Isabelle danced along the boulevard, insofar as that was possible with a wheelalong case.

He stopped outside a heavy green double door, pushed it open – it took all his weight – and suddenly, from the noise and bustle of the street, they fell into a strange nineteenth-century silence, high walls on either side of a dark courtyard, water dripping from ancient drain-pipes, ferns growing in every crevice.

'*Voilà*,' said Will. 'I hope you're feeling fit. We have a long climb ahead of us.'

'No lift?'

'Are you kidding? It barely has stairs. *Allez-oop.*'

The apartment was on the top floor, under the roof, the ceilings at crazy angles. It made the studio in Hoxton look like the Ritz. Running water was restricted to one stone sink in the corner, near the grimy window, over which a single tap (*froid*, needless to say) dripped greenly.

The beds were against one wall – bunk beds, Isabelle noted, with some surprise. She had not slept in bunk beds since sharing a room with her infant brother. Every surface was strewn with debris – plates, cups, books, magazines, CDs.

'Ah,' said Will. 'He tidied up, I see.'

They managed to make a cup of tea – there was a very dusty old box of *tilleul* at the back of a cupboard, and a dangerous-looking electric kettle with worn flex. They cleared two patches on the worn rug, and sat cross-legged, sipping.

'*La vie de bohème*,' said Isabelle.

'You'd better believe it,' said Will. 'It's a *veritable* garret.'

'I can feel my consumption coming on.' Isabelle coughed weakly, put a hand to her brow.

An hour later, sort-of-washed and changed, they were back at Gare du Nord, waiting for another train to take them to Parc des Expositions.

'Christ,' said Isabelle, staring out of the window as the gloomy suburbs slipped past, 'this isn't very glamorous, is it?'

'Wait till you see the hall.'

'I thought it would be like *Moulin Rouge*.'

'More like Milton Keynes, really.'

But nothing could dampen Isabelle's excitement. They were on their way – in Paris – on a buying trip – together. There was money in the bank, enough to buy fabrics for the first Cissé autumn/winter collection. All Isabelle had to do was swan around the trade fair (Will's words) and pick out the stuff she wanted. And if she couldn't find the material she was looking for at Premiere Vision, the fabric fair *par excellence*, it didn't exist.

She had only to use her eyes.

The exhibition hall was like a gigantic steel and glass aircraft hangar, overlit, deafening, filled to bursting with people and cameras, lighting and displays, and miles and miles of stuff. If you knotted all these swatches together, thought Isabelle, you could put a belt around the equator.

Colours clashed, argued and fought. Floaty chiffons flirted with sheer silk satins. There were florals, feathers, stripes, dots and swirls. Isabelle's head flicked from side to side, she darted from one stand to another, 'Oh God! Oh God!', burying her face in swatches, draping them over her arms, feeling the silk slipping over her skin, imagining a thousand outfits, a hundred shows, several millions in budget.

'We've got to do this systematically,' said Will. 'We've got two days. Take notes, talk about prices, and we'll make our choice tomorrow.'

'Well I've got to have this one,' said Isabelle, holding up a hanger of poison green satin. 'It looks like dragon skin.'

Will hustled her on, always looking at prices, scribbling numbers in his notebook, picking up business cards, filing them carefully away in his organiser.

By mid morning, the hall was full – and now the racks of clashing colours had competition from the exotic creatures who had come, it seemed, as much to be seen as to see. There were designers, stylists, photographers, PRs, journalists, agents and models. There were 'wannabes' in all those categories. There were fashion students, who looked young even to Isabelle and Will, earnestly scribbling and sketching, struggling to take it all in. There were the has-beens, the also-rans, the never-weres, positioning themselves at prominent corners, hoping to be recognised, shrieking when they saw someone they knew, ostentatiously kissing, comparing scrawny necks and fake tans, rattling bangles like prisoners rattle their chains.

The women were all underweight, starved and anxious looking. The men had taken steps to eradicate any signs of masculinity – eyebrows were plucked, faces shaven down to the dermis, polished to a high shine with tinted moisturiser. There was enough make-up in the room to paint the Pont Neuf several times over. Perfumes mingled in the air to form a slightly nauseating uniform scent – the smell, thought Will, of fashion. Voices were raised against inappropriately loud sound systems. It was like a cross between a sex club and Heathrow in terminal meltdown.

Isabelle wasn't hearing (or smelling) any of this. She had a faraway look in her eyes, a look that Will had seen many times when they were at St Martins together – a look that told him that Isabelle was a real designer, a woman with artistic vision, while he would only ever be a good businessman. She needed him, to bring those visions to life – and he needed her, her instinct, her passion, her talent. And more? Did he need her for something else besides? They had been skirting around the issue of sex for weeks now. She expected it, he could see that. She would not be the first woman in his life, and she might not even be the last – but what was the point of leading girls on when you had no intention of following through? A quick fuck at fifteen could be put down to curiosity, inexperience or just plain greed. But they were adults. They – he – knew what they wanted. She wanted him, and tonight, in that impossibly romantic garret high above the noise and grime of the boulevard, the dome of Sacré Coeur just visible from the window, she hoped to get him.

But he didn't want her. Not for that, at any rate.

Now his energies were focused on the business of getting a Cissé dress on the red carpet at the Oscars. Okay, so there was unresolved sexual tension between them – so far, so Hollywood. But this was was not a movie. There would be no passionate embraces among mountains of taffeta on the studio floor. This was reality, and one of them was going to be disappointed.

Will looked at Isabelle, her face buried in a pile of sherbert-coloured silks, pinks and oranges and yellows, eyes closed, inhaling as if she could smell colour. She was wearing a simple white dress, broderie anglaise on the bodice, her brown skin peeping through the holes. Her backside filled the skirt. Isabelle was not one of the fashionable skeletons that clattered and chattered around the exhibition hall. She had tits and arse. She was unambiguously a woman. And, as such, she would remain a business partner, nothing more.

But if that's all she was, why was Will getting a hard-on in his jeans?

'Oh Will, look at this!' said Isabelle, holding up a length of yellow organza, the sort of colour that made you think of lemon sorbets on hot afternoons. 'It feels wonderful.' She moulded it against her torso. 'Look how it falls . . .'

It fell beautifully, hanging from Isabelle's breasts, skimming her knees. It would look so much better with nothing on underneath . . .

Will blushed, and cleared this throat. 'Trust you to pick the most expensive one,' he said, sounding gruffer than he intended. 'You couldn't have one of the synthetic weaves, could you? Oh no. Princess Isabelle has to have the very finest Italian silk.'

Isabelle looked at him with a question in her eyes, the joy draining from her face.

'But you're right, of course,' said Will, forcing himself to sound upbeat. 'It's beautiful. You are beautiful.' The words slipped out, hung in the air for a moment. Will started scribbling serial numbers in his notebook. Isabelle watched him, her eyebrows drawn together, as if she was trying to work out a complicated bit of mental arithmetic . . .

It was hard, sometimes, not to wonder 'what if . . . ?'.

Am I being a fool? Am I just another middle-aged, only-just-pre-menopausal woman, allowing herself to be taken for a ride by an unscrupulous, gold-digging toyboy? Is Joel really interested in me – as he gives a very good impression of being – or does he just want access to my wallet, my lifestyle, my 'other rich girlfriends'? Am I setting myself up to be a victim? Worst of all, thought Christine, am I making an idiot of myself in the way that Linda does every six months? Will it be me sobbing into a bucket of booze, stuffing my face with comforting bars of Green and Black?

Banishing such thoughts, Christine poured a glassful of white wine into a saucepan, where it sizzled with garlic and onion and oil-coated arborio rice. She stirred gently, savouring the aroma. Joel was due in twenty minutes, and she thought it would create a good impression if she was at the stove, whipping up a simple risotto – delicious, classy, but easily dismissed as 'Oh, this? It's nothing, just the sort of supper I have all the time . . .' She did not want to appear to be making too much of an effort. She did not want him to think that this oh-so-casual dinner invitation, given almost as a throwaway at the end of a training session, accepted in the same light manner, was a big deal.

But it was a big deal. This wasn't another sociable dinner in a restaurant, a kiss goodnight and home alone. This time, Christine was inviting him into her house. She knew, or at least bloody well hoped, that she would end the evening breaking what had become an embarrassingly long sexual drought. And if she was going to break it with anyone, it had to be Joel. He was just so . . . fit. In every sense of the word. Physically fit. Sexually 'fit'. And fit for her purposes – an attentive, appreciative and intelligent young man who had made it abundantly clear that he was available for her enjoyment.

She took a ladle of simmering stock and added it to the pan, stirring, stirring, counting the minutes. The rice started to turn soft and creamy.

Christine poured another glass of wine, and this one did not go into the risotto.

'Don't look now, but guess who's just walked in with an entourage of about twenty?'

Isabelle peeped through the hangers on a rail of heavily beaded swatches; they clacked and rattled like curtains in a brothel. 'Oh Christ, it's bloody Maya Rodean.'

'Pretend we haven't seen her.'

But it was too late. Maya Rodean, resplendent in a sheer black Versace dress (it was well known that she was in talks about a job with Versace), black shades perched on top of her sleek blonde bob, the only touch of colour the impossibly thin heels of her Jil Sander shoes, in bright pink, walked towards them with her hands outstretched, as if she owned them.

'What on earth are you doing here?' she squawked, as if it was a delightful but incomprehensible surprise.

'The same as you, I imagine,' said Will.

'I very much doubt that,' said Maya, who had spent one whole term at college trying to persuade Will to be her unpaid PA.

'Isn't it wonderful?' said Isabelle, whose enthusiasm was not to be dampened even by Maya Rodean's flared nostrils. 'All this beautiful stuff . . .'

'That?' Maya looked as if someone had just farted under her nose. 'Oh . . . well, I suppose it has its charms. Bridal wear, perhaps . . .' She flapped a hand in front of her face, as if to disperse a foul smell.

'I'm looking for stuff for our first big collection,' said Isabelle, oblivious to the daggers that Will was shooting at her. 'I want to go for full-on evening wear. Great big fantasy fondant creations. The sort of dress that makes a woman feel . . . What's the matter, Will?'

'Nothing,' said Will, with a look that said 'Shut up now!'

'Well I think that's marvellous,' said Maya, who might have been jealous as hell of Isabelle's talent — but celebrity offspring don't need talent. 'I wish you all the luck in the world. Do send me an invitation to your . . .'

She snapped her fingers at a young man in a distressed white denim jacket, with the word MAYA spelt out in candy-red buttons on the back. He handed Will a card with a website address on it.

'Now, I really can't stop,' said Maya. 'We're on our way to see . . . Well, least said soonest mended.' She took a swatch from Isabelle's hands, and said 'Aaaaw,' in a way that is usually reserved for child cancer patients, and moved on, entourage and all.

Isabelle and Will looked at each other.

'Aaaaw,' they both said, and burst out laughing.

Joel arrived five minutes early, standing on the doorstep looking up at her with those puppy dog eyes, always so wet and white, as if he'd just administered eyedrops, a bottle of wine clutched in one hand, a bunch of chrysanthemums in the other. Not the chicest of flowers, thought Christine, especially when they're yellow, and wrapped in cellophane, from some garage forecourt or supermarket stand, but flowers nonetheless. And it was a long time since anyone, other than herself, had brought flowers into the house. She took Joel's offerings, which included a kiss on the lips, his mouth slightly open, tasting of spearmint.

'Come down to the kitchen,' said Christine. 'Dinner won't be long. I hope you're hungry.'

'You know me,' said Joel, bounding down the stairs five at a time, hoisting himself aloft on the handrails, 'I'm always hungry.'

'Do you like risotto?'

'Strictly speaking, I don't eat carbs after five,' he said, walking into the kitchen and rather unnecessarily raising his pale blue polo shirt to rub a hand over his six-pack, 'but for you, Christine, I'm willing to make an exception.'

Why did everything he say sound like an invitation to sin? Christine busied herself with the illicit carbohydrates.

'Any chance of a drink?'

'Oh, I'm so sorry.' Christine, the Iron Lady of the divorce courts, the barrister with twenty years call, felt flustered. 'I'm forgetting myself.' Was that sweat she could feel at her temples? She hoped not – but it was hot in the kitchen. 'Wine all right?'

'Whatever you're having.'

'It's quite nice,' she said, slopping Chardonnay into a glass. 'Cheers.'

They clinked. 'Looks like you've got a head start on me.' He downed
half his glass in one, smacked his lips. 'That's better. Never let a lady
drink alone.'

He held her eyes for a moment. He's right, said Christine. I shouldn't
drink alone. I shouldn't be alone. Especially in bed. The bed where I
will take him later.

Dinner went well, insofar as Joel ate every grain of rice, asked for
more and ate that too, complimented Christine on her cooking, her
presentation, her house. He did rather have a tendency to bang on
about himself – for the fifth time at least she had to listen to his plan
to open a chain of health clubs, sell them for a massive profit, move
into property/travel/hotels, retire at fifty and travel the world etc – but
at least he had passion, enthusiasm, self-belief. So many of her peers
were jaded, and masked their ambition with that peculiarly English
form of self-deprecation, possibly the most unsexy quality known to
man. Joel knew what he wanted. And if he carried on looking at her
tits like that, thought Christine, he'd get it.

Plates cleared away, they took drinks out into the garden. The air
was cool, the sky already dark, summer long gone, the chill of autumn
getting a grip. Christine put on a little woollen shrug, but even so, she
shivered. Joel put his arm around her shoulders, drew her to him. She
felt the heat from his body, felt her knees go weak, and allowed herself
to sink into his arms.

They kissed – not for the first time, there had been pecks on the
cheek, then on the mouth, even a suggestion of lips parting – but this
time they meant it. Joel's lips were soft, the skin around his mouth
slightly scratchy with stubble. His tongue was firm as it came into
contact with hers, his teeth smooth and shiny, a pleasant shared taste
of garlic and good wine.

God, it had been so long. Not since that time with Andy . . . And
how long since she had had any man other than Andy? Not since her
early twenties. Not for most of her adult life. She did not know how
to act – how aggressive to be, how much to steer the encounter, how
much enthusiasm to show. She did not want Joel to think she was
uptight or prudish; on the other hand, she didn't want to come across
as some randy old lady who'd sacrifice her dignity at the first sniff of
young meat.

She needn't have worried. Joel took control, setting the pace, reacting to the slightest hint like a mindreader. He took the drink from her hand, set it down on a table, and kissed her on the neck, working his way down her throat, pulling her hips into his with one hand in the small of her back. She could feel how hard he was, and gasped. He pressed against her, moving in rhythm, as if they were dancing, feasting on her neck, those soft lips and firm tongue setting her body on fire. She needed to sit down, to lie down, her legs were giving way, drawing him down on top of her. They would have sunk to the ground had Joel not broken this kiss, held her by the hands and said, staring into her eyes, 'I've waited so long for this, Christine,' then leading her back into the house, through the kitchen, and into the living room, as if he owned the place.

He lowered her on to the sofa, and himself on to her, gently opening her legs, his shoulders bunched up as he kissed her breasts through the soft wool of her sweater. She pushed him back, unbuttoned the front, opening herself up to him. For a while, he just looked, a rapt expression on his face, his eyes half closed, glinting through those eyelashes, and then he came down again, kissing, undoing her bra, sucking her nipples.

'I want to see you naked,' she said, surprising herself. 'Please.'

He jumped to his feet, just as he did in the gym, and with one swift movement pulled the polo shirt over his head, revealing a mat of dark hair on his stomach, a little on his chest, deep dark patches under his arms. His torso was lean, defined, like a swimmer's. All that talk about exercise and diet was not in vain. Pink nipples peeked through the hair; Christine wanted to kiss them.

'And the rest.'

She was sitting up now, her breasts exposed, her skirt pushed up around her hips. He kicked off his shoes, hopping from foot to foot as he removed his socks, and then stepped out of his jeans. His underpants looked at least one size too small for him – two sizes, perhaps, given his current state of arousal. They sat around his hips, the fur on his stomach fanning out into a broader delta then disappearing inside the elastic.

He pulled down his pants as if he was taking a bow, plucked them from the end of this feet and threw them over his shoulder, extending his arms in a 'ta-dah!' kind of gesture. His cock smacked up against his stomach, bounced back down, moving with every beat of his heart.

And all this is for me? What's the catch?

Even at times like this, Christine remained above all else a lawyer.

Isabelle lost Will around two thirds of the way through the show. He said he'd seen someone he knew, and disappeared in the crowd. She carried on through the stalls, lost in a thousand wonderful couture visions, but at the back of her mind was a niggling feeling that something was wrong. She did not really trust Will, she realised – and then, a split second later, she realised that she was treating him as if he was her boyfriend. Rather than her – well, her what, exactly?

'Isabelle Cissé?'

She spun round, and saw a familiar face that she couldn't quite place, blond hair, glasses, a check shirt that rather screamed 'non-iron'.

'Dan. Dan Parker.' He extended a hand. 'Walker Parker. Remember?'

'Oh yes . . .' She kind of remembered.

'We came to see you in your studio a few weeks ago. Me and my business partner, Fiona Walker.' There was the tiniest stress on that word 'business'. 'I'm delighted to see you here. I thought your graduate show was a knockout, and your business plan's good.'

'Thanks.' Yes, she remembered, that overlong day of meetings with faceless sales agents and PRs, none of whom they could afford.

'So, I guess you've got the funding together for your first collection, then.' He grinned.

'Yes, that's right.' Isabelle didn't know what else to say. She wanted to talk about colours and cuts, about ruffles and hemlines and beading, but she didn't think Dan Parker would understand. She needed Will, and looked around for him.

'Your partner in crime not here?'

'Oh yes, he's around somewhere. Always doing deals, you know.'

Was that a smirk on Dan Parker's face?

'So, what can we look forward to in the spring? Any clues?'

'Not yet, I'm afraid.' *And I very much doubt you'd understand even if I told you.*

'Smart girl.' Patronising knob. 'Best to keep your ideas to yourself. There's plenty round here that would love to rip off talent like yours.'

Was that a warning? 'Well, I guess I'll see you back in London,' he said, after what Isabelle realised was rather a rude silence. 'Enjoy the rest of your visit.' He sounded like a holiday rep – and, thought Isabelle, dressed rather like one as well.

Dan Parker faded into the crowd.

Where was Will? She hadn't seen him for nearly half an hour. Supposing something had happened to him? She didn't even know the address of the place where they were staying, she didn't have a key, Will had the Eurostar tickets, she was stranded . . .

'Ah, here she is!' Familiar hands gripped her shoulders. 'Isabelle! I want you to meet some people.' Will's eyes flashed a message – don't ask questions, just be charming. She understood, and extended a hand to a handsome, grey-haired man in a beautifully cut dove-grey suit.

'Massimo Rivelli, this is Isabelle Cissé. Isabelle, Massimo Rivelli.'

'*Piacere.*' He bowed slightly, took her hand as if he would kiss it.

'Rivelli?' said Isabelle, looking into twinkly blue eyes in a tanned face. 'As in . . . well, as in Rivelli?'

Rivelli inclined his head.

'And this,' said Will, indicating a vampy-looking blonde in a Chanel suit, 'is . . .'

'Victoria Crabtree,' she butted in, as if afraid that Will had already forgotten. 'Pleased to meet you, Isabelle. I thought your graduation show was terrific.'

'You saw it?'

'Of course. I make a point of checking out the stars of Graduate Fashion Week.' She nodded towards Rivelli. 'He says I'm the best scout in London.'

'She has an eye,' said Rivelli, nodding and rubbing his chin.

'And so when this young man told us that he was your business manager . . .'

Will waggled his eyebrows in a '*don't contradict me*' style.

'Thank you very much,' said Isabelle. 'I had no idea I'd made such an impression.'

'Never undersell yourself, young lady,' said Rivelli, his perfect English accented with a curious mixture of Italian and American. 'That's the first lesson to learn. If you don't stand up and tell the world that you're the best, there's plenty of others that will. Even when, perhaps, their talent is . . . What shall we say? Lesser.'

'Oh, God,' said Victoria, lowering her voice to a just-us-girls tone, 'this place is packed with 'em. Talentless nobodies who cling on to the fringes of the fashion industry through family connections or God knows what else. You know who I'm talking about.'

'Mmmm . . .' said Isabelle, whose mother had instilled in her a habit of never bitching about people in public.

'Not you, though. I can see the potential. When you're ready, I want you to call me. Your . . . business manager has my card.'

'Thanks. We will.'

'Come on, Massimo,' said Victoria, taking Rivelli's arm in a proprietorial fashion, 'we've got an hour before the helicopter picks us up. Let's make it count.'

Victoria led him away.

'God, Will, *the* Massimo Rivelli.'

'The very same.'

'You don't think . . .'

'Why not? He needs us just as much as we need him.'

'But to have our clothes made by Rivelli . . . That's like a dream.'

'It's a dream that's just come a little bit closer to being reality. They like you. She's seen your stuff.'

'I don't remember her.'

'She was wearing Chanel. And you can bet she didn't pay for it.'

'You mean . . . Rivelli?'

'Sure. She's his . . . what would you call it?'

'My mother would say "mistress".'

'I like your mother. She always has the right word.'

'Yes. And usually she has the last word as well.'

They carried on around the stalls, but Isabelle's head was starting to ache. 'I can't look at any more,' she said. 'I'm going colour blind. I just want to wear beige for the rest of my life. Can we go?'

'Any time you like. We've got what we need. And you may have done yourself a better turn today than you know, charming the pants off Massimo Rivelli.'

'Don't be ridiculous.'

'Hey, if Rivelli fancies you, don't knock it. Come on. Let's blow this joint. There's a bar in Pigalle that we need to go to. They have trannie waitresses.'

Isabelle was not in the mood. Her head ached, her feet were sore, and she could not stop herself from wondering where Will had got to for the missing half hour. God, thirty minutes of mystery and she was behaving like a jealous wife . . . This would never do.

'Trannie waitresses?' she said, forcing a smile. 'How fabulous! Let's go!'

They made love for the first time right there on the sofa – and partially on the floor – grappling with each other, clinging on as if their lives depended on it, Christine making more noise than she could ever remember making with a man before, crying out 'Oh!' and 'Oh God!', trying to stop herself, forgetting to stop herself, forgetting everything but Joel and what he was doing to her. He was simultaneously soft and hard, tender and aggressive. He knew exactly how to give her pleasure, taking his time, putting her first, her enjoyment setting the agenda for his.

They lay together for a while, drifting in and out of sleep, kissing, caressing, holding each other.

Eventually they got cold.

'Let's go to bed,' said Christine. 'You are staying, aren't you?'

Joel bounced to his feet. 'Yeah. I even brought my toothbrush.'

They climbed the stairs, arms round each other's waist. As they reached the landing, Christine heard the key in the lock of the front door.

Ben, who was supposed to be 'with mates' for a couple of nights, had come home.

She hurried Joel into her bedroom and prayed that her son and her lover would not meet in the morning. Joel would have to get up early for work – he had a client at eight, she knew – and Ben seldom surfaced before ten.

They did not get much sleep. But Christine, conscious of Ben's presence, was much less vocal in her appreciation.

Isabelle lay awake as dawn broke over the Boulevards. Will slept in the upper bunk. Every time he moved, the springs twanged a staccato passage and silence fell, but for his deep breathing, a semi-snore. He had kissed her goodnight – this was it, she was sure, her lips parted, his hands heavy on her shoulders, and when she opened her eyes he was staring into them, uncertain, troubled. She moved closer – and he slipped away, elusive as smoke, up the ladder to the safety of his own bed.

Grey light filtered into the room, and the sound of traffic rose, the dull roar of another working day. Finally, exhausted and miserable, Isabelle slept.

Chapter 5

'News obviously travels faster than I thought.'

'For God's sake, Mum. He's practically the same age as me.'

'He's thirty. Eight years older than you, to be precise.'

'And I suppose that makes all the difference.'

'It's just a statement of fact.'

'Can't you stop being a lawyer for a moment and actually talk like a human being?'

'All right. I will. As far as I'm concerned, what I do in my private life is absolutely none of your business.'

'But you're my . . .'

'As you've made it perfectly clear for several years that what you do in your private life is none of mine.'

This 'discussion' had been going on in the same vein for some twenty minutes. The moment Isabelle heard from her brother Ben that Mum had been entertaining younger men in the family home, she was round there like a shot. She also had to broach the eternal subject of money – costs for the collection were spiralling out of control. She didn't want to piss Christine off too much – but on the other hand she had to find out if her mother had really gone off the rails and started screwing toyboys.

'Yeah, but there's one big difference,' said Isabelle, sipping the coffee which her mother had just served. 'You're not interested in my life. You haven't been for years.'

'That's absolute nonsense.'

'Really? Well I don't remember seeing you around the studio recently.'

'I don't remember being invited.'

'Since when do you need inviting anywhere?'

'Oh, I can just imagine the welcome I'd get if I turned up un-announced. I made that mistake once too often when you were a student.'

'Anyway, if I do invite you to things you don't turn up.'

'I told you a thousand times, I couldn't come to your graduation show because I was in the middle of an extremely important case.'

'More important than my career, quite clearly.'

Christine held up a hand to silence the opposition – it was a technique she used to great effect in court. 'I would not expect you to drop everything in order to come and see me at work. You can't expect me to either.'

'Even though you are my mother.'

'In case you hadn't noticed, Isabelle, I have a job.'

'Here we go.'

'A job, I might add, which pays for all this.' She gestured around the kitchen, with its gleaming fittings, its hardwood work surfaces, its terracotta floor tiles. 'Which paid for you to go through college, and which still seems to be paying for you to set up in business. If you'd like me to tell the clerks that I can only take briefs that don't happen to clash with your diary, I'd be happy to do so – but it might lead to a slight drop in our standard of living.'

'Rubbish,' said Isabelle into her coffee. 'You don't pay for everything. Dad pays his share.'

'I know exactly how much your father contributes.'

'What's that supposed to mean?'

'Look, darling, I don't want to get into this. Your father and I are trying to behave like civilised adults, largely for your and Ben's sake. The financial side of things was dealt with by lawyers . . .'

'Oh, that's your solution to everything.'

'And one of the main areas of discussion is how much each of us contributes to your education and upkeep.'

'You make me sound like a farm animal.'

'Don't try to wind me up, Isabelle.' Christine looked severely at her daughter – a look that could quell high court judges. 'If you want a war of words, pick on someone your own size.'

'Is that a threat?'

'No, darling. Just advice.'

'Advice! Advice! God, you just can't stop yourself, can you?'

Isabelle stood up, pushing her chair back over the floor. It made an unpleasant scraping sound. She'd been engaged in this battle with her mother for as long as she could remember – always going through the same moves, whipping herself up into a fury while her mother remained irritatingly, glacially calm, freezing her out. Why couldn't Christine just blow her top, say what she meant, instead of holding on to her words like a miser, saying only what would stand up in court? Andy, her father, was a hothead like her – they argued rarely, but when they did, it cleared the air, they hugged – and Isabelle usually got her way. Fighting with her mother was like fighting with a wall of solid steel.

But even as she realised how useless and pointless it all was, Isabelle could hear herself going into the next phase of the game.

'I'm sick of this, Mum. You're always pushing me away. It's not my fault that you and Dad split up, but you seem to think it is.'

'I beg your pardon?'

'Ever since I can remember, you've been like this with me.'

'Like what?'

'Like a fucking lawyer!'

'There's no need to swear, Isabelle.'

'Do you think I came between you and Dad? Do I remind you of him too much? You don't seem to be like this with Ben. No, Ben can do no wrong. Comes and goes as he pleases, does whatever he fancies, and does he get the third degree? No he doesn't. It's just me, isn't it? Everything I do, you're always niggling away, having a go, trying to undermine me.'

'Excuse me, Isabelle,' said Christine, starting to sound heated at last, 'but it was you who barged in here and started firing off impertinent questions about my private life.'

'Barged in? Oh that's very nice. Into the family home.'

'And just because I don't choose to tell you who I see . . .'

'You do more than see him, apparently.'

'That does not concern you.'

'It does.'

'Well, that's your opinion.'

'You're making a fool of yourself, and . . .'

'And what?' Christine was getting angry now, her eyes flashing. 'You think that I'm going to make you look uncool in front of your fashion friends? Is that it? I would have thought it would be rather to your credit to see your mother on the arm of an attractive man.'

'Don't be . . .'

'You don't like it, do you? The fact that I've got a new man in my life who just happens to be young and very good looking, and you . . .'

'What?'

'And you haven't. There.'

They both picked up their coffee cups simultaneously, and buried their noses in them. They shared so many gestures and habits of behaviour that they could never forget that they were mother and daughter.

Silence fell, both of them fuming, both guarding their tongues. A cross word now would have led to a far greater estrangement than either of them wanted.

Isabelle broke the silence first.

'I have, as a matter of fact.'

'Oh, really?'

'Don't you want to know who?'

'I know better than to ask, darling. You always jump down my throat.'

'I don't.'

'Well then?'

'His name's Will.'

'Will? *The* Will?'

'Yes.'

'I thought he was gay.'

'So did I.' Isabelle sipped coffee again. 'So did he.'

'Oh. I see.'

'Do you?' It was worth telling a lie if it helped to calm her mother down. 'Well I wish you'd explain it to me, because I'm damned if I do.'

The ice melted, and Christine put a hand on her daughter's shoulder. 'Be careful, darling. I don't want you to end up getting hurt.'

'Thanks for not saying "again".'

'You said it. Not me.'

'I know I've got rubbish taste in men. I can't seem to help it. I always fall in love with the wrong ones. After all those wasters I dated at college, I've finally found myself someone I really like, we really click, he's hard-working, presentable, intelligent, he makes me laugh.'

Christine felt giddy; she and her daughter were suddenly talking. Not arguing.

'But are you and he . . . ?'

'Yes.'

'So how gay is he?'

'I don't know. That's the trouble. He always has been, up till now.'

'That doesn't bode very well.'

'People change.'

'Hmmm.'

'Oh please don't start with the lawyer stuff again. I know you have a very low opinion of human nature.'

'I see the bad side of it, darling. It becomes a habit.'

'But Will's not like that.'

'I never said he was. I'm just saying that leopards tend not to change their spots. How old is he?'

'Twenty-four.'

'I would have thought that by twenty-four most young men know what they want in that department.'

'And you're suddenly the expert on young men, of course.'

Their eyes met, their jaws set, they both took breath to resume the argument – and they laughed.

'Shall we start this conversation again, Isabelle?'

'Yes.' They kissed each other on the cheek. 'Lovely to see you, Ma. You're looking marvellous. Have you by any chance taken a much younger lover?'

'Yes I have as a matter of fact. And look at you! Positively glowing! You must be dating a homosexual.'

'How clever you are.'

They raised their coffee cups to each other.

'Oh dear,' said Isabelle, 'I'm not making much of a go of things, am I?'

'Don't feel too bad about it, Isabelle. We all make mistakes. Remember – I married your father.'

And for the next hour, they were friends – not just mother and daughter, warring and worrying and winding each other up. When they said goodbye, they both wondered why it could not always be like this.

Victoria and Adele had regular lunches at a little French restaurant hidden away behind Harrods, where they talked fashion, gossiped about mutual friends and, in their breezy way, counselled each other through the latest drama. Adele, for all her financial stability, was still a tender-hearted old girl, and easily bruised by men who thought she was tougher than she really was. As for Victoria, there was only one song in her repertoire, and it went to the tune of Massimo Rivelli.

It was a foggy day in London town, the morning mists thickening rather than clearing, leaves falling from the trees and a sense of decay in the air. Victoria, who didn't have a job or a family to take her mind off such things, was morbidly sensitive to the changes of the season.

'It all seems so hopeless,' she said over a salad of warm duck and endive. 'The closer we get, the further he seems from any idea of leaving his wife and marrying me.'

'But surely you don't expect him to do that. I mean, they don't.'

'He said he would.'

'Oh, *chérie*, how many times have I told you that what men say and what they do are two completely different things.'

'But how can he stay with her? He doesn't love her. They don't have sex.'

'Says Massimo.'

'I know when he's telling the truth, darling.'

'I'm not sure that you do. Okay, he says he doesn't love her. What does that mean? He's not in love with her, maybe. He doesn't feel the urge to buy her expensive presents, to be with her all the time. He doesn't want to sneak off from work to see her for a couple of hours. But she is his wife, the mother of his son, the centre of the family. He loves her – but in a different way.'

'How do you know? You haven't spoken to Massimo in years.'

'I know because I know men.' This was Adele's answer to everything. She was a self-certified expert on men and their funny ways – and, irritatingly, she was nearly always right. Listening to Adele give her advice on man-management was like reading one of the longer, more ruthlessly cynical French novels of the 19th century.

'But the woman is a religious maniac. She won't eat meat if it's some obscure saint's day. As for having sex – well, that's strictly for procreation. And she's well past that. How can he possibly love her? You, with your knowledge and understanding of men, must know that they are led by their . . .' She wouldn't say 'dicks' in a nice restaurant, so wiggled her little finger instead. A highly inappropriate digit, she thought, to represent Massimo's peppermill.

'If you believe that, Victoria, you are a fool.' Adele had a habit of laying down the law in this way, which made Victoria crazy. But she knew, after all these years, that it was worth listening when Adele talked. 'Only a simpleton would think that men are only interested in sex. Yes, of course, it's important to them, and sometimes it makes them forget all the other things. But that's only for a while. The rest of the time, they are interested in position and status and reputation. A man like Massimo wants an easy life. And so, he must have the wife and the home and the reputation of a good family man. At any cost.'

'Then why does he have me?'

'Because, of course, he wants that as well.'

'It's not fair. Why should he get everything he wants, and I have nothing?'

'You have plenty.'

'I don't. Nothing is in my name.'

'Then you have played a bad hand.'

'The only way I can see to change my situation is to get him to marry me. And if I have to force the issue, I will.'

'You will not.'

'Watch me.'

The waiter came, refilled their glasses.

'Victoria, listen to me. Never, never force a man's hand. If he thinks for one minute that you're putting pressure on him, he'll jump the other way.'

'So what would you advise? I just sit tight, and wait for him to get bored of me, and then, when I'm too old to start again, I find I've got nowhere to live and no means of support? I don't think so.'

'Why would he get bored of you? Only if you nag him about this, I think.'

'Oh, it's all right for you,' said Victoria. She rarely lost patience with Adele, but sometimes the older woman's self-satisfaction needed slapping down. 'We all know that you got the wonderful settlement, you're sitting pretty. But it's not like that for the rest of us. Some of us have to think about our future.'

'And you think that forcing Massimo to divorce his wife is going to give you some kind of security?'

'He loves me. He tells me so all the time. In France this time, it was different.'

'It's always "different", *chérie*, every time you go away you tell me this.'

'And I love him.' There was defiance in Victoria's voice.

'Ah, as for that . . .' Adele sighed. '*Dommage . . .*'

Victoria was in a bad mood when she returned to the flat. The weather, the wine and Adele's infuriating advice conspired to give her a headache. Oh, London was ghastly at this time of year, especially with the memory of the Provençal sun on her skin. But the tan was fading, along with the intimacy they'd shared, replaced by the routine of occasional visits, discreetly paid credit card bills, lavish gifts. But never the man himself, all hers, for keeps. Adele said that what she had was enough, but it was not. Victoria needed more. There was a hunger in her that could not be satisfied by occasional lovers, like the Polish plumber, delicious as he was. He'd been back for seconds, claiming that there was a pipe in urgent need of attention, and it had been great. The next time – if there was a next time – Victoria would send him away with a flea in his ear. The boy was taking altogether too much for granted.

And such things were a distraction that she could ill afford. She needed to concentrate on the one thing that mattered – getting Massimo. And while he stayed with his wife and his disabled son in that prison of a house in Surrey, Victoria would never be happy or secure. Yes, she knew perfectly well that he spent as little time there as he could, or so he said. He was always in Milan, or New York, or Paris, or in London with her, he said; visits 'home' were nothing more than duty calls. But now she thought he was lying. Adele had sown a seed of doubt. Perhaps he did still love Janet. Perhaps he valued his home life, saw it as a refuge from the hurly-burly of his professional existence. Perhaps she, Victoria, was a part of that hurly-burly from which he was glad to have some respite. Perhaps there were others like her, dotted around the world – all of them hanging on to the false promise that one day he would be theirs.

Well, if Massimo thought that she was content to be strung along and then dumped, he'd backed the wrong horse. Victoria wasn't just some starstruck fashion bimbo. When he'd met her, she was a promising journalist. Editors always told her that she had an eye for the truth in a story. She hadn't lost it, in all those years wallowing in the honey trap that Massimo had got her in. She could see what was going on – the lies, the avoidances. It was a shame that she had fallen so deeply in love with Massimo. It wasn't just the sex that she was addicted to – although that was a great part of it, she thought, feeling slightly woozy at the memory of some of the things he'd done to her. It was the man himself. Everything about him – his looks, his money, the fashionable world to which he gave her access, even his dishonesty and emotional avoidance. But she would have to push that love aside for a while, if she was going to get what she wanted for the long term.

How, though, to precipitate a divorce? Of course it couldn't appear to come from her; Adele was right about one thing. Any hint that Victoria was rocking the boat would be completely counterproductive. And Massimo wasn't going to act; he'd have done so in the first, fine, careless rapture of their affair, when Victoria's star was in the ascendant. Now she was a familiar part of his life, jogging along very nicely; why would he want to change things?

That left only one person in the equation: Janet. Signora Rivelli. The wife. She would have to be the one to sue for divorce. Yes, it was improbable, Victoria could see that; the woman was a devout Roman Catholic, the mother of Rivelli's son, besides which she enjoyed the considerable material advantages of being married to the owner of a prestigious manufacturing company. The house in Surrey was rumoured to be palatial, and there were other properties all over the world. Even with the most generous divorce settlement, Janet could never have the kind of life she enjoyed as Rivelli's wife.

This might have defeated less determined women, but Victoria had a pragmatic turn of mind, and once she'd realised that Janet was the only one who could under any circumstances precipitate a separation, she knew that she would have to provide her with a damn good reason for doing so. Without, of course, being in any way to blame. Her hands must be cleaner than clean.

* * *

'And this is the silk tulle that I'm going to use for the skirt, like a huge kind of tutu.'

'Oh, gorgeous.' Victoria ran her fingertips over the fabric, an exquisite pale yellow, almost cream. 'It will look absolutely perfect.'

'And at the other end of the scale,' said Isabelle, flicking through the hangers on her rail, 'we have my absolute favourite, this is going to make what I call the dragon dress.' She pulled down a swatch of poison-green satin. 'It was the first thing I saw at Premiere Vision, and it was the best. It's very simple . . .'

'But it's also very special.' Victoria took the hanger, held it up beside her face. 'The colour! It's like . . . poison.'

'That's exactly what I thought!' Isabelle clapped her hands. 'Oh, it suits you.'

'I'm not sure how I should take that.'

'I don't mean . . . Just . . . with your hair, and your colouring. Your eyes.'

'And how will this "dragon dress" work?'

'A simple bodice, just covering the bust, halter neck, leaving the shoulders and the sides bare to the waist. Heavy vertical gathering around the waist, and then . . .' Isabelle threw her hands out. 'Sheeyooo! Straight to the floor. Huge.'

'I can see it! I can see it! Oh, you must show it to Rivelli. He'll be so impressed.'

'Really?'

'Absolutely. It's just what he needs. Bold and young but with good tailoring.'

'Yes, that's the general idea.'

'I tell you what,' said Victoria, in whose mind a plan was forming, 'you should get it made up and send it to him. Like a calling card.'

'I'd have to talk to Will about that. He takes care of all the business stuff.'

Victoria clapped her hands, spun round on the balls of her feet. 'In fact, have it made up in his wife's size. He'd *love* that. It's *just* her colour.'

She'll look like mud in it.

'Wow . . . Well, if you really think . . .'

'We'll pay for it, of course,' said Victoria. 'I know how tight money is. And I tell you what – how about if I take one for myself as well.

It's just too perfect. We'll just have to be very careful not to wear it at the same time.'

'I'd need measurements.'

'Leave all that to me,' said Victoria. 'Oh, and hurry. I can't wait to wear it.'

Christine felt confident enough to call Andy and arrange a meeting. There were things they had to discuss – the children, mainly – but she had been putting it off, not trusting herself to keep up the 'I'm doing fine' act. Now she really was, she called – and Andy accepted immediately, almost eagerly. She suggested a restaurant, neutral territory, away from reminders of their life together, and he proposed that he would treat her to dinner. She was about to protest, and then thought – well, why not? It excited her. She chose not to analyse this too much. She was busy with another big case in the daytime, and with Joel in the evenings. Why waste time worrying about an ex-husband?

Andy turned up for their meeting – she did not let herself think of it as a date – looking as if he'd actually made a bit of an effort. He had a tendency, during their married life, to dress like a tramp, especially when he was in the middle of a big project, as she knew he was now. He was designing a conference centre in Dubai, he said on the phone. So much for the eco-warrior she married. On this occasion he was wearing a crisp white shirt – either fresh from the packet or actually ironed, which would be a first – and a nice dark brown suit with the faintest of grey pinstripes running through the fabric. It suited him well. He always did look handsome in a suit. Well, he looked handsome in anything, with that bone structure and that wonderful black skin . . .

'You look amazing,' Andy said, standing up when Christine walked into the restaurant. That was a first too: being on time for something.

'Thank you, kind sir.'

'The single life obviously suits you.'

A few weeks ago, that would have needled Christine, and they'd have been bickering even before they'd ordered drinks. Now she just said 'Yes, I rather think it does.' He pulled out a chair for her, and she sat down. Her lawyer's mind wondered briefly 'what does he want?', but then she saw the drinks menu.

'Oh, cocktails! Shall we?'

'Why not? That'll be a blast from the past.' As students, they had blown their grants on trips to then-smart cocktail bars for over-garnished drinks with embarrassing names.

'I don't suppose a classy joint like this would do a Slow Comfortable Screw Against the Wall,' said Christine, half under her breath.

'And I don't imagine they could give me an Orgasm either,' said Andy. 'Would you settle for a Manhattan? You used to like them.'

'I still do.'

Andy ordered the drinks, allowing Christine a moment's reflection. Were they here to talk about 'us'?

They made small talk about work. Both were doing well. He justified his work in Dubai by saying that the conference centre would be carbon neutral. She said that she was only interested in taking silk because it would allow her to spend more time concentrating on the cases that really mattered. They both nodded in agreement, and withheld judgement.

They did not ask about their personal lives. Christine could not know whether Ben or Isabelle had told their father about Joel; it was possible, but Andy was too polite to mention it. He said nothing about his mistress – the one for whom he had sacrificed his marriage – although Christine had heard through mutual friends that the grass had not turned out to be so green on that side of the fence. Perhaps that's why he was being so attentive . . .

'I'm glad to get you on your own for once,' he said, when they'd had a few mouthfuls of the main course.

'Well that certainly makes a change,' said Christine, narrowing her eyes mockingly.

'My dear ex-wife, let's not argue.' Andy's accent, which rarely suggested his Nigerian origins, could swing from cut-glass British to the richest West African. On this occasion, it was the former. 'There is something I want to discuss with you.'

'Oh yes.'

Was he about to drop a bombshell? 'It's . . .'

'Yes?'

'It's Isabelle.'

'Oh.' She realised how disappointed she sounded, and rallied quickly. 'I thought it might be. What's she done now?'

'It's not what she's done, it's what she wants to do. This business that she's starting up.'

'I thought you'd be proud of her. She's named the label after you.'

'Well, after herself, but . . . Anyway, that's not the point. It's the money.'

'She's been round cap in hand again, I take it.'

'Yes, and . . .'

'And you caved in as usual?'

'I gave her something, yes. Is that a problem?'

Of course it's a problem you bloody idiot, she's playing us off against each other again, and you just buy her good opinion by chucking money at her every time she bats her eyelashes at you. 'No, it's not a problem at all. I just think we need to establish some boundaries.'

'She's not three years old any more, you know.'

'Thank God for that.' Isabelle had been a particularly ghastly three-year-old. 'But she still needs to learn that she can't have everything her own way.'

'Do you think this design business of hers is a real goer?'

'Yes.' Christine didn't mention that Isabelle was in love with her business partner; Andy didn't like to hear anything about his daughter's sex life. 'She's got talent. They seem to know what they're doing. They've got a bank loan, apparently there's money coming from the Fashion Council, and they're seeking sponsors.'

'So why is she still asking me for money?'

'I don't know, Andy. What did she say?'

'She said that production costs for the show were far greater than she'd imagined. She said that she wanted to do the best show in London Fashion Week. I don't know. Lots of reasons.'

'She needs to learn to work within a budget. As long as we keep bailing her out, she'll never do that.'

'Well . . . I know. You're right. I just don't want her coming to me in two years' time, when her business has gone bust, blaming me because I didn't invest when she needed it.'

'If her business goes bust, it will be nobody's fault but Isabelle's. Personally, I don't think it will.' Christine was far from feeling this confident in reality, but it felt good to be fighting her daughter's corner for a change. Usually Andy was Isabelle's champion.

'Right. I don't need to worry then.'

'No.'

'Thanks.' Andy put his hand on Christine's – a familiar gesture from days gone by – and pulled it away again, as if he'd touched something hot. 'That's put my mind at rest. How's your chicken?'

'Absolutely delicious, thank you. And how's your trout?'

'A bit disappointing, to be honest.'

Christine sipped her wine. 'Mmmm. I thought it might be.'

Chapter 6

'Yes, hello. This is . . . er . . . Signora Rivelli's personal assistant, calling from England.'

'How can I help you, miss?'

'I just wanted to check that you have madam's correct measurements on file. Signora Rivelli thought the last few dresses were a little tight.'

'Perhaps madam has put on . . .'

'Certainly not,' snapped Victoria, delighted to think that the rumour would be all over Milan within the hour: Janet Rivelli was porking out. 'Madam takes great care of her figure. Now, if you would just check for me . . .'

It had been a punt, but it turned out to be a sound one. Of course Rivelli's wife would get her dresses direct from her husband, the manufacturer. Of course someone, somewhere in the head office in Milan, would have her measurements on file.

'Hello, Miss . . .'

A woman's voice this time, with an American accent. She sounded young. Victoria experienced a pang of jealousy. Was this one of the attractive, ambitious 'interns' who bobbed along in Rivelli's wake at fashion shows?

'Ah, hello. Janet Rivelli's PA here. Just need to check on . . .'

'I have them right here.' She sounded efficient, and eager to prove it. The girl rattled off the vital statistics, and Victoria scribbled. Ha! *Her* waist was narrower, *her* breasts bigger, than Janet's. How could Massimo possibly stay with such a flat-chested, shapeless old bag?

'Yes, that appears to be correct. There must have been some error in the tailoring.' She had better not push this too far, or word would get back to Rivelli. 'However, she is happy to overlook it on this occasion.'

She hung up before the girl could start asking questions. She had what she needed; no point in trying to cause more trouble, however great the temptation. Stage One of Operation Divorce was complete.

* * *

Stage Two necessitated a return visit to the Cissé studio in Hoxton, where Isabelle and Will were happily working away, she on designs, he on funding applications. She had mentioned Victoria's strange request, and Will was taking his time to think it over. Two women, powerful and well connected, both wearing Cissé – that, surely, was too good an offer to turn down. An *entrée* to the very best Italian garment manufacturer in the world – not just as another pushy newcomer, but hand-picked by the women closest to him. And if it worked out as it should, then Rivelli would want them – might even take them under an exclusive licence. Then they would have the best tailoring possible, the standard to which all the big fashion houses aspired. They would have a label in their clothes – 'Made in Italy by Rivelli' – a guarantee of quality, and a sign that they had arrived. Instead of spending their time chasing pattern makers and cutters and seam-stresses, they would hand the order books over to Rivelli and sit back, secure in the knowledge that the orders would be fulfilled to the highest standards. It was a step towards the red carpet. A big step.

On the other hand, it could all be bullshit. Victoria could be using them as bait. Will knew the type – ageing cokeheads racing towards their sell-by date – and had an instinctive distrust.

'Princess.'

She didn't hear him. She was absorbed in her work, her mouth full of pins. Around the studio, like a silent guard, stood the tailor's dummies, swathed in fabrics, covered in chalk and bulldog clips, the lines of the collection starting to emerge on their lifeless trunks.

'You do trust her, don't you? This Victoria woman.'

'What? Sorry, I was miles away.'

The doorbell rang. Will did the meeting and greeting.

'Oooh!' squealed Victoria, rushing into the studio and clapping her hands together, 'this is my dragon dress! I just know it!'

As I suspected, thought Will. *Cokehead.*

'Yes, that's it,' said Isabelle. She was not expecting interruptions today, and had been working hard on four different dresses, variations on a basic theme of opulent evening-wear, lavish explosions of silk in luscious colours. But Victoria was not someone to dismiss lightly.

'I love it, love it, love it! I can't wait to see the finished results. Rivelli will just die.'

'And you really do want two, do you?' asked Will. 'It's a bit unusual.'

'I know,' said Victoria, 'but I can't resist. I'm being a bit naughty. I'm putting it all on Rivelli's account. You won't tell him, will you?' She put a hand on Will's arm. 'It's one of the perks of the job. I get to help out talented young designers, and I get some lovely dresses to wear.'

'Okay,' said Will. He could not very well say more. With the bank being rather circumspect about extending their overdraft, and the Fashion Council taking ages to decide on their funding, they needed all the help they could get. Like it or not, Victoria Crabtree was throwing them a lifeline. 'We'll need all the measurements, of course . . .'

'Victoria fished in her handbag. 'I've got them right here.'

Will took the paper, filed it away. How much could he charge for two dresses? Enough to cover the rent and a few bills . . . And if Rivelli was paying, perhaps a bit more . . .

'I think the colour is very me, don't you?' Victoria stood behind the dummy on which the dragon dress was forming, sticking her head above its truncated neck.

'I'm getting Veronica Lake,' said Will. 'Jerry Hall. Classic stuff.'

Victoria embraced the dummy, lifted it off the floor, danced around with it. Pins and clips clattered to the floor, undoing a morning's work, but she didn't seem to notice.

'Is Mrs Rivelli the same sort of colouring? Not everyone can carry that off.'

'Oh, yes, darling,' said Victoria, thinking of Janet Rivelli's drab brown hair and sallow complexion. 'She'll more than live up to it.' *She'll look like a corpse dredged out of the river.*

Isabelle crawled round after Victoria, picking up pins, trying to repair the damage. 'Please . . . if I could just . . . I don't want you to . . .'

'Oh, sorry, darling. Have I done something?' She dropped the dummy, which would have fallen on the floor had Isabelle not caught it. 'Now this is nice.' She moved on, like a bee to another flower, stopping before a yellow sheath dress that was being modelled on the other side of the room. 'Is this me?'

'That, I'm afraid, is strictly work in progress,' said Will, before Isabelle could open her mouth. 'And I'm not really sure if yellow . . .'

She wasn't listening. 'Who wants lunch?'

'I've got to get on,' said Isabelle, who was looking forward to sand-wiches and coffee in Hoxton Square, where they were now regulars.

'My treat,' said Victoria. 'Call it a down payment. Now, where does one go round here? Or does one? Sorry, but I can't get used to all this east London thing. It's not my stamping ground.'

'There's the Great Eastern Dining Rooms,' said Will, who knew the *maître d'* rather well. 'That's always . . .'

'Let's go into town!' said Victoria. 'Surely you can take a couple of hours off? It's so much nicer, don't you think?'

'Really, I must get on . . .' Will shot a glance at Isabelle. 'But then again, I suppose it would be nice to have a change of scene.'

Victoria was already on her phone. 'Darling, it's Victoria. Table for three at one-thirty? Oh yes you can. You can. That's a good boy. See you later! *Ciao-ciao.*' She put her phone away, powdered her nose. 'There. Does one get taxis round here?'

'It's only twelve,' said Isabelle. 'If the table's not till half past one . . .'

'They have a very nice cocktail menu. Come on. This is on Rivelli.'

And with that magic word still ringing in their ears, they went out to hail a cab.

'Well of course, he's always on the lookout for new talent. I mean that's his absolute lifeblood.'

'You make him sound like a vampire.'

Lunch was a strain. They all drank too much. Victoria got more animated with every visit to the loo.

'Oh, darling, but he is! He sucks and he sucks and he sucks and then he discards the corpses like so many . . . What's the word, darling?' She put a hand on Will's arm.

'Husks?'

'Marvellous!' Her voice was a little too loud; people were looking. 'Husks.' She made a muddle of the sibilants and the gutturals. 'What a wonderful word! I shall have to phone you every day for a word of the day. My *mot du jour.*'

Isabelle and Will looked at each other, signalling with their eyebrows. *Get me out of here. No – behave yourself.*

'Well, here's to us.' Victoria raised her glass for the third time. '*Cin cin,* as we say in Italy.'

'Shall we order?' said Will. 'I'm starving.'

'Oh, they know what I want. I always have the Caesar salad here. Not very imaginative I know but they do it just the way I like it, without parmesan and without too much dressing.'

'Perhaps you should try it without lettuce,' said Isabelle, wishing with all her heart that Victoria would starve to death before their very eyes.

'What a marvellous idea! But of course you don't watch your weight, do you?'

'I think I'll try the lamb tagine,' said Will, eager to change the subject. The waiter, an attractive young Berber boy who had cruised him the moment they walked in, was immediately by his side.

'Lamb tagine for you, sir?'

'Yes please, and I'll have . . .'

'Just my regular,' interrupted Victoria. 'Where's Laurence today? He knows what I want. Tell them in the kitchen that Victoria is here.' She thrust her menu at the waiter like a blade to the stomach.

'And for you, ma'm'selle?'

'Well, I'm hungry,' said Isabelle, determined to get her money's worth. 'I'll have the steak. Rare. With chips.'

By the time the food arrived, Will was feeling like an umpire at a particularly hostile cricket match. Victoria talked endlessly about Rivelli, and what he could do for them. Isabelle countered with acidic little remarks which were either unheard or ignored. Will could feel the goodwill evaporating on the fumes from their wine glasses.

They ploughed through three bottles. After the second, Will cared less that his two companions seemed to hate each other. After the third, he pushed back his empty plate, excused himself and went to the toilet, making sure that he caught the waiter's eye on his way. Let them fight it out between themselves, he thought, looking forward to a dessert that was not on the menu.

Victoria and Isabelle ran out of conversation quickly. Without a man at the table, Victoria's batteries seemed to go flat.

'Thank you for lunch,' said Isabelle, falling back on good manners as a last resort. 'I'm very grateful.'

'Oh no really, darling,' said Victoria, bucking up, 'it's me that's grateful. When I get you to sign with Rivelli, he'll be very pleased with me.'

Isabelle sensed bitterness in Victoria's voice, and hoped she wasn't in for a drunken tirade. Where the hell was Will?

'But enough about me.'

Thank God.

'Tell me about you. Who you are, where you come from, all the juicy details about absolutely everything.'

'Well, I'm twenty-two ...'

'I forgive you.'

'I grew up in London.'

'You must have madly exotic parents.'

'Not really. My dad's an architect. He's from Nigeria.'

'Hence . . .' Victoria gestured vaguely at Isabelle's hair, face, body.

'Yes. And my mother is a lawyer.'

'Gosh. How very professional you all are. And how useful! Daddy can design your Paris showroom, and Mummy can take care of all the contracts and so on.'

'She's not really that sort of lawyer. She specialises in divorce.'

Victoria opened her mouth to speak, registered the word *divorce* and abruptly shut it again. For a moment, she drew patterns in the condensation on the side of the wine bottle.

'A divorce lawyer, you say?'

'Yes. One of the best, or so she tells me.'

'Is that so.'

'Not that she could keep her own . . .'

'What's her name?'

'I'm sorry?'

'Your mother. What's her name?'

'Christine Fairbrother. Why?'

'Darling,' said Victoria, rummaging in her bag for a piece of paper, 'my motto in life is be prepared.' She wrote the name on the back of a receipt. 'A girl never knows when she might need a good divorce lawyer.' She snapped her bag shut, topped up their glasses. 'Now, where has that attractive young man of yours disappeared to? I do hope he's not a drug addict.'

'No, absolutely not. He just has a rather delicate digestion.'

'Oh Christ. He's not . . .' She motioned sticking fingers down her throat. 'Is he?'

'Definitely not,' said Isabelle, wondering exactly what Will was sticking down his throat. At that moment, he emerged from the toilet, smirking.

'Ah!' said Victoria. 'Talk of the devil. Now, what about a naughty little pud? Isabelle? Will?'

'Not for me,' said Will. 'I couldn't eat another thing.'

'She's a bloody nightmare,' said Isabelle, stomping upstairs to the top deck of the bus. Will followed wearily, and rather drunkenly, after her.

'She's no worse than the rest of them. You have to get used to this.'

Isabelle threw herself into the back seat. 'You mean I have to kiss her arse like you do? No thanks. I know where it's been.'

'What's the matter with you?'

'Nothing.' Isabelle crossed her arms, and started fishing her headphones out of her handbag.

'You look like a sulky six-year-old. Now I see what your poor mother had to put up with.'

'Leave my mother out of this!'

'All right!' Will held up his hands. 'No need to shout. Christ. Chill out.'

'Fuck off.'

They rode back to the studio in silence. The postman had been in their absence.

'It's from the Fashion Council.'

Their differences, real and imagined, were quickly forgotten.

'You open it,' said Isabelle. 'I can't. I feel sick.'

Will tore the envelope open. 'Shit.'

'What?'

'I don't believe it.'

'*What?*'

He paused, looked up from the letter, looked down again. 'They've given us twenty thousand pounds.'

'Twenty . . .'

'Thousand . . .'

'Quid. Oh my God.'

They embraced. Isabelle went to kiss Will on the mouth, but he moved his head aside.

'You know who we have to thank for this, don't you?'

'If you say Victoria Crabtree, I'll fucking brain you.'

'No, my dear,' said Will. 'Your little boyfriend. Dan Parker.'

'What?'

'Chair of the awards committee. Or didn't you know?'

'He's not my . . . Wow. That little nerdy one?'

'I would have said the cute blond with the nice arse, but yes. Him.'

Isabelle nodded. 'And what will twenty grand get us, in terms of production values?'

'Oh, she's businesslike now, all of a sudden. Bells and whistles, my dear. Bells and whistles.'

'Ring a ding ding.' Isabelle felt strangely deflated. The alcohol was wearing off, and the prospect of a properly budgeted show now seemed like a burden of responsibility, rather than a fantastic fantasy.

'I'd better get on, then.' She heaved a deep sigh. Was it all going to be like this – the excitement of beginning gradually chipped away by the reality of work? By the responsibility of budgets? Having to be nice to people she despised? Watching as Will slipped away, tiring of her? She saw herself in five years' time, putting together her umpteenth collection, too busy to have a social life, still holding a candle for a man she would never have, still struggling . . .

'It is all worth it, isn't it?' she said, tying her hair back with an offcut of the poison-green satin.

Will was busy texting. 'Hmmm? What?'

'Nothing,' said Isabelle. 'Just talking to myself.'

On the same sunny morning in October, postmen in London and Surrey delivered two green silk evening dresses, identical in all but size, to Miss Victoria Crabtree and Mrs Janet Rivelli. Each was accompanied by a postcard bearing the Cissé logo on one side and the words 'With best wishes, Isabelle Cissé' on the other. Mrs Rivelli hung hers in the closet along with dozens of other free samples; she got two or three a week, and wore them as instructed by her husband, depending on whom he wished to encourage or impress. Victoria tried hers on straight away, dancing round the apartment like a little girl raiding her mother's wardrobe.

* * *

It wasn't a huge do – just drinks and canapés and DJs and a micro-fashion show to celebrate the latest round of Fashion Council grants. There was a Cissé dress ready for the catwalk – the gold tower dress, which Isabelle insisted went on a black model. There were about three hundred guests, about half of them designers and their friends, the rest the usual opinion-formers, freeloaders and hangers-on of the fashion industry. Most of them were there to see Maya Rodean. It wasn't enough that she'd got the job with Versace – she must also hog the biggest of the Fashion Council payouts. The press were already shadowing her every move, turning up to her shows not to see the clothes, but to report on the famous friends who turned up. Maya was already dating rock stars – and there was always the chance that her father might turn up.

Dan Parker greeted Isabelle and Will at the door. He'd already phoned twice that day to make sure they were coming.

'Ah, there you are! The star of the show!' In a suit, he looked rather better than usual, thought Isabelle. Obviously his Fashion Council colleagues had vetoed the Blue Harbour casuals.

'Hi Dan!' Will unhooked his arm from Isabelle's, extended his hand. 'Great to have a chance to thank you in person. We really appreciate your support.'

'My pleasure,' said Dan, shaking Will's hand but never taking his eyes from Isabelle. She was wearing one of her own 'little creations', as she called them – a dress knocked up from the end of a roll of violet chiffon, cleverly cut and exquisitely stitched, the front of the bodice an exotic garden of ruffles. It looked a million dollars. It looked very 'Cissé'. It cost about five pounds.

'Well,' said Will, 'I'm going to work the room, as they say. I'll leave you two young people together.'

He strode off, an irritating grin on his face, and was absorbed by Maya Rodean's entourage. The bitch is trying to poach him, thought Isabelle, frowning.

'So, Isabelle,' said Dan, still goggling at her.

'Looks like a lovely party.'

'You're the loveliest thing at it.'

'Oh, come on. I bet you say that to all the designers.'

'Not at all. I don't really do all that fashion stuff.'

'I thought you were on the board.'

'I am. Chair of it, in fact. But they don't want me for my fashion sense, that's for sure. I'm the token bean-counter.'

'Oh.' Isabelle felt crestfallen. 'So it wasn't my wonderful designs that got us the award. It was Will's brilliant business plan.'

'The Fashion Council doesn't give grants to business plans,' said Dan. 'They think you're the bee's knees. They were raving over your stuff.'

'But you weren't.'

'I know when something looks good.' He smiled; Isabelle always had the impression that he was, somehow, taking the piss out of the whole lot of them.

'Well, thank you,' said Isabelle. 'Now, introduce me to some of those people who think I'm the bee's knees.' She scanned the room in search of Will, and couldn't find him. 'I could do with an ego boost.'

The whole strategy was ridiculous in some ways – and yet what better weapon to use against Rivelli's wife than couture? If Victoria could turn up unexpectedly at a party where Janet would be present, wearing the same dress, that might provide the spark that ignited the tinder of their long-dead marriage and burn the whole rotten edifice to the ground. And then Victoria, like a better-dressed Jane Eyre, would nurse her scorched Rochester back to health and happiness.

There were risks, of course, but Victoria was not risk averse. First of all, she was only guessing that Janet would wear the Cissé dress to the party – but she knew how Rivelli's mind worked, and if he was really keen to snare one of the two stars of the show, he would dress his wife either in Maya Rodean or in Cissé. It was his way of expressing interest. And if Maya really was going straight to Versace, then there was nothing for Rivelli there.

Secondly, Victoria's presence at the party would anger Rivelli – it was always understood that she would not attend any function where he was bringing his wife. Fashion Council parties were usually off limits, unless the Mrs was out of the country, and Victoria was usually happy to comply; Massimo was always generous with the gifts afterwards.

But the time had come for action. Victoria prepared the ground carefully, establishing her 'innocence' well in advance. She'd asked Rivelli for a date on the night of the party, and was told that he'd be in Italy – accepted code for being unavailable. Italy, to Rivelli, was more a state of mind than a state in Europe. It could be anywhere he was required to be a good married Catholic. There were large parts of Surrey, and several restaurants in London, which Rivelli counted as 'Italy'. But this time, Victoria decided to take him at his word, and to accept the invitation. If challenged, she was there as Isabelle and Will's guest, scouting new talent, working tirelessly for Rivelli – certainly not trying to make trouble. She thought the boss was out of town. She practised her look of surprise and dismay. If she could squeeze out a few tears as well, the effect would be stunning.

She arrived at the party early and talked to everyone, making sure they all registered how good she looked in the dragon dress. 'It's a Cissé original,' she said, 'hot off the sewing machine.' She span round, showing off the way the skirt billowed up around her. 'Isn't it wonderful? I love the colour so much.'

And when they see her – well, if that doesn't precipitate a divorce, nothing will.

Dan was running out of small talk. Isabelle did not seem to be in a party mood, despite the fact that the Fashion Council was funding her debut show so generously – largely at his insistence. There were some on the board who thought that spending twenty thousand on an untried designer was throwing money away, but Dan had talked up the soundness of the business plan, the originality of the designs, and managed to secure funding that was usually reserved for designers in their fourth or fifth year.

He wasn't expecting sycophancy, but a decent show of gratitude would have been nice. Instead, Isabelle was distracted, monosyllabic. He introduced her to his colleagues on the board, who made all the right noises, but she just smiled and said very little. Perhaps, thought Dan, she preferred to let her designs do the talking – but that wasn't enough in an industry so based on networking. She looked marvellous, and Dan was sure that, somewhere beneath the sulky teenager exterior, there lurked a heart of pure gold. But it would take some mining.

Champagne glasses were being topped up, but this did nothing to improve Isabelle's mood, and Dan realised with a shock that she had spent the entire evening watching her business partner like a hawk.

So that's the way the land lies, is it?

'Dan. There you are.' It was Fiona Walker, Dan's rather stern colleague. 'You're wanted.'

'Ah, Fiona. Here's Isabelle Cissé . . .'

'Quite so, quite so.' She looked Isabelle up and down as if she was wearing a bin liner. 'Nice to see you, dear.'

Dear?

Fiona dragged Dan away, leaving Isabelle alone. The party was a disaster. She hated being there, she hated these people, she hated the fact that they were going to talk loudly while her designs were being shown on the catwalk, that they were only interested in money and status and publicity and not really interested in beauty at all . . .

Her miserable little reverie was interrupted by a commotion across the room. There was a shriek and a gasp. Every head in the room turned towards the eye of the storm, where a space had cleared around two women dressed identically in green.

In Cissé.

Victoria, her cheeks burning, her eyes wide and filling with tears.

An older woman with brown hair and pearl earrings.

And between them, a handsome man in a sharp Italian suit . . .

Oh Christ. Rivelli.

'My dear,' whispered Maya Rodean in Isabelle's ear, 'you've made a bit of a boo-boo.'

Isabelle couldn't look away.

'Who is this person?' said Janet. The dragon dress, that looked so good on Victoria, did not suit her at all. It fitted badly – had the measurements been wrongly given? Deliberately? Where it should have accentuated the bust, it seemed to sag. Where it should have skimmed the hips, it pinched and stretched. It did not fall properly; it hung like a carrier bag caught in a gorse bush.

'This should be fun,' said Maya Rodean, her mouth a tight little cat's arse.

'This is Victoria Crabtree,' said Will, rushing in where angels wouldn't be seen dead. 'What a coincidence that you're both wearing

Cissé.' He laughed, tried to make light of it, but even Will could not defuse this bomb.

'Massimo?'

'Yes, my dear?'

'How does this person come to be wearing the same . . . garment . . . as me?'

'I have absolutely no . . .'

'I understood, when you suggested I wear it, that it was as a favour to some new discovery of yours. And I have worn it without comment, although' – and now Janet Rivelli raised her voice – 'it is badly designed, badly made, and badly finished.'

'I hardly think that's fair,' said Will.

'And now I see why it does not suit me,' said Janet, warming to her theme. 'It is a dress fit only for a prostitute.'

'Good shot, *Signora*,' said Maya, quite audibly.

Victoria recoiled as if slapped. She was still playing the little sparrow, her breast heaving lusciously, as if it would burst out of her *décolletage* at any moment. 'But Massimo,' she said, 'you told me you'd be in Italy.'

Rivelli's face was dark with anger. 'This is clearly a misunderstanding,' he said. 'I will speak with you later, *Miss* Crabtree.'

He took his wife's elbow to escort her out of the party. All might yet have been well, but Janet, on turning to make a dignified exit, caught the hem of the dragon dress on her heel, tripped and ripped and only just managed to save herself from going arse over tit.

Victoria giggled.

'Don't you dare laugh at me!' Janet was as white as a sheet, the blusher on her cheeks standing out like clown make-up.

Victoria put her hand to her mouth, but could not stifle her laughter, which broke out through her nose.

'You little whore,' spat Janet, and threw a nearly full glass of champagne in Victoria's face. Victoria screamed as the wine bubbled over her cleavage, soaking into the satin and turning it an unpleasant algae colour. She wiped her face with the back of her hand, then drew back her arm as if to slap her rival's face – and would have done so, perhaps, had not Will restrained her.

Maya Rodean jumped up and down on the spot, clapping her

fingertips together. Her celebrity pals joined in. Janet Rivelli left on a wave of applause.

'What the bloody hell did she think was going to happen?' Isabelle's voice was harsh from crying and shouting. The taxi rolled through the empty streets.

'Oh come on,' said Will. 'You can't think that she set this up deliberately.'

'I can believe anything of her.'

'Be sensible. Why would she want to piss off Rivelli like that?'

'Jealousy?'

'Don't be silly. She's dependent on him. And besides everything else, she's just ruined two couture dresses which cost a great deal of money.'

'It was her idea. She got me to send the dress to Rivelli's wife. Now it looks as if I set the whole thing up. And did you hear what she said? Badly made, ill fitting. Christ. It's a disaster.'

'You don't think it could have just been a ghastly mistake?'

'Oh come on, Will. Nobody makes a mistake like that. Thanks to Victoria, we've lost any chance of a licence with Rivelli, we've been made fools of in front of the whole of the British Fashion Council, and worst of all we had Maya bloody Rodean laughing at us. God, they'll be talking about this for months.'

'Look on the bright side, Princess. At least they'll be talking about Cissé.'

'And I suppose you're going to say any publicity is good publicity. Don't bother.'

The taxi took Old Street roundabout at speed.

'It'll all blow over. Don't take it so personally.'

'I can't believe Victoria would do this to me. I thought she was my friend.'

'Look, love, I wouldn't trust Victoria Crabtree as far as I can throw her. She's useful in her way, but if she's going to start using us for her own devious little purposes, then forget it. Typical cocaine behaviour. Did you see her eyes? *Pinpricks!*'

'But what's she trying to do? Piss off Rivelli? Doesn't she work for him?'

'There's more to this than meets the eye, Princess. Don't worry about it. Look. We're here.'

They stopped outside the studio.

'Coming in?'

'No,' said Will, pecking her on the cheek. 'I'm going on. See you in the morning.'

'It's morning already . . .'

He waved from the window of the moving cab as Isabelle put her key in the lock.

Chapter 7

'He's just a solicitor, Joel, for God's sake. He's been briefing me for years. That's all.'

'But I want to see you tonight.'

'Well I'm sorry, but you can't.'

'Why does it have to be dinner? Can't you see him in normal working hours?'

'Because that's the way the world works. You train clients in the evening, don't you?'

'Yes, but that's . . .'

'And sometimes I have to work late as well. We can meet afterwards, if you like.'

Joel sat on the edge of the bed, naked, the early morning sun hitting his broad, smooth shoulders. His black hair was a mess. Later, when he had his shower, he would spend several minutes with product and hairdryer restoring it to a more artful version of this exact mess.

'Oh, I see. You'll fit me in when you've finished with someone who's more important that I am. Right. I get it.'

'Or we can go for dinner tomorrow night.'

'Yeah, but tomorrow night isn't tonight.'

'And what is so special about tonight?' Christine put a hand on the top of his back, let the fingertips slide down the smooth, taut skin towards the wings tattooed above his arse.

'You've obviously forgotten, so it can't mean much to you. It's our three-month anniversary.'

Christine stopped her kneading, and allowed her hand to fall back on to the sheet. She hadn't realised that this – whatever 'this' was – meant so much to Joel. He'd made her feel like a new woman, that was for sure, and she enjoyed every second of their frequent, athletic lovemaking – but on an emotional level, she thought of him fondly at best. His endless autobiographical monologues bored her. She'd long since tired of his plans for world domination through health clubs.

He took little interest in her career – seemed, in fact, to resent her vastly greater achievements – and he certainly didn't want to hear about her family life. As far as Christine could make out, she represented money, class, access to nice restaurants and regular, uncomplicated sex. It was a shock to discover that Joel, naked and rumpled and smelling like a freshly mown field of hay, was so keen to celebrate their quarter-anniversary.

'Oh, Joel . . .'

He turned to face her, the muscles on his sides forming elegant diagonal lines down his torso. 'You'll cancel him?'

'I can't. You know that.'

'Right. I'll get a shower, then.'

'No, don't.' She pulled the duvet back, patted the sheet. 'Come back to bed. We can celebrate now.'

'I don't want to, now.'

'You do from where I'm sitting.'

'That's just . . . you know. First thing in the morning thing.' He stood with his back to the window, rotating his hips slightly. Christine bit her lip. 'You want it?'

Yes, of course I do.

Christine put her hands behind her head, tried to smoulder. This was his cue to pounce. He missed it.

'If you want it,' he said, leaning on the dressing table, groin thrust forward, 'come and get it.'

So this was his game, was it? Making her work for it?

'Oh, for heaven's sake, Joel.' She scowled at him, and realised that she sounded very much like a mother. And so, to undo that unwelcome impression, she got out of bed, and crawled on her hands and knees across the carpet to where her young lover stood, his eyes half closed, his lips curving in a smile.

'You look very beautiful this evening, Christine.'

John Ferguson pulled out a chair, got Christine comfortably seated.

That'll be because only twelve hours ago I was having sex on the bedroom floor, on the landing, in the shower and against the sink.

'Thank you very much. You're not wearing too badly yourself, John.'

'How you can tell such lies and still look so convincing I will never know. But I suppose that's why we keep instructing you.'

John Ferguson was doing himself a disservice, and had it not been for the fact that he was so resolutely married, and so very important a part of her professional life, Christine would have been quite happy to have him in her bed rather than Joel. But he and his firm, Ferguson McCreath, were her most important clients, and instructed her in some of her most lucrative cases. He'd asked her here tonight not for the pleasure of her company, but to sound her out over a bit of business which could, depending on several factors, be coming her way.

'You say the sweetest things, John. You could turn a girl's head.' This was a new sensation for Christine – flirting with colleagues. Did they think she'd turned into a randy menopausal old bag, a stock character from English comedy, a legal Wife of Bath with Mrs Slocombe tendencies?

John laughed; he looked handsome when he laughed. He was about her age, maybe a year or two older, also the father of two kids, born around the same time. After they had discussed whatever he'd asked her here to discuss, they would doubtless catch up on family life. She would tell him a little about Isabelle's new business, but not about their increasingly frequent rows, and about Ben's imminent departure to university, but not about her guilty feelings of relief that she would finally have the house to herself. John would trade similar reports. They knew each other very little, after all these years. They exchanged highly censored information. They were, after all, both lawyers.

They ordered food and wine, drank, ate soup and bread, chatted about changes in the law.

'Now, I have a ticklish little case coming up that I could do with an opinion on.'

'Officially, or unofficially?'

'Officially.' He smiled, and half-winked. 'You'll be paid, if that's what you're worried about.'

'Don't be cheeky, John. I've given you more than enough freebies over the years.'

'I think this one's going to go all the way.'

'Oh, goodie. Is it messy?'

'Potentially, very.'

'I'm all ears.'

'Well,' said John, once the main course was served and the waiters had retreated to a discreet distance, 'at this stage both parties are still negotiating, but I suspect the wife won't settle.'

'And you're representing the husband, I take it?'

'Correct. Massimo Rivelli. Extremely successful Italian garment manufacturer, factory in Milan, makes clothes for some of the biggest names in the fashion business.'

'I must ask Isabelle if she's heard of him.'

'Oh, she will have. He's one of the top three or four, apparently. Anyway, it's the same old story. Married for twenty-plus years, big house in Surrey, one grown-up child who, unfortunately, has special needs . . .'

'Hmm. That complicates matters.'

'Properties dotted around Europe and America. Everything hunky dory, he does his thing, she does hers.'

'And I take it that his "thing" is the usual?'

'Yes. The mistress is set up in a penthouse in Kensington, leads a very nice life, and Rivelli picks up the tab.'

'Ah. The Kept Woman motif.'

'Sounds familiar?'

'Extremely. So, let me guess. Mistress gets restless and grabby, starts making demands, sparks a confrontation . . .'

'That's uncanny.'

'Hardly, John. How many of these have we worked on now? Do you want me to cite cases?'

'No need. So – Mrs Rivelli gives him an ultimatum – ditch the bitch or pack your bags. Rivelli promises her faithfully that he's done so . . .'

'Oh God. This is so depressing.' Particularly so, thought Christine, as he could easily have been talking about the former Mr and Mrs Andrew Cissé.

'Then she finds text messages on his mobile phone, she gets a private detective on the case . . .'

'Ouch.'

'And she finds out exactly where the mistress is living, flaunting her status as Rivelli's wife-in-waiting – which is presumably what he's led her to believe, although he denies it strenuously. Relations break down irrevocably, and Mrs Rivelli instructs her solicitors.'

'Who are?'

'Pennington and Blythe.'

'She means business then.'

'Oh yes. She asks for everything, he instructs us to offer next to nothing, and here we are today.'

'What sort of assets are we talking about?'

'That's the problem,' said John. 'He's a very cunning man, Rivelli. He's got fingers in an awful lot of pies which he, being Italian, thinks he has an absolute right to keep secret.'

'Well, John,' said Christine, dabbing her lips on her napkin and putting her knife and fork down, 'if you want my advice, I would say that no counsel worth their salt is going to touch a case like this unless there is a full and frank disclosure of assets.'

'That's what I'm telling him.'

'Because if he's involved in anything dodgy . . .'

'Which he undoubtedly is.'

'Then she is going to find out.'

'He doesn't believe me.'

'Okay, John. I'll sum up my advice at this stage in five very simple words. The Proceeds of Crime Act.'

'Quite so.'

'If Pennington and Blythe suspect for one moment that your client is concealing assets, they're going to go after him hard and fast. And it's not difficult to get that kind of information. He'll not only lose his case, he'll find himself in the dock.'

'But, of course, he doesn't want to disclose the full scale of his assets because if he does, then his wife will feel that she's entitled to a great deal more.'

'Which I have no doubt she is. So we're in for a spectacular court case.'

'Out of which we could do very well indeed.'

'Precisely.' They raised their glasses. 'This is what you might call a win–win situation.'

'Isn't it always?' said John. 'Here's to Justice, and big fat fees.'

* * *

Rivelli agreed, after some persuasion, to allow Victoria to tell her side of the story. He turned up at the flat looking like a whipped dog; his home life was obviously horrific. Normally, he'd have been round like a shot at the first sign of a row with the wife; Victoria could always tell, by the tone of his conversation and the style of his fucking, when things weren't going well with Janet. But this time she'd been turned down three times before he agreed to sneak over.

'I promised her I wouldn't see you,' he said, glancing down from the windows as if he expected to see spies.

'You promised her a lot of things when you married her, Massimo.'

'Don't remind me.'

'Well? What's so different now?'

'She's threatening divorce. She's seen her solicitors.'

Victoria wanted to jump up and down, punching the air and saying 'Yessss!', but instead she composed her face and said 'Oh, hell. I'm sorry.'

'What did you think you were doing, Victoria?'

'What did . . .' She looked shocked, put a hand to her breast. 'My God, you don't think that I . . . That it was deliberate, do you?'

'What am I supposed to think? You turn up at a party to which you are not invited . . .'

'I was invited.'

He ignored her. 'Wearing the same dress as my wife. These things do not happen by accident.'

Victoria brought an indignant flush to her cheeks. 'Wait a minute. Are you suggesting that I set all this up to spark some kind of confrontation? Is that it?'

'Well?'

She opened her mouth to protest, then closed it again, walked across the room and took three deep breaths. 'You'd better leave now, Massimo.'

'I'm not going anywhere.'

'If you seriously think that after all these years of playing the game by your rules, being the good, discreet mistress who sacrifices everything to make your life easier, I'm suddenly going to turn around and . . . Jesus, Massimo.' A tear spilled over her cheek. 'I've tried so hard to be what you want me to be.'

'Okay, okay . . .'

'And yes, it's true, I did hope that one day you might realise how much I love you, and that you might . . .'

'What?'

'Come on!' She laughed; more tears fell. 'Don't make me say it. Okay – that you might one day divorce Janet and marry me. There.' She wiped her face, looked around for a tissue to blow her nose. Rivelli gave her a handkerchief. 'Thanks.' She blew. 'I may be a fool, Massimo, but I'm not completely stupid. I know that women in my position have nothing to gain by forcing anyone's hand. I had my romantic dreams, but they were just that – dreams. I know you'll never really divorce Janet, and I know I'll never have you to myself. I've learned to be content with what I've got.'

This was going better than Victoria expected; Rivelli looked positively stricken.

'Then how . . . How did it happen?'

'I don't know. I really, truly went to that party believing that I could help you get a deal with the best new designer of the year. I even went to the trouble of ordering one of their dresses to wear, and paying for it myself.'

Was this pushing it too far? After all, Victoria's money was Rivelli's money.

'Then how come they sent the same one . . .'

'I don't know. It was a ghastly mistake. They're young, Massimo. Inexperienced. They may have misinterpreted something I said. Oh God, it's probably all my fault. I told them how much you'd like it. They must have thought . . .' More tears, more sniffling. 'Oh, Massimo, what have I done? I'm so sorry.'

He put an arm around her shoulders. 'It's okay. It's not your fault. I see that now.'

'I would never do anything to hurt you. You know that. I've always tried to be . . .' Her voice went small and girlish. 'Good . . .'

Rivelli's arms encircled her, warm and strong, and his lips found hers.

Benedict left for university on a Sunday morning, packed his books and clothes and instruments into the back of a hired van and cleared out. Joel was on hand to help him load up. Christine found this extremely awkward – the two young men treated each other as equals, spoke the same language, dressed in similar clothes. They chatted about music, about sport, about clubs. They were quite at ease with each other. When Ben was ready to leave, there was much back-slapping and shoulder-gripping and use of the word 'mate'.

'Alone at last,' said Joel, peeling off his shirt, which was dark with sweat. 'Fancy a bath?'

The rest of the day passed pleasantly, cooking, eating and making love, until, at about nine in the evening, Isabelle arrived unannounced, wide-eyed and, thought her mother, far too thin.

'I've just had a text from Ben,' she said, stepping into the house, not even acknowledging Joel, who was, fortunately, wearing some clothes at this point. Christine was in her dressing gown.

'Oh yes?' said Christine, trying to keep her voice from scaling the octaves. 'Has he arrived safely?'

'Yes he has,' said Isabelle, in a way that implied *no thanks to you.*

'Would you like a glass of wine, darling? We're just . . .'

'I need to talk to you, Mum.'

'Right.'

'Alone.' She glared at Joel, who jumped up.

'I'll just go and make myself useful in the kitchen,' he said, springing over the back of the sofa in characteristically athletic style. 'Don't mind me, ladies!'

'What the *hell* is he doing here?'

'What does it look like? As if it's any of your business.'

'Ben was terribly upset.'

'No he wasn't.'

'Yes he was. I can tell. He's my brother, you know.'

'I had noticed.'

'Don't try to be funny. How do you think he feels being kicked out so that you can move in a boyfriend who's only a couple of years older than him?'

'He's not moving in.'

'Oh! So you admit he's your boyfriend, then?'

'Have I ever tried to deny it?'

'I can't believe you, Mum. Do you have any idea how embarrassing this is for me?'

'Isabelle, darling, you're not fourteen any more. You're an adult. Allegedly.'

'You fucking bitch. I'm sorry, but you drive me to it.'

'I see,' said Christine. 'It's my fault, as usual, like every other thing that seems to go wrong in your life. What's the matter this time, Isabelle? Bank not coming up trumps? Need another couple of thou to tide you over? Will not quite the surefire bet he appeared to be? Or is there something else that you're not telling me?'

'Like what?'

'It hasn't escaped my notice that you're losing weight, you're as thin as a rail, and you look . . . Well, you don't look well.'

'What are you implying, Mum? That I'm on drugs?'

'Well? Are you?'

'Of course I'm not bloody on drugs.'

'I hope not, because I've seen the damage that drugs can do to people . . .'

'Here we go again. Spare me the lecture, Mum. I've heard it a million times.'

'But you haven't listened, apparently. If I suspected for one moment that you're using drugs – that you're spending money that I give you to buy drugs – I would . . .'

'Oh, I see. It's not the fact that I might just accidentally kill myself. It's the fact that it's your money. Great. Thanks a lot.'

This sounded, to Christine, uncomfortably like an admission. Whenever she tried to express serious concern for her daughter, she usually ended up sounding authoritarian. She tried to soften her voice.

'Darling, if you are having problems . . .'

'My only problem right now is that my mother is shacked up with a man half her age.'

'Right.' Christine felt tears rising, and swallowed hard. 'Well, if that's your only problem, you can put your mind at ease. I can look after myself.'

'And what about Ben?'

'What about Ben?'

'How do you think he feels, having his nose rubbed in it? God, he'll be scared to bring any of his friends home in case you pounce.'

'You really can be incredibly hurtful when you try, Isabelle.'

'I'm only telling you what everyone is thinking.'

'Well thank you. That's very dutiful of you, I'm sure. And now you've discharged that duty, perhaps you can either tell me what you've come here for, or leave me to enjoy the rest of my weekend.'

'You're throwing me out?'

'Well, you're welcome to join me and Joel . . .'

Isabelle put her hands over her ears. 'I don't want to hear his name, thank you very much.'

Christine regained her *sangfroid*. '. . . To join me and Joel for a civilised drink and a chat. Who knows? You might actually like him.'

'That's disgusting.'

'I see.' The two women stood, facing each other. 'Well, if that's how you feel, I don't think there's much else to say. Please go before we say something we both regret.'

Isabelle opened her mouth to give one of her standard responses – like 'You're not in court now, Mum' – but thought better of it, and walked out of the house.

'Safe to come out?' said Joel, peeking around the kitchen door a few minutes after the front door had slammed. Christine's hands were still shaking, but she put on a bright smile and held them out to him.

'Am I allowed in?'

Victoria put her head timidly round the studio door, as if afraid that she was going to be thrown out. Isabelle was alone.

'Oh. It's you.'

'Yes, I'm afraid so. Can we talk?'

'About what?'

'You know.'

'Yes. I don't think there's anything to say, is there? I hope you got what you wanted, whatever that was.'

Isabelle was going to be harder to manage than Rivelli, thought Victoria.

'Look, I just wanted to say sorry. I realise that I put you in a very awkward position.'

'That's the understatement of the century. You've made us into a laughing stock.'

'I wouldn't go quite that far.'

'No?' Isabelle looked steadily at her. 'I don't suppose you would.'

'If it's any consolation,' said Victoria, 'Rivelli thinks you're great.'

This wasn't strictly true. Rivelli had said an awful lot of things about Cissé, many of them in highly colloquial Italian, before conceding that Isabelle did know her way around an evening dress.

'Oh come on, Victoria. If he thinks of me at all, it's as the idiot who stuck his wife and his girlfriend in the same dress. Great. Cheers. Thanks a lot.'

She'd hit the nail on the head, but this did not suit Victoria's purposes. It was important that Isabelle thought well of Rivelli, and he of her. Any friction between the two would be sure to expose Victoria as the author of dragongate.

'I haven't come here to argue,' said Victoria.

'Oh, really? Then you might as well leave,' said Isabelle, 'because I don't have any other ideas.'

'I wanted to tell you what really happened.'

'It's perfectly clear what happened. You set me up. You used me as a way of getting at Rivelli and you didn't give a damn about the damage to my reputation.'

'That's not true! I didn't know they were going to be there. I swear to God, I did not know. He told me they were out of the country.'

'Yeah, right. And the identical dresses? Whose bright idea was that?'

'Mine. And it was a good idea. That dress is your best piece. I wanted to show him what you were capable of. Believe it or not, I was trying to help you. But I can see where that's got me. Both you and Rivelli think I'm some kind of jealous lunatic who's got nothing better to do than engineer embarrassing social situations that actually hurt me more than anyone else. Oh, it's okay for you, isn't it? People will talk for a couple of weeks, just long enough to get the Cissé brand in everyone's mind, and then they'll forget it. Rivelli will be in the doghouse for a while, but then she'll take him back, like she always does. But me? I'm the one who got a drink thrown in her face. I'm the one who was made to look like a scheming bitch. That kind of mud sticks, you know. Unless I'm very lucky, Rivelli will drop me. And then I'll be . . .'

Her voice cracked, and she stopped, took a deep breath.

'Can I smoke?'

'No.'

Victoria's hands fidgeted, picking at strands of hair.

'Look. You probably know anyway. Rivelli and I are . . . lovers.'

'No. Really?'

'It's not easy being with someone as successful and powerful as him. I'm walking on eggshells all the time.'

'Look, I don't know anything about the personal side of things.'

'Of course not,' said Victoria. 'Forgive me. It's so hard sometimes having nobody to talk to, but . . .' She rummaged in her handbag for a tissue, and blew her nose. 'You don't want to hear my problems. Here,' she said, holding out a small, fat, rectangular wrap of white paper, 'take this. Call it a peace offering.' She put it on the table. 'You're always working so hard. You look as if you need it.'

She left. Isabelle listened to the receding clack-clack-clack of her heels, staring down at the small white packet in front of her.

It was really not appropriate to be taken for lunch by a prospective client, thought Christine, but the whole thing happened so fast that she didn't have time to say no. And, for once, it was nice to put pleasure before business, and blow the consequences. Was she, after all these years of circumspection, becoming spontaneous? Well, that much she had Joel to thank for.

She met Massimo Rivelli in the Ferguson McCreath offices; he was coming out of a meeting with John, she was going in. John introduced them, they shook hands, Rivelli looked her up and down with an appraising eye, and liked what he saw. Christine experienced a slight flutter at the sight of those ice-blue eyes, the perfect white teeth, shining out of that tanned, handsome face.

And that was that – she thought.

When she emerged from an hour with John, discussing other cases, nothing whatsoever to do with Rivelli, he was still sitting in the outer office, making calls, scribbling notes, sending emails. He sprang to his feet the moment she appeared, gabbled 'okay, okay, ciao' into his phone, blocked her exit.

'Hello again,' said Christine, wondering what he wanted.

'Miss Fairbrother.' He put the stress on the second syllable. 'I want to thank you.'

'For what?'

'For saving me a lot of trouble.'

'Ah.' That full disclosure business. So, he had taken his medicine like a man, then. 'My pleasure. All part of the service.'

'And I would like to show my gratitude by taking you to lunch.'

Christine was about to trot out the usual excuses, but then Rivelli touched her on the arm, just above the elbow. Even through the black wool of her jacket, she felt a tingle, and found her mouth saying the word 'yes'.

Well, after all, she thought, as Rivelli steered her out of the office and into a cab that seemed to materialise out of thin air, he was not a client yet, nor, if John Ferguson was doing his job right, would he ever be. If Rivelli had taken her advice, and given a full disclosure of assets, then there was a good chance that a settlement could be negotiated without the courts being involved at all. And so – what was he to her? A chance acquaintance, really, little more. Someone to whom she had done a good turn. She would be paid for her opinion, of course, by Ferguson McCreath, and thus, indirectly, by Rivelli himself, but there the matter ended. Didn't it? Yes, she told herself, it did, as Rivelli held the cab door open for her and handed her in.

He took her to L'Escargot.

Sitting across the table from him, it was hard not to make an inventory of his charms. The well-cut, greying hair. The immaculate clothes, the blue checked shirt with the charcoal suit, the open collar revealing a few tufts curling up on to the thick, tanned throat. The hands, neatly manicured but large, masculine, the hands of a working man, not some effete academic or *lawyer* . . .

'It is very charming to kidnap you in this way, Miss Fairbrother.'

'Am I being kidnapped?' She looked around the light, airy opulence of the L'Escargot dining room. 'I had no idea it could be so agreeable.'

'Of course, you are free to leave at any time.' His eyes twinkled – it was the only word for it – and he smiled, flashing those perfect white teeth again. Christine felt slightly light headed. He ordered wine without looking at the wine list, and certainly without consulting her, which she found surprisingly pleasant; with Andy, there had always been long deliberations over grape, vintage and price, although neither of them really knew the first thing about wine. Rivelli may be an unreconstructed Italian macho, she thought, but he's rather refreshing. As was the wine, when it arrived, a light tangy little number that slipped down very easily.

'Your health,' he said, 'and thank you again. John tells me that you take a very hard line on these matters.'

'Ah, now if we're going to drift into professional waters, Mr Rivelli, I shall have to make my escape.'

'No, no. Nothing of the sort. I understand your sensitivity. I say only one thing, and you say nothing. That I have learned a lesson. My business dealings are . . . complicated, I suppose, as all business dealings are. Some things are here, some things are there, we do not always want people to know too much.'

Christine put her hands over her ears. 'I must not hear this, you know.'

'Okay, enough.' He playfully, but firmly, pulled her hands down. 'But just to say that I am taking your advice, John's advice, and I go like a lamb to the slaughter.'

'It is better that way.'

'Because, as you say, I do not wish to find myself under investigation for any suspicion of . . . what? Irregularity?'

'Quite so. Delicious wine. Have you tried this olive bread? It's perfect.'

'I admire your discretion, Miss Fair . . .'

'Please. Christine.'

'*Piacere*. And you will call me Massimo, of course.'

They clinked and drank again, maintaining eye contact. This was starting to seem a great deal more like a date than Christine was anticipating – and, at the back of her mind, there was the delightful knowledge that she, for once, would not be picking up the tab. Impoverished thirty-year-old personal trainers with abundant sexual stamina were all very well, but there was much to be said for a man of substance. Besides which, Joel was becoming unpredictable. Sometimes he was clingy and demanding; at other times he broke dates, ignored her calls. The time had come to draw down the curtains on that particular episode.

'You are, John tells me, the number one in your area.'

'That's very kind of John,' said Christine.

'How long have you been in family law? It must be hard to make a mark in your profession.' Massimo showed more interest in her career in two sentences than Joel had in several months.

'Oh, I've been practising for ever,' she said. 'Family law was something I just fell into.' This wasn't strictly true: she'd seen which side her bread was buttered on a long time ago, and opted out of the less dependable criminal cases. 'But it's something I enjoy . . .'

'And which you're very good at.'

'Well, my clients seem to think so.'

'And yet, for all that, you remain, if I may say so, a very beautiful woman.'

Christine was about to protest, but found she did not want to. Yes, he was a smooth-talking Italian. No, it probably wasn't a good idea to start anything with a somewhat crooked, not-yet-divorced businessman. Who may, she had to remind herself, yet end up being her client.

'Thank you.' She blushed, and looked down at her napkin, just as the food arrived. Rivelli never took his eyes off her.

Chapter 8

Autumn wore into winter, the hours of daylight dwindled, and even in the studio with all those windows it was sometimes hard to distinguish between day and night. Isabelle spent so much time there that she began to feel that she lived there. By the middle of December, she actually did live there. She gave up her flat in Bethnal Green, and persuaded her father to carry on paying the rent into her bank account as before; money saved was money to spend on the collection. The collection. All that mattered was the collection. Isabelle breathed, dreamed, drank and ate the collection. Well, perhaps not ate. She was losing more and more weight. The curves that made her look so emphatically like a woman were disappearing. She looked like a model. She looked like a boy. Will didn't like it.

There was another reason for Isabelle's weight loss, besides stress: she had developed a serious cocaine habit. It started with Victoria's little 'peace offering', just to keep going late at night, and when that ran out she got more. There was no shortage of cocaine in Hoxton and Shoreditch. You didn't have to hang around dodgy council estates waiting for teenagers on bikes, like the crackheads did in Bethnal Green. You got it from a friend who worked in a bar, who gave it to you for free at first, but then, with deep regret, explained that he had money troubles of his own and would really appreciate a token payment, say forty quid a gram. And suddenly, the money that you were saving by sleeping on a mattress on the studio floor had gone up your nose. But, Isabelle persuaded herself, the cocaine was a means to an end. It helped her to work, to cope with deadlines, to blot out the longing for Will. As soon as the collection was on the catwalk, she would stop.

She put everything into the collection – all her dreams and frustrations, all her love for Will, because it was love by now, all her anger at her mother, her craving for approval, her loneliness, her fear that the whole thing might just go up in smoke. The dresses that emerged were extraordinary, surprising even Will – great explosions of colour and texture that somehow, when worn, managed to be chic, even severe. 'It looks like a little girl's dream of what a princess would wear to a fairy-tale ball,' he said of one particularly extravagant pink satin confection, 'tailored by Coco Chanel.'

'You're starting to sound like a publicist,' said Isabelle.

'Darling, when they get a look at this' – he ran a hand over her bare shoulder, down the bodice of the dress, which she was modelling on an improvised catwalk – 'they're going to have to invent some new superlatives. Roll on February. They'll be eating out of our hands. And speaking of eating, it's nine o'clock. Don't you think we ought to call it a day and get some dinner? My shout.'

'No, you go ahead,' said Isabelle, stepping out of the dress. In her white bra and panties she looked painfully thin, the ribs sticking out down her sides. 'I'm going to carry on for a while.'

'You must eat.'

'I will! I do!'

'It doesn't look like it, from where I'm standing.'

Isabelle bundled herself into a fleece, a cast-off of her brother's that came down to her knees. 'I can't help it if I lose weight. I always do when I'm working hard. Remember before graduation? I went down to a size four.'

'You still had tits, as I recall. Where have they gone?'

Isabelle nearly said 'Fat lot you care,' but did not want to sound like a bitter fag hag. 'They're still in there somewhere,' she said, trying to make light of the situation. 'Now run along and leave me in peace. I want to get this finished tonight.'

'Princess . . .'

'What?' She hoped he might want to stay tonight, sharing their little corner of Bohemia, as they had in Paris.

'Are you . . .' He wiped his nose and sniffed. 'You know.'

'Oh for Christ's sake.' She busied herself with pinning a hem. 'You're as bad as my mother.'

'I'll take that as a yes.'

'Don't be ridiculous.'

'Don't bite my head off. I'm just concerned, that's all.'

'Well don't be.'

There was little else to say. Will kissed her on the top of her head, which felt unusually hot, and muttered 'Goodnight.'

'I don't have a . . .'

'What?'

She was going to say 'cocaine problem', but it sounded ridiculous. 'Nothing. I don't have enough pins, that's all. I'll find them.'

'Okay. Goodnight, Princess.'

As soon as she heard the street door closing, Isabelle chopped out a fat line on the cutting table.

She'd got away with it, or so it seemed. The poison had been administered; now she just had to wait for it to work. Rivelli was in Italy for Christmas – the real, geographical Italy, not one of those psychological provinces of his – with Janet and his son, putting on a show of unity for the family, hoping that a return to normality would persuade Janet to forgive him. He'd left an expensive present for Victoria, and told her that things would be better in the New Year. Victoria said she hoped so too – and prayed with all her heart that Janet would keep the divorce alive. But Rivelli had swallowed it hook, line and sinker. Whatever happened next was Not Her Fault.

Cissé had served their purpose, and could flourish or perish, it didn't matter to Victoria. Supposing, just supposing they recovered from the notoriety of the dragon dress fiasco, and became a force to be reckoned with at London Fashion Week, she would keep on their good side. Isabelle was easily talked round, and Will – well, Will was a gay man, and she could wrap gay men round her little finger. She'd keep them sweet; they might be useful in the future.

With Massimo out of town, Victoria occupied herself with lunches and launches, shopping and spa, and, it being December, endless parties. All the buyers and agents, the PR agencies, the magazines and even the more successful designers, had a Christmas party, and Victoria was invited to them all. Weeks passed in a tsunami of champagne and a blizzard of cocaine, where breakfast, lunch and dinner could, if you planned it right, consist entirely of canapés. In between times Victoria slept, went to Pilates, and took the occasional lover; there was no shortage of waiters or couriers or models to be snapped up at this time of year. In a designer dress, a good pair of shoes, with coke in your handbag and a clutch of invitations to the best parties in town, Victoria would never be short of company.

Adele could read her like a book, damn her.

'So, darling, you have your Christmas holiday,' said Adele, tasting the first drink of the day over brunch at Century. 'I hope that Santa is bringing you lots of nice presents.'

'I can't complain. My stocking is quite stuffed.' Just a few hours ago, Victoria had been enjoying the dual attentions of a pair of athletic young waiters who, for reasons known only to the party planners, had been serving drinks dressed as football players. This had put Victoria in mind of the popular sport of spitroasting.

'You are a greedy girl, Victoria. You want too much.'

'Just a salad for me,' said Victoria to the hovering waiter, who seemed to be looking straight down her cleavage. 'I'm watching my figure.'

'And so was he,' said Adele, when the waiter had gone. 'You flirt too openly, my dear. You are becoming . . . forgive me for saying, this. You are becoming coarse.'

'Oh fuck off, Adele.'

'You see? Coarse.'

They drank in silence.

'If I have a little bit of fun on the side,' said Victoria at last, 'if I take advantage of the opportunities that being Massimo's mistress gives me, then I have you to thank, Adele, for teaching me that men are to be used.'

'Not in this way. One must keep up appearances.'

'You're starting to sound like Massimo.'

'And we are both right. You can't go around like a child in a sweet-shop, grab grab grab. Especially now.'

'Well I'm bored. I get lonely.'

'You'll be a great deal more lonely if you lose Massimo.'

'I won't. He's getting divorced, isn't he?'

'Maybe.'

'What do you mean, maybe?'

'I mean . . . what is the English expression? Don't count your chickens?'

'All right. I know. And there's many a slip twixt cup and lip. You can trot them all out.'

'There is wisdom even in cliché you know.'

'He's been saying for years that he wanted a divorce so that we could be together all the time. He said it repeatedly when we were in France. It was wonderful . . . it was like being married to him for real.'

'But it is not real. It is a fantasy.'

'The only thing that's been preventing Massimo from getting a divorce is the fact that he and his wife and his family are all such bloody good Catholics. He would not instigate divorce proceedings simply on the grounds that he had fallen in love with someone else. The Pope wouldn't like that at all. But now that she's started it . . .'

'If she has.'

'You know she has. You told me that everyone was talking about it. All those big high-powered lawyers who hang around your parties. They should know, shouldn't they?'

'I would be very careful about planning my future on the basis of gossip, Victoria.'

'You just can't stand the idea that Massimo and I might be happy together, can you?'

'And *can* you?'

'Of course we can.'

'Darling, there is a big difference between being a mistress and being a wife.'

'Huh. Like you'd know.'

'Just because I have never married does not mean I do not have eyes in my head. I watch. I observe. They all say they want the divorce. But when it finally comes, they are not always so glad. Maybe they are unhappy, even. They lose a lot of money, paying the lawyers and the settlement and the alimony. Maybe they start looking for someone to blame.'

'It's not my fault they're getting divorced, Adele.'

'Isn't it, darling? Are you sure?'

'Of course. I'm not stupid.'

'I hope you're not, darling. I really do.'

They ate their salads.

'Now, *chérie*,' said Adele, dropping her folded napkin on to her empty plate, 'please say that you are coming to my little party.'

Adele's pre-Christmas *soirée* was one of the fixtures of Victoria's social calendar. 'I'm not sure if I'm welcome.' Victoria dabbed her lips. 'Me being so coarse and all.'

'Don't be silly.'

'You might think I'm going to steal the silver. Grab, grab, grab, that's me, isn't it?'

'I am sure you will behave *chez moi*, won't you? And there are some nice people coming this year.'

'That usually means that you've lined up some man that you think I ought to transfer my affections to.'

Adele waggled a hand. 'It pays to have options.'

'I'm not like that, Adele,' said Victoria. 'I'm a one-man woman.' She had a sudden flash memory of herself, on all fours in the middle of her king-size bed, a cock at each end.

'You put all your eggs in one basket.'

'If you're going to start talking in proverbs again, I shall ask for the bill.'

'As you wish.' Adele attracted the waiter's attention, flicked a credit card from her purse. 'No, darling, this is on me. The way you're carrying on, you will soon be glad of a free meal.'

They kissed, without meaning it.

'See you at the party,' said Adele, heading for the stairs. 'Or not, as the case may be.'

Christine was not missing Joel at all, neither at the gym, nor in bed, not even inside her. He'd gone back to Australia, cursing the English winter, teasing her with the fact that it was summer down under, that he would return with a tanline, which he'd be glad to show her the minute she picked him up at Heathrow in January.

Which she had no intention of doing.

Joel had become a drain on her energies. After those first few months in which she'd felt reborn, reactivated, like a new woman and every other cliché, she tired rapidly of his endless egotism, his casual assumption that she would pay for everything and be grateful for what she got in return. He was behaving like a gigolo. A very handsome, sexy gigolo, who still made her feel fantastic when she could shut off her mind, stop listening to his endless shifting plans for the future and concentrate on the sensation of being with him – but that was getting harder and harder. When he left, she was glad.

Work was always quiet in December. Nobody wants to start divorce proceedings at Christmas, whatever the soap operas tell us. There were cases to be prepared, schedules of assets to be drawn up, which kept the solicitors' noses to the grindstone, but there were few cases big enough to keep a barrister of Christine's seniority busy. And so, undistracted by Joel or by complicated briefs, Christine was free to concentrate on the thing that really mattered at the moment – her application for silk.

The coming year, she thought with confidence, was the one in which she would become a Queen's Counsel. She would put all else aside in pursuit of her goal. She spent her days in chambers, doing research, preparing her application. She spent her evenings at home doing the same, enjoying the solitude, looking forward to Ben's return from college – if he came. There had already been talk of spending most of the vacation with indeterminate mates. She hoped to have the company of at least one of her children on Christmas Day, but if not – well, it was another day on which to work on her application, wasn't it? A day like any other.

Linda was becoming a nuisance. After successfully avoiding her for several months, screening her calls until she finally gave up ringing, Christine took pity and agreed to meet her for 'Christmas drinkies', as Linda would have it. Well, it would do no harm to have a night off, if it made Linda happy. She had been a good friend over the years, in her way, and a great help in the early stages of Christine's career, when she'd been her pupil mistress. Pupil had long since leapfrogged mistress, a fact that both of them knew but neither cared to acknowledge to the other, for reasons of tact or pride. Linda would always be senior, if only in years of call.

Since putting the date in the diary, Linda had been calling at least once every day, in and out of working hours, sometimes late at night when she was a good deal the worse for wear. She seemed to know, although Christine had not told her, that they were both 'single girls' again, and suggested that it might be fun to go out 'on the pull' at one of the disgustingly overcrowded, overpriced bars that were popular with the younger, rougher end of the legal profession, where one was pressed up against bumptious clerks and sleazy solicitors and those junior barristers who still thought that drinking ones way to red-nosed obesity was still a professional requirement.

'Come down,' Linda bellowed into her mobile, barely audible over the baying and braying that surrounded her. 'I'm in Daly's. It's fun!'

'Linda, I'm in bed.'

'How boring, it's only . . . my God it's half past ten.'

'Exactly. I'll see you on Thursday, as arranged. Goodnight, Linda.'

'But Lindy's lonely . . . Lonely in a crowd . . .'

'Good night, Linda,' said Christine, through gritted teeth, and then could not get to sleep for hours.

When they did finally meet, on the dreaded Thursday, it was at a party at Linda's chambers. The plan was to have one drink there, then go on for dinner, after which it would be acceptable to bail out without causing too much offence – although Linda would certainly want to go on. But when she arrived at chambers at six o'clock, it was clear that Linda had already been drinking for some time, possibly since lunch. Christine recognised the symptoms. Linda's pupils were tiny pinpricks in their pale blue irises, the retinas a horrible greyish red. Her long, wiry hair, black with a good deal of grey, was hanging loose, parting at the back, dragging her head down with a weight that her neck could apparently not support. And yet she had a hectic kind of energy about her, an off-putting gaiety. She was holding forth to an embarrassed group of pupils and junior barristers when Christine walked in.

'Chris, darling!' Linda shouted, waving above her head, slopping her wine. 'Over here! Everyone, this is Christine Fairbrother. Chris, this is . . . everyone!' She threw back her head and laughed. People stepped back a little. The fumes could have knocked you over.

'Christine Fairbrother,' said one of the younger men, a reasonably attractive chap in a cheap suit – he was not yet earning enough to afford better. 'I was just reading about your work in *Macdonald v Macdonald*. Absolutely amazing.'

'Thank you very much,' said Christine, flattered that her most recent success was already being studied at the lower end of the profession. 'I think luck had a lot to do with it, but . . .'

'Nonsense!' said Linda, interposing herself between Christine and the attractive young man. 'No such thing as luck in this game, that's what I keep telling 'em. Now come on, Chris.' She took Christine by the arm and dragged her away. 'People-I-want-you-to-meet.' She stumbled forward, and might have tottered had not Christine held her up.

'No point in wasting our time with the small fry,' said Linda, quite audibly. 'Let's talk to the big boys.' She approached a group of tall men in well-cut suits, and blundered her way into their circle. 'Hello, big boys.' She hiccupped loudly, covered her mouth with an unsteady hand, said 'Oops. Room for a couple of little ladies?'

The men shuffled apart, clearly embarrassed. Christine recognised a couple of Linda's long-suffering colleagues, who were all too familiar with her drunken rampages. Both, she was sure, had put a semi-conscious Linda into taxis home, fending off her drunken pawings and maudlin cries of 'Lindy is lonely . . .'

'Is thissa private party or can . . . hic! . . . anyone join in?'

'Of course, Linda,' said one of the colleagues, recoiling from the stench of wine.

'Hello, Christine.'

'Hi, Gerry.' She recognised the face, now fat and pouchy, of a senior partner at Pennington and Blythe, one of the biggest law firms in town.

'Drumming up a bit of business, Christine?'

'Really, Gerry, you make me sound like a whore.'

'Well, darling, barristers are self-employed too. And you all specialise in unhappily married men.'

Christine had heard the same tired joke on an annual basis for too many years.

'Toodle-oo, Gerry. Happy Christmas, and all that. Me 'n' my mate Chrissie are on the pull tonight, so you better watch out,' said Linda, her fingers digging into Christine's arm. 'She was my pupil, you know. Taught her ev'rything she knew. Knows. Ev'rything she knows.' She pointed unsteadily towards her bust. 'Listens to me, you know. Takes my advice.'

Christine, who had been too horrified to look up from the floor, decided to put a brave face on it, raised her head – and looked straight into the amused grey eyes of John Ferguson, her most important instructing solicitor.

Oh God. Let the ground swallow me up.

'Really, Miss Fairbrother,' he said, cocking an eyebrow. 'On the pull? I'm shocked.'

Christine smiled, nodded her head from side to side, desperately hoping that he did not think this was what she was like.

'Shocked, but quite pleased. Can I get you a drink?'

'Oh yes,' said Linda, waving an already-full glass, warm white wine sloshing on to the carpet, 'you certainly can. What a gen'l'man.'

'Thanks, John.'

'A girl could do a lot worse, Chrissie,' said Linda, in a pungent stage whisper, 'than John Ferguson.'

'Come on,' said John firmly, disengaging Christine's arm. 'Let's go and see what they've got.'

He led her across the floor, away from Linda, who simpered at the remaining men.

'Now,' he said, when they reached the table where drinks were laid, 'what would you like?'

'How about a hole in the head?'

'Ah. Bad as that?'

'Worse.'

'Well, we all have our crosses to bear, I suppose. I think it's rather nice of you, actually.'

'What?'

'Looking after the old girl.' He nodded across the room, where Linda was now left alone, but apparently unaware of the fact. 'A jolly good advocate, once upon a time. Couldn't hack it, I suppose, like so many of them. Hit the bottle.'

'And the bottle hit back.'

'Sad.'

'Very.'

John handed her a drink. 'Well, here's to the survivors,' he said. 'Those of us who can take the heat.'

'I'll drink to that,' said Christine. There was a sparkle in John's eye tonight that she had not seen before. Perhaps he, too, had been drinking.

'So, how are you? Don't answer that. I can see. You look extremely well. Almost indecently well, I might say.'

'Thank you. I am. Extremely, rather than indecently, I hope.'

'Hmmmm . . .' John looked pensive, as if trying to work out the cause of Christine's apparent well-being. 'And what does Christmas hold for you?'

'Oh, you know me, John. Work.'

'Don't be daft. You've got to take some time off.'

'Couple of days, I suppose. See the kids, I hope.'

'How are they?'

'Fine. Yours?'

'Fine.'

The old barriers were up again. It was frustrating, thought Christine, but then again those professional barriers existed for a reason. Kick them down, and you end up like Linda.

But with John, she'd be prepared to make an exception . . . If he wasn't so married.

'And what about you? Going up to Scotland?'

'Not this year, no.'

'Oh. That's a shame.'

'Sue's not too well, actually. So we're taking it easy.'

'Nothing serious, I hope.'

'Well, yes, I'm afraid it is. Cancer.' He looked at the carpet. 'Not looking terribly good.'

'I'm so sorry, John.'

'But, you know, we do what we can.'

'If there's anything . . .'

'Thanks.'

It would be wrong to flirt with a man whose wife is dying, thought Christine. A sadness descended over them both. The sparkle had gone from John's eyes.

'Chrissie!' Linda approached, crossing the room in a controlled fall. 'You naughty, naughty man, John Ferguson. Monopololising my friend. Issa party!' She showered more wine. 'Come on, Chrissie. Le'ss talk to s'mother people.'

Christine smiled weakly as Linda dragged her away, but John was intent on the bottom of his glass.

'His wife's dying,' whispered Linda, again for all to hear. 'You know what I mean? He'll be back on the market . . .'

'Linda, for Christ's sake,' said Christine, snapping her hand away.

Linda stopped, wobbled for a second, looked up at her with wounded, mad-child eyes, and burst into tears.

'I'm sorry, Chrissie. I'm so sorry. Don't be angry with me. Lindy's very vunnerable. Very fragile . . .'

The party dragged on until Christine slipped out, alone, half pissed and starving hungry, at nine. John was nowhere to be seen.

Chapter 9

It was not a Christmas to remember.

Victoria was in disgrace, after getting coked off her head at Adele's party and getting off with one of the hostess's son's friends – which Adele regarded not only as a *faux pas* but also an insult to her as a mother. The boy left Victoria's flat the next morning with a smirk on his face, and Victoria watched him as he walked down the street, already texting. She refused to be ashamed of what she'd done, in public at least; if Adele couldn't handle it, that was her problem. Perhaps it made her feel old. Well, she was old – while Victoria was still young and beautiful enough to attract a young man at his sexual peak. Admittedly that peak was not particularly high, although that may have been due to the drugs. It was certainly not worth falling out with Adele over – but Adele would have to be the one to apologise. Victoria had done nothing to apologise for. Who, after all, was Adele to be telling anyone not to have sex when they felt like it?

It did, however, leave Victoria at a loose end on Christmas Day. Normally, she would go to Adele's, enjoy a good dinner, give and receive a few small but expensive gifts, drink too much, stroll home and straight to bed . . . But not this year. This year, she told anyone who asked, she was going to enjoy a day of rest – she'd been running around so much that Christmas Day was actually the only time she'd get to put her feet up, pamper herself, catch up on sleep and reading and *relax* . . .

Christine was contemplating an empty nest on Christmas Day. Isabelle was not coming home; that much had been established beyond all reasonable doubt during another heated discussion about money/drugs/sex, which ended with slamming doors and little prospect of reconciliation. Ben, meanwhile, announced in a typically oblique way that he was 'working' over Christmas, and would be staying with mates, that he'd be back 'some time' over the festive period and they'd 'play it by ear'. Christine had no idea what this 'work' was – DJing, perhaps, or gigging (she had yet to be invited) – but for all she knew he could be a drug-dealing male prostitute, he gave so little away. He didn't look the type, but then neither do half the defendants in the criminal courts.

And so Christine prepared a nice healthy dinner of which Joel would approve, if he had the chance, which he probably wouldn't get, and in any case he had been suspiciously silent despite parting vows to email, text and call at every available opportunity. She ate alone, had a glass of wine (Dutch courage?), called her mother, called her son, and finally called her daughter, to wish them all a happy day. Her mother didn't seem to know who she was. Her son made all the right affectionate noises but was clearly busy with other people and didn't talk for long. Her daughter was on voicemail, and so Christine left her Christmas greetings there.

In the early evening, as she was going over her QC application for the umpteenth time, the TV on with the sound down, some Bruckner on the stereo and another glass of wine in her hand, the phone rang.

It was Andy.

'Couldn't let the day go by without wishing you a happy Christmas,' he said. He sounded rather drunk.

'Thank you. And a very happy Christmas to you too.'

Their last Christmas together had been anything but happy – Christine remembered furious arguments in whispered voices, burnt food, too much drink and Isabelle doing one of her silent-but-deadly acts. She shuddered.

'We had some good times, didn't we?'

What do you want?

'Remember those New Years we spent in Scotland, before the kids came along?'

'Yes, of course. Those were the days.'

Andy sighed. 'Yup. Those were the days . . .'

In an attempt to steer the conversation away from nostalgia, Christine asked 'So, have you had a jolly day?'

'Jolly!' He expelled air quickly through his nose – a typical Andy laugh. 'Not exactly jolly, no. Working.'

'Dubai project.'

'Yeah.'

'Talk to the kids?'

'Yeah. Both seem well.'

'Do they? It's so hard to tell.'

'Yeah . . . When did they grow up, Chris?'

'While we weren't looking, I suppose.'

There didn't seem to be much else to say.

'Well, thanks for call . . .'

'Fancy a drink? For auld lang syne, and all that.' He put on his ridiculous posh English accent.

'That would be nice. We'll get a date in the diary.'

'I meant now. Tonight.'

'Oh, I don't know . . .'

'A bit of Christmas cheer. Two lonely people together, and all that jazz.'

You're alone on Christmas Day? It was hard not to feel a surge of delight at the news. 'Oh, I'm afraid not tonight, Andy. I'm . . .' What? Working on my QC application? Planning an early night? 'I'm going over to Dave and Sally's in a minute for supper.'

'Oh God. You poor thing.'

'Now now, goodwill to all men.' Dave and Sally were old friends, whose over-elaborate parties had been a source of amusement throughout their married life.

'Oh well,' said Andy, 'just a wild, unstructured thought. I'll see you soon, ex-wife. I'm sure we have all sorts of exciting child maintenance issues to discuss.'

'Andy, don't be . . .'

He'd gone.

Isabelle spent Christmas Day at the studio, although she told everyone, including Will, that she'd be at her mother's. There was no point in letting on that she was going to be alone in the cold, dark studio, without even a telly for company, perhaps working on a few dresses, more likely passing the day in a Valium haze. Valium was the only thing that got her to sleep these days, just as cocaine was the only thing that woke her up – and she'd run out.

She would sleep and read and maybe do a bit of work and listen to some music and sleep again, waiting out the day, like a siege.

Eating didn't figure in her plans, even though she knew that she was hungry in a generalised, chronic sort of way. She hadn't eaten properly for weeks, even months, and could feel her hip bones digging into the mattress. Oh well, a meal skipped was a few quid saved, and that, under the circumstances, was no bad thing.

Money was tight – so tight that she and Will had decided not to buy each other Christmas presents, and had taken advantage of as much seasonal hospitality as they possibly could. The Fashion Council grant was all spoken for, every penny dedicated to the show in London Fashion Week, a couple of months away. The bank would not lend any more. Will's savings had all gone on studio rent. They were living on the money that Andy gave her – and that just about paid for electricity, transport and a few essentials like coffee and toothpaste. They didn't eat at the café any more. Meals, such as they were, consisted of sandwiches made from the cheapest ingredients. This, Isabelle told herself, was why she was off her food.

Oh, and cocaine, of course. That was the other major expense. But without cocaine, no work. No show. It was not a luxury. It was a necessity. She must get some.

Hope had reared its ugly head when a music promoter offered to sponsor Cissé to the tune of four thousand pounds, with promises of stage and video work next year, and for a while Will was hopeful, but then Christmas intervened, people went on leave with no deals signed, calls unreturned.

Isabelle wondered, dreamily, if this was all just a temporary illusion . . . If, this time next year, she'd be living with her mother or her father, looking for a lowly job alongside all the other unemployed fashion graduates, frustrated, bitter, her health screwed and her career over.

She was dozing off again when she heard the key in the door. She did not move or call out. Nobody knew she was there. It could only be Will. She would surprise him.

She heard voices – Will's voice, and another man's.

'Well, this is it. The Cissé studio.'

'Very nice.'

'It's a dump, but it'll do for now.'

She made herself very small under the duvet. She was so thin that she wouldn't show.

'I'd offer you a drink or a cup of tea, but . . .'

'I haven't come round here on Christmas Day to drink tea, have I?'

'No.'

Silence, heavy breathing, the occasional click of wet mouth parts interlocking. Isabelle peeled back a corner of the duvet and peeped out. She could see Will's back, in a denim jacket with a bright knitted scarf around his neck, his arms around another body, another pair of hands feeling his back, his arse.

Thank God for the Valium, thought Isabelle. I feel nothing.

She shuffled forward, quiet as a mouse, and peeped through the join in the screen.

If Will decided to use the bed, he would get a hell of a shock, she thought, stifling a giggle. She felt rather breathless. It was so funny, so funny, watching him like this . . .

The two men broke apart, and she got a good look at *him* for the first time – *my rival*, she thought, and nearly sniggered again, but it was caught up in a strange gulp that might have been a sob if she'd let it out.

He was about thirty, red haired, pale skinned, freckly, good looking in a slightly puggish way, wearing a black navy pea coat, a pair of suit trousers and a well tailored pink shirt that shouldn't have gone well with his colouring but, irritatingly, did.

They stood apart, looking at each other, arms hanging by their sides, breathing heavily, like boxers.

Ding ding! Thought Isabelle. Round Two!

And they were grappling again, Will pushing him back towards the cutting table, where a length of black satin was laid out, ready to be marked up and cut. It was going to be a very simple, nineteen-forties-style cocktail dress, with beaded detailing on the bodice . . .

The redhead's backside hit the edge of the table, and he half sat. Will pushed him back, still kissing him. Hands went up the back of Will's shirt, lifting his jacket, exposing his broad, pale back.

Isabelle carried on watching. One hand moved down inside the duvet, inside her pants.

Will was on his knees, unbuckling the man's belt, unzipping his trousers, moving around in his crotch. Isabelle could not see 'it' – but she knew what Will was doing. As did he, evidently, judging by the moans his partner was making.

They changed places; the redhead knelt in front of Will, pulling his trousers down, exposing his arse, the arse that she had admired so many times, kneading the buttocks, exploring, caressing . . . Will's hands rubbed the short-cropped red hair, pulling him inwards, fucking his mouth.

Isabelle was wet, fingering herself, and suddenly, unaccountably, starving hungry for the first time in weeks. The Valium fog was clearing. This was not entirely welcome. All her appetites, all her feelings, seemed to be returning at once.

Will lifted the other by his armpits, kissed him roughly on the mouth, turned him around, yanked his trousers and bent him over the table. The redhead struggled and kicked to free his feet, pulling his shoes awkwardly through his trousers, finally freeing one. Will kicked his feet apart, and fumbled with a condom packet, tearing it open with his teeth, spitting the foil on to the floor, spitting into his hand and rubbing around the other man's arse.

This is what he wants, thought Isabelle. *This is what he does.*

Will thrust forward and grunted, and the redhead sighed as if in relief. The black satin slipped and skidded over the surface of the cutting table with every thrust.

Isabelle felt tears running down her face, soaking into the warm, dirty duvet cover. She stuck out her tongue and tasted salt.

They were getting faster, harder, their bodies striving, Will's feet planted firmly between the other's, his hips slamming and slapping into the white buttocks.

The man swore – 'oh, fuck' – again and again, and then Will slammed into him one last time, held his breath, let it out in a great long 'sssssshhhhhhhhhh', and they lay still, panting, Will bent over the other's body, his back heaving.

Isabelle came silently.

They wiped up, dressed and left quickly, giggling like schoolboys.

Isabelle took a Valium, washed it down with half a bottle of red wine and slept for hours.

She woke vaguely to the sound of the door buzzer, then slept again. It was the phone that woke her properly, a text arriving. From Will.

Happy Xmas Princess! Guess what? We've got that 4k sponsorship. Tell you all tomorrow. Best to your mum. XXX

So that's who it was.

She got up, surveyed the wreckage of the cutting table, the stained, creased satin, useless now for anything other than mopping up spilt coffee. Unless she made a feature of it ... A huge semen stain right at the front ... Instead of beading on the bodice ...

She laughed until she cried again, and sat down quickly, weak with hunger.

From the corner of her eye, she noticed an envelope stuck under the door.

A Christmas card, hand delivered, a cartoon picture of penguins having a snowball fight.

Love from Dan.

She had to think for a while. Dan? Who's Dan? Oh – Dan. From Parker Walker, or Walker Parker, or whoever. What were they? A PR company? Selling agents? Loan sharks? Will dealt with all that sort of thing. She had a rather blurred image of a smart, dull young man with blond hair and glasses, and she had a surprisingly warm, agreeable feeling in her stomach.

Craving for cocaine kicked in suddenly. She had to have some – now – or she would scream. Will – the redhead – Dan – the money – work – Christmas – it was too much. She needed cocaine.

She called Victoria.

'Be right round,' she said. 'We'll have a party.'

Victoria arrived with a bottle of champagne in one hand and, judging by the clinking, plenty more in her bag.

'Happy Christmas, darling.' She produced a chic little alligator wallet. 'Let's make it a white one.' Two fat lines were chopped out on the table where Will had so recently, and so energetically, secured their sponsorship deal.

'Forget your troubles,' said Victoria, handing Isabelle a stylish silver tube – the sort of thing Alessi might have come up with if they designed drug paraphernalia – 'come on. Get happy.'

Chapter 10

The collection was ready.

Twenty-eight pieces of evening wear, from white to black – without spunk detailing, Isabelle decided) – via every colour of the rainbow, severe or elaborate, all clearly the work of one hand, like the plays of Shakespeare of the symphonies of Mahler – said Will. Out of that uncertain autumn and miserable winter had come a burst of fashion fire. Will was ecstatic. Dan Parker was delighted. Victoria was effusive. Even Isabelle, insecure and coke addled, admitted that she was not displeased.

It was late January, and they were having a little preshow in the studio, roping in friends as models, before an audience of supporters and sponsors, including both Victoria and Ricky the redhead, who was clearly hoping for a repeat performance.

It was chaos, with models changing behind the screens, the music a mix from Will's iPod, no lighting, no lasers, no dry ice – but it was, undoubtedly, a smash.

Victoria was dancing around, high as a kite, grabbing dresses from the rails and trying them on, until Will stopped her.

Dan Parker hovered on the sidelines, sipping a drink, smiling at everyone, trying to get a word with Isabelle and being frustrated at every turn. But he was patient. He would wait.

Ben was there, having come down specially from university; he was going to DJ at the London Fashion Week show itself, for free, and sat there scribbling notes, beating out rhythms on his thighs, occasionally fending off the attentions of Victoria or one or two of the other over-refreshed guests who seemed rather taken with his dark skin, brushed-up Afro hair and full, shapely mouth . . .

Even Will was not immune to Ben's charms, despite Isabelle's threat to castrate him if he even so much as breathed in his direction. Rejection she could handle, but not for a family member.

The guest of honour, in fact the whole reason for the pre-show, was

Cherry Lucas, self-styled 'legendary' stylist, who worked for everyone – including *Vogue*. Cherry was more important than a publicist, more important than an agent, more important than the Fashion Council or the buyers for Selfridges or the bank manager. Cherry was a gate-keeper. And boy, did she know it.

She arrived late, but nobody would dream of starting without her. She made an entrance as if she owned the place, with an entourage of eight – six ridiculously overgroomed gay men, and a couple of dumpy girls with too much make-up, her 'Mini Mes' as they were universally known. Cherry herself was built on generous lines, and looked rather like her name, round and juicy and black. She was famous for her make-up, her penchant for white eyeshadow and yellow eyelashes, bright pink circles drawn on her plump cheeks, glitter thrown over everything as if by an overexcited child at Christmas. On anyone else, it would have looked insane. On Cherry it worked. She was every-thing the fashion world told you not to be – fat, loud, opinionated – and somehow, she ruled it. Designers quaked in her presence. If she put you in a shoot, you were made. She liked to announce that she was dressed entirely from charity shops and Primark, because designer clothes were 'a rip off' and 'ugly'. Cherry was a loose cannon, and for that reason she attracted malicious gossip – but all of it was behind her broad back. Nobody was ever anything but pleasant to her face. Pleasant, tinged with grovelling. Cherry lapped it up.

On this occasion, Cherry was dressed in what Will referred to as her 'Mama Africa' look, a clashing collection of batiks wound round her body and head, her shoulders and arms bare but for half a hundred-weight of ivory bangles, straw sandals flapping off her feet. It was rather an odd choice of outfit for late January, but then Cherry didn't spend a great deal of her life outdoors. She'd been known to turn up to shows in Garfield slippers and a highly styled dressing gown.

'I see,' said Will, when Cherry and her people arrived, 'we're playing the ethnic card.'

'Oh God, she doesn't expect my collection to be all *Nigerian*, does she?'

'I shouldn't have thought so. But if you can be just a little bit blacker than usual, it might help.'

Isabelle rolled her eyes and sighed.

'Oh come on, Princess,' said Will. 'You're always telling me that you're your father's daughter rather than your mother's. Just this once, put your money where your mouth is. Oh, look. She's seen your brother. Marvellous. Beeline.'

Cherry planted herself in front of Ben, hands on her hips, swaying in time to the music. Understanding without being told that this was someone whose good opinion was worth cultivating, he got to his feet and started moving his hips with hers. Whoops broke out from Cherry's delighted entourage, who clapped their smooth hands in front of their shiny faces and made ill-advised attempts at African dance steps themselves.

All this was conducted to a soundtrack of Girls Aloud.

'Remind me to download some Youssou N'Dour,' said Will.

'He's Senegalese, not Nigerian.'

'Well what do they play at Nigerian parties?'

'Mostly Michael Jackson, in my experience.'

As soon as Cherry was sitting down with a drink in her hand (and drinks in the hands of all her friends – this was goodwill at a price), the show began. Will gave a running commentary, using a beer bottle as a microphone, and got more laughs than, Isabelle thought, was really necessary. The 'models' squeaked and giggled behind the screen, which fell over at one point, discovering bony knees and boyish breasts. The show opened in black and white, evolving into more colour and more fantasy, the fashion version of Dorothy's arrival in Munchkinland.

It began, as these things usually do, with a certain amount of indifference, as if the audience were rather annoyed at having their chit-chat interrupted. Conversation continued, competing with the music; some people even had their backs to the 'catwalk', as if to pay attention was beneath them. But gradually, the chatter ceased, heads turned, eyes focused on the collection. By the time the last three dresses emerged from behind the screen – three flamboyant *jeux d'esprit* in lime green, electric blue and gold – they were cheering. Will grabbed Isabelle, brought her on to take a bow, kissed her and hugged her and signalled for quiet.

'Ladies and gentlemen,' he said, 'I give you Isabelle Cissé.'

They expected a speech. She could have killed Will.

'Thank you all for coming,' she said, acutely conscious of forty, fifty pairs of eyes taking in every detail of her clothes, her hair, her body. 'I don't really like speaking in public.' Will had told her off about her habit of self-effacement; if she didn't flog her wares, nobody else would. 'But I think I can safely say, on this occasion, that I've let the clothes do the talking for me. Please come to our show at London Fashion Week. Please tell all your friends and colleagues about us. And if any of you happen to know any heterosexual millionaires, please send them my way.'

They laughed, and Will kissed her again.

'I've got one,' screamed Victoria above the hubbub, 'and I'm keeping him!'

After they'd all gone, Isabelle and Will rescued the dresses, put them back on hangers, opened the windows to air out the smoke, collected up the plastic cups and empty bottles.

'Well, Princess, we pulled it off.'

'Don't count your chickens. That wasn't the show itself.'

'But the collection is ready, the money's in the bank, the invitations have gone out and tonight, my dear, we made sure that everyone that matters will be there. Cherry Lucas is your new best friend.'

'She's my brother's new best friend, God help him.'

'She said you were fabulous.'

'Oh, headline news! "Stylist tells designers she's fabulous" shock. People like her say things like that to people like me a thousand times a day.'

'But she meant it.'

'Today, maybe. But will she remember in the morning? Or, more to the point, next week?'

'Yes, if we send her flowers and nice choccies.'

'Whatever it takes, I suppose.'

Will busied himself with bottles, emptying dregs of wine down the sink, filling the recycling crate. He could feel her eyes on him, too big in her skull, too hungry.

'And Victoria came, of course.'

'Why wouldn't she?' snapped Isabelle.

'So, maybe we're still in with a chance with Rivell, after all.'

'I suppose so. Let's see if he comes to the London Fashion Week show.'

'It's a good thing, Princess,' said Will. 'Don't be so touchy.' He put his coat on. 'Right. I'm off.'

'With Ricky, I suppose.'

'Yes, with Ricky. Wish me luck.'

She nearly said 'Go to hell.'

Everyone came to the London Fashion Week show.

Christine was there – not with Joel, nor with Andy, but with John Ferguson, her instructing solicitor, who had known Isabelle since she was a baby.

Andy was there – not with his girlfriend, of whom he never spoke, nor with any other woman, but with his best friend/best man Steve, with whom he'd been to college. Steve was now big in town planning.

Ben was there, with a few mates of both sexes, with a smile for everyone from the DJ booth.

Cherry Lucas was there, in the front row, strategically positioned so that she could see Ben, as well as the dresses, to their best advantage. She was wearing a reinvention of the puffball skirt in blue PVC, gathered above the bust and below the knee. She looked like a ghetto-fabulous Smurf.

Dan Parker was there, nerdily smart as ever, with Fiona Walker in tow, looking as if she'd been on a lemon-only diet for several weeks.

Maya Rodean was there with her celebrity boyfriend *du jour*, ignoring everything except the paparazzi who buzzed and clicked around her.

Victoria was there, telling everyone that Cissé was 'my fashion story of the year', and that Rivelli was determined to take them under exclusive licence.

Rivelli himself was there.

And so was his wife.

Christmas had gone well enough. He'd made a large settlement on their son. He had shown his contrition at endless family lunches, endless masses. Janet had said a lot about 'swallowing my pride' and 'things being different' – and hinted that she might even drop divorce proceedings.

Victoria saw them arrive together, and was a mess.

Christine watched Janet Rivelli's eyes – perfect blanks, until they lighted on Victoria. Then they widened slightly, flared, sparkled – like a candle flame where salt is sprinkled, thought Christine, remembering an old snatch of Browning.

'The co-respondent?'

'Mmmm,' said John, who could say more with less than any man she knew. She liked that. She had got into the habit of thinking of him as a maybe, an almost, a not-quite . . . That he was accompanying her tonight, albeit in the role of Isabelle's 'Uncle' John, was heartening. And he had made an effort with his dress, looking ridiculously well preserved for his years in a charcoal grey Dolce & Gabbana suit.

Isabelle and Will watched the two women avoiding each other.

'Bloody hell,' said Will, through a clenched grin, 'handbags at dawn.'

'Not again,' sighed Isabelle. 'Can't they just leave us alone?'

'Notoriety isn't a bad thing.'

The room held its breath as the two stars came close to a collision. Even the sound system seemed muted.

But Janet passed by, her eyes fixed on some distant horizon, her face unflinching. The room exhaled, the music returned to full volume.

For all his poise, Rivelli was clearly rattled. Perhaps if they could get through this party without any more dramas — and Rivelli loathed dramas above all — the marriage might survive. He hoped so. He liked his present arrangement very well indeed — and if Victoria was disappointed, well, so be it. There were others to take her place. She could have the flat, maybe. Something to show for the last ten years. Yes, that might be an idea. He could sacrifice Victoria to keep his marriage . . . If only they could get through tonight . . .

The show was in a club just north of Oxford Street, once an elegant members-only establishment that had been decaying picturesquely for decades before being rediscovered by the Hoxton set as the ideal ironic West End venue. There were still remnants of the original mouldings on the ceiling and pillars — great swathes and flourishes and Corinthian toppings that were once gilded but were now a dusty green. The walls were deep red; somewhere underneath the varnishing of time and use there was some suggestion of damask. The floor was an original worn parquet, almost black now; high, churchlike windows disappeared into the cobwebby murk above. A catwalk thrust from the rear of the room, almost the entire length, twinkling with yards and yards of fairy lights.

Backstage, there was barely room to swing a cat, let alone wrangle two dozen models and attendant stylists, make-up artists, hairdressers, journalists, photographers and hangers-on. Isabelle was jostled and trampled at every turn. But gradually from the chaos emerged the spectrum of colours and cuts that would soon be the talk of fashion town. The preview show had done its job, just as Will said it would. Cherry Lucas had talked of nothing else – her infatuation with Ben had lasted long enough to ensure that she'd brought everyone along. Considering that this was a first show by a new designer in a small venue – and considering it clashed with a very big catwalk show by one of the major Paris houses – there was some serious firepower in the room. Will was handing out cards like confetti, and getting other people's back in even greater numbers. As well as launching a fashion label, he could have set up a dating agency.

Things did not go smoothly; they never do. Models missed their entrances, zips tore and lighting cues were confused – but the audience didn't seem to notice. From the moment the first little black dress shimmied down the catwalk, to the squelching, clicking electro soundtrack that Ben had selected, the crowd was cheering. Pens raced across the surface of notebooks. Cameras flashed, cameraphones clicked, voices gabbled into digital recorders. Three men with movie cameras ran up and down the room; whatever footage they captured would be little more than an abstract sequence of light and colour. 'Film students,' thought Will, shaking his head.

Christine and Andy caught each other on opposite sides of the catwalk, beaming up at the show, pride and surprise writ large on both their faces. Christine's heart did a little leap, then a little flutter – surely Andy would not make the mistake of thinking that she was 'with' John?

The Cissé collection evolved before enraptured eyes from severe beginnings to flamboyant finale, and when the models did the final line up, sashaying out *en masse* to show the key pieces again, the applause drowned the music. Cherry Lucas was on her feet, and so were all her people – and soon everyone was up and stamping, clapping, cheering. Isabelle was dragged into the spotlight, grinning, blinking, apparently stunned by the lights, her eyes huge and wet. The models applauded her, applauded the audience. The lights got brighter. Everyone loved everyone.

Cut to black.

There was a strange, ferocious energy in the room afterwards, as if everyone felt the need to make their own mark, to show that they were just as important as the fashion, to say 'I'm fabulous too.'

Everyone was waiting for the big stand-off between the current Signora Rivelli and the heir presumptive. It was not long coming. Rivelli was jittery, fiddling with his wedding ring, his cufflinks, his tie, bouncing on the balls of his feet as if he wanted to run out of the room. Janet was serene – horribly, icily serene, her champagne untouched, the only sign of tension a whiteness around the eyes. Victoria was the first to greet Isabelle when she came out, intercepting even her parents, grabbing her in an ostentatiously physical embrace, kissing her on the lips.

'We did it!' she cried. 'We bloody did it!' She stuck by Isabelle's side, hoping, perhaps, to be shielded from Janet Rivelli, and so she had to be introduced to Christine and Andy. She more or less ignored Christine, extending a languid hand and looking away while Christine shook it. *The woman is on drugs*, thought Christine, who had seen more than her fair share of stinking junkies when she was knocking about the magistrates' courts at the start of her career.

When Andy was introduced, things were very different. 'Now I see where Isabelle gets her looks from,' she said, holding on to Andy's hand and caressing his sleeve. 'You must be very proud.'

'Yes, I am.' Andy tried to concentrate on his daughter, who was looking lost and fragile and far too thin.

'Well, of course, I always knew she would go far, this one,' said Victoria, gesturing expansively. 'One develops an instinct. I would almost say a fashion sixth sense.' People were looking at her, laughing, talking behind their hands. 'And it's so gratifying to see what a little faith can do, just at the critical moment, when the rest of the world is turning its nose up . . .'

Nobody was listening, and Victoria was quite clearly *de trop*, but she would not let go of Andy's arm. Even when Isabelle was swept off to be photographed and interviewed, she commandeered him. Christine's attempts to get a few words with her own ex-husband and co-parent were thwarted; the look Victoria gave her would have discouraged anyone.

'So,' Christine heard her say, 'you're single these days, I understand. That's fascinating . . .'

Christine went to find John. 'I think Andy's been vamped,' she said.

'Who is she?'

'I have no idea. Bad news, I suspect.'

'A note of jealousy?' said John, with half a smile.

'Of course not. I just don't like the look of her.'

'Andy's a big boy,' said John. 'He can take care of himself.'

'Let's get a drink.' Christine sounded too bright. 'I'm finding it a little odd to see my children being so . . . I don't know. Successful. Sought-after. They don't seem to have time for their old mum.' The DJ booth was surrounded by admirers; Ben's hair, half mashed down by headphones, was all that was visible of her son.

'Miss Fairbrother.' A hand on her elbow.

'Ah, Mr Rivelli.'

'I did not realise that you were interested in fashion.'

'I'm Isabelle's mother.'

'You?' His eyebrows shot up. 'Surely, impossible.'

John hovered behind Christine, holding fresh drinks.

'All too possible, I'm afraid.'

'You are married?'

'Not any more. But my husband . . . my ex-husband . . . Is here, somewhere . . .'

'Hello, Massimo.' John sounded rather stern.

'Ah, Ferguson! Keeping an eye on me?'

'Not at all. Friend of the family.'

'Very cosy.' The two men eyeballed each other across Christine. 'Well, I must not abandon my wife.' Rivelli said it without irony; perhaps, thought Christine, irony does not translate. 'Ferguson.' He extended a hand, the two men shook. 'Christine.' He took her hand, kissed it, bowed.

'Who's been vamped now?' said John.

'A note of jealousy?' asked Christine, mimicking him.

'Frankly, yes. And I'm not sure that one's client should be flirting with counsel.'

'It doesn't look like it's going to court from where I'm standing.' Mr and Mrs Rivelli were reunited, chatting to friends, to all appearances a perfect team.

'Don't be deceived. Rivelli is quaking in his boots.'

'Will they settle, then?'

'Who knows?' said John. 'You're witnessing a very civilised power struggle. The stakes are high.'

'It's exciting,' said Christine, squeezing John's arm. 'How will it all end?'

'That depends on what happens now.'

Janet and Victoria were keeping as much space between them as possible – for now. One moved, the other moved. Little by little, the distance between them diminished, like two stars set on a collision course, impelled by gravity. They drifted towards the end of the catwalk, and then, like duellists who had chosen their ground, both stopped and turned.

Victoria engineered the collision, manoeuvring backwards until Andy stumbled against the steps, and, when he did, massively overreacting so that she swerved in a semicircular movement and sloshed her drink at Janet Rivelli's feet. Not on them, of course – she knew better than to drench her rival's Louboutins. Just in front of them.

Victoria shrieked as if she had been attacked, righted herself by using Andy as a sort of climbing frame, brushed the hair out of her eyes. 'Massimo!' she said, loud enough for all to hear. 'How lovely.' She went to kiss him, but Janet interposed. The battle lines were drawn. Conversation stopped. Ben really should have turned the music down, so that everyone could hear – but you didn't need to be a lip-reader to follow the gist. Janet stood her ground.

'Get out of my way,' said Victoria. She was almost six inches higher than Janet, although much of that was hair.

'You'd like that, wouldn't you?' said Janet, her voice sounding computer generated.

'What you do is a matter of complete indifference to me.' She was going to say 'us', but thought it better to keep her powder dry.

'My dear . . .' Janet began, then put her fingers to her forehead. 'Sorry, what is this one's name? I find it hard to keep up.'

Rivelli was trying to shrink into the background, but such was the press of onlookers behind him that he was obliged to make the introductions.

'Victoria Crabtree,' he said, signalling to his mistress with blazing eyes.

'Of course. How could I forget that name. Crab. Tree.'

'And this,' said Victoria, bringing Andy forward, 'is Andy Cissé, the designer's father.' Hands were shaken. 'And the husband of a very famous divorce lawyer.' Hands were dropped. 'But I expect you know all about that, don't you, Massimo? I think you've met Christine Fairbrother.'

'I have . . .'

'Well good for you. Nothing like being prepared. Is there, Janet?'

Janet took a sip of wine. She was not a drinker, but the sheer audacity of the woman unnerved her. 'If I were you, Miss Crabtree, I would watch my tongue.'

Victoria laughed far too loud, gesticulating with her empty glass. 'Is that a warning? Oooh! Look at me shaking.'

'Victoria, for God's sake.' Rivelli's face was darkening, but Victoria was high on cocaine and combat.

'Come on,' said Andy, trying to drag her away – but Victoria's feet were welded to the floor.

'No, really,' said Victoria, 'it's good to see what I'm up against. Poor Massimo. I see what you mean.' She put so much intimacy into that line, almost a caress . . . 'No wonder you can't bear to go home.'

'Victoria, this is not helping.'

'Massimo.' Janet turned her back on Victoria. 'We are leaving.'

'No wonder it's me you take on holiday, not her.' Victoria knew she was hurting herself more than anyone, but she could not stop. It felt so good, so liberating, like skydiving without a parachute – fun at first.

'No wonder he hasn't fucked you for four years.'

The words were out. Janet cringed beneath the blow. Massimo looked as if it was only by extreme self control that he refrained from socking Victoria on the jaw.

Janet turned, stepped into spilt champagne, wobbled dangerously – Victoria laughed – and righted herself.

'Listen to me, you cheap little whore.'

'Cheap! How dare you!'

'When I have finished with Massimo . . .'

'You finished with him ten years ago, darling.'

'There will be nothing left of him but the clothes he stands up in.'

'Oh, Janet, don't you know? Massimo doesn't need clothes when he's with me.'

Janet drew breath, thought better of it, slammed her drink down on the catwalk, snapping the stem of the glass, and walked away with as much dignity as a wounded wife could muster. The crowd parted to let her through. Around Victoria, a *cordon sanitaire* had been established. No one would stand within three feet of her. Andy slipped away. Rivelli backed into the shadows. She was left alone, positioned under a yellow light that made her look infectious.

'Interesting strategy,' Christine said to John.

'I don't think she's done herself any favours.'

'No. I would describe it as a sort of suicide bombing.'

'I suspect that I may be briefing you in *Rivelli v Rivelli* after all.'

'Oh, goodie,' said Christine, who could only say such things to John. 'That's just what I need. Lots of reporting, lots of profile, and lots of lovely money.'

'Handy, just now?'

'Yes, but don't breathe a word,' said Christine. 'I'm going for silk.'

'Clever girl,' said John. 'And about time, too.'

'What do you reckon? Is this the one?'

'Oh, yes. I think Miss Victoria Crabtree has just done you an immense favour. She may have hurt herself, and she may have undermined our chances of actually winning, but if you were looking for a high-profile case to leverage your application, you couldn't have picked better.'

'And on that note,' said Christine, 'I feel as if I have the confidence to face my super-successful daughter. Shall we go and find her, Uncle John?'

But Isabelle was not so easy to find. After being interviewed and photographed by *Vogue*, and patted on the back by the assembled guests, she felt desperately tired and emotional, and wanted nothing more than to sleep. This, of course, would not do at one's own London Fashion Week debut, and so she repaired to the lavatory to powder her nose.

Twenty minutes later, she had not come out.

Will was worried; Isabelle had been distant and disjointed all day, which could be explained by preshow nerves, but didn't look good. He'd interpreted for the *Vogue* reporter, managing to make Isabelle's *non sequiturs* sound charming and insightful – but he should not have to do this. If Isabelle was going to do an Amy Winehouse, he would have to think very seriously about their future. Perhaps it was his fault – perhaps he'd led her on, let her down, hurt her. Was she really that fragile? She was no longer the bubbly, energetic, curvaceous girl he'd known and loved at St Martins. She was becoming 'difficult' – and, although she had the talent to back it up, it was not a combination that interested him.

Will told everyone that Isabelle was backstage, packing up, 'you know what a perfectionist she is,' he lied, thinking of the chaos of the studio. Christine waited and waited – surely Isabelle was not avoiding her own mother? – but finally decided to leave when she saw Victoria getting Andy in her clutches once again. She did not like the woman from the first glance, and the scene with Janet Rivelli had done nothing to endear her, whatever the professional advantages.

And so Christine left without being able to congratulate Isabelle. 'I hope she saw me in the audience,' she said to John, as he handed her into a taxi. 'I mean, she does know I was here, doesn't she?'

'Of course she does,' said John, and they drove away.

Dan Parker stood around all night with an untouched drink in his hand, waiting to congratulate Isabelle, who, he figured, must surely pass within hailing distance at some point. While waiting, he had fended off eight offers of cocaine, five offers of dinner and two offers of blowjobs in the bogs, all of them from men. And, while Dan was of the 'never say never' persuasion, he had a definite preference for women, and one woman in particular – the one woman it seemed impossible to get within eight feet of.

This was a shame, because he had something to tell her. Two things, in fact, but London Fashion Week shows were no place to say 'I love you'. But he did hope to make her happy by telling her that Walker Parker were fully committed to offering Cissé a very advantageous deal – and had already had expressions of interest from big stores in London and New York.

Instead, he had to make do with Will. Will was not immune to

Dan Parker's charms, and under different circumstances might have completed the hat trick of blowjob offers. But for now, things remained friendly and professional.

'That's fantastic news, Dan,' said Will, putting an arm round his shoulders and being surprised at the firmness of the muscles. 'We couldn't have asked for a better end to the evening. Wait till I tell Isabelle.'

'Where is Isabelle?'

'Oh, you know. Backstage.' He was sick of trotting out the same lie. Where the hell *was* Isabelle?

'Is she okay?'

'Course she is.' Will cleared his throat. 'She gets very nervous. She's not used to all this. I think she's probably hiding.'

'That's cool,' said Dan. *He says cool*, thought Will. *How uncool*. 'I know how she feels. I can't stand these parties myself.' He laughed, showing white, regular teeth.

Will almost said 'Well, why don't you let me help you relax?', which often worked. Instead he said 'Listen, Dan, I'd better go and check on Isabelle. Thanks for the good news. Can we have lunch next week?'

'Course.' Dan looked worried. 'Look, give her my . . . love, right?'

He turned and left before Will could reply.

The party was over. The fashion pack was on its way to the next one. Backstage, the models were kissing each other, texting each other, trying to nick things.

Isabelle was not there.

Will felt a surge of panic. Maybe she'd just left . . . But of course that was nonsense. She wouldn't leave without saying goodbye.

He knew without thinking where to look. In the ladies' loos, a few stragglers checked their look for the next party, sounds of sniffing came from behind locked doors, one couple was braced awkwardly against the hand dryer in deep congress. Nobody turned a hair when a man walked in. This was a fashion show, after all.

'Isabelle?' Will didn't want to cause a fuss, but he was now seriously worried. Most of the cubicle doors were closed. 'Are you in here?'

A toilet flushed, a door opened – but it was not her, just one of the models.

'Have you seen Isabelle?'

The model shrugged, pulled out her mascara and went to the mirror.

'Isabelle!' More urgency in his voice now. Another door opened, and another. Never her.

He texted her, WHERE R U?, and listened for an answering beep. The reception here was bad, the noise levels high. He strained his ears. Was that . . . Was it? Or just another of Ben's electro mash-ups?

Now there was only one door left. It was like a sinister game show. The last model left, and the loo was empty, but for Will and . . . whoever.

He checked that he was alone, and got down on his hands and knees.

The feet were bare, the jewelled sandals (Top Shop, customised) kicked aside, the chiffon of the skirt damp with water from the floor.

He reached in, grabbed her ankle, shook it.

No response. She felt cold.

'Shit.'

There was a distinct smell of vomit. Will dialled 999.

Isabelle left her own show on a stretcher, under the searching eye of a flashing blue light.

Part Two

Spring/Summer

Chapter 11

She had not been invited to New York, and under normal circumstances would have welcomed Massimo's absence to catch up on sleep and long, gossipy lunches with Adele. But these were not normal circumstances. After the fiasco of Fashion Week, Massimo had banished Victoria to the Siberia of his affections, further than ever from Italy – calls were unanswered and unreturned to the extent that she suspected that he'd changed his number just to avoid her. Dates that had been in her diary for weeks were cancelled by a call from Rivelli's PA. The salary was still going into the bank, the credit cards still being paid off, but that was all. Rivelli had gone to ground as the divorce which Victoria had precipitated with such careful, strategic planning got underway.

Now was the time for her to stake a claim in Rivelli's future. Desperate measures were called for.

And so Victoria sat on an American Airlines Boeing 777 – economy class, if you please – watching the Manhattan skyline wheeling beneath the wing tip. Her stomach turned over, and not just from fear of falling. Somewhere down there, somewhere in the middle of the island, making a deal over lunch, perhaps, or screwing one of his Stateside whores, was Massimo. She had to find him, woo him and win him back. This was not some crazy romantic gesture. Victoria was fighting for her future.

There was no one to meet her at arrivals, and she pushed her own luggage cart, just like any other tourist. Normally, as an ambassador of Massimo Rivelli, she was chauffeured to her destination, after flying first class, well rested and looking forward to the receptions and shows that gave her an excuse to travel. Now, tired and aching after seven hours in a small seat, her guts sour and churning, her teeth coated and her skin greasy, she made her to way to the strange terrain of the airport bus station. She dared not take a cab. The bus to Grand Central Station would only cost fifteen bucks, and from there, if necessary, she could walk to the little hotel off Seventh Avenue. Thank God she had her hair tucked up under a cap, no make-up and a huge pair of shades. It really wouldn't do to be recognised on a bus. Slumming went only so far.

An hour and a half after leaving the airport, Victoria was throwing herself on to the shiny satin cover of a creaky double bed in a room rather too small to contain it. The window didn't open, but that scarcely mattered; New York at this time of year was so cold that anything you could do to keep the elements out was welcome. She lay back, tore the sunglasses from her face for the first time since she'd landed, and stared up at the light fitting, an elaborate affair of brass rods and fluted glass that would have benefited from dusting. She wanted to sleep – her body was crying out for it, from her gritty eyes to her throbbing feet – but sleep would not come. There was too much to think about. She needed a drink, but this was not the sort of hotel that had room service. Fortunately, she'd had the foresight to pick up a bottle of brandy and several hundred cigarettes at the airport. She poured a generous slug into one of the bathroom tumblers, sat in the window and sipped, watching the world go by, four storeys down. It was still early in the morning. People were on their way to work. The brandy went straight where it was needed, untying the knots in her intestines, warming her heart and deadening the generalised pain in her limbs. She lit a cigarette, assuming, rightly, that smoking was forbidden on hotel premises, and daring anyone to do anything about it.

Let 'em try.

Victoria was in combative mood. And she'd need to be – Rivelli was not going to be a pushover. She may have liberated him from an unhappy marriage, but she knew in her heart that he would never have made the break unless it was forced on him, and that it would be a long time before he could forgive her for causing a scandal. Rivelli abhorred scandal, and had managed his life very well in order to avoid it – and now she, Victoria, his long-term mistress, the very person on whose discretion he relied, had turned him and his wife into figures of public amusement. She would not blame him if he never wanted to speak to her again. But Victoria would not give up at the first hurdle. Nobody said that the metamorphosis from mistress to wife would be easy. Like any major change, it involved pain. If you were going to be put off by scandal and sulking, you weren't cut out for the job.

Four hours later, she awoke with a start, her head falling on to her chest then snapping back with a crack. The empty tumbler was on the floor, a cigarette burnt to a long white column in the ashtray. She could not remember falling asleep, and for a moment had no clue as to her whereabouts. What was it, this dingy room, the dirt, the nasty décor, the hum of traffic? There was a split second of panic, as if the last ten years had all been a dream, and this was reality . . .

Victoria pulled herself together and headed for the bathroom. A shower, and a caseload of make-up, would make her feel better.

Rivelli was not difficult to find; she had only to call the New York office to get a run-down on his diary. They wouldn't know about his current *froideur*; as far as the employees were concerned, Victoria and Massimo were friends, colleagues, no more. That was the party line, and the staff would stick to it if they wanted to keep their jobs. What they said about her behind her back, Victoria neither knew nor cared. So unless Massimo had given explicit instructions to banish her to the outer darkness . . .

'He's seeing Saks this afternoon,' said a girl with a Vassar accent, 'and then he's going to a reception at the Whitney.'

'What time does that start?'

'Six.'

'Right.' Victoria made a note. 'RSVP for me.'

'Yes, Miss Crabtree.'

No nonsense about 'you haven't been invited'. Rivelli had not declared a fatwa – yet. What a surprise he was going to get.

She'd packed only a capsule wardrobe, confident that she'd be spending a good deal of her time in New York naked. The bulk of her luggage was a large *faux*-fur coat – it wouldn't do to die of hypothermia on the streets of Manhattan in March – and a selection of shoes. There were three dresses, each variations on a basic theme of Dress to Kill. Plan A, for the subtle, sophisticated approach, was a pewter-grey Stella McCartney with a jewelled neckline, which showed off her legs and had the added advantage of making her look young. Plan B was a fitted black knee-length sheath by Jasper Conran, with transparent lace across the upper chest and the shoulders, more obviously seductive.

And she was ready for emergencies with Plan C, a tiny little black Marchesa number, the lightest, sheerest silk, the tiniest straps, flaring gently around the knees. All it needed was the diamond earrings and the Azzedine Alaia shoes and for Rivelli to use his imagination – not that it left much to that.

Which one to wear? It was the Whitney, not a nightclub, and therefore good taste seemed to dicate A or, at a pinch, B. But then again, if she failed tonight, she could kiss her future goodbye. It would be back to London, and the long uphill slog to find another boyfriend, starting at the bottom again, ten years older, less able to pick and choose.

She stepped into the Marchesa, jabbed in the diamond earrings, a dab of *Envy* behind each, and she was ready to hail a cab. She'd thought of calling the office to arrange a car – but that might be pushing it.

She had not thought of walking. In Azzedine Alaias?

Middle Temple Hall is the Holy of Holies of the legal profession, the inner sanctum, the place that most perfectly expresses the mixture of tradition, conservatism, fair-mindedness and fogeyism that makes up life at the bar. When Christine first stepped into that four-hundred-year-old, wood-panelled interior, the walls lined with shields, the elaborately vaulted ceiling leading the eye up to the stained-glass windows, she felt simultaneously humbled and hysterical. Humbled that she, a law student in her early twenties whose idea of a posh night out was Pizza Express, could possibly have got to such a place on her own merits. Hysterical because – well, because it was all so fake, like a film set, everyone pretending that there was nothing odd about a profession in which men still wore wigs, in which sitting down to oxtail soup in the room where *Twelfth Night* was first performed was the most natural thing in the world.

Over the decades, she had become accustomed to dining in Middle Temple Hall, like those crusty old benchers who looked down her blouse. Dining, then as now, was a rite of passage through which all would-be barristers had to pass, and could be a useful way of meeting and impressing those who could smooth your passage in the turbulent early years of your career. It didn't do any harm to be sexually attractive, and able to hold your liquor. Christine had worked it well, charming her way into chambers after chambers – and now she returned regularly as a guest of honour, addressing tomorrow's legal hotshots on the ups and downs of family practice.

Tonight she was back, another year older, the gap between her and those depressingly fresh-faced students wider than ever. She was singing for her supper, giving them her standard routine before they were allowed to tuck into the first course. It was not difficult. Half an hour was all that was required, and she could do it with her eyes shut. A few words about some of her recent successes, naming no names, of course, but anyone who had done their homework would know to whom she referred, and then a bit about the absolute importance of the very highest standards of personal probity, bla bla bla, confidentiality in an age of increasingly intrusive media, the contract between advocate and client no matter who that client may be, drop a few hints and let them guess about the roster of the rich and famous that she had steered out of miserable matrimony into the happy-ever-after of fabulous settlements. The students would ask questions, she would demonstrate the verbal dexterity that served her so well in court, and then they would all get fed. She was astonished to see that oxtail soup was still on the menu.

Christine enjoyed dining. The food was comforting, the surroundings beautiful, the company occasionally distracting – but this year there was more reason than ever to do one's bit. With an application for silk in the pipeline, one had to be seen to be giving something back. Extending a hand to the young – those few who would actually make it in the profession – looked good.

The Master introduced her, and she stood in her place at the High Table – that historic chunk of oak, cut down in Windsor Forest on the orders of Queen Elizabeth I, floated down the Thames and installed, all twenty-nine feet of it, before the building could be completed. There was some polite applause from the four long tables that ran down the length of the hall. Every seat was taken. She was a draw. Most of those students would kill for a chance to be taken on in her chambers, to bask in her reflected glory for their first six months' pupillage. The chance of representing a major celebrity, even if it only ran to fetching the coffee and doing the photocopying, was irresistible.

'The family bar,' she began, her voice well modulated, her hands at rest, 'shows us human nature at its very worst.' A ripple of laughter. 'Affairs, infidelity, sexual perversion and mental cruelty – these are our bread and butter.' More laughter, some of it uneasy. She had them where she wanted them. 'And the lower our clients sink, the higher our professional standards must be. Those of you who have any serious ambition to practise at the family bar had better sow your wild oats now. Because the minute you start working, you'll be under the most intense scrutiny you can imagine. The press will try to bribe you or blackmail you. People you thought were your friends will ply you with an extra glass of wine at dinner to get you to spill the beans. And woe betide you if you're caught *in flagrante* with someone who is not your lawful wedded spouse.' She paused, took a sip of water. 'I hope I am painting for you a thoroughly depressing picture.'

The tension broke, and laughter rang around the double hammer-beam roof, just as it had, perhaps, over Feste's clowning at Candlemas 1602.

She heard her voice droning on, and found her mind wandering to scenes from her recent liaison with Joel. They see me now, she thought, in my tailored suit, with my legal face on, and they would not believe that just a few weeks ago I was rolling around underneath, and frequently on top of, a muscular, sexually instatiable thirty-year-old fitness instructor. Would they think me a fit and proper person to practise at the bar if they knew about that? And what of the QC selection panel? How would they take it?

'You were very good tonight,' said John Ferguson, Christine's dinner date – as he so frequently was these days – when the soup was being served.

'I hope I impressed the right people.'

'You don't have to worry about impressing anyone,' said John. 'The job is done.'

'You're very gallant, my dear, but you know perfectly well what I mean. I want silk within the year. I've waited long enough.'

'Slowly slowly, and all that jazz.'

'If I go any more slowly slowly, I'll be a King's Counsel rather than a Queen's Counsel by the time I finally take silk.' She lowered her voice. 'They drag their feet so. It's a miracle that anything gets done at all.'

'As an institution,' said John, 'the bar is not known for snap decisions.'
'I'm impatient.'
'You're bored.'

John had never spoken so directly before; the elegant euphemism was much more his style. Perhaps his wife's illness made him less inclined to beating about the bush.

'Bored? Am I?' She looked around her, at the room that had once seemed like an enchanted fairy palace, and which now, for all its history and beauty, was just an extension of the office. 'I suppose you're right. You usually are.'

'But what happens when you get what you want? When you finally take silk. What will you want then?'

'I'll cross that bridge if and when I come to it.'

'Is it really enough? All of this?' John was looking at her very directly, as if a declaration was in the offing, and then soup was slopped into their plates, and the moment was gone. When Christine could see John's face again, the shutters were down, and they were lawyers once again. Had she hoped for more? Well, if she had, this was neither the time nor the place to pursue it – especially given her recent remarks about professional standards and personal probity.

It would really never do, would it? Dating a colleague. Dating a man who was largely responsible for keeping her in work, whose wife was dying. They would both know that there was nothing improper about it, that Ferguson McCreath briefed Christine Fairbrother because she was the woman for the job. But it might not look like that to the outside world, to the hundreds of pairs of eyes watching them as they ate and chatted at the High Table. And, in a world where one watched what one said anywhere within a five-mile radius of the Inns of Court, where one could never be too sure that someone connected with a case couldn't overhear even the most discreet allusion, it was important to have very clean hands.

Particularly when one was going for silk.

Particularly when one is about to represent an extremely wealthy garment manufacturer in a multi-million-pound divorce case, by whom one has already been taken for lunch at L'Escargot and to whose easy Italian charms one is far from immune . . .

Christine applied herself to her soup, and looked down the hall at the hundreds of students, all of whom would give their right arm to be at the High Table, the Queen Bee, the hottest name in family practice, the one whom pop queens and movie moguls counted themselves lucky to get.

Nothing must be allowed to jeopardise that. No distractions, no affairs, nothing that would shift her focus from the one thing that mattered: taking silk. And if that meant lonely nights, so be it. She'd rather be successful and single than miserable and married. She'd been through one divorce; from now on, she'd restrict herself to other people's.

There had been a great deal of last minute discussion about who, exactly, Amelie Watts was going to model for – Cissé, or Maya Rodean, or both, but in the end the decision was made by Cherry Lucas, who was styling the 'New Generation' shoot for *Vogue*. Amelie would appear exclusively in Cissé. Amelie was made for Cissé, said Cherry, and Cissé for Amelie, who should never wear anything else. Maya Rodean could have her pick of the leftovers. It took a lot of flouncing, and several threats to boycott the shoot, before Maya saw sense.

'She's shitting herself,' said Will. 'She knows how bad she's going to look next to you. I don't know why she doesn't just pull out of the whole thing and bugger off to Paris.'

'Because it's *Vogue*, dear. Even the Maya Rodeans of this world need *Vogue*.'

'Perhaps this will take her down a peg or two. Bitch.'

'Will,' said Isabelle, whom the last few weeks had taught a short, sharp lesson in tolerance, 'I think, under the circumstances, we can afford to be generous.'

Despite her dramatic departure from her own London Fashion Week debut in the back of an ambulance, two nights in hospital and a further week's bed rest at home, Isabelle found herself, at the age of twenty-two and only six months out of college, the hottest story in the British fashion world, eagerly courted by stylists, editors and PRs desperate for her business. The morning after the show, Cherry Lucas had called Will, telling him that Cissé was her 'one to watch' for *Vogue*'s 'New Generation' feature, which she was styling. And while Cherry couldn't exactly ignore Maya Rodean, who was already a fixture in the newspapers and designing her first collection for Versace, she implied that she was only there on sufferance. Any lingering resentment over Maya Rodean's rapid rise, or her 'theft' of Amelie Watts at the St Martins graduation show, was swiftly disappearing.

It was one of those complicated shoots that involved ten models draped elegantly over antique furniture wearing creations by Cherry's three favoured designers. Getting ten models, a small army of make-up artists, hairdressers and assistant stylists into the same studio at the same time was a logistical achievement not far short of building the Great Wall of China. Cherry Lucas, for all her cultivated wackiness, knew how to get things done. Even the photographer, a sexually preda-tory forty-something with ice blue eyes and a permanent tan, did as he was told – and so did his people, another battalion of assistants and runners. There was someone to do everything. You only had to look thirsty and someone was hovering with coffee.

Will's eyes were all over the place.

'Could you stop lining up your next shag and help me?' said Isabelle, who no longer resented Will's sexual rejection as sharply as she once did, but preferred not to be left alone while he followed butch little runners towards the toilets. 'This is supposed to be about furthering our career, not your love life.'

She'd given up on Will, and much else, during the interminable forty-eight hours that she'd spent in hospital. Oh, he'd been there beside her, of course – he was her right hand man, her best friend, never too tired to get her a magazine or some fresh fruit, coping with her grouchy come-down with his usual even temper. He didn't even tell her off for the massive drug consumption and borderline anorexia that landed her there in the first place. He made little jokes about it, cut it down to size, dissipated the shame like a struck match disip-pates the smell of a fart. Other people visited, of course – father, mother, brother, a few friends – but nobody else called her a coke-addled slapper or pinched her bum under the covers or gave unkind names to the nurses and patients like Will did.

He'd given her so much – he'd saved her life, really – but there was one thing he would never give her, and that was himself. Whatever it was that made his pants swell up and propelled them on to the mattress had gone, just a passing phase, something to be laughed off. 'Oh God no,' she would say, perhaps in interviews, 'we got all that out of the way years ago. Friends are so much more important than lovers, aren't they? Will's part of my life, it would be like incest!' – great soundbites, fun for parties, end of story.

Of course, that left Isabelle alone, boyfriendless, at a time when she could do with arms around her at night, a sympathetic ear, someone to love . . . But she'd have to face that emptiness and fill it with work, rather than cocaine. Another soundbite. 'Drugs? They're everywhere in the fashion world. Been there, done that, had the near-death experience. I prefer limos to ambulances these days.' Edgy. Experienced. Urban. The grit beneath that glamour, and so on. Very Cissé.

The photographer's studio was huge, the size of two tennis courts, in what had once been a warehouse by the Regent's Canal just north of Kings Cross station. One entire wall had been knocked out and replaced with glass, to afford impressive views of the water. The opposite wall was white-painted brickwork, exposed pipes and old-fashioned radiators, handy for that sought-after post-industrial look with which the photographer had made his name. Today it looked as if a Jane Austen adaptation had been airlifted in – a ballroom's-worth of Regency furniture was lined up along the floor, variously draped with ethnic throws and punctuated by potted parlour palms. The colour story was cream and gold – devised, said Cherry, to make Cissé look good. 'Maya's stuff is going to look washed out against that background,' she said with a shrug, 'but if she uses those sludgy colours for everything, it really isn't my fault.'

The third designer was a nervous young lad from Liverpool with a penchant for 'street styles', ripped seams, mohair sweaters and appliqued bits and pieces that might have come from his nan's dressing table. The clothes looked good on him – he was so beautiful that anything would have. On the models they looked awkward, 'but we can stick them at the back,' said Cherry, with embarrassing clarity. The Liverpudlian fashion prodigy scuttled away with flaming cheeks and wet eyes. Will followed him with words of comfort.

They had been there since eight o'clock in the morning waiting for something to happen, and by noon Isabelle was wondering why she had been asked along at all. If she went anywhere near the models she was shooed away by Cherry or one of her assistants. When she suggested she might iron something, they looked at her as if she was mad, as if the Queen had suggested she'd serve drinks at a Royal Garden Party. Her work was done; now, the stylist took over. It was just as well Isabelle concentrated on tailoring; there wasn't much you could do to 'style' a Cissé dress. It fitted where it touched, and could only fall in the right way. She saw Maya Rodean's collection being pulled unceremoniously off shoulders, hitched up over knees, accessorised with huge pieces of jewellery that completely obscured the line. Isabelle's designs went unadorned.

A pudgy young woman with lopsided glasses and dirty hair held back with a scrunchie was running around scribbling in a spiral-bound notebook, and eventually made her way to Isabelle, who thought she was taking orders for coffee and was on the point of saying 'Black, please, no sugar.'

'Hi, Isabelle, right? I'm Ginny Pagett, I'm, like, doing the words.'

'Oh,' said Isabelle, composing her face into a welcoming smile, 'right, pleased to meet you. What can I tell you?'

'What sort of inspires your designs?'

'Great colours, great fabrics, and a desire to create dresses that modern women of all ages can wear without the fear that they're going to look like frumps or tarts.'

'Why do you think you've been so sort of successful in so short a time?'

'Because I've worked my bloody socks off.' Isabelle had kicked the habit of self-deprecation along with the cocaine. 'There are lots of people in this business with great ideas, but not that many who are willing to put in the hours.'

'Are you talking about anyone in particular?' asked Ginny, with a glint in her eye.

'Of course not. I just mean that if you haven't got the patience and dedication to learn about tailoring yourself, you can't really expect the clothes that you create to stand out.'

Her words were being taken down like holy writ.

'And finally, where do you see Cissé in like a year from now?'

'My business partner says we'll be on the red carpet at the Oscars.'

The journalist scuttled away, her lips moving as she read over her notes. God knows what she'll make of that, thought Isabelle.

She probably thinks I was being bitchy about Maya Rodean. And I probably was.

The models issued from the dressing room *en masse*, like a football team coming out of the tunnel. They were herded and prodded into place.

'Not there!' screamed Cherry. 'You'll have the gutter running right between your legs!'

One piece of furniture, just right of centre, remained unoccupied, a beautiful cream velvet *chaise longue*, studded with worn brass upholstery nails, the elaborate wooden scrolling under the headrest a deep rich brown, almost black. It was set a good two feet forward from the rest of the line.

'Everyone ready?' shrieked Cherry, taking her place at the photographer's elbow. 'Right, bring her on.'

Two assistants held the doors, and into the studio floated Amelie Watts, a fragile porcelain doll draped in a Cissé creation so light it should have melted under the lights. Layers of chiffon parted like cobwebs to reveal a deep red floor-length sheath, above which Amelie's perfect shoulders, long white neck and golden *chignon* rose with heartbreaking fragility.

'And that,' said Cherry Lucas, 'is why we're here. Let's shoot.'

'But Cherry,' came a voice from the ranks, 'Maya's not arrived. We must wait for her.'

'She's four hours late. And besides,' said Cherry, 'I don't think she needs to see this. It would be unkind.'

Victoria collared Massimo as he was leaving the Whitney and about to get into a waiting car. Throughout the reception he had acted as if she was invisible – perhaps he really hadn't seen her, surrounded as he was by business associates, although, Victoria noticed, his head turned when any pretty woman walked past. Well, she looked better than all of them, of that she was sure. She had not been the mistress of a high-powered garment designer for ten years without learning a thing or two about dressing to impress.

'Fancy seeing you here,' she said, blocking his exit to the street. 'We really must stop meeting like this.'

She watched his eyes, knowing every hidden meaning in those flickering brown depths. Would he simply say 'excuse me', and make his escape? Would she see the greenish sparks of anger beneath the contracting black brows?

'I am going to dinner,' he said, 'and then to a party at Diane von Furstenberg's.'

Much depended on what Victoria said, or did, next. She decided to keep her mouth shut, and to let her coat fall open. The Marchesa did its work, and Massimo's eyes dipped rapidly to her legs.

'Would you like to accompany me?'

Antony, once again, had fallen for Cleopatra. She took his proffered arm, and followed him to the car. Perhaps she looked less like marriage material than she might have liked – but at least she was in the back of a chauffeur-driven limousine, with Massimo's mouth on her neck, and his hand travelling up her thigh to discover – how this would please him – that she was not wearing underwear.

Dinner was dreary, and the party an unpleasant crush, but Massimo remained by her side, whispering obscenities in her ear. He did not say that he had forgiven her for what happened in London, and for all she knew he intended to drop her like a stone when the night was over, but for now, at least, he was hers, and she had every intention of leaving a lasting impression.

'That girl over there is cute,' she said, nodding towards a curvaceous twenty-year-old that Massimo had been ogling ever since she walked in the room.

'She is pretty enough.'

'Shall I go and talk to her?' She knew just how much Massimo liked a threesome, and while it was not something she regularly encouraged, the current situation called for extreme measures.

'If you like her, baby.'

'I think she's lovely.' He was excited by lesbianism, although, as a good Catholic, he was disgusted by it too. 'Don't you think we'd look nice together?'

'Sure.' He tried to sound cool, but she could hear the gruffness in his voice. Let this be a night to remember, she thought, as she crossed the floor to where the plump little brunette chicken was waiting, ripe for the plucking. When he's back in London, meeting with the lawyers, sorting out the dreary business of his divorce, let him think about the joy that I can bring him.

'Darling,' she said, touching her lightly on one tanned shoulder, 'you look very lovely in that dress.'

'Thank you . . .' An American accent, breathy, excited.

'I bet you'd look even lovelier out of it.'

'Oh . . .'

'My friend over there' – she nodded towards Rivelli, who raised a glass of champagne – 'would love you to join us for a drink in our hotel room.'

They left the party almost immediately, and took the car back to Rivelli's suite at the Carlyle.

Victoria's room remained unoccupied.

Chapter 12

'So there's absolutely no hope of a negotiated settlement?'

'None. I have made a generous offer, which she refuses.' Rivelli shrugged his shoulders, held his palms upward. 'I did not want a fight, but I suppose that is now inevitable.'

'And why,' said Christine, 'do you think Mrs Rivelli is holding out for so much more money than you are offering?'

'Revenge.'

'Ah, that, of course. But does she believe herself entitled to such a sum?'

She had asked these questions many times, of many men desperate to conceal the real nature of their assets from discarded wives. Nothing must be hidden; no nasty surprises in court. They would deny it once, twice, even three times before admitting that, perhaps, there was a little something salted away in the Caribbean . . .

'Oh, as for that,' laughed Rivelli, 'Janet always believed that I am worth more than I really am. She is very good at spending the money and not so good at counting it. She is not what you would call . . . What is the English word?'

'Thrifty?'

'*Sriffi,*' essayed Rivelli. 'No, she is not *sriffi*. She likes to believe that Rivelli is a bottomless well of money.'

'And is he?'

'Alas, no. I am afraid that I very much have a bottom.'

Denial Number One.

'And the offer you have made to your wife is, you would say, a fair settlement?'

'Very fair,' said Rivelli. 'She gets the house, there is money in trust for my son, and she has an annual allowance of two hundred thousand for as long as she remains unmarried. That is generous, no?'

'I would consider it generous, Mr Rivelli, but we must ask ourselves why your wife does not.'

'Because she wants to punish me, of course. She wants to ruin me.'

'But the sum she is asking for . . .' Christine ran her finger down a column of figures. 'Ten million pounds. That seems like an awful lot. What would lead her to believe that you could afford that?'

'I can't.'

Denial Number Two.

'Then why is she asking for it? Your wife is represented by Pennington and Blythe, Mr Rivelli. They are an excellent firm. They brief me on occasion. They would not advise a client to ask for a sum that she had no hope of getting. That would be a waste of time, and counterproductive.'

Rivelli waved his hands in front of his face and made a choking noise at the back of his throat. 'Aaach! Do not complicate matters. She is angry, I have hurt her, she wants to hurt me back.'

'We do not hurt people by asking for sums that we can't get, Mr Rivelli. Divorce is a game, and like all games, it has rules.'

He started to look angry. 'There are no rules! This is war! She wants to . . .' He joined his fists, made a breaking gesture. 'You are here to fight for me. That is what I pay you for.'

'No, that's not quite the case.' Christine always remained impassive during these tirades. She was used to them. 'If I stand up in court and say that my client is unable to meet his wife's demands, I have to be sure that I am telling the truth. That is what one's reputation is built on.'

'Are you suggesting . . . ?'

'Does your wife know something about your financial position that your solicitor does not?'

'My wife knows nothing about my financial position!' He stood up, the better to gesticulate. 'She lives in a dream world! She has never understood business!'

'Sit down, Mr Rivelli.' No 'please'; Rivelli looked shocked, but did as he was told. 'If your wife believes you can pay this money . . .'

'Which I can not!'

'Then I would imagine she has a good reason for doing so.'

'I told you. There is no hidden money. She wishes there was. She believes there is. But there is not.'

Denial Number Three. Perhaps, after all, he was telling the truth.

'And are you willing to state under oath that the schedule of assets you have given Mr Ferguson is true and accurate?'

'Of course I am.'

'Because if it is not, you are going to lose a great deal more than ten million, Mr Rivelli. You may find yourself under investigation . . .'

'This is bullshit.'

Christine put down her pen, took off her glasses and crossed her arms. The silent treatment. It had worked on her children – even Isabelle, at her most ghastly, and it worked on clients.

Rivelli blushed. 'Forgive me.' He poured himself a glass of water. 'This is very upsetting for me, as if I am under suspicion.'

'Get used to it. A performance like that in court will go very badly for you.'

'Yes.' He drank. 'It has been a lot of stress . . . Staying away from home, from my boy.' He pinched the bridge of his nose, closed his eyes for a moment. 'Now, I am ready. I will remember my manners. Please, Miss Fairbrother, ask your questions and I will answer like a good boy.'

'There is only one question.' She held up a four-page document. 'Is this schedule of assets true and accurate?'

'Yes, it is.'

'Thank you, Mr Rivelli.' She put the document away in a buff folder. 'Now, I think, we can get on with the business of winning.'

The Hoxton studio, which looked so big when they first saw it last summer, was starting to feel small. There were too many clothes hanging on too many racks, too many samples waiting to be sent out to shoots, to PRs, to buyers. Swatches were piling up in corners like glamorous snowdrifts, and every flat surface was covered in magazines and books. Will kept one tiny corner tidy, a table and a filing cabinet and a phone, and tried to stop important paperwork from being sucked into the surrounding chaos, whence it would never return. And in the middle of it all was the cutting table, piled high with fabric, with Isabelle perched at one end, bent over a sketch book, her tongue sticking out of the corner of her mouth as she scribbled down notes and drawings, frowning in concentration.

'You'll need Botox if you carry on like that, Princess,' said Will, grabbing her shoulders and starting to massage.

She swatted his hands away. 'And you'll need a stretcher if you carry on like that. Leave me alone.'

'It's nearly two o'clock.'

'I know! I know! They can wait!'

'No they can't. This isn't some silly bloody journalist, you know. This is Dan and Fiona. Your selling agents.'

'Don't nag me!' She sounded cross, but she put her pencil down and closed the sketch book. 'You know I hate to be disturbed when I'm working.'

'I told you two hours ago that they were coming in.'

'Right.' She looked at her watch. 'It's two. Where are they? Late?' The buzzer went.

'No, as a matter of fact,' said Will, 'they're on time.' Isabelle had been tetchy of late – but at least she was clean and sober, and eating properly, if he reminded her.

'Darling,' said Fiona Walker, all warmth and smiles now that she could see the figures mounting up in the sales column, 'how are you?'

'Never better,' said Will. 'Would you like a–'

'Isabelle!' Fiona stood, her arms outstretched. 'You look fantastic.'

And you still look like you shop at Asda, thought Isabelle, but accepted the embrace. 'Where's Dan? Is he coming?'

'Oh,' said Fiona, an irritating twinkle in her eye, 'he's on his way, don't you worry.' Isabelle caught a glance between Fiona and Will, and hated the implication.

'Just if we're going to be running late, I've got stuff to do.'

'Sorry . . .' Dan bumbled through the door, dropping things, carrying a bunch of dark blue hyacinths, their thick white stems wrapped in tissue paper, tied with raffia. 'These are for you.' He handed them to Isabelle; cold water from the soggy stems ran down her arms.

'Oh! Thank you!' The scent of the flowers hit her, and she sneezed suddenly, and needed a tissue. Dan rummaged in his pockets, dropping more paper, finally found something crumpled but clean, and handed it to her.

'Thanks.' Isabelle had a good blow. 'They're beautiful. I love them.'

'I thought they were like that dress . . . That blue one you showed . . .' Dan was blushing furiously. 'Well, I hoped you might like them.' He pushed his glasses back up his nose, ran a hand over his bristly blond hair.

'Well then,' said Fiona, cocking an eyebrow, 'shall we get down to business? I know how busy you both are.'

'We've always got time for you,' said Will. 'Haven't we, Isabelle?'

She stuck her tongue out at him, and busied herself with clearing space on the cutting table. Hundreds of pounds' worth of silk slipped to the floor.

'So,' said Will, 'what have you got for us?'

'Nothing but good news,' said Fiona. Ah, thought Will, what a difference six months make . . . 'We've got Selfridges.'

'Right.'

'And we've got Harrods.'

'Okay.'

'And we're ninety percent certain of Browns.'

'Ninety percent?'

'Well, their buyer's been on holiday, and so we haven't . . .'

'Right,' said Will, not waiting for excuses. 'What about Milan? Paris? New York?'

'We're working on it. As I said at our last meeting, I'll be taking samples out there next month . . .'

'The thing is, Fiona,' said Will, 'we've had a direct approach from Saks Fifth Avenue as a result of the *Vogue* feature.'

'It's not even out yet.'

'Which makes it all the more exciting. And so, obviously, we're looking for the most advantageous deal possible.'

'And that's what we'll get you, Will,' said Fiona, who would have given a very different reply if she had not been so cravenly eager for Cissé's business. Dan and Isabelle kept out of the discussion, avoiding each other's eyes.

'Good. Now, on to other matters.' Will turned away from Fiona, as if she had outlived her usefulness. 'Manufacturing.'

'Yes,' said Dan. 'I'm glad you mentioned that. You do realise, don't you, the volume that you're going to have to turn out when these orders start rolling in?'

'Yes, of course,' said Will.

'So have you appointed a manufacturer yet?'

'No.'

'That's . . . I mean, potentially, that's a bit of a problem,' said Dan, looking up at Isabelle, his brow furrowed. 'These things can take a bit of time, and if you're late with fulfilment . . .'

'We're on the verge of signing with Rivelli,' said Will.

'Ninety percent certain?' said Fiona. 'I only ask because I've seen Rivelli screw designers over before, and I'm not going to stake my reputation on another of his fuck-ups.'

'Rivelli is the best manufacturer in the business,' said Will.

'He's also the most crooked.'

'What makes you say that?' Isabelle sounded worried. 'I thought he was the one everyone wanted.'

'He is,' said Fiona, 'and that's why he can pick and choose. He plays people off against each other. He makes a lot of money and nobody asks too many questions about what he does with it. A contract with Rivelli is a pact with the devil.'

'A contract with Rivelli is a passport to the most important buyers in the fashion world,' said Will. 'He's made an offer, which we've accepted. We're just waiting for the paperwork to come through.'

'Well, good luck,' said Fiona, much more her old self. 'Just let us know when the ink's dry on the contract.'

'Thank you, Fiona. I will.'

'You don't think there's really anything wrong with Rivelli, do you?' Isabelle asked Dan, when they were breaking up and saying goodbyes, Will and Fiona still bickering over diaries. 'I mean, he's the only one anyone talks about. That's all we ever dreamed of at St Martins. Made in Italy by Rivelli.'

'He's the man for the job all right,' said Dan. 'Don't you worry. Fiona's super-cautious because Rivelli's going through this divorce business at the moment.'

'Oh, that,' said Isabelle, who had heard of her mother's part in the proceedings, and was still wondering if that was a good thing or a bad thing. 'Is there something I ought to know?'

'If there was, I'd tell you.' He put a gentle hand on her arm, pulled it away, grinned and exhaled through his nose.

'Thanks, Dan,' said Isabelle, and sighed. They stared at each other's feet for a moment. 'Well, this won't do,' she said. 'Goodbye. Thanks for coming in.'

'Oh, I don't mind.'

'And thanks . . . you know. For the flowers.'

'That's okay . . . I just thought . . . The colour.'

Fiona bustled past, crackling with static. 'When you're ready, Dan.'

Dan saluted behind her back, and followed.

'I need to know about Victoria Crabtree.'

Another day, another conference, this time in the more congenial surroundings of Rivelli's London office. Christine had objected at first, but then – well, why not? It was good to get out of the legal ghetto once in a while. And if Rivelli insisted on sending a car to take her to Marylebone High Street, it would be rude to refuse. Solicitors' offices, even those as high-end as Ferguson McCreath's, were functional spaces that exhaled the misery they'd witnessed. Rivelli's office was like an expensive hotel suite, right down to the fresh flowers and lovely views over desirable addresses and budding plane trees.

'Ah. Miss Crabtree.'

'Indeed, ah Miss Crabtree. What is she to you, and what are you to her?'

'We were lovers.' He pronounced the word with a heavy Italian accent: *loffers*.

'Were? Or are?'

'Were. Most definitely *passato*.' Rivelli smacked his hands as if knocking off the dust from a dirty job.

'Because, as I'm sure you know, your wife is citing your relationship with Miss Crabtree as one of the major grounds for divorce.'

'It is ridiculous. She knows that is not true.'

'Again, Mr Rivelli, if that was the case your wife would not be committing large amounts of money to prove it, not to mention jeopardising her divorce settlement.'

'You do not trust me yet, I see.'

'I am a lawyer, Mr Rivelli. I trust nobody.'

'I told you. I am a good boy.'

Christine paused for a moment. 'Do you want to win this case?'

'Of course.'

'Do you think I know what I'm doing?'

'Your reputation is good.'

'And do you think I have never encountered, in twenty years at the bar, husbands who deny things that their wives swear are true?'

'No, I . . .'

'If you don't want to tell me the truth, Mr Rivelli, just say so now and I shall withdraw from the case. John Ferguson will find you alternative representation. The way I work, you see, is always from the basis of truth.'

'But the truth is . . . complicated.'

'It usually is.'

'And if it all comes out in court it might not look so good.'

'Who said anything about it coming out in court?'

'You . . .'

'Mr Rivelli, perhaps you have never been through the British judicial procedure before. We say things in court that we think will win our case. We conceal other things. We do not tell outright lies, except in extreme cases. What we do – what you are paying me to do – is to present the truth in a certain way.'

'I see.'

'So you need to lay your cards on the table. Then you let me play them as a winning hand. Do you understand me?'

'I do.'

'Very good.' Christine pulled her chair closer to the table. 'Where were we? Ah, yes. I need to know about Victoria Crabtree.'

Massimo hadn't called since they got back from New York, but Victoria wasn't panicking – yet. If that's what it took for him to win his divorce case, to come out with his fortune intact, she was not going to throw a spanner in the works. He'd be back when he wanted her – and she'd made damn sure, during those coke-fuelled New York nights, that he wanted her, and all she could do for him. He loved her. He told her so repeatedly, rhythmically, sometimes while banging an eager twenty-something under her very nose. And he meant it. Of that, Victoria was sure.

* * *

'Would you say she is a habitual drug user?'

'I don't know . . . I don't like the word "habit". It sounds like a junkie in the street.'

'There's very little difference between the models taking cocaine to keep their weight down and the addicts injecting in the park. They're all part of the same depressing criminal network.'

'You take a hard line on this sort of thing,' said Rivelli.'

'Of course. Do you?'

'In the circles I move in, it's hard to avoid.'

'I see,' said Christine. 'And does your wife know about this?'

'About what?'

'Your drug use.'

'Oh, for God's sake!'

'Once again we encounter that concept that you seem to find so difficult to grasp – the truth.'

'But you disapprove of everything! You bloody English woman!'

'I assure you that I do not. It may surprise you to know that there are some things that I actually enjoy. A nice cup of tea and a cross-word, for example. Or a spot of knitting. I mean, we English women can get pretty wild sometimes.'

They stared at each other across the green leather desktop. Rivelli sighed, shook his head and laughed.

'I see I must do as I am told.'

'It would save an awful lot of time.'

'Very well, mistress.'

'I am not your mistress, Mr Rivelli. The question is, is Victoria Crabtree?'

A formal offer from Rivelli Srl came through a few days after that prickly encounter with Fiona Walker. He would take Cissé under exclusive licence at very advantageous terms, manufacturing all Isabelle's designs and sending them out with that all-important 'Made in Italy' label inside them. In return, Rivelli Srl would enhance its reputation in the fashion world for signing up the hottest new designers just before they became world famous. Everyone was happy, doubts were swept away and Will made damn sure that everyone in the business knew about it.

'And now,' Will said to Isabelle when they had signed the contracts, 'the final piece of the jigsaw is in place. World domination is within our grasp.'

'It makes my head ache.'

'Never you mind, Princess. I'll take care of everything. Watch the money-go-round. This time next year . . .'

'Don't say it! It's bad luck!'

'Okay. But mark my words, that old bag Fiona Walker will be all sweetness and light next time we see her. Just watch the orders rolling in!'

'Do you really think a deal with Rivelli means that much?'

'You bet it does,' said Will. 'In this business, it's not just about making nice dresses. It's about having the right players on your team. We've got Walker Parker, and we've got Rivelli. Couldn't be better. Aren't I clever? I feel a bit like Madonna, surrounding myself with talent.'

'And there the resemblance ends.'

'So now the buyers at the shops know we're in the big league, they'll start ordering like mad. Walker Parker will send all the orders on to Rivelli, who will make up the clothes and send them out to the shops, and collect the money and pay it back to us, minus their commission, of course. And then we pay Walker Parker their commission . . .'

'I hope there's enough left for us. I'm rather bored of baked beans.'

'Trust me,' said Will. 'We've made it. You laid the golden egg, Princess.'

'And we do trust him, don't we?'

'Rivelli? Sure. As much as we trust anyone in this business.'

'Which is about as far as I can throw him.'

'Leave all that to me,' said Will. 'You do your job, and I'll do mine.'

'Absolutely not. We are finished.'

'And how has Miss Crabtree taken it?'

'Ah . . .'

'And you have told her in no uncertain terms?'

'Well . . .' Rivelli waggled his hand. 'Not in so many words.'

'Right.' Christine gathered up her papers, tapped them into a neat pile and loaded her briefcase. 'In that case, Mr Rivelli, I am going to assign you a piece of homework before our next meeting. I expect you can guess what it is.'

'I must tell Victoria that it is over.'

'Precisely. And, I might add, in terms that admit of absolutely no misinterpretation. This is not a time for ambiguity.'

Chapter 13

Christine had seen very little of her daughter since London Fashion Week. She visited her in hospital, where she was greeted with sulks and grunts and a face turned to the wall; it reminded Christine of when Isabelle was six, and hadn't been bought a pony for her birthday. Will relayed messages with his usual good cheer: your mother wants to know how you're feeling, she says she's feeling all right, your mother says she'll come back tomorrow, she says not to bother. Christine liked Will. He winked and sighed at her daughter's bad manners. It was good to know he was beside her – boyfriend or not.

But too many weeks had passed without civilised mother–daughter interaction, and so she invited Isabelle for Sunday lunch, 'and bring a friend', she said, hoping that would mean Will, to keep the peace.

Things went well at first. They arrived on time, both of them fit and healthy – a far cry from the pasty-faced shadows of a few weeks back. Isabelle had put some weight back on; she was still too thin for Christine's liking, but she no longer looked like a junkie. Her eyes were clear, and her hands did not shake. She'd even brought a bottle of wine, something that Christine did not remember happening before. She guessed, rightly, that this was Will's idea.

'Darling!' Christine kissed her daughter on both cheeks. 'You look wonderful. Thank you so much for coming.'

'My pleasure.' Isabelle went ahead into the kitchen as if she expected to see half-naked twenty-year-olds sprawling on the work surfaces.

'It's all right, it's just family. Oh, how lovely! Is that for me? I'll open it right away.'

They talked about everything and nothing, Will asking questions about Christine's working life, as a result of which Isabelle learned more about her mother than she'd ever known before.

'A QC! Wow, that's really something. You didn't tell me your mother was going to be a QC, Isabelle.'

'It's not happened yet! The application is being processed.'

'Yeah, but you're sure to get it, aren't you? I mean, with the kind of cases that you do. I've read about you in the papers a lot.'

'Have you?' asked Isabelle. 'You never told me.'

'Princess, you never read the newspapers. She takes about as much interest in the outside world as she does in . . . I don't know. Golf, or something.'

'She was always the same. Head in the clouds, playing with dolls, painting, drawing.'

'And she's turned it to good use. Your daughter is the hottest name in British fashion at the moment.'

'Really? I'm so proud of you, darling.'

'We're in *Vogue*.'

'Seriously?'

'Of course,' said Isabelle, sounding defensive for no reason.

'Well that's wonderful! Why didn't you tell me?'

'Why didn't you tell me you were going to be a . . . whatever it is?'

'Queen's Counsel. Because you didn't ask.'

'Neither did you.'

'Oh dear.' Christine topped up glasses, gladder than ever of Will's company. 'We don't communicate very well, do we? Must try harder in future. Now, I hope you're both hungry. I've made lasagne. All the wrong things in lasagne, I suppose, but I do like it.'

'It's my favourite food,' said Will, who seemed to know exactly where to find table mats and serving spoons. 'Isabelle said you were a great cook.'

The meal was a success. Will steered them away from the reefs – boyfriends, husbands, fathers, divorce, drugs, drink, sex. Only after dessert, when they were sipping coffee in the lounge, did he take his eye off the ball.

'So tell me, how are you going to satisfy the demand for your clothes? I mean, now you're in *Vogue*, you're going to have a lot of orders, aren't you?'

'We've got selling agents to take care of that side of things,' said Isabelle.

'But the actual manufacturing. I mean, you don't get it all made by child labour in Korea, do you?'

'Of course not. We're under exclusive licence to the biggest manu-facturer in Italy.'

'Oh,' said Christine, and even as she said the next words she had a horrible feeling that she knew what the answer would be. 'And who is that?'

'Rivelli.'

She got up and started clearing away coffee cups.

'Oi!' said Isabelle. 'I haven't finished with that yet!'

'I'll get you a fresh one.' Their hands jangled over the cup, and spilt the remains over the upholstery.

'Don't try telling me it's inappropriate because you barged in and decided to represent him. He's the best in the business. You should be happy for me.'

Will sat with his hands on his knees and his mouth open. He had steered them through the reefs, straight into an iceberg.

'I suppose you're going to tell me that you know something about him but you can't possibly tell me because it's all highly confidential, bla bla bla.'

Damn her, she's a mind reader, thought Christine. 'No, of course not. It's just he has a bit of a reputation.'

'Oh please,' said Isabelle. 'He's old enough to be my father.'

'I didn't mean in that way. Why do you interpret every remark on a crude sexual level?'

'I can't imagine, Mother. You've got far more experience of that sort of thing than I have.'

'Mmm, lovely coffee,' said Will, 'any chance of a top-up?' Christine and Isabelle ignored him and so, grateful for an excuse to leave the room, he fled to the kitchen and looked out of the French windows at the crocuses pushing their orange heads through the dark London soil. Blue tits pecked nuts from a feeder. A black cat stalked along the fence, and disappeared into a thicket of ivy. The rest of the world just got on with it. He was tempted to join them. The living room was ominously silent. He waited for the explosion.

Christine barged in with a tray full of cups and glasses which she dumped, almost dropped, on the table. A glass fell over, causing a domino effect.

'Here, let me . . .' Will sprang into action, saved the day, avoided breakages.

'How do you cope with her?' asked Christine, her voice lower than normal.

'Oh, lots of stroking. Lots of avoidance. You know,' he said. 'Tact.'

'Tact!' Christine snorted through her nose. 'I'm famous for my tact. I've reduced internationally famous celebrities to tears with my tact.'

Will tried to think of a suitable platitude, and was about to say 'The cobbler's children go unshod.'

'Tell me honestly,' said Christine. 'Is she still on drugs? Is that it?'

'What, mood swings and all that? No. I assure you, Isabelle does not need drugs to have mood swings.'

'I'm glad to hear it.'

'I think she's just very sensitive about the business side of things.'

'I see. So I'm to be kept in the dark. Only to be called on when money is needed. I'm surprised I haven't been tapped for a loan already.'

'Those days are over, I hope,' said Will. 'And you needn't worry. We'll pay you back. Every penny.'

Christine glared at him, and for a moment Will felt almost total sympathy for Isabelle. But then the face softened, and she smiled. 'Didn't she tell you? I'm made of money.'

They didn't hang around to chat. By six o'clock, Christine was alone, the washing up done, wondering what to do with her Sunday evening. There was nothing on television, and the prospect of opening another bottle of wine and watching a DVD was a bit too Lindaish to be contemplated.

Face it, Christine, you're lonely. You need a man in your life. But who?

John was out of the running; he was at his sick wife's bedside, and however much Christine liked the idea of spending her declining years in his company, she wasn't quite ready to step into a dying woman's shoes. Joel – tempting, but too much trouble. He'd stopped calling, at last, and Christine was relieved. If she could have him without all that went with him, just on tap, as it were . . . God, she was thinking like a man. That would never do.

If only the phone would ring . . .

The phone rang. It was Andy.

'Hello, ex-husband. Are you as bored as I am?'

'What? Oh, no.' There were sounds of revelry in the background; obviously Andy was not sitting at home wondering how to fill the hours before an embarrassingly early bedtime. 'Listen, I just wondered what you were doing on Wednesday night.'

'Oh! Right, hang on.' Another date? Where was all this leading? Christine fetched her diary, more for form's sake than anything; she knew she was free. 'Okay, Wednesday. Hmmm . . . Let me see. Well, if I juggle a few things around I suppose I could make it.'

'Great. I want to come over and pick up my rolltop desk, and it's the only night I can do next week.'

Not dinner, then. She tried to keep the bitterness out of her voice. 'Hang on . . . Actually, no, Wednesday's no good. I was looking at the wrong week. I'm speaking at City Law School,' she improvised.

'Oh, right.'

'Have to keep my public profile up, you know.'

'Yes, of course. Oh well. Shame. It would have been nice to see you.'

Damn – was the desk just a pretext? Had she jumped to the wrong conclusion? She'd instantly imagined him wanting to furnish his flat, to make it look nice, more like home, which must mean that he had *someone to share it with* . . .

But it was too late to backtrack. 'Is that the only night you can do?'

'It's okay, Chris. It really doesn't matter. I'll see you soon, no doubt.'

He hung up. It was not even seven o'clock. She opened another bottle of wine.

Now then: *An Affair to Remember* or *The English Patient?*

Oh God, has it really come to this?

She chose *The English Patient*, on the grounds that it was longer.

Adele had finally forgiven Victoria for seducing her son's friend at Christmas; their spats never lasted longer than a month. Victoria even started going to Adele's parties – not, as Adele suggested, because she was in the market for a new boyfriend, but simply because she had nothing better to do. For the first time in ten years, she did not have the word MASSIMO in her diary. There were no trips in the offing, no long weekends to look forward to. Invitations to shows and parties had dried up; officially, Victoria blamed the economic climate, but in her heart she knew that Rivelli was keeping her on ice.

Well, two could play at that game. She wasn't stupid enough to think that she could make Rivelli jealous – she'd tried that in the past, and it hadn't worked – but it wouldn't do any harm for him to know that she was out and about, enjoying herself, not moping at home waiting for him to call, sticking pins into voodoo dolls and forgetting to shave her armpits.

And at the back of her mind, Adele's voice always whispered 'Get yourself a new one before you're too old . . . too old . . . too old . . .'

'Darling' – kiss, kiss, kiss, *trois fois*, Adele being Swiss – 'you look lovely. Well done.'

Victoria was wearing the sky-blue Cavalli, a souvenir of happier times with Massimo, and selected largely because it was the most expensive piece in her wardrobe. If she was going to appear in public as a single-ish girl, she might as well look like quality goods.

'Who's here?'

'The usual gang,' said Adele, waving her hands towards the middle-aged professional men who made up her current stable. 'You might like Gerry.' She lowered her voice. 'He's a lawyer, darling. Don't say a word, but his firm are representing Massimo's wife.'

Right on cue, Gerry approached.

'Ladies, my ears are burning.'

He wasn't bad looking – not a patch on Rivelli, who was an Arab stallion in comparison to this old carthorse, but encouragingly well dressed, and flashing a Rolex.

'Allow me to introduce a dear friend of mine, Victoria Crabtree.'

Gerry kissed her hand. The women's eyes signalled across his head.

Go on!

Shut up!

Gerry steered her to the kitchen, where there was champagne. No staff tonight, Victoria noted; this was one of Adele's informal at-homes. No one to overhear. No need for discretion.

'So,' began Gerry, 'how do you know Adele?'

Victoria felt as if she was being interviewed for a job. 'Oh, we go way back.'

'Did she pluck you out of school?'

It was a clumsy compliment, but a compliment nonetheless. 'Something like that.'

'I've not seen you here before.'

'No . . . I suppose I've been rather out of circulation.' Like a library book, thought Victoria. Does that mean I'm now back on the shelf?

'Me too,' said Gerry. 'But things change, don't they? Adele tells me you work in fashion.'

How much, exactly, had Adele told him?

'Yes, that's right.'

'That must be very rewarding.'

Had he heard about her imminent redundancy?

'Well, it has its ups and downs, like any job.'

'I'm a lawyer myself.'

'I rather imagined you were.'

'I expect you've heard of Pennington and Blythe.'

'Indeed I have. You're representing a friend of mine.'

How much had Adele told him?

'Oh, really?'

'Janet Rivelli.'

'Mmm hmm.' Damn his professional discretion.

'Will she win, do you think?'

Gerry's eyes goggled. 'That's a very direct question.'

'I'm a very direct girl.'

He looked her up and down, licking his thick lips. 'I bet you are.'

'So? What's the forecast?'

'Stormy,' he said. 'The husband is instructing Christine Fairbrother.'

I know that name.

'You might have heard of her daughter,' continued Gerry. 'She's in fashion, apparently. A designer.'

Ah. That Christine Fairbrother. Isabelle's mother.

'Yes, of course. Dear Isabelle. Well well. Small world.'

Victoria left quietly, without causing a scene.

Christine was walking along High Holborn, on her way back to Middle Temple after successfully demolishing another marriage, when her mobile rang.

'Christine Fairbrother.'

'Miss Fair*bro*ther.' The emphasis was unmistakeable.

'Mr Rivelli.'

'I am sorry to disturb you . . .'

'Where did you get this number from? If you need to speak to me, you should go through Ferguson McCreath.'

'You will forgive me.' An order – or just a foreign word order? 'I obtained it through a little white lie. Your PA was very helpful.'

'We don't have PAs, Mr Rivelli. We have clerks. Now what do you want?'

'I have an urgent matter to discuss.'

'Call John Ferguson.'

'I don't think it would be of much interest to him.'

'What is it?'

'Your daughter.'

She stopped in front of a shop window, saw herself standing with her mouth open.

'I don't think that's really appropriate.'

Apparently, he didn't hear this. There was a crackle on the line, and then she heard the words 'dinner tonight'.

'You know I can't do that, Mr Rivelli.'

'Ah, but I have booked a table at Le Gavroche.'

Le Gavroche? How obvious! 'I told you . . .'

'At eight o'clock. I will see you there.'

'Mr Riv–' The line was dead.

'Cheeky bastard,' Christine said aloud to her reflection, and walked back to chambers in a fine foul mood. She hadn't been to Le Gavroche for years, and wondered if they still did that divine lobster salad.

They opened the studio doors to celebrate the publication of *Vogue*, and invited everyone in Hoxton. It was like a St Martins reunion. Graduates recent and not so recent, tutors, heads of department, a smattering of current students, all the denizens of the studios and workshops in fashion's square mile descended on Cissé to share in the glory. The bandwagon was rolling.

'Knock knock,' said Will, when the party was at its height, two hundred people crammed into the space.

'Who's there?'

'Maya.'

Isabelle took her cue. 'Maya who?'

'Ah,' said Will, 'that's show business.'

Maya Rodean was nowhere to be seen, having retreated to lick her wounds in Paris, where, it was said, relations with the house of Versace were not as cordial as they could be. The air was thick with *Schadenfreude*. People who would have sold their souls to be Maya's friend at college, who had used desperate measures to crash her inner circle, were enjoying their moment of revenge.

'Her drawing was always terrible. I mean, terrible. Like a five-year-old's drawing of mummy.'

'Well, I tried my best to teach her about pattern making, but you can tell by looking at her clothes that I was wasting my time.'

'I heard that Versace rejected the whole of the spring/summer collection and told her to go back to the drawing board.'

'I never saw Maya at a drawing board in my life.'

'What's that you're wearing? Did you make it?'

'It's Matalan. Customised, you know.'

'Of course!'

'How long will it be,' Isabelle whispered to Will, 'before they're picking over the corpse of Cissé?'

'Oh, I think we'll give them a run for their money. Why do you think they're here?'

'For the free booze, I assume.'

'No. Because they want to be able to say to all their friends and colleagues and students "Oh, when I was at the Cissé party, Isabelle said to me . . ." You've done what they're all desperate to do. They hate you for it, of course, but keep doing it and they'll kiss your arse.'

'What a lovely world we work in.'

'Darling,' said Will, 'if you want *lovely*, you're in the wrong job. *C'est la mode!*'

Copies of *Vogue* – they'd ordered a couple of bundles – were seized upon and scrutinised, torn, dog-eared and stolen. A couple of young fashion students, dressed, for reasons best known to themselves, in geisha drag, even asked Isabelle to sign the appropriate spread.

'I'd better not see that on eBay,' said Will, as the odd couple shuffled off, giggling behind their hands.

Dan Parker arrived late, full of apologies, and Isabelle was pleased to see him. At least he didn't feel the need to raid the dressing-up box. His M&S shirts and slacks were a relief after the relentless tailoring and distressing.

'You've arrived!' said Isabelle, kissing him on the cheek. He was the only man in the room who did not have some kind of designer stubble. It was nice not to have that sensation of being attacked by a piece of Velcro. Dan was smooth, and smelt of soap.

'I'd say it's you who's arrived,' said Dan. 'Look at all this! You've come a long way in a short time.'

'Hope we're making lots of lovely money for you and Fiona.'

'You certainly are.'

'Glad to be of service.'

'Perhaps you'd let me spend some of it on you some time?'

'Are you going to ask me for a date?'

'Yes, I think I am. Here goes. Isabelle,' said Dan, standing rather stiffly, 'would you let me take you out for dinner?'

'I certainly would.'

'When suits you?'

'Let me think,' said Isabelle, chewing the end of the pen she'd just used to sign *Vogue*. 'How about . . . let me see . . . in about an hour? I think they'll have drunk us dry by then.'

'Oh, right! I'd better nip home and change, then.'

'Please don't,' she said. 'I like you just the way you are.'

The lobster salad at Le Gavroche did not disappoint.

Rivelli made small talk, all of it subtly flirtatious. He spoke very little about himself, but was interested in every detail of Christine's life. By the time the main course was over, he was familiar with her career history, knew about her divorce and shared her excitement over her elevation to Queen's Counsel. It made a very refreshing change from Joel and his incessant monologues.

They said nothing about his divorce, which was only right and proper, and allowed Christine to silence the nagging voice that told her she should not be here at all.

They did not even mention Isabelle until dessert had been ordered.

'Now,' said Rivelli, 'I have an awkward question to ask you.'

'Yes. I thought you might.'

'You know, perhaps, that I have a professional interest in your daughter.'

'So I hear.'

'I want very much to take her under exclusive licence.'

'I understood that you had already done so.'

'I do not want to complicate matters, however. I know how important it is for you to be above the table.'

'Well, that's not quite what we say, but . . .'

'So if you feel that there is a conflict of interests, I will of course abide by your decision.'

'Meaning what, exactly?'

'If you think it would be inappropriate for me to give your daughter a contract, I will withdraw my offer. Alternatively, if you think that it is improper for you to represent me, I will instruct Ferguson to find me someone else. Which would be very sad for me, of course.'

Very clever: he had made it her decision. She had used the same technique herself a thousand times. So – either she lost a huge, high-profile job at a time when she really needed it, or she scuppered her daughter's best chance at a successful and sustainable career.

'I don't think there's a conflict, provided we are quite clear about where we stand,' she said, wondering how she could compromise her own professional standards quite so glibly. Perhaps it was the wine, the luxurious comfort of the Gavroche dining room, the inspiring effects of the lobster. Perhaps it was Rivelli's eyes, his broad shoulders, his strong jaw . . .

'I am in your hands,' he said, and she rather wished he was. Dessert arrived, and there was much clearing of throats.

'I appreciate your concern,' said Christine, 'but I don't think it's a problem. It's not as if your interest in Isabelle is contingent on our professional relationship.'

'Of course not.'

'In that case, I will treat you exactly as I would treat any other client.'

'Thank you, Miss Fairbrother.' He had chosen a very delicious, very expensive dessert wine.

'I wish you'd call me Christine.'

'Ah, thank you.' He put a hand on hers. 'Christine. *A te.*'

'*A noi,*' replied Christine, who had been to Italy often enough to have a basic grasp of pronouns.

He smiled, and drank.

It was nice to talk about something other than fashion – stupid stuff, like the pets they'd had as children, what sort of holidays they liked, how bad they both were at driving. Dan, who could be so awkward and gauche in his professional life, was relaxed and relaxing over pizza and pasta in a restaurant by the river. Nobody shrieked when they walked in, no cameras flashed, nobody started furiously texting or scribbling. He insisted on paying, and afterwards they walked along the south bank, the lights strung between the dolphin lamp posts reflecting in the cold black water of the Thames. Isabelle jumped on and off the embankment wall, spun herself round on railings and, when she suddenly felt cold, took Dan's arm and cuddled up against him.

'I'm not dressed for a cold March night,' she said. 'I wish I had a big sloppy sweater and a pair of jeans.'

'You can borrow some,' said Dan.

'Oh, I say! Is that an invitation?'

'If you'd like it to be.'

She stopped; they'd walked further than she'd realised, and were almost at the Globe Theatre. There were fewer people around. He looked very handsome, even though his glasses had misted up a bit.

'Not tonight, if you don't mind.'

'Of course, I . . .'

She kissed him, because she did not want him to feel discouraged. His lips were soft, his kisses forceful, and he held her around the waist without groping.

'Oh! Mr Parker!'

'Miss Cissé.' They stepped apart, holding hands. She could see that he had an erection.

'Would you be a perfect gentleman, and see me to a taxi?'

They kissed at length through the cab window. The meter was running, but neither of them cared.

The moment Massimo kissed her, Christine knew that she had crossed a line, and that there was no going back. From now on, for the foreseeable future, she was leading a double life. If she did not resist the gentle pressure in the small of her back, propelling her towards the waiting car, if she did not pull herself together and say 'No, Mr Rivelli. I am your counsel. I cannot do this,' she was jeopardising everything – her application for silk, her professional reputation, her daughter's future.

The inside of the car was warm, the cream leather upholstery smooth.

Massimo's hand was on her thigh, his mouth on her neck, as the streetlights slipped by and they glided inexorably towards Butlers Wharf.

Like everything in Rivelli's life, the apartment looked like a film set, the full-length windows giving vertigo-inducing views over London. Suede furniture stood on deep-pile white carpets. Tropical fish cruised crystal waters in a spotless tank. There was soft music, a delicious scent of lemons.

Their bodies fused together as if each had been designed for the other. They did not tear their clothes off; there was none of that frantic eagerness there had been with Joel. Clothes simply seemed to disappear, and there was just skin on skin, heat and electricity, smoothness and sudden roughness. When he entered her, pressing her pelvis into the soft wool of the carpet, she gasped and closed her eyes, thinking of nothing but the size of him, how hard he was, how she must relax and breathe and let herself adjust to him . . .

And then, when she came to herself and he was fucking her, kissing her hard on the neck, she looked out of the window, across the river, to the lights of the city still burning in the dead of night, and somewhere out there in the dark, silent buildings of the inns of court, brooding, inward-looking, heavy with tradition.

Chapter 14

Life settled into something disturbingly like a routine. They got to the studio every morning by nine – Isabelle was no longer sleeping there, but had taken a flat in Spitalfields, twenty minutes' walk away, crucially passing at least three good coffee shops *en route* – and were working by half past. What breaks they had were taken up with business discussions. Will partitioned off his little area, so that he could talk on the phone without having to compete with Isabelle's music.

They ordered in sandwiches or salads, when they weren't obliged to go for a business lunch, something Isabelle delegated to Will as much as possible.

In the evenings, they were nearly always out, at openings and shows, launches and galas. Invitations poured in with every post; Will recycled ninety percent of them, and informed Isabelle of his decision late in the afternoon. She relied on his judgement, right down to choosing what she should wear. They did what was necessary in the kissing-and-being-seen department, and always made a point of saying goodnight to each other before going home or, often in Will's case, to someone else's home. A few hours' sleep and then, providing they stuck to their two-drinks limit, back to work at nine the next morning.

The next collection was coming together. Perhaps some of the spontaneity had gone – this was not Isabelle's first, fine, careless rapture, she now had a reputation to live up to, and certain expectations to meet, from her agents and manufacturers, from critics and buyers. But she was designing better than ever, buoyed up with the confidence of success. There was no more second-guessing the market, wondering if this was commercial, if that was too *outré*. Now she could follow her instincts, secure in the knowledge that this collection would be snapped up as quickly as she could design it. She could afford the best of everything.

Will raised his eyebrows when the bills came in.

'You certainly aren't cutting corners this time round, Princess.'

'We can afford it, can't we?'

'We'll be able to afford it when Rivelli pays up.'

'What do you mean? There's nothing wrong with the contract, is there?'

'No. The contract's sound as a pound.'

'You mean they're late in paying?'

'I mean they're not paying at all. Yet.'

'Should I be worried?'

'No. It's just how the world works. Rivelli won't pay us until he absolutely has to, just as the shops won't pay Rivelli, and we won't pay Walker Parker. We all hold on to the cash till the very last minute.'

'It makes my head spin.'

'It's the same in the haulage business, if that's any comfort.'

'I'm not sure that I wish to hear about the haulage business. Where are we going tonight?'

'Breakthrough Breast Cancer fundraiser at the Café de Paris. You're donating a dress.'

'Am I? How kind of me. Is it very décolleté?'

'No, Princess, under the circumstances you thought it would be more appropriate to give them something with a high neckline.'

'I'm considerate like that, aren't I?'

'Be ready by seven.' Will retreated into his office.

A uniformed chauffeur with a handwritten sign stood outside the arrivals gate at Glasgow airport with a sign reading CHRISTINE FAIRBROTHER. He saluted when Christine made herself known, and took her suitcase.

'This way, madam,' and the crowds parted as she followed his highly polished shoes across the marbled floor. A long black BMW was waiting at the terminal doors.

'How long will it take?'

'About an hour and a half, madam. I have Mr Rivelli on the phone for you now, madam.'

He handed a tiny handset back over his shoulder.

'Massimo? This is very naughty of you.'

'You told me you had a couple of days off.' She could hear rooks cawing, possibly the sound of running water.

'I said I didn't have to appear in court for a couple of days. That's not quite the same thing. I have an awful lot of work to do.'

'Then I hope you managed to get some done on the plane.'

'I did, but . . .'

'You will be here in time for a nice cup of tea. *Ciao.*'

The plane ticket had arrived at chambers by courier, first thing this morning, along with a note, 'See you later, M.' Her head light with exhilaration and the fear of being caught, she told the clerks she would be away on urgent business for two days, and took a cab all the way to Heathrow. It was a reckless extravagance, such as she had never allowed herself before. She felt as if she was falling.

After that first night, they had hardly been apart. She spent nights in the Butlers Wharf apartment; he never came to her, and that seemed, somehow, less of a risk, the unreality of that picturebook stretch of river frontage matching the fantastical nature of what she was doing. *Having an affair with a client . . . On the eve of a big divorce trial . . . When your application for silk hangs in the balance . . .*

And now, a long weekend in the Highlands, far away from prying eyes . . . Surely there among the heather and the grouse, or whatever else populated those remote regions, nobody would see them, nobody would care . . .

Up and down they went, along lochs, through mountain passes, heading north west, the city giving way to small, desolate towns, then villages, then nothing . . . Finally a glimpse of the sea, the tattered coastline of seaweed as brown as stewed tea, tossed up on beaches crunchy and sparkling with crushed shells. She opened the window and breathed. When had she last breathed air as clean as this?

'We will be there in a few minutes, madam.'

I've got nothting to wear, thought Christine. *But then again I suppose I won't need much . . .*

She giggled, pinched her nose and looked out of the window. They were turning down what looked like a mud track, under trees that interlaced bare branches above their heads. The tyres bumped through rain-filled potholes. A gap in the rhododendron hedge to her left revealed a flash of a fairytale castle, all grey stone and pointy turrets, blind broken windows looking down on an unkempt garden – and then it disappeared, and they bumped on towards the glare of the white sky and the sea.

A square box of a house, in the same grey stone as the castle, but smart and spruce where the castle was decaying, all the slates in place, the window frames freshly painted against the corrosive salty blasts of the Atlantic west wind.

Rivelli stood at the door, holding a steaming mug in his hands. In a thick navy blue fisherman's sweater, and a pair of comfortable old jeans, his feet bare, he looked very different from the Massimo Rivelli of London, Paris, New York and Milan. She ran a hand up inside his sweater, feeling the fur on his flat, hard stomach and chest.

'You're a very bad man,' she said, then kissed him.

'Would you like to see the private beach?'

'In a minute,' she said, and pushed the door shut behind her. They heard the car crunching and bumping back along the muddy lane.

This was exile, of that Victoria was now sure. How long, or how permanent, she could not tell – and, like Napoleon on Elba, she was determined to use her exile wisely. She would go out. She would keep herself connected, her ear to the ground. She might learn something to her, or Rivelli's, advantage – something that would persuade him to take her back. Or, if that was not to happen, some means of revenge.

She wasn't getting the A-list invitations any more. Tonight, for instance, while the rest of the world was going to the Breakthrough Breast Cancer party, Victoria had to settle for the launch of a new range of sportswear by a high street store that had long outlived its fifteen minutes of fashionability. Well, there would be drink and photographers, and that was enough to get the pushy socialites and former soap stars along.

Victoria wore Cissé. She had two pieces, besides the ill-fated dragon dress, which was consigned to mothballs. One was yellow, the other blue, both from the first collection. She wore them whenever she could, and talked up the brand to anyone who would listen. It was good karma. Tonight was a blue night. She saved the yellow for events when she thought she had a good chance of pulling.

The party was held in an unpromising basement off Baker Street – hardly a fashionable address, thought Victoria, whose heart sank as she descended into the overdecorated hangar. Drinks were being served by waiters dressed in the new sports range – really horrible shirts with far too much lycra in them, flashes of dayglo around the shoulders, the sort of thing that had surely gone out in the nineties, shorts and funny little skirts that made everyone look like they had stunted legs. Like all bad clothes, they looked good only on those lucky few who could get away with a bin bag. That guy over there, for instance, standing by that pillar with a tray of champagne balanced on one hand, the other hand dangling in front of his shorts . . . The clothes seemed to fit him better, to be tight in all the right places. He'd probably snuck off to the toilets to style himself. He was probably an out-of-work model, and almost certainly gay. Well, he'd have the best gossip and the best drugs, thought Victoria, waving aside other offers of drinks and making for the pillar.

'Drink, love?'

Cocky little sod. Perhaps they'd been told to act like chavs; it was sportswear, after all.

'I'm gasping for one.'

'Have two if you like. It's all free.'

'I'm aware of that. I have been to launch parties before, you know.'

He didn't sound particularly gay, although that could have just been the Australian accent. She knocked back the first glass, licked her lips and took another. This one would have to last longer.

She looked around the party for people she knew. They were all there, the same hangers-on, those who lived on champagne and peanuts.

'Nice dress.'

'What?' The waiter, still hovering. 'Oh, thanks, it's . . .'

'Cissé, isn't it?'

First impressions were obviously right. He must be gay. 'Clever boy. Go to the top of the class.'

'I'd rather go to the bottom.'

'Would you indeed?' Talk about mixed messages. 'So what's a nice boy like you doing serving drinks in a dump like this?'

'Making money and looking for pussy.'

That cleared that one up, then. 'I see.' Victoria did not particularly like being referred to as pussy, at least not on so brief an acquaintance. 'Well, I hope it's your lucky night.'

'And what about you?'

'I beg your pardon?'

'Stylish bird like you . . . If you can afford to wear a dress like that, what are you doing at a shitty sportswear party like this?'

'If it's any of your business, I'm working.'

'That makes two of us.' Damn him, he had a beautiful smile, even white teeth, and the body . . . Those muscles . . .

'As for the dress, it was a gift from the designer.'

'Isabelle Cissé?'

'Yes. I know her, you see.'

'That's very interesting.' He stared at her cleavage, and licked his lips. 'So, as a matter of fact, do I.'

A snippy supervisor intervened at this point, interposing herself between Victoria and her new friend, precluding any further conversation – for now. Still, thought Victoria, the night is young, and he'll keep. Obviously ambitious to get on in the fashion world. Probably went to St Martins with Isabelle and Will and is desperate to trade on the connection. A little too old to be their contemporary, but one never knows with Australians. All that ruinous sunshine: half of them look like leather before they're thirty.

She cruised around the party, chatting here and there, and would have been bored out of her mind if the alternative – sitting at home listening to the phone not ringing – had not been so much worse. She kept the waiter in the corner of her eye at all times.

'Hello you,' he said, when the scramble for goodie bags had begun. 'Still here?'

'Couldn't tear myself away,' said Victoria. 'I mean, from a party as fabulous as this . . .'

'Bad, isn't it?' He grinned, and her stomach tightened a little. 'Which makes me wonder what you're up to.'

'Espionage,' improvised Victoria. 'Have to see what the high street's doing.'

'Seen enough?'

'More than.'

'Fancy a drink?'

'I thought you'd never ask.'

'Your place or . . . your place?'

'Now then.' She discreetly smacked him on the arm; it was very hard. 'We'll go to Soho House.'

He whistled. 'Smart. What's your name, gorgeous?'

'Victoria.'

'Pleased to meet you, Victoria,' He pumped her hand firmly. 'I'm Joel.'

The Breakthrough Party was all about arriving and leaving; photographers had not been allowed inside the Café de Paris, so half the guests drifted purposelessly around the club, shouting in each other's ears, paying no attention at all to the speeches and the band. There was a great deal of couture under that domed ceiling.

'Did you know,' said Will, 'that in March 1941 two German bombs fell directly through the roof of the Café de Paris and exploded on the dance floor?'

'You're full of cheerful facts.'

'Eighty people were killed, including the band leader Ken "Snakehips" Johnson. And most of the his band, come to that.'

'Well,' said Isabelle, eyeing up the forlorn jazz trio who were tootling above the chatter, 'let's hope history doesn't repeat itself tonight.'

'Think of all those designer dresses drenched with blood. All these celebrities blown to smithereens. What a way to go.'

'You're a ghoul.'

'Think of the headlines the next day. "Mangled corpse wears Cissé frock".'

'That's the kind of publicity I can do without.'

'Speaking of publicity . . .'

Heads were turning all over the club, and for a moment the parrot-house clamour was silenced, just as the clarinet hit a long, high wail.

'I can't see!' Isabelle jumped up and down. 'Who is it?'

'It's Jessica Rodean.'

'Maya's mother?'

'Stepmother, to be precise. Rocky Rodean's fourth wife. She's only in her thirties, you know.'

'They don't get on, do they? Maya and Jessica.'

'Of course they don't. And from what I hear, Jessica doesn't get on so very well with Maya's dad any more, either.'

'What? I thought they were showbiz's most loving couple. The old rocker and the gorgeous model.'

'Not according to the papers. Apparently they're . . . Oh my God.'

'What!'

Will grabbed her by the hand and led her through the crowd, so she had a good view of the huge staircase. An elegant woman with loose, shoulder-length blonde hair was coming down, the fingertips of one hand gently skimming the banister, her fingers sparkling with diamonds. She was dressed in a simple sheath in fuchsia pink, slashed to the thigh.

'Fuck me,' said Isabelle, 'she's wearing Cissé.'

They spent the day making love in every room of the cottage – it was the kind of 'cottage' that could sleep eight people in considerable comfort – and then, at twilight, walked through the woods, across a couple of fields, jumping over cowpats, listening to the curlews wheeling above their heads, and down to the beach, a tiny crescent of white sand fringing a perfect miniature cove. They stood at the water's edge, arms around each other's waists, looking out to the west, where the last purple light faded over the hills of Jura and into the Atlantic Ocean.

'Is this all yours?' asked Christine.

'Alas, no. Only the house and the woods and the fields. I do not own the islands or the ocean. Yet.'

'I see. A little rural hideaway. Very nice.'

'Don't worry, Miss Fairbrother, my wife knows all about it. It's all there in black and white on your schedule of assets.'

'I'm very glad to hear it.'

'You like it?'

'It's beautiful. So far away from everything.'

'Ah, yes. We must all escape from reality from time to time. You, for instance. How often do you get away from your job? From your tailored suits and your black shoes and your briefcase?'

Christine was wearing an an old red fleece that she found hanging by the cottage door, a pair of Massimo's jogging bottoms and some battered black wellington boots.

'Not often enough.'

'We must always have pleasure in our lives, as well as duty.'

'Is that your philosophy?'

'Yes.'

And what does your wife think of that? She bit her tongue, and walked along the sand. 'You realise how silly this is, I suppose?'

'You mean you and me, here, together?'

'Precisely. We're taking a terrible risk.'

Rivelli shrugged. 'We take risks every day. Crossing the road, taking a plane. In business it is all one hundred percent risk.'

'You're a gambling man, I suppose.'

'Only if the odds are very much in my favour. And,' he said, coming up behind her, encircling her with his arms, 'the prize is worth winning.'

It was getting dark now, the wind off the sea was colder. She shivered.

'I can't shake the feeling that we're being watched.'

'Out here?' He laughed, rocking her in his arms. 'There are only the birds and the seals. They will not tell. You must relax.'

'It's not an easy habit to break. We have to watch ourselves twenty-four hours a day. What we say, what we do . . .'

'And who we do it with?'

'Precisely. If anyone found out . . .'

'They will not. It's so easy to . . . disappear. You get in a car or on a plane and you are far away from everything. Invisible. Nobody sees you. Nobody knows you.'

'Do you really believe that, Massimo?'

'Of course. We are in control of our lives, not them.'

'Whoever they may be.'

'The millions of little pairs of eyes and wagging tongues. We are bigger and better than they are. We have the power . . .'

The power to disappear . . . To be invisible . . . To do exactly what you want, without fear of consequence . . .

She huddled against Rivelli, let his warm arms enfold her.

'Come on,' he said. 'We go in. You are hungry?'

'I'm starving.'

'Good.' He kissed her on the neck, tucking her hair behind her ear. 'I will cook for you. You like Italian food?'

'Yes,' said Christine, who could already taste the garlic. 'I love it.'

She followed him across the dark fields towards the house, her hands shaking slightly – from the cold, she told herself, but she hoped very much that they could have a drink.

'How do you know her, then?'

'Who?'

'Isabelle Cissé.'

They sat snugly in the bar at Soho House, drinking Whisky Sours which Victoria would put on the Rivelli account – if she could. Out of his chavvy sportswear, dressed in a plain open-necked white shirt and narrow-legged black trousers, Joel did not look out of place – in fact, heads were turning to check him out.

'Oh, I just met her a couple of times,' he said. 'I don't think she liked me very much. She's a bit stuck up. Sorry. You're probably going to tell me that she's your best friend.'

'Not at all,' said Victoria, cosying up a little closer. 'I suppose you know her professionally. I mean, what are you, when you're not serving drinks and managing to look incredibly sexy even in that really horrible crap that they made you wear? A model, maybe?'

'Me? Nah.'

'A photographer then . . . or perhaps a photographer's assistant.'

'Not me, nope.'

'What then?' She wasn't going to let the guessing game go on – she didn't want him to think that he was interesting.

'I'm setting up my own company.'

'Oh yes.' She'd heard this one a thousand times before. 'And what might that be?'

'A chain of gyms . . .'

'So you're a trainer.'

'Not any more, no. I'm more on the business side of things now.'

'And while you're waiting for it all to take off, you wear nylon shirts and pour champagne. Very beautifully, in both cases, I must say.'

'That? No, love, I was just helping out for a friend who runs the events company. We're working together on a few projects.'

He was lying, she could tell, but it didn't really matter. He was good looking enough to overlook that sort of bullshit for a night or two.

'Coming back to our mutual friend . . .'

'Oh yeah. She's a designer, right?'

'You could say that. Do you read *Vogue* at all?'

'Do I look as if I do?' He put an arm along the back of the chair, and gave her a good look down the front of his shirt. He was close enough to kiss, if she so wished.

'Frankly, no.'

'Damn right.' He smelt nice – a woodsmokey sort of smell. She could count the individual hairs in his thick dark eyebrows, and had an urge to run her tongue along his jawline. 'It's not her, really. I mean, I met her.'

'So you don't really know her at all.'

'No.' It was just a line, then. A pathetic attempt to . . . 'I know her mum.'

'Her mum?'

'Yeah. Christine.' Those thick, dark eyebrows knitted together in a frown.

'The barrister?'

'That's the one.' He leaned a little closer. 'Fucking bitch,' he whispered, and moved in for the kiss. Victoria did not push him away.

The crowd parted a little, allowing Jessica Rodean to walk into the room, then to stop, turn and brush her hair back; she may have retired from the runway when she married a millionaire, but she'd never stopped modelling. She saw Isabelle, and put her hands to her face as if in surprise, although, as every film critic and pitifully few movie-goers knew, her acting talents had not been enough to sustain even a one-film career.

'Isabelle Cissé!' She tapped her little fists together in front of her face. 'Wow! I love your stuff! I'm wearing you!'

'Thank you,' was all Isabelle could think of to say, and then she was interrupted by a high-pitched scream from Jessica, as a camera fired off multiple flashes. The cameraman, having got the shot he'd been paid to get, legged it up the stairs.

'Oh,' said Jessica, entirely unconvincingly, 'I thought they told me that we'd be safe in here. I really must have a word with security.' She waved her hand around in a rather royal gesture, as if 'security' would suddenly manifest at her side. 'Well, Isabelle Cissé, I hope you don't mind me gushing, but I just think you're marvellous. Absolutely marvellous.'

'That's very kind of you . . . This is Will Francis, my business partner.'

Jessica Rodean looked him up and down. 'Hello,' she said, and that was all. 'You must come with me to Jamaica,' she said, grabbing Isabelle by the arm and pulling her towards the bar. 'You and I are going to be great friends. What do you think of that stepdaughter of mine?'

Isabelle looked desperately over her shoulder for help from Will, but he shrugged and waved and grabbed another drink from a passing tray.

Christine awoke in the middle of the night with a bump, as if someone or something had just shoved the bed. Her heart was racing. But everything was quiet in the house, no sound at all, not even the hum of traffic that passed for silence in London. This was real, tangible silence, as real as the moonlight that came through the window, casting shadows on the floorboards. When had she last seen moonlight bright enough to cast a shadow? When had she last heard nothing but the sound of her own breath, and the breath of the man sleeping peacefully beside her?

She closed her eyes again, but sleep had gone. Her stomach was heavy and sore, as if there was a lump of concrete inside it; maybe that was the pasta they'd eaten, or the red wine they'd drunk, or maybe it was a reaction to the enormous amounts of sex she'd had in the last sixteen hours. She looked at her watch on the bedside table, quite easy to read by the moonlight; it was four o'clock. It was Friday morning. In three hours, she should be getting up, having a shower, eating a piece of toast and leaving for work. There were papers to be read, research to be done, a speech to be written.

And she was lying here in the west-facing bedroom of a luxury cottage in the Highlands, shielded by the interlacing branches of trees, the black, invisible ocean on one side, a wide tract of empty countryside on the other, insulated, as it were, from the world. Rivelli, the magician who had conjured her there with a wave of his wand, sighed deeply in his sleep, turned over, his thigh coming to rest against hers.

Rivelli: her client. Whose divorce she was handling. The biggest divorce of the year, perhaps – the case that would certainly get her into the headlines. She hoped it would be for the right reasons.

*　　*　　*

'And then she just dropped me like a stone. I dunno what I'd done wrong. But you know what they're like, those older women. They're hot for it when it starts out, but then they feel guilty or something.' He was staring moodily at the fresh cocktail Victoria had ordered.

'When did you last speak to her?'

'This morning, as it goes.'

'Oh yes? And did she tell you anything about work?'

'Nah. She couldn't wait to get rid of me. The only reason she took the call in the first place was because I rang from my mate's phone. If she sees my number she just blocks it.'

'You poor boy. She must have hurt you very much.'

'Hurt me? Bollocks.' He was starting to get frisky again, now a good deal of the fresh round was inside him. They'd have to leave soon. 'Whoever she's gone off with, they're welcome to her.'

'So there is someone.'

'Look, I don't fucking know. All right? She just said she was going off on a case conference, or something. To fucking Scotland, of all places.'

Victoria's ears pricked up. 'Scotland? Where in Scotland?'

'I don't know, babe. Now can we please go somewhere? You're not just some kind of prick tease, are you?'

Victoria had been called many things in her time, but never that. She sent him out to look for a cab.

Scotland, was it? Scotland.

Her mind worked and worked as the taxi took them back to Kensington.

Scotland. Why Scotland, of all places? Christine Fairbrother in Scotland. Surely not. That was not possible. Not possible . . .

Jessica knew exactly where to stand – just this side of the velvet rope, right in front of the door, holding on to Isabelle's hand as if they were the oldest friends in the world, enjoying a girls' night out – so that the photographers could get all the shots they needed. Isabelle's eyes burned and fizzed with the flashes, orange and blue blobs floating behind the eyelids like jellyfish.

And then she was gone. Not even 'call me'. Not even 'goodnight'. Certainly not 'thank you'.

'Well, that's you all over the evening papers tomorrow,' said Will, bringing up the rear with the coats. 'I can see it now. FASHION WARS. Jessica Rodean fired the first salvo in her divorce war against her rocker hubby last night by partying at the Café de Paris with close pal Isabelle Cissé – arch rival to designer stepdaughter Maya Rodean. God, I hope they spell your name right. Accent and everything.'

'Don't be silly. They don't know who I am.'

A few cameras were still clicking and flashing.

'I think they do, dear. Get used to it. You've just become a celebrity.'

Chapter 15

There was press at Heathrow when they left for America – and even press at JFK when they landed.

'That's the power of a rock star divorce,' said Will, as they were whisked off to a waiting car. 'All we need now is for your mum to represent Jessica when it comes to court, and we've got the whole thing sewn up.'

'Don't joke about things like that,' said Isabelle. 'Besides, Mum isn't stupid. She wouldn't represent Jessica Rodean in a million years. She knows which side her bread's buttered on, and she'd never associate herself with a loser like that.'

'Oh. Suddenly full of respect for one's dear mother, is one?'

'Not particularly. But she knows better than to appear against her husband. He's one of the best loved celebrities in the world, however much of a two-timing bastard he may be.'

'But her daughter isn't quite so picky, is that it?'

'Hey, don't knock it,' said Isabelle, as the car glided out of the airport. 'First-class travel, posh hotels, invitations to all the right parties. You're the one that taught me the power of celebrity endorsement. Even if said celebrity is a bit of a car crash.'

'Who cares,' said Will, 'as long as she looks fabulous in Cissé?'

Ten minutes later, they rounded a corner and there, laid out like a jumbo child's toy, was Manhattan. Isabelle squealed with delight.

'Pinch me.'

'I'm too busy pinching myself,' said Will. 'We're really here. Last time I came to New York, I flew with a horrible budget airline and stayed in a bug-ridden hostel on the Lower East Side.'

'How bohemian.'

They approached the mouth of the Midtown Tunnel, and were swallowed up in the darkness, orange lights flashing rhythmically over their heads.

'Oh,' said Isabelle. 'That's a shame.'

'Never mind, Princess. Next time, we'll take a helicopter.'

They were billeted at the Four Seasons, just a few blocks up from Saks Fifth Avenue, and there had been no mention of the bill – 'We must simply assume that they're picking up the tab,' said Will, after they'd checked in, 'and if anyone asks us for money, we turn our pockets inside out and say that we're starving artists.'

The porter gave them a dirty sideways look which they caught in the mirrored walls of the lift. 'Don't worry, Raul,' said Will, reading his name badge and patting the wallet in the back pocket of his jeans, 'I've got plenty for you.'

Delivered to their reservations on the twenty-fourth floor, and with Raul duly tipped and winked at, they reconvened in Isabelle's room, which had the better view of 57th Street.

'This is a superior room,' said Will.

'It certainly is.'

'No – I mean it's a "superior" room, as opposed to a "moderate" room.' He was reading from the leather-bound hotel information.

'Well, we're very superior people.'

'Don't get too excited. We've got a long way to go. Next stop, deluxe. Then deluxe with terrace. Then premium deluxe. Then city view. Then park view.'

'Stop!' Isabelle pressed her forehead against the window. 'I can't take it in!'

'And finally all the way up to the Ty Warner penthouse on the fifty-second floor.'

'This will do very well for now,' said Isabelle. 'I feel like I'm in a movie.'

'You are, Princess.' He came up behind her, put his arms round her waist and rested his chin on her shoulder. 'Didn't I promise you the world?'

'You sure did.' She wriggled back against him, glad of the warmth and human contact, and only experienced a slight pang of regret that the sexual spark had fizzled out so very quickly. Will was for the Rauls of this world, not for her. *Just as well*, she thought. *It would only be distracting.*

'Will this do for starters?'

Isabelle looked down on Manhattan, the bustle of the streets, the dark branches of the trees bordering Central Park, here and there a flush of green.

'I'll take it.'

It had taken a good deal of fucking and drinking before Victoria felt that she had Joel exactly where she wanted him. Her first impressions were right – he was a cocky little sod, and seemed convinced that he was doing her a favour by allowing her to have sex with him. Still, he knew what he was doing, and as long as Massimo was withholding the pepper grinder she might as well keep the cobwebs at bay with a sexually voracious fitness professional who looked as if he had been carved out of marble. Very gratifying for the body, if somewhat less so for the self esteem, which took a bit of a battering every time Victoria lowered herself to boys like Joel. Oh, and he was a boy – treating her penthouse apartment like the kind of ghastly shared flat that he was doubtless more used to, taking the wine and the cabs and the meals for granted, expecting her to pick up after him and to tell him how good he was at everything. It gave her some satisfaction to know that he must have treated Christine exactly the same, or rather, given the greater disparity in their ages, even worse.

Christine was becoming an *idée fixe*. She was in the driving seat now, telling Massimo what to do, who to see, who to drop – and Victoria was quite convinced that his silence was Christine's doing. Ever since hearing the fatal word 'Scotland', she had convinced herself that Massimo was giving Christine far more than just his legal business. Why would he take her there? Surely there was no need . . . And Christine, damn her, was an attractive woman, still younger than Massimo, infuriatingly well preserved and well dressed. True, her tits weren't up to much, and her legs, though good, were a touch on the skinny side – but she was a professional, curse her, and a hideously successful one at that. Massimo, fool that he was, would be impressed by that sort of bullshit. Victoria had done her research, reading up on her rival – as she now saw her – torturing herself with details of one legal triumph after another. Christine Fairbrother may not be in the celebrity magazines – but Victoria was forced to concede that there might be levels of achievement even above that. Well, she would settle her hash. She would make her regret taking Massimo away from her.

She thought she could have it all – Massimo's money, the kudos of another high-profile divorce case and then, after a suitable interval, Massimo himself. She had another think coming.

Thanks to Joel's unguarded mouth, Victoria now knew where Christine lived, where she worked, and who briefed her. Joel had his uses, besides being a sort of warm, hairy dildo on legs. Once Victoria had whipped him up into believing that Christine had done him wrong, it was easy to persuade him to spy on her. All she needed was confirmation of her suspicions – to see Massimo and Christine coming or going from one or other of their homes at a time of day that allowed for no misinterpretation.

Joel took to the espionage lark rather well, and within a week Victoria had the evidence she was looking for – a photo on Joel's phone of Christine and Rivelli leaving his apartment block, together, arm in arm. He texted it to her, and she kept it carefully, backed up on her computer, a ticking time bomb.

Saks Fifth Avenue allocated a PR/PA person to cover them, whatever that meant, for the duration of their stay. He was a fast-talking Bronx Italian in his forties, with a rather obvious weave, who flapped his hands a lot and spent much time arguing with people on his cellphone. He made Isabelle nervous, but seemed to amuse Will, who, after twelve hours in his presence, was imitating his every phrase and gesture to perfection.

The PR/PA's sole function seemed to be to get Isabelle to turn up for her in-store appearance – the twenty-minute slot that she'd flown all the way across the Atlantic for, but which he seemed to think she might either forget or run away from. He'd taken on the additional task of reducing her to a nervous wreck by his incessant talking about problems which didn't yet exist and probably never would; perhaps the clothes wouldn't be there on time, perhaps the journalists would defect *en bloc* to another event, perhaps there would be a fire alarm in the middle of Isabelle's short speech of thanks. 'Perhaps they'll forget to put fifty cents in the meter and we'll all be plunged in to darkness,' offered Will, which set the PR/PA's hands flapping even more.

In the event, Isabelle was there on time, the press turned out in numbers and the event passed off without mishap or *force majeure*.

The line that Saks had bought was simple but striking evening wear, based around the less fantastical items in Cissé's debut collection. There were three key pieces: a black strapless mini dress with a sweetheart bodice, a chiffon halter party dress with a gathered waistband and a floaty skirt, available in half a dozen signature Cissé colours, and, finally, a shirred V-neck dress, sleeveless, ruched all over and plunging way down at the front, that came in pewter or teal. Dull enough on the page, perhaps – but, from the buzz among the journalists and the delighted gasps of the shoppers who crowded around the models, the very thing to get Manhattan ladies dipping deep into their pocketbooks.

The PR/PA shoved a selection of celebrities at Isabelle – he assured her they were celebrities, although she recognised none of them – and got them photographed. Finally, there was a woman whom Isabelle dimly remembered having seen on television, and when she heard Will's slightly vocalised intake of breath, she assumed that she was revered in gay circles, if not globally, and so she smiled a little more brightly for the cameras.

'Now I'm impressed,' said Will as they went down in the elevator. 'I mean, if *she* wore Cissé on one of her shows . . .'

'Then we'd have every drag queen in Lower Manhattan coming up to nick our stuff from the racks of Saks Fifth Avenue,' said Isabelle. The PR/PA stifled a giggle. 'Am I right?'

'Darling,' said Will, 'talented you may be, but you ain't Pat Field. Yet.'

'No, you can't come with me. What would be the point of that?'

'What am I going to do this afternoon, then?'

'I don't know, Joel. I'm not your mother.' He had a pitiful look in his eyes when she said that, which Victoria found slightly distasteful, and so she changed her tack. 'I tell you what, though. I've got a whole load of guest passes to my gym that I've never used. Why don't you go down there and . . .' She was going to say 'work on that nice little arse of yours', but instead she said 'check out the competition? I mean, it's supposed to be one of the best. You could pick up some ideas.'

Joel pushed his lips out in a sulky way, and she wouldn't have been surprised if he'd said 'It's not fair.' Instead he said 'Okay, I could do with some exercise,' although he'd managed some impressive feats of endurance last night.

'Don't spend too long hanging around the sauna. You get all sorts in there.'

'I can look after myself, thanks,' said Joel, although it had crossed Victoria's mind that Joel might not be a stranger to gay sex. He certainly liked her to pay a lot of attention, some of it quite rough, to his rear end. And while Victoria was experienced enough to know that this said nothing at all about his sexual preference, she wondered if a male lover might be better equipped to give him what he so clearly wanted.

'Anyway,' she said, clearing her mind of the not unappealing image of Joel being used by some brawny muscleman, 'I shan't be home late. We can have dinner together.'

He shrugged. He was taking altogether too much for granted – like sleeping at hers every night, letting her pick up the bill for everything, assuming that sex was on tap when he wanted it.

'I tell you what, Joel. Why don't you cook for me?'

'Oh, but . . .'

'Not buts. Let's taste some of your traditional Australian cuisine. Come on, I rather fancy seeing you in the kitchen in a little pinny.'

'And nothing else?'

'Whatever takes your fancy.'

'I could put it on now if you like.'

Oh God, he was indecently keen to dress up in humiliating outfits. What had she done to him? Was she really such a ball-breaker?

'No, darling.' She patted him on his backside. 'Go to the gym, stop off at Waitrose on the way home, and have dinner ready for eight. Here's some money.'

'Can't you cancel?'

'No. I told you.' She'd booked herself in for an art course – not some adult education free-for-all, but a painting class taught by an artist she'd seen featured in *Vogue*. A series of six classes cost enough to feed a family for a year, but what was money – especially when it was someone else's? She'd been meaning to do this for as long as she could remember, and besides, it meant that she had at least six afternoons away from Joel's increasing demands. Something that she could call her own. Something in which to pour all the frustration of the last few weeks – or, come to that, the last ten years. Yes, art was the way ahead. Her creative spark ignited, there was no limit to her potential. She'd always felt that she was wasted in fashion. She'd already picked out a rather nice little gallery off Kensington Church Street where she would have her first exhibition . . .

The artist lived in Notting Hill, one of those white stucco squares which once housed communes and mad old ladies but which had now been reclaimed and tarted up and reserved for the rich. Painting must be financially rewarding as well as glamorous, thought Victoria as she rung the bell. You certainly don't get to live in a house like this if you were struggling to remain true to your muse. Leanne Miller was obviously doing very nicely indeed. Victoria would have to check out what sort of prices her work fetched. Perhaps if they got on well she might be able to arrange a private sale, and have something worthwhile to present to Massimo when he came back. An investment piece.

'Yeah, just coming!' A London accent, possibly Essex – Victoria remembered reading in *Vogue* that Leanne had gone to a comprehensive school somewhere or other, and that she made great play out of her father having been a van driver.

The door opened, and there she stood – shorter than she looked in *Vogue*, and less dressed up – but even in a paint-spattered grey t-shirt and a pair of dark jeans, she looked good. Her dark hair was short, and she wasn't wearing a trace of make-up. *It's so unfair*, thought Victoria. *Some women just don't have to try so hard.*

'Ah! Come in! You must be Victoria.' She had a warm smile, her eyes crinkling up at the corners. 'Is it Victoria or Vicky? Or Vic?' They shook hands, and Victoria felt herself being pulled inside.

'It's Victoria, thank you.'

'Right you are.' She followed Leanne through a huge, newly fitted kitchen and into what looked like an outsize conservatory. Four other women, very much from the same mould as Victoria, sat at easels, laying out their equipment.

'There you go.' Leanne motioned towards the remaining empty easel, where a few brushes and pots of paint were laid out. She glanced to her left, where a box-fresh set of extremely expensive gouaches was being arranged in perfect rainbow order. To her right, a woman with her hair tied back in a Hermès scarf was rubbing Clarins moisturiser into her hands. Obviously Leanne's commitment to the *avant garde* was not without its limits.

'We're going to start today,' said Leanne, carefully dropping Ts and Gs, 'with an exploration of colour. I want you to let yourselves go wherever you feel like going. Don't think about what you're painting, what it's meant to *be*, just take the paint on to the paper and let it speak for itself.'

This was starting to sound a bit like occupational therapy, and Victoria wondered if any of the women would start crying in the next half hour.

She opened up a pot of red paint, stuck the biggest brush she could find right into it, and made a big red circle on the paper in front of her.

'Wow,' said Leanne, squatting down beside her, 'someone's had a bad day.'

'Bad year, more like,' said Victoria, flashing back to the events leading up to Fashion Week. Oh, the nonsense of that fucking dragon dress! She found the green, cut a load out with a palette knife and slathered it across the page. It dragged the red with it in rather pleasing, bleeding lines. She flicked the knife up just before it reached the edge; a few splatters of green showered on to the paper, on to her clothes.

'That's it!' said Leanne. 'Stop right there! Ladies, I think we have a finished piece.' She took the pad off Victoria's easel, held it up for inspection. 'Now *that* is what I'm talkin' abaht!'

When she got home, feeling more exhilarated than she'd felt at any time since getting back from New York, Victoria wanted to talk to someone about the new direction she could see her life going, the untapped talent that had been maturing in her for all these years (so Leanne said), the creative potential that we all have if only we knew how to access it . . .

Instead, she found Joel in the kitchen, putting what looked approximately like a shepherd's pie in the oven, and wearing – no surprises there, then – a little frilly apron that he must have found at the back of one of the drawers, and nothing else. It did frame his arse rather sweetly, she had to admit, and appeared to be rising at the front.

'Dinner will be ready in about an hour,' he said, taking her by the hand and leading her to the bedroom. 'I hope you don't mind, but I've been doing a bit of tidying up and sorting out.'

'What . . .'

'And look what I found in your bedside table.'

A large dildo was lying on top of the duvet. Victoria had bought it for herself one summer, when Massimo was in Italy for longer than usual, and she was full of good resolutions to be faithful to him. She had never got round to using it, not having the need, and had completely forgotten about it.

There was no time for her to wonder who was going to be on the receiving end. Joel whipped off the pinny, threw himself on the bed and raised his legs over his head in a position that yoga enthusiasts would recognise as the Plough.

The after-party, unless it was the after-after-party, was much more fun than the event itself. They were taken down to a club in TriBeCa, which looked very scary and industrial from the outside, but which got plusher the further in you got, and once you were past the velvet rope that cordoned off the VIP area, you might have been in a luxury spa, complete with an illuminated pool and intimate little banquettes in dark corners. There was a dance floor for those who felt like dancing, which Isabelle and Will did, and it all got very *Saturday Night Fever* as he held her hands and spun her around, while people stood round the edges and clapped. 'For my next trick, I'll throw her in the air and you'll all see that she's not wearing any knickers,' said Will, at which point Isabelle decided to beat it to the relative safety of the bar. Will was immediately surrounded by potential partners of both sexes, and Isabelle was offered drinks on all sides. She saw a high bar stool, which commanded a rather advantageous position, and had no sooner looked at it than two pairs of hands lifted her on to it, as if she was weightless.

Will had told her that the men in New York were the handsomest in the world, by which she had assumed that they would all be gay – but, apparently, these ones were straight, or giving a damn good impression of it. They seemed to know all about fashion, which was usually a no-no, and not one of them had the high street wardrobe and lack of personal grooming that made the likes of Dan Parker stand out as the only heterosexual in Hoxton. They were beautifully but not ostentatiously dressed, and some of them even allowed their eyebrows to grow the way nature intended, which, in this world, was little short of revolutionary. They complimented Isabelle on her success, they predicted great things for her, and none of them seemed to want anything other than the pleasure of her company. None of them wanted to tell her that they, too, were putting together their first collection and would, like, really value her opinion not to mention the contents of her address book. They never suggested that her success meant that her designs were second rate and that real talent never got recognised by the commercial mainstream. They didn't even seem to want to be seen with her just because she was black. In short, it all made a very refreshing change from being in London. It was as good as a holiday. All this attention was going to Isabelle's head, and she struggled to find witty, original things to say – so when one of the models from the instore event dragged her off to the ladies' room and insisted that they would both benefit greatly from just the tiniest bump of Ketamine, Isabelle was quick to follow. *When in Rome . . .*

It did the trick. Before she knew it she was back on the dance floor, moving better than she usually did, and being fabulously witty, not that anybody could possibly have heard what she was saying, but they laughed anyway. There was a particularly attentive young man called Marco, wearing a black pleated shirt undone almost to the navel, who danced like a professional and seemed to fit with her extremely well – they made a good couple – the music got louder and faster and higher and harder, and they danced and danced and danced, even when her unsteady feet hit the pavement – sorry, the *sidewalk*, she giggled – she was still dancing, dancing in the lift all the way up to the twenty-fourth floor, dancing her way out of her clothes and into the shower and on to the bed, where they were still dancing, sort of, but horizontally.

'Good news, good news, good news, good news, good news,' said Will, bursting into her room the next morning with a sheaf of faxes and printouts. 'Oh, sorry Princess. I didn't realise you had company. I'll leave if you . . . Oh! Marco! Hi, how's it going?'

'Pretty good, man,' said Marco, stepping out of bed stark naked and making for the shower.

'Shall I come back later?'

'What's the time?'

'Nearly ten.'

'Oh Christ . . .'

'We were supposed to have a meeting at nine, in case you'd forgotten, but under the circs I can hardly blame you. He's gorgeous.'

'You know him?'

'Yeah . . . You don't? He's kind of famous.'

'What for? Fucking? He deserves an Oscar for that.'

'Lucky cow. Actually, he's a dancer. Tell me you know that.'

Isabelle was giggling, and buried her face in the duvet.

'You were having a good time last night, Princess. You weren't by any chance on drugs, were you?'

'Is my mother paying you to spy on me?'

'Absolutely. Well?'

'Of course I wasn't, dickhead. What about you? Where did you disappear to?'

'A club in the Village.'

'Oh, "a club in the Village" was it? And did you catch his name?'

'I certainly did. And I hope that's all I caught as well.'

'You are disgusting.' She sat up. 'Now close your eyes while I find a dressing gown.'

'Come on, I've seen it all before.'

'That's as may be, but I'm famous now, so you can bloody well do as I say.' She was only half joking. 'Right. That's better. You can turn around now.'

'Thank you, Superstar. Now, while you were on your back, some of us have been up since crack of, talking to London.'

'Everything all right?'

'Very much so. You've been in the papers again.'

'Not falling out of clubs with Jessica Rodean, please.'

'No. They're reporting you as a local girl made good, actually. The talk of the New York fashion scene and so on. They'll go mad when they hear about last night.'

'They won't hear about last night.'

'Oh, I think they will, darling. The place was full of press. That was rather the point of it all. I thought you knew.'

'Yeah, right, of course,' said Isabelle, who naively thought that a VIP area was for VIPs. 'What else?'

'Fax from Dan Parker.'

'Oh.' Isabelle wrapped the dressing gown a little more tightly around herself. 'How is Dan?'

'It wasn't a social fax, I'm afraid. Just a long list of sales figures.'

'All good?'

'All very good. Not least because it means that we've got Rivelli over a barrel.'

'How so?'

'If he doesn't pay us the money that he owes, we won't send on the order books. Simple, really.'

'You surely don't think that we can hold someone like Rivelli to ransom, do you?'

'I'd say that's exactly what we can do. You don't seem to comprehend just how famous you're becoming. The balance is tipping. It's now about how much people need us, not how much we need them.'

'Hmmm . . . Nice to be wanted, isn't it?'

Marco emerged from the bathroom, towelling his raven locks; he really did look like something dreamed up by a Romantic Lady Novelist. At least he had a towel round his waist this time.

'What else?'

'Isn't that enough? Oh, there's this.' He placed a page on the dressing table, a printout from the London papers. 'Thought you might like to know. Now, if it's not too much trouble, we have a meeting with the people from Barney's.'

Marco whistled.

'I'll be ready.'

'In half an hour.'

'Okay!'

Isabelle ran for the shower.

The two men looked at each other, nodded, shrugged. Marco picked up the printout.

'Who is this?'

'Oh, she's just some English celebrity. Famous for being famous.'

'Never heard of her. Is she married to a soccer player?'

'Not yet.'

'Made a record?'
'Once, a long time ago.'
'Been on TV?'
'Yeah, a lot.'
This seemed to clinch it. 'She's hot.'
'More to the point, mate, she's wearing Cissé.'
Marco grunted, and headed off to join Isabelle in the shower.

Chapter 16

Reality kicked in somewhere over the west coast of Ireland.

'I don't feel very well,' said Isabelle, who had been nauseous and tetchy for the last few days in New York. Will was starting to lose patience, especially after a delay at the airport followed by six hours in the air. Even flying first class was not enough to improve Isabelle's mood. He'd bitten his tongue so much it was frayed round the edges. Finally he'd had enough.

'Just for a change, why don't you NOT tell me about it?'

'What? Oh, well, fuck you.' She crossed her arms, turned to face the window, but couldn't get comfortable. During the subsequent thrashing around, she somehow managed to give Will a dead leg.

'Ow! What's the matter with you? Is it the time of the month, or something?'

Isabelle grunted and scowled in reply.

'Jesus, what a time to be trapped with a pre-menstrual woman. Do you need chocolate or something? Red wine? Gin and Nurofen?'

This usually did the trick, but not today. 'Oh piss off,' said Isabelle, and snapped the complimentary blindfold over her eyes before Will could be certain whether those were tears he'd seen gathering.

After Scotland, Christine had declared a moratorium on any further personal relations between herself and Massimo Rivelli. It seemed like a crazy dream, undertaken in a stupid, girlish rush of passion, heedless of what people thought, of the possible consequences. She was twenty again, flaunting herself on the arm of Andy Cissé – *a black man*, oh yes you noticed, go on, disapprove *if you dare*. But back then there was nothing to lose – and besides, she really did love Andy, truly believed that a 'mixed marriage' (one of the kinder phrases she heard) was neither here nor there and certainly no bar to her professional advancement, whatever some of the old fools thought. In fact, it could do her good. Marked her out as progressive, ticked a few boxes.

But screwing a client – one from whom she stood to make a good deal of money, one whom she was about to represent in a trial that was bound to attract a mass of publicity? That was a very different kettle of fish, and however good the sex had been – and boy, had it been – there was absolutely no excuse for what she had done other than a reckless urge to self-destruction. She was on the brink of taking silk, for God's sake! If the grapevine got hold of this particular indiscretion, she'd be a laughing stock. *Poor Christine Fairbrother . . . well, I always said when her marriage broke up . . . I suppose she's menopausal . . . One final fling . . . What a shame, she could have gone far, she's betrayed her sex, she's put back the cause of women at the bar by twenty years . . .*

Stop. Enough. That was not going to happen. Focus on the job: Janet's multi-million pound claim was outrageous, a joke, a desperate false step by Pennington and Blythe that she, Christine, the most feared divorce lawyer of her generation, would dismantle with forensic precision. She would point to Janet's long-term tolerance of Rivelli's affairs, her willingness to spend his money, her sudden eager grasping after money that simply was not there. And if Janet cut up rough, there was the sworn schedule of assets in black and white, Exhibit A. Yes, she would say, Rivelli is a philanderer, a bad husband, certainly – who knew that better than Christine? A bad father, even. Admit all that. But he had made provision for his son's welfare in what the court would agree was a very generous settlement. Janet was angry, Janet wanted more – and where, Christine would ask with a mock smile, pointing at the schedule of assets, was that 'more' going to come from?

And there it would end, Janet's greedy hands grabbing at nothing, Rivelli well able to afford the maintenance, and Christine one big step closer to silk.

And they would have got away with it.

Victoria had never ridden pillion on a motorbike before. But then she'd done a lot of new things during the short but intense weeks of her friendship with Leanne Miller.

Leanne was charismatic, energetic, heedless of tomorrow – and lesbian. She'd made that very clear when she first asked Victoria to stay behind after a painting class to discuss her use of pink. The second the door had closed behind the last of the students, Leanne was on her, kissing her neck, squeezing her breasts and telling her in no uncertain terms just what she intended to do. And over the next hour or so, she was as good as her word.

Victoria knew what to do with another woman – but only if there was a man watching. This time, there was no audience. They moved quickly from the hallway to the living room and on to the sofa, rolling around on books and magazines until Leanne had her fingers inside Victoria's jeans and then inside Victoria. She brought her to climax quickly, and only then did she let her come up for air.

'Strip. I want to see you naked.'

She did as she was told.

'Look at your boobs,' said Leanne, whose eyes were popping out of their sockets. 'They're lovely.' Victoria nearly choked at the word 'boobs', but managed to control herself. 'Turn around. Christ. Your arse. It's fantastic.'

So much for soft-focus fantasies of lesbian sex, all tender and romantic, full of sighing, little broken cries and biting of the lower lip. No, this was 'boobs' and 'arse' and hands kneading her flesh in all the places where, ordinarily, Victoria wished she was flatter and thinner.

'You're fucking magnificent,' said Leanne, who had managed somehow to keep on all her clothes except for her shirt. Her torso was tanned and strong, and her breasts, still contained in a white bra, much bigger than they looked when she was dressed. 'I've got to paint you. Here.' She cleared clothes and bags off an armchair. 'Sit there. Make yourself comfortable. I'll be right back.' She darted into the studio for paper and paint, setting up on a coffee table, dipping her brushes into a cup of cold herbal tea that happened to by lying around. She worked fast, driving the paint into the paper, staring ravenously at Victoria, who opened her legs and let her head fall back, exposing her throat.

Either Leanne Miller was a fast worker, or this was just a preliminary sketch, because she hadn't been at it for more than ten minutes when she launched herself on to Victoria again. Victoria held on to the top of Leanne's head and let herself go. Was this what it felt like when she gave a blowjob to a man? If so, it was little wonder they kept coming back for more.

Since then, they'd done everything, been everywhere together. Leanne got around town on a motorbike – 'And not just because I'm an unreconstructed dyke,' she said, 'it also happens to be quicker than a car' – and soon had Victoria perched behind her, blonde hair tucked up under a black crash helmet, thighs open around Leanne's backside. After a few nervous trips around the back streets of Notting Hill, during which Victoria clung on to Leanne's waist in terror, she learned how to balance, to lean into corners, to keep her hands by her side and to enjoy the freedom and speed.

Leanne took her to art openings, private views and gallery parties – oh, this was a step up from the fashion world! This was real talent, not just the ability to sew a straight seam and bung on a few sequins. These were people who could charge six or seven-figure sums for one-off pieces of work that were neither decorative nor representative, things that you often needed a couple of sheets of A4 to explain. Leanne taught her what to like and what not to like, and Victoria, a fast learner in this as in all that Leanne was teaching her, soon realised that one liked things more the bigger the price tag. Art was a game she could play. Not only did she appreciate it – she had talent. Leanne told her so. Under her tutelage, there was no reason why Victoria shouldn't become an artist in her own right. How much more satisfying than fashion, where she could screw as many designers and manufacturers as she liked, and still never get her own line.

For the first time in ten years, she was thinking of a future on her own terms – not just about how she could fit in with Rivelli. He'd learn, soon enough, just how much she missed him. The bastard had thrown her over in favour of that stringy old cow of a barrister – well, they were welcome to each other. Let him go. The divorce will go through, I won't hear from him for a while, perhaps he and Christine will try to make a go of it and then he'll come sniffing around again. Will I take him back? We'll see . . .

She had never felt so at peace with herself. Why, if the opportunity came to hurt Rivelli – if she had a chance to use the evidence of his affair with Christine, that she had so painstakingly accumulated through Joel – she wasn't even sure that she could be bothered. Perhaps it was time to leave the past behind. The art world – Leanne's world – was the future.

*   *   *

'Oh shit. You can't be.'

'Well I am.'

'What are you going to do about it?'

'What do you bloody think I'm going to do about it.'

'Oh shit.'

'You said that already.'

Isabelle waited all day for a quiet moment in which to tell Will. She'd done the pregnancy test first thing in the morning, bowing before the undeniable fact that her period was late. She'd been irregular before, particularly during her cocaine-and-starvation diet, but now there was absolutely no reason for her to be anything other than normal. And this wasn't just a question of two or three days. This was a week.

Journalists and buyers had been in and out all day, congratulating them on their New York success, hoping for a sneak preview of the spring–summer collection, which was still very much under wraps. Dan Parker had been in for a quick catch-up, the first time they'd since him since they got home – but Isabelle had chosen just that time to go out. Will talked him through various figures and contracts, but Dan was out of it. He might just as well have been talking to an empty room.

'I saw the pictures from New York,' said Dan. 'Looks like you had a great time.'

'Yeah, we did.'

'I guess Isabelle has a boyfriend now.'

It was the nearest he'd ever come to a declaration of interest. Will didn't know quite what to say.

'Isabelle's very much in demand.'

Dan sighed – a terrible, soul-shattering sigh that came from some-where around his heart. 'Oh well. I suppose I missed my chance. Sorry, Will. I'll come back tomorrow.'

And now he'd gone, and Isabelle returned – almost as if she'd been waiting for his departure – and she'd dropped the bombshell. She was pregnant. It had happened in New York. It was Marco's.

'Did it not occur to you to use protection? I mean, he's a New York party boy, for God's sake.'

'Thank you for adding that to my list of things to worry about. I meant to. I thought we were going to. It's just that when it happened . . .'

'You sort of forgot.'

'Yes. Don't look at me like that. It's not like I killed someone.'

'I despair. And now what are you going to do?'

'It's none of your business.' Isabelle's voice was high and thready; she was going to cry. Will put an arm round her shoulder.

'Excuse me, madam, but it's very much my business. Am I your best friend?'

'Yes.'

'Well then.'

'Oh God, Will, what have I done?'

She wept at last, big fat tears plopping off the end of her nose and on to her skirt.

'You've done what millions of women do every year. You've gone and got yerself knocked up. It's not the end of the world.'

'But I can't . . .'

'What?' Will thought she was going to say *I can't get rid of it.*

'I can't have it.'

'Oh. No. I suppose not.'

'I mean, not now.'

'Well it's not going to wait, darling. Didn't your mother teach you anything?'

'God, what's she going to say? She'll go mad. She wants grandchildren.'

'Your mother? Don't make me laugh.'

'You might not think it to look at her, but when I turned twenty she told me that this was the best time in my life to start thinking about a family.'

'That's just being practical.'

'No. I've seen the way she looks at babies. She's got that broody look in her eye. I reckon she wants to have another chance – to make up for the mess that she made of me and Ben.'

'She didn't do so badly.'

Isabelle started to wail again, so Will got her a tissue.

'Listen, there's no need for her to find out. We can deal with this quickly and quietly. You get yourself down the doctors right away . . .'

'I can't! I'm so busy!'

'Right away, I say. I'm not having you shilly-shallying around for the next three months. If you really want to do it, do it now. The earlier the better.'

'It sounds so heartless.'

It is heartless, thought Will – and he might have said so if his livelihood didn't depend on Isabelle, at least for the next three or four years. Then, maybe, when Cissé was established, they could afford to sit back and let other people do the work, and concentrate on the fun stuff like having children and boyfriends that last for more than a week.

'Don't be so gloomy,' he said instead. 'Come on, Princess. Chin up. We'll get through this. Trust me.'

She gave him a brave smile, tried to laugh, and had to mop up the resultant mess with a tissue.

All Victoria's good intentions went up in smoke when she discovered that Rivelli was no longer paying off her credit card. There had been no warning, no call, just a final demand for payment, all manilla envelope and red letters, and the horrible realisation that she was being cut off.

How long before he stopped paying the rent on the flat? Before she was no longer on the Rivelli payroll? How long before she lost it all?

Christine was to blame, of that she was certain. Why else would Massimo treat her like this? He should have come crawling back by now – it had been weeks, months even, since they were together in New York, and he'd never gone without her for that long, whatever their disagreements. No – he was under Christine's thumb, and, what was worse, she was taking care of him in the bedroom as well as in the courtroom. Victoria knew Rivelli inside out; he was getting his oats elsewhere. And if another woman was able to satisfy him, then he would not need her any more. She could hardly believe it of Christine, so fucking demure in her tailored suits and her straight brown hair, her dark tights and plain black heels. But if Christine was good at her job and good in the sack, things were even worse than Victoria had feared.

It was time to fight back.

She was not completely without resources. Rivelli could cut off her money, sack her, evict her if he chose to go that far – but there were some things that even he could not take away. One was her friendship with Isabelle Cissé, the hottest name in British fashion whom she, Victoria, had brought to Rivelli. That deal, so easily made, could just as easily be broken, leaving Rivelli in the doldrums, dependent on rich Euro-matrons and their ugly, horsey daughters.

And then, of course, there was the photograph.

Victoria didn't know much about the ins and outs of the legal profession, but she guessed that an affair between a barrister and her client was not the sort of thing that anyone would want made public. She had only to send that photograph to the right person – someone who could hurt Christine, someone on the opposition – and Christine would be destroyed. Massimo would drop her like a hot brick.

Leanne took her to the studio on the bike; she had meetings about a big one-woman show at a gallery in Brick Lane, so it was handy – and Victoria liked the idea of turning up in a crash helmet and a leather jacket.

She found Isabelle alone – so much the better – and in tears. Perfect timing. She went straight to her, and put a motherly arm around her shoulders.

'Darling, what on earth's the matter? Is it stress?'

Isabelle wiped her eyes, looked around for a tissue, which Victoria provided, and blew her nose.

'Sorry . . . I didn't want anyone . . .'

'Come on, you can tell me all about it.'

'I'm just so tired . . .'

And she looked it – all the shine gone from her hair, her eyes sunken and red. Back on drugs? Or something more?

'Tell me about it,' said Victoria, rubbing her back, 'I've been buzzing around like a blue-arsed fly. They work us too hard in this business.'

'It's not that. It's . . .'

'Is it Will?'

'God, no. He's the only thing that's right with my world.'

'What, then? Family stuff? Problems at home?'

'Yeah. Kind of.'

Cut to the chase, damn it.

'Your mum?'

There! That got a reaction.

'I just wish that she could . . .' Isabelle's face crumpled again. 'That I could talk to her.'

'You can talk to me,' said Victoria, very quietly, as if shy of suggesting such confidence. 'I know how much it can help.'

Isabelle desperately wanted to blurt it out, to say the words that seemed to be forming in her mouth like wooden nursery blocks spelling out 'I'm pregant, and I'm going for an abortion.' Instead she said 'She's always so busy. She always puts her career in front of her children.'

Then she understood exactly what she'd said, and started crying even harder.

Victoria was on the scent.

'Oh, I see. Is it this business with Rivelli, then?'

'No. Will's taking care of that.' Isabelle looked puzzled. 'He'll pay up in the end, won't he? I mean he's not . . .'

Victoria laughed. 'I wasn't talking about that side of things. I meant about your mum and Rivelli.'

'Do you think it's a problem?'

'Well, it depends who finds out.'

'I guess it's pretty common knowledge.'

'No, I shouldn't have thought so. They're being very discreet.'

The line between Isabelle's eyebrows deepened, as if she was trying to work something out. 'Hang on. What are you saying?'

Victoria put a hand to her chest. 'Oh God. Didn't you know?'

'They're having an *affair*?'

'Apparently. Shit. I shouldn't have told you.'

'God almighty.'

'It's okay. As long as nobody finds out. I mean, he's very careful,' said Victoria.

'But if they do . . . Christ, what does she think she's doing? This could screw everything up! Why is she always sticking her nose in to my business?'

Your business! What about mine? 'That's mothers for you.'

'Everything I do, she either criticises or screws up in some way. She's always trying to tell me how to live my life. God, it's no wonder I can't tell her anything important.'

'What is it that you can't tell her?'

Isabelle blew her nose again, scrunched up the tissue and walked slowly across the studio floor. She dropped it carefully into the bin, stopped, waited, thinking.

Then she turned.

'Victoria,' she said, 'can I trust you?'

'Of course you can.'

'I've got to talk to somebody, and . . . well, you just came along at the wrong time.'

'That's okay.'

'The thing is, you see, when I went to New York . . .'

She picked up a bulldog clip, fiddling with it, attaching it to her fingers.

'What? Did something happen?'

'I got pregnant.'

Her mouth flooded with saliva, and she wondered if she was going to be sick. She swallowed hard, took a swig from a bottle of water.

'Oh, you poor thing.'

Gotcha.

'Please don't tell anyone. I don't want my mother to find out. She'd go bloody mad.'

'Doesn't she approve?'

'She's always on about grandchildren. She'd want me to have it.'

'That's ridiculous, darling,' said Victoria, filing the information away. 'You have your career to think about.'

Christine had some good news. Her application to become a Queen's Counsel had been well received by the selection panel, and she had been invited for interview. The date was perfect: by that time she would have steered *Rivelli v Rivelli* to its rightful conclusion, and would be, without doubt, one of the top three family barristers at the English Bar. They could not turn her down. If they had called her for interview, then all the professional conduct checks had gone through without a hitch, references had been given and found satisfactory, and her application had gone to the panel of the good and the great, starting with the Lord Chief Justice and working down from there. The first big hurdle was past. Nothing could go wrong now. All she had to do was keep her nose clean, and win the Rivelli case.

The papers were already referring to it as the biggest divorce of the year. It had all the makings of classic Christine Fairbrother: an erring husband who looked like a love rat, and a wronged wife, quietly dignified in her Surrey *château*, nursing her disabled son. Oh, the newspaper readers would be quick to judge that one – but they reckoned without Christine. By the time she had finished, Rivelli would seem like a repentant philanderer, willing to admit his mistakes but driven to it by a cold, grasping wife who used their son as a pawn in her game of emotional and financial blackmail. Her insane demands for money that her husband did not have would be pilloried as the last attempt of a desperate woman to maintain a disgustingly lavish lifestyle that she had never earned. Too greedy to accept Rivelli's generous offer, she would end up with nothing.

'You're absolutely confident of the result,' said John Ferguson as they had one last meeting to discuss tactics.

'Of course. I know what I'm doing.'

'She's got a lot of sympathy on her side.'

'And we have truth on ours, in the form of a sworn affidavit. She's grasping after money which isn't there.'

'I hope you're right.'

'Why? Have you suddenly got cold feet, John?'

Ferguson took off his glasses, rubbed his tired eyes. 'No. I'm just exhausted. Ignore me. I've signed him off, and now it's over to you. If you can make the judge feel sorry for Massimo Rivelli, then you are officially a genius.'

'You don't like him, do you?'

John scowled. 'My personal feelings about my clients never influence my professional judgement.'

Was he trying to tell her something?

'Then relax,' she said, to herself as much as to John. 'As you say, you've done your job. Now let me do mine.'

Chapter 17

It was 'day one', as the newspapers insisted on calling it, of *Rivelli v Rivelli* at the Royal Courts of Justice. It was a popular trial, with more ambulance chasers than normal crowding into the courtroom to wallow in the misery of people richer and better looking than themselves. The press were there in force, which pleased Christine, as long as they referred to her as 'Britain's top divorce lawyer' and hinted that she would soon be representing a certain ageing rock star or his young blonde wife. And she was appearing before a judge whom she knew well – he'd looked at her legs the very first time she appeared before him as a pupil, and had continued to do so at trials and dinners and parties ever since. They were on first-name terms – although never in court, where she was 'counsel for the respondent' and he was 'My Lord'. When it was all over, they would be 'Christine' and 'Malcolm' over a drink in his chambers.

Janet, as the applicant, was in the witness box first. Her legal team had coached her well – Christine expected nothing less from Pennington and Blythe, who had instructed Joseph Greenbaum, one of the few barristers whom Christine regarded as her equal. It would be fun tussling with him. She knew his methods, and liked him tremendously. He was a big, charismatic man with a penchant for waistcoats and fob watches, slicked-back black hair and an appetite for the finer things in life that showed around his well-padded middle. They, too, might laugh about it in a few weeks – but for now they were sworn enemies.

Greenbaum led Janet gently through her examination-in-chief. She was dressed for the occasion in a dove-grey suit, classy but not vulgar – obviously it would not do to look rich – and spoke in a soft but clear voice with a hint of misery. Her face was smooth and matt, powdered down, subtle lipstick, nothing much around the eyes. She looked every inch the wounded wife. Pennington and Blythe had earned their fee.

She told the court that she had been aware of her husband's infidelities for some time, but had tolerated them for the sake of their child. Yes, he had special needs. He was autistic. No, he would never lead a normal adult life. Yes, his father was frequently away from home for long periods of time, and that was why Janet had always felt the need to take particular care of him.

And why had she decided to sue for divorce at this particular time? Because hitherto her husband conducted himself properly in public, and had never rubbed her nose in his affairs. That changed last year, when he started flaunting his mistresses, giving them lavish presents, causing gossip and humiliating his wife in public.

And why had she been unwilling to settle out of court? Because she considered her husband's offer to be risible. There was a ripple of interest around the court; Janet had gone on the offensive. Yes, she said, £200,000 a year plus the house and the son's trust fund might seem like a lot of money to some people, but it would not go very far when one considered the kind of lifestyle to which she was accustomed. By the time she had paid for staff, cars, clothes, gardeners, holidays for her and the boy, there would be very little left . . .

Did she believe that her husband could afford more? Yes, she most certainly did.

Rivelli heard it all without betraying an iota of emotion. Occasionally he whispered to John Ferguson, who passed notes to Christine. It was all very businesslike.

Greenbaum finished. Over to Christine for cross-examination.

'Mrs Rivelli, how old is your son?'

'Twenty-eight.'

'And he lives with you at home, is that correct?'

'That's right.'

'Is he in any form of education?'

'He needs a lot of care . . .'

'But is he going to college? Or doing a course in something?'

'No . . .'

'And yet you're claiming a substantial amount for his education. Some hundred thousand pounds a year.'

'He needs to be looked after all the time.'

'Which, I assume, is why you are claiming a salary for two, sorry, three part-time carers.'

'Quite.'

'Who take care of him at home?'

'And take him out on trips.'

'I see. He leads a busy and active life, then.'

'Yes.'

'I wonder how he manages to fit in this very expensive education as well?'

'As I said . . .'

'And then there are the holidays. How many holidays do you take a year, on average, would you say?'

'Three or four.'

'For how long?'

'The normal sort of time. A few weeks.'

'A few weeks.' Christine made a play of looking at her notes, although she had no need to. 'Four weeks, last year, in the south of France, followed by a further three weeks a couple of months later in Florida. A fortnight in Greece, and another fortnight in Andalucía just before Christmas. I believe it's lovely at that time of year.'

'Yes, it is.'

'And you took your son with you, I assume.'

'Some of the time. At other times he remained at home.'

'I see. With his carers.'

'Quite.'

'Did he come with you to Florida?'

'Yes, he did.'

'In term time? That must have been inconvenient.'

There was a murmur in the public gallery – a sound that Christine loved. The sound of the tide turning.

'It was important that he came with me. He loves waterskiing.'

'Waterskiing! That's an expensive hobby, isn't it?'

'He's always done it.'

'Every time you go to Florida?'

'Yes.'

'I see.' That was enough – the seed was sown. Regular holidays in Florida, for the waterskiing. It looked greedy.

'And the south of France . . . Another expensive holiday destination.'

'Very expensive,' said Janet, essaying a smile. Christine remained stony faced.

'Not so expensive, however, when you stay at your husband's property in Sainte-Maxime.'

'Well, no . . .'

'And when the flights are paid for by your husband.'

'No . . .'

'But of course, if you divorce him, you will have to pay for all that sort of thing yourself, won't you? Your holiday accommodation, your flights, your spending money. Not to mention clothes, meals, cars, even helicopters.'

'Everything adds up . . .'

'Certainly it does, Mrs Rivelli. We can see that these necessities of life could easily cost well over the two hundred thousand pounds a year that your husband is offering – not including the house that he's giving you in Surrey, which I believe is an eight-bedroom property. And the the money he is putting trust for your son.'

'You don't know . . .'

'And then, of course, there's your art collection . . .'

It was very interesting, watching a divorce trial in process, even though Victoria watched it through a large pair of dark glasses, her hair concealed under one of Leanne's large flat caps. It was a novelty to see Massimo acting the part of the humble, wronged husband, to see his lover – 'That Bitch Christine' as Victoria always thought of her – mincing around the court in her black gown and silk stockings. It was so tempting to stand up, whip off the disguise and scream 'Tell 'em about your holiday in Scotland, Christine! Hey, Massimo! Remember snorting coke off the tits off a nubile twenty-year-old New Yorker?' But she kept her powder dry. Victoria had other ways of hurting them. She had information – what Isabelle had told her would surely wound her mother – and she had evidence.

And it was extremely interesting to see, sitting on Janet's side, that odious creep Gerry from Pennington and Blythe. She really would have to call him to discuss a small matter of a photograph. Adele would have his number.

She dismantled Janet piece by piece, and when she asked her for the umpteenth time why she believed that her husband was able to pay her more than he had originally offered, Janet simply hung her head. Joe Greenbaum asked the judge for an adjournment to advise his client, and the day's work was over. Tomorrow, thought Christine, the case would collapse and Janet would agree to settle. Whether Rivelli kept the same offer on the table as before the trial was between him and his solicitors.

Christine was leaving the RCJ when she heard the click of heels on the marble floors behind her, and a female voice calling her name.

'Christine.'

She recognised the clothes (Chanel) before she recognised the woman who was wearing them – someone she didn't like – something to do with Isabelle – and what was it? Rivelli? – of course. Victoria Crabtree. What the hell was she doing here? Surely Rivelli had chucked her out for good? Was she here to cause trouble?

'Oh, hello. I'm just on my way . . .'

'You're doing a wonderful job in there. Massimo must be very pleased with you.'

Where was this leading?

'Thank you.' Christine waited for her to say something else, and then, after five seconds of silence, carried on walking. Victoria followed, out of the building, along the Strand.

'It must be very hard for you.'

'Sorry?' Christine quickened her pace; Victoria kept up with her. Damn her, she could probably sprint in those heels.

'With all the worry about Izzy.'

Izzy? Nobody called Isabelle *Izzy*.

'I don't think that's any of your . . .'

'Have you spoken to her today? How is she? I saw her yesterday and she was very tired but she seemed to be bearing up all right.'

Christine stopped and turned. 'What's the matter with her?'

She's back on drugs.

'Oh, gosh,' said Victoria, 'have I put my foot in it? She said she was going to tell you. I'm so sorry. Please . . .' Victoria started backing away, holding her handbag in front of her like a shield. 'Sorry. Forget I said anything.' She waved a hand in front of her face, turned away and melted into the crowded street.

Christine hurried back to chambers, and called her daughter.

*   *   *

Isabelle opened the door rubbing her eyes, very grey in the face, wrapped in a filthy dressing gown. There were clothes and dirty plates balancing on top of unpacked boxes in the hall.

'You didn't say you were coming.'

'Would you have tidied up?' asked Christine, sniffing the air. The place needed a good airing.

'What do you want, Mum?'

'I'm worried about you. I've come to see how you are.'

'Well that's a first.'

Isabelle didn't throw her out, so Christine went into the living room. The curtains were drawn, the television on, and something had been nesting on the sofa.

'Is Will here?'

'No. He's at the studio.' Isabelle sat down, pulled the duvet over herself. Christine perched on the arm of a chair.

'You're not well.'

'I'm fine.'

'Don't be ridiculous. Look at you . . .'

'If you've come round here to shout at me, please don't bother. I appreciate your concern, but you really shouldn't have bothered. I'm sure you have more important things to attend to.'

'Isabelle . . .'

'Look, I'm just tired. Okay? I had a very late night and I'm trying to catch up on my beauty sleep.' She curled her legs up under the duvet, shifted her weight on to one elbow, winced in pain.

'You're not well.'

'I've got period pains.'

'You? You've never had period pains in your life.'

'Well I have now!'

This is ridiculous, thought Christine, arguing with my own daughter about her menstrual cycle. Has it come to this? Can we really communicate so little? Have I lost my own daughter for good?

'Darling,' she said, modulating her voice to a softer key, 'if there's anything you need to talk about . . . If you need help.'

'Here we go again. I am not on drugs. Okay?' She pulled back the sleeves of her dressing gown. 'Look. No track marks.' She pushed her nose up like a pig snout. 'Septum still very much intact. I would give you a urine sample but I just went.'

Christine breathed out, counted to ten, watched the silent faces on the television screen. She had never consciously seen daytime television before.

'So, how was New York?'

'What?' Isabelle seemed unnecessarily defensive.

'Your trip to New York. Saks Fifth Avenue, wasn't it?'

'Yeah . . .'

'Your father bought me a cocktail dress there once. Our first holiday in America. I've still got it somewhere. Nice little black thing. Armani. You probably remember it. I used to wear it all the time.'

'Hrrrmph.'

'So, were you the talk of the town?'

'It was okay.'

'Okay. Good. Great. You flew to New York to launch your own range at Saks Fifth Avenue and it was okay.'

'It was! Okay? It was okay.'

One more try. 'And now I suppose it's all hands to the pump for the second big collection.'

'What?'

'You know . . . Next year's spring lines. Is it? Or the year after? I get confused.'

'It's all under control.'

'Good.'

Silence fell. Isabelle scowled at the TV. Christine wished she could open the curtains, let some light and air into the room.

'Right.' She stood up, smoothed down her skirt. 'I suppose I'd better be off. I'm not wanted here.'

Isabelle said nothing, her frown deepened.

'Goodbye then.'

One stared at the telly, the other stared at the curtains. Silence.

'You would tell me, wouldn't you, if anything . . .'

'I had an abortion. All right? Are you satisfied?'

Their eyes met for a moment, and a flashgun seemed to go off in

Christine's head. She looked back at the window, the after-image of Isabelle's pinched face burning on to the curtain.

'An abortion.'

'You heard.'

'I didn't even know you were . . .'

'Oh come on, Mum. Let's drop the niceties for once. I don't suppose you came round here just for the pleasure of my company, did you?'

When did she become so hard?

'I was worried about you.'

'Somebody told you.'

'No. Someone said you were ill. I didn't know about . . . that.'

'I didn't want you to know. I didn't want anyone to know.'

'Well people have a way of finding out. And whether you like it or not, people care.'

'I'm fine. Just leave me alone. I'm trying to get some sleep.'

Christine was about to reply, but her breath jumped in her throat, and she had to close her mouth to stop herself from crying. An abortion. *A dead child.*

Eventually, she managed 'Can we talk about it?'

'Not now, Mum.'

'Come over for dinner at the weekend.'

'I'm busy.'

'Please.'

'Mum, I'm sorry. I didn't want you to find out. I didn't want you to know.'

'Don't I have a right . . .'

'No, you don't. Here's the deal, Mum. Don't ask about my private life, and I won't ask about yours. Okay?'

'What makes you think I have a private life?'

'Oh come on. Did you really think that nobody would find out? It's all anyone can talk about. My mother and my manufacturer. Very cosy.'

Isabelle jabbed at the remote, and the sound came back on. One middle-aged woman was interviewing another about her portrayal of a rape victim in a primetime soap.

Christine held her tears back until she was safely in the back of a cab.

*   *   *

My mother and my manufacturer.

They knew, then, the gossips. How far had it gone? The fashion business, obviously – but how much further?

Christine lay awake, staring into darkness, the blue-green figures of the digital clock doing strange dances in her peripheral vision.

My mother and my manufacturer.

I had an abortion. Are you satisfied?

My mother and my manufacturer.

An abortion. An abortion. Are you satisfied?

A dead child – like the child she had lost after Ben was born, miscarried at three months when Andy was away on a job and she had been burning the midnight oil over an important new case, wondering if this time, with baby number three, it was time to give it all up and become a proper full-time mother. To put her career aside and give all her energy and her time and her love to her children.

Faces rose before her in the darkened room – Rivelli, Andy, Isabelle, Ben, the faces of unknown babies, of Joseph Greenbaum in court, of Janet Rivelli, of Victoria, and of the judge watching them all, recording, judging.

Adele was easily persuaded. Victoria let her believe that she wanted Gerry's number for romantic purposes, that she was abandoning Rivelli and lining up a replacement. That's what Adele would have done.

Victoria had other plans. She texted Gerry, with the photograph of Christine and Massimo attached, and a little message saying 'Show this to Janet. She will recognise the location. Tell her they went to Scotland.'

That would put the cat among the pigeons.

Goodbye, Christine.

'Where were you last night?'

'At home.' Christine dabbed powder under her eyes in the robing room mirror, concealing dark rings.

'You didn't pick up the phone. Your mobile was turned off.'

'I had some bad news, John.'

'Well you're about to get some more.'

'What do you mean?'

'Have you seen the way that Greenbaum is strutting around this morning? Like the cock of the bloody walk.'

'He's always like that,' said Christine. 'Ignore him. Ah, good morning, Joseph. You're looking pleased with yourself.'

'And well I might be,' said Greenbaum, all smiles and winks and rosy-cheeked good humour. 'I've not looked forward to a day so much for a long time.'

'I hope you're not disappointed.'

'I won't be,' he said, waving chubby fingers over his shoulder. 'See you in court, Christine!'

'See what I mean?' hissed John. 'Trouble's brewing.'

'They're just trying to psyche us,' said Christine. 'I can handle him, don't you worry.'

'They've got something up their sleeve. She's given them something new. I can feel it.'

'It's not like you to be jumpy, John. Buck up. Can't go into court looking like we've already lost.'

Rivelli was waiting in the lobby, sharp-suited as ever.

'We do trust him, don't we, Christine?'

'I have no reason not to. Do you?'

'I don't know. I tried to call him last night too. Couldn't get hold of him either.' Rivelli saw them, smiled and started walking over. 'Was he by any chance with you?'

Christine had no time to ask what he meant. Rivelli was upon them.

Victoria was grateful to Joel, and eager to get rid of him now that he had served his purpose. She had a new distraction in the shape of Leanne, who had money as well as love to offer. Let someone else listen to Joel's incessant babble, let someone else satisfy his increasing appetite for sexual sumbission. At the end of a long, drawn-out row, she patted him on the backside and suggested he found himself a sugar-daddy.

'I'm not a whore,' he said.

Victoria looked horrified. 'Oh! The very thought!' She put on her jacket, arranged her hair, put on some lipstick and snapped the compact shut. 'Now, if you don't mind, I have a meeting with a gallery owner.'

She had nothing of the sort, but it sounded good.

'Can't I come?'

'Darling,' she said, stroking the side of his handsome, stubbly face, 'you'd be bored out of your mind.' He stuck out his lower lip, and looked so pitiful that Victoria felt obliged to do something for him.

'Look, I tell you what. I'll phone up a girlfriend of mine who works for a model agency. They're always looking for sexy boys like you.'

'Really?'

'Sure. If you're not going to use your arse to make money, you might as well use your pretty face. You could do very well. You've certainly got the temperament of a male model.'

Joel seemed to take this as a compliment.

Examination-in-chief went well. Rivelli gave the answers he said he would give, making no bones about his persistent infidelities, expressing surprise and dismay that his wife would suddenly sue for divorce just when he was on the verge of signing a batch of lucrative new deals, and looking suitably remorseful on the subject of his son.

Christine would have been delighted had she been able to ignore Joseph Greenbaum's constant smirking on the edge of her field of vision. Whichever way she turned, he was always there, a knowing twinkle in his eye, his gold watch chain flashing in the light.

It didn't take long. Rivelli reiterated his offer, and told the court that it represented a very substantial percentage of his annual turnover, as detailed in the schedule of assets.

And then it was time for the cross-examination.

Rivelli stood in the witness box looking relaxed and confident.

'Mr Rivelli.' Greenbaum drew himself up to his full height – a dreadful old advocate's trick, thought Christine, any minute now he'll hook his thumbs behind his lapels or consult his fob watch. 'We have heard a great deal about the success of your garment manufacturing business in the last couple of days.'

Rivelli nodded graciously. 'It turns over well.'

'Your business card,' said Greenbaum, producing said card rather as a conjurer would, 'boasts offices in New York, Paris and Milan, as well as London.'

'That is correct.'

'And you are registered for income tax in all these places, I take it.'

'Alas, yes,' said Rivelli. 'A considerable amount of my . . .'

'Mr Rivelli,' said Greenbaum – Rivelli hated being interrupted, and for a moment his eyes flashed – 'what is your connection with Egesta Holdings?'

Rivelli's mouth froze. And then, 'Who?'

'Egesta Holdings. A company registered in Liechtenstein.'

'I do not know this company.'

'What is your connection with Knightway Holidays, a company registered in . . . let me see . . .' Greenbaum made a play of peering at his notes, then looking up and saying, with an incredulous tone, 'The Cook Islands?'

'I . . .'

'And Mr Rivelli.' Rivelli was looking to Ferguson for guidance. 'What is your connection with the Iambic Property Development Company of Antigua?'

Ferguson slowly shook his head.

'Mr Rivelli?'

Rivelli said nothing. Christine's hands felt cold.

'I am waiting, Mr Rivelli.' And there they were – the thumbs behind the lapels.

No response. Ferguson was scribbling.

'There are many other companies, Mr Rivelli, all of them registered in territories known for their generous tax arrangements. I could go on.'

John passed Christine a note, with the word ADJOURNMENT writ large upon it.

'I suggest, Mr Rivelli, that your activities as Rivelli Srl are what we might call the tip of the iceberg.' Out came the fob watch. 'And that your real assets are distributed in tax havens in every nook and cranny of the world.'

Christine rose to her feet. 'My Lord,' she said, before an increasingly red-faced Rivelli could make some blustering denial and land himself in contempt, 'I would like to adjourn to advise my client.'

The judge understood.

The game was up.

They beat a hasty retreat to Ferguson McCreath's office on High Holborn.

'What happened, Massimo?'

'She did it. I can't believe she did it.'

'Did what?'

'She told them.'

'About your offshore holdings? Hmmm? I'm waiting, Mr Rivelli.' John Ferguson was as cold as ice. 'You have forced me into a potentially very awkward position.'

'You?' said Rivelli. 'Why should I think of you? I'm the one who just lost the case.'

'You don't seem to understand. Under the proceeds of crime act...'

'Ah, pfff, your legal jargon.'

'I am obliged to make a full report to HM Revenue and Customs of any suspected tax evasion.'

'Everyone evades tax.'

'No, Mr Rivelli,' said John. 'Everyone tries to avoid tax; that is perfectly legitimate. That's what we have accountants for. Evading tax is a different matter entirely. Evading tax is a crime.'

'And who says I have been doing this? My wife? You believe her, all of a sudden? The judge...'

'Ah, the judge,' said John, pressing his fingertips together. 'I would not concern yourself too much with the judge.'

'Why not?'

'Because you will never see him again. The case is over, Mr Rivelli. You just lost.'

'This is an adjournment. Yes?' Rivelli sought Christine's eyes.

'That's a polite way of getting out of the courtroom before you say something that we will all regret,' she said. 'I'm afraid I've done all I can.'

'What? Wait a minute. I am paying you good money for...'

'You have lied to us, Mr Rivelli,' said Christine. 'You presented us with a schedule of assets that turns out to have been almost entirely a work of fiction.'

'No. This is the holdings of Rivelli.'

'And these other companies? These holiday companies and property developers littered all over the world, in every tinpot little tax haven? When were you planning to tell us about them? Afterwards? Hmmm?'

'They are nobody's business but my own.'

'And your wife's, it appears,' said John. 'I assume that is where the information came from. Did you think she would keep quiet?'

'She knows nothing.'

'On the contrary. She appears to know everything. You banked on her keeping her mouth shut because she's implicated as well as you. She's been enjoying the benefits, and she hopes to carry on enjoying the benefits. As long as she was asking for ten million pounds, as long as she had a hope of getting it, she would keep quiet about all of that. But something made her change her mind, it seems. Something persuaded her to go on the offensive.' John looked from Rivelli to Christine, and back to Rivelli. 'Do you have any idea what that might have been?'

'She is a fool.'

'Unfortunately for you, Mr Rivelli, I am not.' John stood up. 'The best I can do is make a full declaration to Revenue and Customs in the hope that they will allow you to settle your tax affairs . . .'

'You will do no such thing.'

'In the hope that they will allow you to settle your tax affairs without prosecuting you, Mr Rivelli. If you do not wish to retain my services, I will make a much simpler report and allow your new legal representatives to sort out the mess. Do inform me of your decision.'

He held the door open.

'Christine,' said Rivelli, but she could think of nothing in reply.

There was a long silence after Rivelli left the room.

'I blame myself,' said John, finally.

'What? Oh no. You mustn't.'

'I took my eye off the ball. I should have followed my instincts.'

'How could we know?'

'Oh, I think we knew,' said John, looking Christine steadily in the eye. 'But there were factors that blinded us to our better judgement. In my case, it was dealing with my wife's illness. I've allowed personal factors to compromise my professional conduct.'

And in my case? How much do you know? How far has it gone?

'I suppose they will settle now,' said Christine, after swallowing hard.

'Yes, I suppose he will.'

'And you will make your report?'

'I have to, unless I want to face prosecution myself.'

'What a mess,' said Christine, staring at her feet.

'Yes.' John held the door open for her. 'What a mess.' She put on her coat. 'Goodbye, Christine.' They shook hands. They did not kiss.

Chapter 18

The letter came without warning, not from Rivelli but from the managing agents, informing Miss Crabtree that they would require vacant possession of the property on the first of August, fixtures and fittings, bla bla bla, telephone and utilities, yours faithfully, not even sincerely, a blue squiggle, *pp* somebody she'd never heard of.

Victoria tried to speak Rivelli, but she knew it was useless. His mobile had long since been answered by a robotic voice informing her that the number she was calling was unobtainable, and if she rang the office she was passed from one extension to another until she fell into the void.

So she was out in the street. How long before they put a stop on her salary as well? Another six months? Three months? One? She was in freefall, without a parachute.

Rivelli had lost – the trial, his reputation, perhaps his fortune. Janet would demand, and get, millions in settlement. The legal fees would be astronomical, and the taxman would get the rest. Rivelli was sinking fast, and he was throwing everything overboard in a desperate struggle to keep afloat. Over the side went the properties, the companies, the speedboats and cars – everything would have to go to pay for his misdemeanours and keep him out of jail. Goodbye, penthouse flat in Kensington. *Au revoir*, Le Mûrier. *Arrivederci*, Victoria.

And now Janet was sitting pretty in that huge house in Surrey with more money than she would ever know what to do with, while Victoria could count herself lucky to get a room in a shared flat in zone four. She would grow old and ugly in a squalid tower block overlooking a railway line, dressing herself in worn-out designer dresses, getting the bus up to town to sit in pubs and sweet-talk drinks and meals out of short-sighted elderly men . . .

This would not do. She was not some clapped-out old tart in a post-war novel – she was Victoria Crabtree, taste maker, opinion former, fashion muse, talented painter (said Leanne) and once considered a promising journalist. She was young enough to start again. And not, this time, as the plaything of some man who would dump her at the first sight of trouble. This time she would make it on her own terms, men be damned. And while she was waiting to launch her art career, she would return to journalism, pick up where she left off, brush up her contacts and place a few features; she'd soon be back in the swing of it, reporting from the shows, interviewing the stars and the up-and-coming talent, doing the rounds of the launches and lunches as she did before Massimo sidetracked her . . .

What a fool she'd been! What a blind, wasteful fool! All that talent, all that hard work thrown away for what? For an illusion. A dream, and a bad dream at that. Massimo Rivelli, and all that bunch of sad married businessmen with their stale breath and flatulence and piles that hung around Adele's sordid knocking shop like ghosts at the feast − she didn't need them any more. The scales had fallen from her eyes. Being evicted was the best thing that could have possibly happened to her. A wake-up call. And now it was time to start living − on her own terms.

But first things first. She phoned Leanne Miller, and asked her if she could stay in her spare room for a while. Leanne was absolutely delighted to have her.

Work was the best medicine, which was just as well, because Isabelle had precious little else in her life. She was back at the studio, busy with pins and shears and patterns, as happy as she could be among the hangers of silk, the racks of samples, one of Ben's mixes playing on the iPod. All she had to look forward to was another London Fashion Week in September, showing the new collection, waiting for the next lot of orders to come in, the next round of interviews and spreads in the glossies. She had fallen out with her mother − terminally, it seemed, judging by the stinging silence that followed their last encounter − and only heard from her brother when a CD dropped through the letter box. Her father spent more and more time in Dubai; it looked as if he might have to move out there for a couple of years. She didn't even have Dan; surely by now he'd have given up on her, and be dating someone more suitable. All that was left was design, and a mixture of over-the-counter painkillers and prescription

Diazepam that she'd managed to sweet-talk out of her GP after the abortion.

Will knew better than to bother her with 'business shit', as she liked to call it, and they spent more and more time in separate parts of the studio, absorbed in their own worlds. She was back, she was designing, and the designs looked good to Will – as good as anything she'd done, if not better – and that was all he needed to know.

Besides which, he had other things to think about. Rivelli was not paying up. Will tried to play hardball, withholding the orders until the account was settled; Rivelli hit back by stonewalling him, refusing to answer calls. Soon there would be recourse to the law. And now, after the collapse of his divorce, Rivelli had gone to ground completely. Rumour had it that he was ruined – taking with him thousands of pounds that he owed to Cissé. Could Cissé withstand a setback like that? Will looked over at Isabelle, her frail figure hunched over the cutting table. How much more could she take?

On the plus side, they had been approached by a major Hollywood studio to tender for a design job – dressing a New York rom-com that would basically be a shop window for Cissé. Will hired a photographer and a stylist to showcase the clothes for a portfolio that he'd send out to LA. Amelie Watts was up for the gig – she had her eyes on Hollywood too. All they needed was a handsome young man to drape around her, and the job was done. To that end, Will arranged a casting call with one of the smaller agencies; he didn't want to spend too much money, after all. They had lined up a dozen young men in various colourways for his consideration. It's a tough job, thought Will, but someone has to do it.

There was no direct suggestion that Christine was to blame for the collapse of the Rivelli trial, and his financial misconduct did not reflect on her in any way at all. If anyone was in trouble, it was John Ferguson, who might be accused of conspiracy to defraud HM Customs and Excise. Christine's hands were clean. She had accepted the schedule of assets, at face value. She had interrogated Rivelli at length on that very subject. She had nothing with which to reproach herself, nothing at all.

But she knew what she'd done. She'd broken every rule in the book, and if it didn't all blow up in her face and wreck her career, she would be the luckiest woman alive. No one in chambers had said anything about the nature of her relationship with her former client – perhaps they genuinely didn't know. Perhaps the story had gone no further than a confidential conference between Janet Rivelli and her legal team. But stories like that had a way of getting around, in the casual commerce of Inns gossip. Christine had heard enough of it in her time. It was just a matter of waiting for the whispers to begin. If Isabelle knew, then others knew. The story was out there; someone had talked. Who? A driver? A PA? It didn't matter.

She sat alone in chambers, long after everyone else had left. The room was quiet. No chat, no phones, nothing to distract her from the latest developments regarding equality and contribution in the field of ancillary relief – something she really needed to get on top of.

The words sat on the page, meaningless as hieroglyphs, then taking off, flying around her eyes like birds, flocking, forming patterns, faces, the faces of babies . . .

Christine snapped back, shaking her head, concentrating her mind.

It did not work. The paper was too white, the print too small, too dense. She would have to book herself in for an eye test . . .

Don't think about the abortion. The dead child. The grandchild you will never know.

A deep breath. Funny how her eyesight had deteriorated in the last few days.

Her phone rang; it was Linda.

'Hello Linda, how are you?'

She was in a bar, of course. Christine could hear the braying, the clink of glasses, the glug of wine, the din of the legal profession at play.

'*I'm* fine.'

Christine did not like the emphasis. 'Good. So when . . .'

'But how are *you*?'

'Very well, thanks. Just swotting up on the new ancillary relief stuff. God, it's complicated.'

'That's not what I hear.'

Christine declined to be drawn. 'So, we really must get together some time, Linda.'

'How about right now?'

'As I said, I've got a bit of work to finish off, and . . .'

'Don't worry. I'm not suggesting you should come out anywhere *public*.'

'Look, Linda, I've got to go, my . . .'

'I'll come to you. Be there in five minutes.' She put the phone down, and silence fell again.

Linda was as good as her word; she must have run up the Strand. She was drunk, of course, but not at the falling-over stage. She'd had a bottle and a half, maybe; that, for Linda, was a basic operational level. She'd appeared in court with much more inside her.

'Who's been a silly girl, then?' she said, as soon as she walked into chambers.

Christine felt her cheeks burning, her scalp contracting. Thank God she knew how to keep her voice even. 'Where shall we go, then? I feel like getting out of here. All this new legislation is doing my head in.'

'Sit down, Christine.'

'I beg your pardon?'

'Sit down. Lindy needs to talk.'

She stood there, her dry, bushy hair sticking out from her head, her smudged glasses perched unevenly on her nose, smelling of wine – a ridiculous figure, one of the sad by-products of the legal system, a person to pity rather than respect.

But Christine sat.

'You know what everyone is saying, don't you?'

'I shudder to think. The usual vicious nonsense, I suppose.'

'They say that you and Massimo Rivelli were lovers.'

The words hung in the dim, golden light like a fart in a lift.

'Oh,' said Christine, at length. 'Do they, indeed.'

'Yes. And what's more, they're suggesting that you knew . . .'

'Careful, Linda.'

'That you knew about Rivelli's . . .'

'That's enough.' Christine slammed a hand down on her desk. 'How dare you come in here repeating the drunken slander of the clerks?'

'Drunken?'

'If you have something to say to me, Linda, come out and say it. You think I've been guilty of some kind of professional misconduct? Is that it? You believe that I'm part of a conspiracy?'

'I didn't say that . . .'

'What exactly are you saying, then? That I screwed my client?'

'That's what they're saying at Pennington and Blythe.'

'Go on.'

She stared straight ahead, waiting for the words to come.

'Chris, I'm just trying to help . . .'

'No you're not, Linda. You're trying to get the story from the horse's mouth, so that you can go back to your little witches' coven and drop hints and suggestions that you know more than you can tell, and that if someone buys you a drink, you might . . .' She stopped abruptly, aware that she was being cruel.

'Is that what you really think, Chris?' Linda fiddled with a loose button on her jacket; it came off, and she could not find a pocket to put it in.

'I'm sorry. I just don't want to hear it.'

'More fool you, then.' Linda shouldered her handbag. 'You would have listened to me once upon a time. Now it's too late.'

Victoria wound her hair up into a knot on top of her head, secured it with a big tortoiseshell clip and dropped her dressing gown to the bathroom floor. It was Leanne's dressing gown really, a white towelling number that had obviously been liberated from a hotel room some-where in the world, somewhere expensive, by the look of it, by the feel of the cotton. Leanne spent a good deal of time travelling, promoting exhibitions of her work all over the world – that was one of the reasons Victoria had accepted Leanne's offer of a place to live. The house was big and comfortable, and she would be alone for much of the time, able to think about her future. Money was never mentioned. The arrangement suited Victoria – for now. It couldn't last for long, of course – but for the time being, Leanne offered a refuge.

She spent a lot of time in the bathroom. The tub was huge, the towels soft, the shelves crammed with every sort of top-end gunk with which to pamper herself. A sound system was built into a recessed alcove. Diptyque candles, one in every flavour, thousands of pounds worth of scented wax, covered every surface. Victoria slid into the hot, foamy water and reclined on soft cushions of bubbles.

She lay back and dozed, half-hearing Donald Byrd on the stereo, the fumes of the candles mingling into one thick fug of perfume, mint fighting with gardenia fighting with lavender fighting with freesia fighting with tuberose . . .

She woke with a start, the bubbles gone, the water chilling around her. She could hear Leanne talking on the phone downstairs; another interview, probably.

She climbed out of the bath, shivering slightly, her body covered in goosepimples, her nipples so hard they were almost sore. She picked up the towelling dressing gown from where she'd dropped it on the slate floor, wrapped it tightly around herself.

The mirror was misted over, but she cleared it with a swipe of the hand and looked at the face it reflected. Make-up had run around her eyes, sweat taking it down her cheeks in long grey lines. She wiped it away, a dirty mark on the white sleeve.

Was this what she was – a plaything to be passed from one rich, powerful lover to another, adored at first, soon tired of, never to know security or stability, never to enjoy the satisfaction of achieving something for herself, of making even a modest income by her own efforts and talents? Rivelli had dumped her – and how soon before Leanne, who seemed like a saviour, grew tired of their one-sided lovemaking and found someone else to inspire her? While paintings of her hung on gallery walls all over the world, Victoria herself would be back on the shelf. The art career – the journalism – all of it seemed as insubstantial as steam. She opened the window, scent flooding out into the chilly evening air. This was reality, then – a woman with no real friends, no family of her own, facing her late thirties with no visible means of support. Time was running out.

Beyond the screen of trees and the high wall at the front of Leanne's house, Victoria could see cars gliding quietly along wet streets, headlights and tail lights illuminating the fine drizzle, occasionally the tap-tap-tap of feet on the pavement, people on their way somewhere, busy, happy, with hopes and disappointments and excitements and problems of their own. And she was here, at the top of a house set far back from the traffic of life, trapped – so she felt – in a strange, unreal bubble, powerless, drugged by luxury, half asleep, cut off.

I must get out of here. I must escape.

* * *

Will was enthroned like an Eastern potentate on a high-backed chair. Drinks had been brought to him, an assistant hovered at his shoulder, recording his opinions as a long line of the most beautiful men in London paraded before his eyes. Will decided he rather liked castings. It certainly made a change from the atmosphere at the studio. Since Fashion Week – especially since the abortion – Isabelle was not fun to be around.

'I'm sorry,' said the head of the model agency, 'that last one was absolutely dreadful. I was only giving him a chance as a favour to a friend of mine. Never again.'

'Oh, I don't know,' said Will. 'I thought he was kind of cute.'

'Darling, cute counts for very little in this business. There are millions of cute boys with nice bodies and handsome faces . . .'

'Great!'

'But if they have a bad attitude and they don't know how to behave in front of the camera, they're best off flipping burgers or turning tricks or however else they've been making a living up to now.'

'You're right,' sighed Will, 'he didn't have a clue. What was his name, by the way?'

The head of the model agency consulted her list. 'Joel Warner,' she said, in a voice that she might have used to say 'you've trodden in something'.

The photographer and the models were packing up and preparing to leave, the agent and her assistants were poring over polaroids and CVs, looking for the face that would take Cissé, and, with a bit of luck, Amelie Watts, to Hollywood.

Will ran down the corridor. 'Joel, isn't it?'

'Yeah . . .' Joel looked sullen and suspicious; she was right, he did have a bad attitude.

'Thanks for coming in to see us.'

'Right.' He scowled, and Will hoped this wasn't that *rara avis* of the fashion world, the straight man who was unwilling to swing.

'For what it's worth, I thought you were great. You've got real charisma. You look amazing in that suit.'

'And even better out of it. Is that what you want to say?'

He wasn't smiling, but he wasn't exactly scowling any more either. Will decided on the direct approach.

254 • *Rupert James*

'Yes. That's exactly what I wanted to say. You've got a great body. Very sexy.'

'Right.' A pause, while he appeared to be thinking. 'Thanks.'

'Look,' said Will, 'if by any chance you don't get this gig . . .'

'I won't. You don't have to bullshit me.'

'I could do with some help getting the new show off the ground.'

'For real?'

'Sure. Why not. Nothing very glamorous – a lot of running around and sorting out problems and ordering bikes and taxis. But we'd pay you and, you know, it might be fun.'

'You mean,' said Joel, without moving away, 'you might get to fuck me.'

He was bigger than Will, taller and broader and certainly stronger. If he wanted a fight, Will would come off much the worse.

'Yeah. That was the general idea.'

Joel furrowed his brow and said 'Okay,' as if he received this kind of offer every day of his life. 'It's a deal.'

Chapter 19

It didn't come as a surprise, but all the same Christine felt sick with disappointment and anger when her application for silk was turned down. Of course she should have expected it – after that night with Linda the chorus of whispers had grown, and soon it seemed that everyone knew that there was more to the collapse of *Rivelli v Rivelli* than just the irregularities of the respondent's accounting. She'd gone through the selection interview as a formality; they'd been horribly polite, nodding and pursing their lips and not even taking notes. She could have argued for a return of the death penalty and they'd have carried on smiling and nodding.

Never mind, was the general consensus; if at first you don't succeed, and all that jazz. Give it a few months and reapply. They just want to make you jump through a few more hoops. They want to be sure they're making the right decision. *They want to see if anything comes of the Rivelli scandal.* They didn't say it, of course, but they thought it. If Rivelli goes down and if, God forbid, he takes John Ferguson with him, *then you're next . . .*

She had been taken for a ride, it was as simple as that. Rivelli believed – rightly, as it turned out – that if he distracted her with sex and romance and meals and holidays, she would take everything he said on trust. She would calm any doubts in John Ferguson's mind, she would use her skills to persuade the judge, and he would get out of an embarrassing divorce scandal financially unscathed. And if she needed any further persuasion, there was the small matter of her daughter's career, for which he could do so much. Oh, he'd been clever. But not clever enough – he hadn't counted on his wife's jealousy. She'd put up with his infidelity for years, but now her nose had been rubbed in it, and she'd seen red. Her legal team saw this as an opportunity. It was a classic strategy – get the wife angry, get the final piece of information that you need to win the case. They'd been beaten fair and square – and Christine had handed Joseph Greenbaum the weapons on a silver plate. Her career was ruined, Rivelli was ruined, and now, perhaps, Isabelle was ruined as well. What would Cissé do without a manufacturer? By one rash act, Christine had brought the whole house of cards tumbling down. She, of all people, with her high regard for personal probity. Oh, the laughs that would give them, Linda and her cronies in the wine bars.

She took a week off work, officially to visit her sister and her family, but really because she was finding it difficult to face the clerks without a tremendous desire to burst into tears.

Surrounded by life and noise and children, dragged out for country walks, constantly pestered by her nephew and niece, she had no time to dwell on bad things. At night she flopped into bed exhausted, and had at least three hours' sleep before she awoke again with a racing heart and a mind as tight as an overwound watch.

What have I done?

What have I done?

What have I done?

Over and over again, like a tune she couldn't get out of her head, like an itch she couldn't scratch, lying alone in the narrow guest bed while her sister and her husband and children slept silently in the house around her . . .

Everything that Isabelle had said was right. She was a hypocrite. A fool. A liar.

A liar.

A liar.

A liar.

She called Andy, and to her astonishment he answered.

'Yeah . . .' The voice sounded sleepy, but close. As if he was just around the corner.

'Hi. It's Christine.'

'Chris.' The sound a dry mouth clacking, water being sipped. 'What's up?'

'Nothing . . .'

'Are you okay? The kids?'

'Yes. Sorry, I didn't mean to panic you. I just wanted to . . . sorry, I thought you were in Dubai.'

'No. Last week. Came back. Waste of time.'

'Is it going all right, though?'

'Chris, you didn't phone me up in the middle of the night to ask how my current project is going.'

'No . . . Sorry . . . I just . . .'

'What is it? What's the matter?'

God, did it sound that obvious? 'I just wondered if I could . . .' Her vocal cords were getting tight, her eyes prickling. 'See you.'

A brief silence, and then 'Of course you can, darling. Any time you like.'

Summer that year consisted of one lovely week in August, just enough to get everyone accustomed to the idea of heat and short sleeves and flip-flops before reverting to the mild grey misery that had characterised July. But for that one week, Londoners woke to Wedgwood blue skies and a lemon yellow sun, light breezes that kept the humidity at bay, a warmth that penetrated the bones and made everyone feel like they were on holiday. In Hoxton, the squares and greens were crowded with naked flesh, the complicated trousers and arch little jackets discarded in favour of t-shirts and shorts; everyone was too happy to be fashionable.

Even Isabelle, a hermit since the abortion, started venturing out of the studio at Will's suggestion, for little walks, breaths of fresh air, picnics in the park just like in the old days. In a pair of dark glasses, her hair concealed under a twisted, knotted offcut, she went unrecognised. For the first time in months, she smiled spontaneously. She started looking forward to the future, planning things for Fashion Week, joining in the lunchtime gossip that did the rounds of the Square. Gradually, she was coming back to life. She stopped taking prescription painkillers and immediately started looking less like a zombie. 'It's a great look for the catwalk, Princess,' said Will, 'but in real life, it sucks.'

The light hurt her eyes. Isabelle had spent so long indoors that she couldn't bear to go out in the sunshine without shades – and if they stopped people from talking to her, so much the better. The first time she sat in the square with Will, she had to concentrate on her breathing in order not to run straight back to the security of the studio. Little by little, she became accustomed to the light, the air, the happy chatter, the noise of traffic and life around her. The pain that had gnawed away at her entrails for the last few weeks, untouched by analgesics, was gradually fading. If she thought about 'it' – the baby she had lost, the abortion, the madness of New York – she had a sensation of breathlessness, her heart beating too hard in her ribcage. But she thought about it less now. She trained herself to keep painful matters at bay – the medication was useful for that, at least. And if she suddenly thought of her mother, her father, her brother, her baby, her hopes for Dan . . . Well, she could switch those feelings off like a light.

Maya Rodean was back in London, her Paris venture having fallen through – 'We don't mention the "V" word in her presence', said Will, who had heard all the details of her departure from Versace from friends of friends of friends. Maya's failure, as everyone was calling it, added spice to Isabelle's success; she didn't think of herself as a vindictive woman, but there was something particularly delicious about seeing Maya walking through Hoxton with her press portfolio over her shoulder, just like a human being.

They met one day, as they inevitably would, at a gallery opening in Shoreditch; yet another St Martins graduate was putting on yet another show of dreary conceptual nonsense to which they all flocked, just in case this was the one. Isabelle went alone; Will had a date with a mysterious new boyfriend that he was keeping well out of her way, perhaps in deference to her tender feelings. Probably some airhead model. She didn't care. She had trained herself not to.

Maya made a reasonable attempt to cut her dead, which was quite an achievement in such a small space, made even more crowded by the 'art', which consisted of huge squeezed-out tubes of paint and gigantic blobs of pigment like brightly coloured cow dung. But eventually they were obliged to confront each other across a tray of drinks. Maya Rodean was dressed head to toe in Maya Rodean, and looked like an ageing child prostitute.

'Well well,' said Maya, flashing her eyes, the upper lids heavy with false eyelashes, which were enjoying a comeback that week. 'It's the *enfant terrible*.' She pronounced 'terrible' the English way.

'Hello Maya,' said Isabelle. 'How are you?' She didn't want to pick a fight, but everyone seemed to expect one.

'I'm fabulous, thanks,' said Maya, grabbing a drink from the tray with one lace-gloved hand, throwing it down her neck and taking another. 'But we all know that. What about *you*?'

'Great, thanks. Just working hard on my next collection.'

'Oh, *Cissé*,' said Maya, drawling the second syllable as if it was the most pretentious name in the world. 'That's all I ever hear about. I don't know who you had to sleep with to get all that publicity.' She laughed, a little kittenish laugh that meant 'Let's pretend that was just a camp joke but we both know that it wasn't.'

'You know me, Maya,' said Isabelle, 'I'll fuck anyone to get ahead.'

'So I gather.' Maya was looking around the party as if hoping to see someone more interesting – a tried and trusted method of putting one's companion in his or her place. The next step would be to walk away in mid-sentence.

'Well,' said Isabelle, who was an experienced enough partygoer to pre-empt a cut, 'it's lovely to see you, I do hope that . . .'

'How's your mother, Isabelle?'

She hadn't seen this one coming. 'Fine . . .'

'I don't suppose she'll be representing my dear stepmother after all.'

'I didn't know she was intending to.'

'Oh come on, darling. Why else do you think poor Jessica was going around wearing *your* clothes all the time?'

'For the same reason as everyone else wears them,' said Isabelle. 'Because she has great taste and she looks fabulous in them.'

'Pffff!' Maya waved a hand, slopping wine on her floral-print top. 'She was just trying to get publicity, as ever. You know,' she said, lowering her voice and becoming horribly confidential, 'she'll do anything to get publicity, that woman. Anything at all.'

'Like marrying your father?'

'Precisely. And now she's desperate.'

'Oh. I see. So that's why she was wearing my clothes. She was *desperate*. Thank you so much for pointing that out, Maya, especially in front of all these people.' Isabelle felt more alive than she'd felt for months.

'Well come on, darling,' said Maya, assuming that everyone was on her side, 'why else would anyone wear them?'

'You're right, of course. I've always said that Keira Knightley was desperate.'

Maya opened her mouth to say 'Keira is a good friend of mine,' but stopped, wrong-footed. 'Keira . . . ?'

'Oh, didn't you know? I thought someone would have told you. Cissé are dressing her for her next movie. The one with . . .' She snapped her fingers, frowned as if racking her brains. 'Who is it, Will? The bloke who's starring opposite Keira Knightley in that film we're being paid so much to do the costumes for?'

'Paul Rudd.'

'Oh, that's right. Paul Rudd. I'd never heard of him, but Will wants to shag him.'

Like all great social tacticians, Maya simply ignored what her opponent was saying, and resumed her original line of attack.

'Jessica has been tarting herself up in your dresses because she's desperate to advertise herself to your mother. She thinks that's the only way she's going to come out of this divorce intact. But it's back-fired, hasn't it?'

'Has it, Maya?' Isabelle folded her arms across her chest.

'Well, I mean your mother's not much good to anyone these days, is she? Not since that business with Rivelli.'

'I don't know what you mean.'

'Of course you don't, darling.' Maya composed her face into that special look she reserved for idiot children. 'Well, I really must be getting along.' She had a momentary advantage, and thought it best to make a tactical withdrawal. 'I leave you to the art. Enjoy!'

She might have won the round had she not tripped on a giant squeezed-out tube of paint and fallen on top of the art critic from the *Guardian*, who didn't know who she was, and called her a clumsy bitch.

Andy was waiting in the pub when she got there. The venue was signifi-cant – neutral territory, neither at her house nor his, a place they went together in happier times, when the kids were young and they counted themselves lucky to get a babysitter for a couple of hours, a stroll over the Heath and a couple of pints before returning to reality.

Christine watched him for a moment from the doorway before step-ping forward and making herself known. He looked tired, leaning on the table with his elbows, staring into space, a pint of bitter barely touched. Older, she supposed – well, we're all getting older. Happy? Not happy, no. Alone. Lonely. She must look the same. Disappointed, bitter, depressed . . .

She took a deep breath, thought *this won't do* and put a smile on her face.

'Mr Cissé, I presume.'

He looked up as if waking from a dream. 'Ah. My former wife, unless I am very much mistaken.' He stood, pulled out a chair for her, got her settled. 'I don't suppose a woman of your status drinks London Pride any more.'

'On the contrary, that's just what I want.' *And it's what I'd better get used to*, thought Christine, who feared that the champagne days were over. 'And a bag of crisps.'

'Salt and vinegar?'

'Of course.'

He walked to the bar, and Christine felt a hideous tug in her stomach. They knew each other so well, all their preferences, their history, their little moods and foibles. Why had they thrown that away over . . . what? An indiscretion? A *mésalliance*?

Andy returned with drinks and crisps. He opened the bag out, placing it between them, salt and grease glistening on the silver foil. They crunched and sipped.

'This is nice,' he said, almost sighed.

'Yes.'

'Quite like old times.'

'Andy . . .'

'What?'

'Nothing.'

Sip, crunch.

'I just wondered how your Dubai project is going.'

'Oh. That. Fine. Hideous place. Lots of money. Goes against everything I ever stood for. End of story.' He watched a woman walking towards the toilets; he could never stop his eyes from wandering.

'Sounds a bit grim.'

'Is a bit grim.'

Crunch, sip.

'And you? Read about the Rivelli case.'

'Oh.' The newspapers had been kind; there was no reason why he should know more than they had printed. 'Yes. Ghastly business.'

'Ghastly man, by the sound of it.'

'Absolutely.'

'Is he the one who . . .'

'Yes. He makes Isabelle's stuff up for her. I don't like it at all.'

'I don't suppose he's any worse than the rest of them.'

'The rest of who? Garment manufacturers, Italians, crooks or philanderers?'

'All of the above.'

'He's bad enough.'

The crisps were finished, the pints going down fast. There was no need to hurry, no babysitter to relieve, and yet Christine felt the urge to move on. Away from the pub, certainly. Away from Andy? 'I haven't seen her for a while, you know.'

Who? Your mistress? Or . . .

'Isabelle, I mean. She hasn't called for ages. Now she's a big star and all.'

'She doesn't need handouts any more, I suppose.'

'You've not seen her either?'

'No.' Christine thought back to her last disastrous discussion with their daughter. 'She seems to be very busy.' She had not told Andy about the abortion; neither had Isabelle, she assumed.

'And Ben?'

'Oh, he calls once in a while.'

'Hmmmm . . .'

The drinks were getting very low.

'What happened, Chris?'

'I don't know. They grew up, I suppose, just like we always told them to.'

'I don't mean that. I mean what happened to . . .'

Not *us*, surely.

'To the family. Everyone getting on together, being jolly.' He did that ridiculous English accent, but she knew he meant it.

'We got divorced, Andy, remember? That's what happened.'

He finished his pint, wiped his lips, got up and headed towards the toilet. 'I know,' he said. 'You don't have to tell me.' He walked away, muttering something that sounded like 'worst mistake of my life'.

'Game, set and match to Miss Cissé,' said a man's voice behind her. She had a sense of agreeable expectation.

'Hello, Dan. Long time no see.'

'I heard you were . . . busy.'

He knows about New York. Marco. The abortion.

'Yes. Horribly so.' He was waiting for more, but he wasn't going to get it – not here, not now, surrounded by eavesdroppers. 'What about you?'

'Oh, yes.' He pushed his glasses up his nose. 'It's a full-time job just coping with all the orders for Cissé. Congratulations, by the way.'

'Thank you. It's kind of weird.'

'Will okay?'

'Sure.' *Why is he asking about Will?* 'He's taking care of business for me.'

'Right.' Dan's blue eyes caught hers, then flicked quickly away. 'Get him to give me a call some time, would you? Small matter of money.'

'Oh. I hope everything is . . .'

'Yes, fine. You know what it's like. Cash flow, and all that.'

'Will calls it the money-go-round.'

'Yeah.' He rubbed his chin, making a scratching sound. She remembered how his stubble felt on her face when he kissed her once – when? Before New York . . . 'The thing is, not much money is going round at the moment. Which isn't much fun for any of us.'

'Is there something I should know?'

'I'm sure everything's fine. But you might want to have a word with Will about the Rivelli account.'

She scowled. 'Oh, Christ, that bloody man. Sorry. It just seems that everywhere I go, he's there. He's already . . .'

Stop. He might not know about Mum.

'He's done this sort of thing before,' said Dan, who knew exactly how much financial trouble Rivelli was in, but did not listen to the gossip about *why*. 'You just have to watch him.'

'You told me he was okay.'

'He is. He's more than okay. He's the best manufacturer in the business. But his services come at a price.'

'Oh God . . .'

He put a hand on her upper arm. 'It's nothing to worry about. Just get Will to call me. I will sort everything out. I promise you.'

He had that look in his eyes, as if he was about to ask her out again, and Isabelle suddenly felt afraid. 'Well, Dan, thanks for the tip.' A waiter came between them, offering drinks, giving her the perfect chance to escape. 'I expect I'll see you around.'

Andy came back from the loo looking twice the man he had been before; Christine almost wondered if he'd taken something. His back was straighter, his eyes brighter, the old spark reignited.

'I've come to a momentous decision,' he said, lowering himself into his seat in a way that contrived to show off the strength of his arms. He'd always had strong arms, Christine remembered. 'I'm going to ask you out for dinner.'

'Oh.'

'Is that all you can say? "Oh"?'

'No. I mean, what do you mean?'

'For a professional advocate, you're pretty crap at asking questions.'

'Don't you start,' said Christine, who had not yet shared her recent disappointment. 'I shall rephrase. When you say that you are going to ask me out for dinner, Mr Cissé, do you simply mean that you want to discuss our children, or do you have an ulterior motive?'

'Very ulterior, I'm afraid.'

'In that case, I have no choice but to accept.'

'Good show.'

They ate in a small Italian restaurant that had already been old fashioned when they were first going out together, but the food was good. They both had *saltimbocca* and ice cream.

Andy walked her home. They kissed on the doorstep, and Christine invited him in, and repeated the mistake that she had sworn a thousand times never to make again. The minute she was in his arms, she felt safe. The world – the gossip – Rivelli – could no longer harm her.

Will's phone was switched off. Unlike some people he knew, he did not like it to ring or beep in the middle of sex. It was enough that one person wanted him; he didn't need to show how popular he was. And at the moment, all that mattered was that Joel wanted him. Will usually avoided so-called straight men – but this one was different. As conversions went, Joel was right up there with Saul on the road to Damascus.

They had sex when they got home, and again in the middle of the night, when Will awoke to find Joel climbing on. They did it again in the shower, and it was only when breakfast was finished and they were on the second cup of coffee that Will switched his phone on. There were several voice messages and texts, nearly all of them from Isabelle.

'Shit.'

'What's the matter, mate?' asked Joel, massaging Will's shoulders, pressing himself into his back.

'Business crap. You don't want to know.'

'Try me. I might be able to help.'

'Isabelle's freaking out about our manufacturer.'

Joel hadn't felt the need to mention his connection with Isabelle or her mother; he'd cross that bridge if he ever came to it. For now, the secret amused him, gave him a feeling of power. 'Why? What's he doing?'

'Usual thing. Not paying up.'

'Who is he?'

'Rivelli.'

'Yeah,' said Joel, who had also failed to mention Victoria Crabtree, 'I've heard of him.'

'So you should have. He's the biggest name in the business. He also turns out to be the biggest bastard.'

'Is he good looking?' Joel was nibbling Will's neck.

'In a daddyish sort of way, I suppose.'

'Perhaps we could persuade him to . . . play ball.'

'God, Joel, you're insatiable.'

'Why not? Call him up. Give it a go.'

'Thanks, but no thanks. Things are quite complicated enough in that department as it is.'

'Wouldn't you like to get me in a sandwich?'

'God,' said Will, turning his phone off again, 'you straight men are so promiscuous.'

As they made love on the kitchen table, both men were thinking, for very different reasons, about Massimo Rivelli.

Chapter 20

Seven months is a long time in fashion.

Since the first fine careless rapture of February Fashion Week, Isabelle felt as if she'd aged ten years. How fast it had gone from innocence to experience, from the heady rush of 'Can we do it? Yes we can!' to the grinding reality of not enough hours in the day, not enough money in the bank, the pressure of expectation. The first Cissé collection had been an explosion of colour and energy and the sheer delight of dressing up; the second collection has to prove that Cissé was not just a flash in the fashion pan. Everyone was waiting for the outcome, ready to pick over the carcass if she failed – or, if she succeeded, to be her best friend. Isabelle worked hard, methodically, joylessly; and somehow, from that dark and dreary time, Isabelle created clothes that put the first collection in the shade. Will said they were on course for the Oscars – and if the money troubles continued, they would simply sack Rivelli and find a better deal. All that mattered were the clothes, and the clothes were perfect.

And then, three days before the London Fashion Week show, the entire collection went missing.

Will was in New York, showing samples and negotiating terms with Saks, the film studios and a couple of advertising agencies who were sniffing around for their business.

Isabelle was in Paris, doing press for *Mode à Paris* and taking the time to visit a few fabric suppliers and be lunched and wooed by representatives of the big couture houses who were eager to employ her.

The Hoxton studio was locked up, the spring/summer collection ready to be shown, barring last-minute zhoozhing, on rails inside.

They were both due back on the same day.

Will was the first to arrive on that fateful Tuesday morning.

The first thing he noticed was that the chain on the door was missing. He didn't panic immediately; Isabelle kept peculiar hours, and could easily have come straight from St Pancras without going home first. He would tell her off for being a workaholic, tell her to get some rest, a shower, some breakfast . . .

He opened up. The studio was empty. Not just of people, but of clothes as well.

Will went through a rapid mental checklist.

Isabelle could have taken the clothes to the venue for a lighting rehearsal. No – she would never think of that, let alone have the energy to do it.

Isabelle could have organised a photoshoot with . . . no. Scratch that. She hated photoshoots. What else?

He might have forgotten some arrangement he'd made with someone for something . . . He rushed into his office, knocking into one of the partition walls as he did so; it wobbled precariously. There was his diary, on the desk . . . But wait. Things had been moved. Drawers were open, a folder of invoices on the floor, disruption in the filing department.

There was no longer any doubt in his mind. They had been burgled. The entire collection, and God knows what else, was gone.

He started calling Isabelle's mobile, then stopped and dialled 999 instead.

Isabelle sat in the middle of the floor, nervously shredding a scrap of chiffon that was all that was left of her spring/summer collection. She had not yet cried, nor even said very much; Will could see that she was in shock. This was the end of Cissé – he knew that, she knew that, but they could not bring themselves to admit it. For now, they could only process what had happened and try to piece together any ideas that might help the police. It was some consolation that the police had taken the matter very seriously indeed. But no amount of official interest would put clothes on the catwalk. Maybe they could recover in time for next year – but by that time they would have been overtaken, forgotten, or, if remembered at all, only as the people who lost everything in an unsolved crime. The success of the last few months, all the hard work of the last year and a half, had disappeared like a mirage.

Finally, after she'd reduced her little piece of pink chiffon to threads, Isabelle awoke from her miserable reverie and said the words that had to be said.

'Who would do this?'

'I don't know, Princess,' said Will, who could think of any number of people who might have done it, all of which were appalling and unthinkable in different ways.

'Was it Rivelli?'

'Why do you say that?'

'He's a crook. Dan tried to warn me.'

'Rivelli is many things, including a crook, but he wouldn't do a thing like this. What does he stand to gain? He ruins us, he loses any hope he has of making money.'

'Maybe he's so desperate to hold on to the money he owes us that he . . .'

'What? Think about it, Isabelle. Rivelli's in a hole, and everyone knows it. He owes millions to the taxman.'

'All the more reason to hold us to ransom.'

'Don't be daft. The police would be down on him like a ton of bricks. He can't afford any kind of unwelcome attention.'

'Then who?'

'Maya Rodean.'

'Oh come on! Don't be ridiculous!'

'Think about it. She hates you. She's eaten up with jealousy. You had that big row with her . . .'

'She started it!'

'And she made a complete tit of herself in public. She won't forgive that.'

'But you don't really think she broke in here in the dead of night and took all our stuff?'

'Not her, maybe – but one of her people, quite possibly. She's surrounded by mad hangers-on, all those desperate wannabes who think they can ride on her coat tails. If she's been bitching about you – and believe me, she will have been – then one of them might think it was a great way of getting Queen Maya's approval by coming in here and taking the collection to lay at her feet. Wiping out the competition. The one person who can show Maya Rodean up for the charlatan that she really is. You.'

'It's completely implausible.'

'Do you have a better idea?'

'I don't know. Have you pissed anyone off recently? Any mad bits of rough trade round at the flat who might have nicked the keys and decided to help themselves? They're probably flogging the dresses at some ghastly car boot sale in Essex.'

'I don't entertain mad bits of rough trade, as you so charmingly put it.'

'Well, you've been seeing someone . . .'

'Yes, I have, and that's all you need to know, thank you very much. Okay, try this for size. Victoria Crabtree.'

'You're just being silly now, Will.'

'I don't think so. She's unhinged. She's obsessed by you, always has been. She's living with that crazy bloody Leanne Miller now, so God knows what ideas she's put in her head. She's in and out of here all the time, she knows where everything is. I reckon she's nicked the stuff, and then a day before the show she'll phone up and say she's "found" it all and will pretend she's saved the day.'

'And why would she do that?'

'Revenge.'

'For what? I've done nothing to her.'

'Not you. Your mother.'

'Now you've really flipped.'

'She blames your mother for screwing up her relationship with Rivelli . . . And who knows, maybe with good reason.'

'And so naturally she comes and steals our stuff because that's really, really going to hurt my mother, isn't it? Quite honestly, Will, I think my mum is a much more likely culprit. She disapproves of my career and so in a moment of menopausal madness she snuck in here under cover of darkness and . . .'

'All right! Take the piss. This isn't helping us get the stuff back.'

Isabelle got to her feet. 'You don't need to tell me that.' She stormed over to the door, ripped it open, turned and shouted 'It's my fucking collection that's been stolen, you know. Not yours. My reputation that's going to be destroyed. Not yours. My fucking career.'

She flounced out, slamming the door behind her, still shouting.

'Not yours!'

Neither Christine nor Andy wanted to rush. They didn't see each other for a few days after that first night. But both of them sat in their respective offices smiling, feeling good about themselves for the first time in ages, not worrying about gossip and failure and money and contracts, just looking forward with calm anticipation for one of them – it didn't matter who – to pick up the phone and arrange the next date.

'I feel a bit like Elizabeth Taylor,' said Christine, when Andy cracked first, 'being re-wooed by Richard Burton.'

'I'm not sure "re-wooed" is a word, but I take your point. Just don't expect any diamonds.'

'Oh. You disappoint me.'

He hadn't denied that he was re-wooing her.

'I can, however, run to dinner.'

'Lovely. Where?'

'My place?'

Christine felt her hand gripping the phone tighter, felt the saliva suddenly leave her mouth. His place? *His place?* The place that he had got for . . . that woman? She took a deep breath.

'That would be nice.'

And why not, after all? Perhaps he wanted to show her that the past was in the past, that 'she' and her successors had moved on, that there was no one else in his life . . .

She would be gracious. She would say nice things. She would try not to notice any signs that he was struggling, financially or domestically. But beyond that, she didn't have a clue how to play it. She knew perfectly well that there was a lot of trust to be regained, that he had been a bastard throughout all the years of their marriage, made a fool of her, smashed up the family and alienated the children, and that she should move on and never have anything further to do with him.

But then there was the inconvenient fact that she loved him, that she wanted him back in their home, back in their bed, back as a father to Isabelle and Ben and back as her husband. And having a husband by your side, even an ex-husband, was a very good way of stilling the wagging tongues of the wine bars. Perhaps her fortunes had changed at last. Perhaps she could still hope for silk.

'It's nice . . .'

'Smaller than you imagined?'

Why lie? 'Yes. I rather got the impression it was palatial.'

'Hmmmm.' Andy took her coat, led her through to the combined living room/kitchen/dining room and poured her a drink. 'Palatial it ain't. But the views are nice.' Yes, the views were nice, out over Docklands, cranes exploding from the ground like fireworks, everywhere the hustle and bustle of change.

'It seems strange being here.'

They chinked glasses before he replied.

'I've missed you, Chris.'

'Really . . .' She walked over to the window, looked over, a long, rather alarming perspective of indefinite space ahead of her. 'Well, here I am.' She didn't want to sound too keen, but on the other hand, there was no point in putting him off. Renunciation and regret were all very well for the young, and people in the long dreary romantic DVDs she'd been reduced to watching, but in real life . . .

'I never stopped loving you, you know.'

This was more like it. She didn't turn round, carried on looking at the view, half expecting golden evening sunlight to break through the clouds. An agreeable shudder made her roll her shoulders.

'Andy,' she said, finally turning, nursing her glass, 'before I say anything else, there are one or two things that I have to get off my chest.'

'Here we go.'

'Don't worry. I'm not going to cause a scene.'

He looked devastated.

'And I'm not going to walk out on you, either.'

He still looked crushed.

'And I think it's only fair to tell you, Andy, that I have every intention of getting back together with you as soon as is humanly possible.'

He made a move towards her, but she held up a hand.

'But first, let me have my say. You'll probably think me an angry old woman, and I might very well put you off . . .'

'I doubt that.'

'You say you love me, Andy. That you never stopped loving me. But if that's true, why did you do it? Why all the affairs and the lies? Why did you have to cause me so much pain?'

The last words came out in a jumble, her voice rough, as if she'd voided something poisonous. She felt better for it. Andy looked worse.

'I never meant to hurt you.'

This time she moved towards him, to offer comfort; it was Andy who kept his distance.

'The honest answer, Chris, is that I don't know. Sex was a habit I got into. I told myself that it had nothing to do with "us", with our lives together and the family and the kids. But it was so easy, when I was away on a job or something, and there were always women . . .'

'And you just couldn't say no.'

'I'm not proud of it.'

'You must have enjoyed it.'

'What do you want me to say, Chris?'

'I don't know. I suppose I just want to hear it.'

'Yes, I enjoyed it. It was like a little bit of freedom, a little thing that was mine, nobody else's. I didn't have to share it, I didn't have to think about other people's feelings.'

'Clearly not.'

'And, you know, the more you do something the easier it becomes to ignore your conscience.'

She was about to say something, but thought better of it.

'In the first years, when you were working to support me, when the kids were growing up, I felt terrible about it. Every time was supposed to be the last time, but it never was. I went back for a bit more, one more last time, and then usually they'd get pissed off with me and take the decision out of my hands. And that was that, over and done with, and I'd be a good boy from now on.'

'But you never were.'

'Someone else would come along, and it would just seem that little bit less important, almost part of going to work.'

'What a delightful picture you paint.'

'I'm not trying to defend myself. What have I got to prove to you? Nothing. You know what I am. When my business started taking off, and I was working all the hours God gave, it seemed like a perk of the job. I deserved it, God damn it! And I'd come home to you and the kids feeling refreshed and ready to be part of family life again.'

'You mean you needed those other women in order to be able to stand living with us?'

Andy frowned. 'I suppose so.'

'Right.'

Silence fell. Andy stared at his sound dock, hoping that it might burst into life and block out the noise of his own too-heavy breathing.

Christine turned to the view again. The curving line of the river, still just visible in the failing light, on and on and out of sight on its long journey to the sea . . .

She spoke first. 'Well, that's better out than in.'

Andy looked up. His hands were braced against the kitchen counter, as if to prevent himself from falling.

'Chris . . .'

'I wish we'd said all this three years ago.'

'Me too.'

'We might have saved ourselves a lot of heartache. And money.'

'Yeah. Sorry.'

'I'm sorry too.'

Silence again, but not such a bad one.

'How much is this place worth, do you imagine?'

'I don't know,' said Andy. 'There's always some sucker who wants to live in Docklands. Not all it's cracked up to be, actually.'

'Yes,' said Christine. 'Always some middle-aged husband looking for a cool new bachelor pad after the divorce.' She smiled. 'That was unkind, but I must say it felt very good.'

'I'm glad.' His eyebrow was raised. They both smiled.

Victoria was on the phone.

'Joel? It's me.'

'Oh, hi.' Joel got out of bed, naked. Will stirred beside him, awoken by the phone, groaning and annoyed. 'It's okay, mate,' said Joel, ruffling his hair. 'Go back to sleep. It's family from down under.'

Will mumbled and turned over. Joel went to the bathroom, shut the door.

'What do you want?'

'I need to see you.'

'That's over, Victoria.'

'Not for that, you little prick. I know who you're with now. I know you're fucking him.'

'Vice versa, actually.'

'God, it didn't take you long to roll over, did it?'

'Yeah? Well I have you to thank for that, Victoria.'

'Okay, okay.' She sounded conciliatory; obviously something was wrong. 'Is it true, about the collection?'

'What?'

'Don't play dumb. That someone's nicked it.'

'Apparently so.'

'And you wouldn't have any idea who, would you?'

'Me? Do me a favour.' Joel stood in front of the mirror, checking his muscles.

'If you knew something,' said Victoria after a while, 'you would tell me, wouldn't you?'

'Would I?'

'You know how important it is for me.'

'Yeah?' He ran a hand down his abdomen. 'Why the sudden interest?'

Victoria mouthed a silent curse. 'Because Isabelle is my friend.'

'Yeah, right. And I'm Kylie Minogue.'

'Look, you little . . .'

'I know what this is about,' said Joel. 'It's your friend Rivelli, isn't it? I'm not stupid.'

Damn him – he's not.

'That's ancient history.'

'Whatever. Anyway, not that it's any of your business, I don't know anything about what's happened. I don't know anything about your precious Massimo Rivelli. I've never met the man. But if I do, I'll send him your love, Vicky.'

'Oh fuck off back to your boyfriend.'

'Thanks, darlin', I'll do just that.' He pressed the red button without listening to what Victoria was saying, and called a new number.

Making love in that flat laid a few ghosts for Christine. She woke up feeling quite refreshed, and ready for an encore. Andy, unstoppable in his youth, laughed and got out of bed.

'Old man!' said Christine, as he headed for the shower, his broad black back reflecting daylight.

'Have you received one of these?' he asked when they were both drinking coffee in the kitchen, handing Christine a postcard with the Cissé logo, white out of orange, on one side, details of the London Fashion Week show on the other.

'Yes. From Ben.'

'From Ben? Not from Isabelle?'

'Good lord, no. She doesn't want me there. Fortunately our son is DJing, and he wants his dear old mum to see him play.'

'Do you think they get together and discuss these things? Who's in favour, who's out of favour?'

'God knows,' said Christine. 'I gave up trying to figure out what goes on in our children's minds a long time ago. I see you have "plus one".'

'Yes. Don't you?'

'Yes.'

'Would you like to be my plus one, Miss Fairbrother?'

'I will if you will, Mr Cissé.'

'Good. We can plan what we're going to wear. Show them that there's life in the old folk yet.'

'Oh, I can't wait to see her face,' said Christine, allowing herself the rare pleasure of getting one over on her own daughter.

The police were working too slowly for Will's liking, and so, without telling Isabelle, he turned Sherlock Holmes, with Joel as his Watson. He went straight to the people he most suspected.

He left Maya Rodean's office with a bright red handprint on his face, and the feeling that his left eye was starting to swell up, and a reasonable certainty that, whatever else Maya Rodean may have done, she had not been responsible for the theft of the collection.

He called Victoria Crabtree, and listened to her irate ramblings about Rivelli, London Fashion Week, how much she could do for them even after what had happened, and what about lunch, right now? She was a drunk, thought Will, but he found it very hard to believe that she was a thief.

Rivelli was next on the list – but how could he confront him? He talked it over with Joel.

'I've had enough of Rivelli's bullshit,' he said, as they sprawled on the couch half-watching TV. 'If he's behind this, I want to know. What does he want? A ransom?'

'Come on, babe,' said Joel, stroking Will's thigh. 'It can't be Rivelli.'

'Then who is it? I've ruled out all the other suspects. Christ, some detective I turned out to be. Someone walks into the studio and steals our entire collection and I don't have the first fucking clue who it is.'

'Let the police do their job.' He put his arm round Will's shoulders, leaned his body weight against him. 'They'll get their man.'

'You don't understand. This isn't about catching the thief. This is about the fact that we're not going to show at London Fashion Week.'

'So? There's always the next one.'

'Yeah, right. And how are we supposed to do that? With all our stuff gone, with no money coming through from our fucking manufacturer, with the whole industry laughing at us. Someone wanted to put us out of business and they knew exactly how to do it. Just walk in to the studio, scoop up the stuff off the rails, into a bin bag, and away you go.'

'What did the police find?'

'Nothing. No sign that the lock had been tampered with or the chain cut. They reckon someone had a key.'

'Who has keys?'

'Only me and Isabelle.'

'Did she do it, then? She's mad enough.'

'She's not fucking mad.' Will pulled away.

'But it was all insured, right?'

'Wrong. The insurance policy was hopelessly fucking out of date.' Will sat forward with his head in his hands. 'It's my fault. I bought what we could afford at the time, when we started up last year, and I never got round to changing it. The insurance money won't even begin to cover what we've lost.'

'Shit.'

'Yeah. Shit.'

Joel massaged Will's neck. 'Come on . . . Relax . . . Everything's going to be fine.'

'How can you say that?'

'All right, man! There's no need to take it out on me! I didn't nick the fucking stuff!'

'I know. I'm sorry. It's just . . . Someone did.'

'Look, Will, you've got to start thinking about yourself. This isn't the end of the world.'

'What do you mean? It's the end of Cissé.'

'Yeah. Maybe. But you . . . I mean, you could do anything you want. Get a job anywhere. You're the golden boy.'

Will was about to reply, but something prickled in the back of his throat, and he swallowed hard.

'I'm going to get a drink of water,' he said. 'Do you want anything?'

'Make it a Scotch and you're talking.'

'No,' said Will, halfway out of the room, 'just water, I think.'

Victoria lay awake in bed. Leanne had been away all week. Plenty of time to think. At first, she wanted to call Rivelli, just to hear his voice, to beg for forgiveness, to grovel – anything, just to be part of his life again. But she had no idea where he was, who he was with, what he was doing. She had no way of reaching him – as if the last ten years had been a dream.

And so she started wondering about Rivelli, about Cissé, about the stories that were flying around the fashion world. The missing collection – that could only be the work of one man. By Rivelli's standards, that was nothing, a warning, a slap on the wrist. He was capable of much worse: had done it, many times, she imagined, from hints he had dropped.

It's about crushing anyone who stands in your way, so that you can have all this.

That night at Le Mûrier, the food, the wine, the bright lights illuminating the blue water of the swimming pool . . . The chill air on her naked breasts, and then the hellish pitter-patter of larvae . . . And Massimo's horrid, cruel smile.

It's about cutting your competitor's throat.

Anything to make a profit, to lower your overheads. She'd heard the rumours often enough to believe that they were true.

'Darling,' Adele had said with that infuriating air of authority, 'you don't for one minute believe all that stuff about dear old Italian *nonnas* making up the garments in their cosy little workrooms? He ships it all off to the Far East, pays them a pittance and pockets the difference.'

She suspected everything, and could prove nothing. All she could do was wait, and hope, and think.

'I'm going to see him today,' said Will, as they lay side by side in bed. 'I don't care what you say. I've got to ask him a few questions.'

Joel, his head resting on Will's chest, rising and falling with each breath, said nothing. He's very good at avoidance, thought Will. Am I going to have to spell it out? *I know you did it, Joel. I know you stole the collection, and I know you did it for Rivelli.*

'Do you hear me?'

'Mmmmh . . .'

'You're not asleep, Joel. I know you're not.'

'Yeah . . .'

'I'm going to go into the office and I'm going to tell him exactly what I think.'

'Don't, babe,' said Joel. His voice was small and frightened.

'I'm not scared of him, you know.'

'Well you should be,' said Joel. 'He's a dangerous man.'

'And you know all about him, I suppose.'

'Yeah.'

Will's chest rose and fell, and with it Joel's head. They were suddenly cold, and Will pulled the duvet up with his feet, then his knees, then his hands, until they were covered. Joel seemed to burrow beneath it, to make himself smaller against Will's body.

'Joel,' said Will, after a while.

'Yes?' The voice quieter, muffled by the duvet.

'You know what I'm going to ask him, don't you?'

Joel said nothing, just burrowed further, his mouth and nose squashed into Will's armpit.

Will pulled the duvet back.

'You do know, don't you?'

There was a long pause, and then Joel said:

'Yes.'

Chapter 21

There was nothing ironic about the venue for September – this time it was right in the heart of London Fashion Week, at the British Fashion Council tent, pitched in the grounds of the Natural History Museum in Kensington. It was no longer 'New Generation'. It was no longer 'edgy'. In just over a year, Cissé had gone from nowhere to the very top, and this show would put the seal on it.

Would have put the seal on it, thought Isabelle, as she woke to a lovely late summer morning. *But now . . .*

Will had called in the small hours to assure her that the show would go on. The clothes would turn up at the venue at ten a. m. exactly as arranged. No one would be any the wiser – apart from those to whom the show would be even more of a surprise than they intended.

And it was going to be a surprise – 'a revelation', Will said, after the final run-through with the producers. There was no talk, this time round, of cutting corners or calling in favours from friends. This time, they'd gone straight to the best, no expense spared, and the best were more than willing to work with them. True, if they'd known the parlous state of Cissé's finances, they might have been a little less eager. Will was far from sure that he'd be able to pay for everything, come invoice time – but he was willing to take a gamble. If the show went well, orders would come in at such a rate that the coffers would be overflowing, whether Rivelli paid up or not. Success of the scale that Will anticipated was better than money in the bank. It gave leverage.

But without the clothes . . .

'Don't worry, Princess,' said Will. It sounded as if he was outdoors; she could hear traffic, the occasional siren, even though it was the middle of the night. 'The collection will be there in time for the show. I stake my right ball on it.'

He rang off, and Isabelle slept for a few more hours, better sleep than she'd had for days.

But now she must get up and get dressed and get down to the

museum for a full day of press and photo calls and backstage panics and breakdowns and air kisses. And she still didn't know what she would find there.

There was a full programme of events in the BFC tent from nine a. m. onwards. Crowds ebbed and flowed in the morning, then flowed without ebbing from about noon, when the first of the big names was up. From that point on, it was a furious buzz of activity, like a well dressed anthill; if you'd viewed it all in slow-motion you might have been able to make some sense out of what was going on, but to the naked eye it seemed like highly coloured chaos. Every hour or so there was a blur of movement around the front-row seats, which were vacated and swiftly cleaned by a little army of fashion students, getting some valuable practice for the type of career that lay ahead for so many of them.

The Cissé show was the highlight of the day – not officially, as the last evening slot was reserved for a designer who had been hot stuff in the eighties and still managed to command crowds, if not head-lines. But everyone knew that the seven o'clock slot was the one to watch, the one towards which all the others were building, after which anything would be an anticlimax. It allowed the journalists enough time to file their diary pieces for tomorrow's papers, and it allowed the models enough time to change, stick their fingers down their throats and take their drugs in time for the after parties.

Massimo Rivelli was in and out all day, as much to be seen as to see; this was a public relations exercise, to show people that rumours of his ruin were greatly exaggerated. He had reached an understanding with HM Customs and Excise, put a number of properties on the market, fired his old accountant (who was immediately re-employed in one of the companies that they hadn't found out about), done the sackcloth-and-ashes routine and was now ready to resume his position as the major powerbroker of the European fashion world.

Two pairs of eyes watched him from opposite sides of the room as the crowds arranged themselves for the Cissé show. Christine was with Andy, both of them beaming with pride, not just for their daughter but also for their son – Ben was DJing for Isabelle's show, happy and beaming in the DJ booth, eyes closed, headphones squashing down his hair. Christine tried not to stare when Rivelli came into view, a thirtyish blonde on his arm; her heart pounded, but her face retained its customary courtroom composure.

Victoria, who had managed to get herself out of bed, scrubbed up and arrayed in her best Chanel, waited like a statue for Rivelli to notice her. She tried not to let him see her looking, to see the hunger in her eyes. There was That Bitch Christine, the author of her misfortune, with man who looked like – damn it, *actually was* – her husband. And there in the DJ booth was her handsome son with his dazzling smile and his caramel skin. And somewhere behind the scenes was Isabelle, the cause of all the fuss, waiting for the applause, if it came. Well, hurrah for happy families. By the time Victoria had finished with them, Christine and Andy would wish they'd never met.

Isabelle had sat backstage all day waiting for Will, fending off questions from the stylists and models, telling everyone that the clothes were on their way.

She took a Valium – her last one. Under the circumstances, she didn't think Will would mind.

At five o'clock, he texted her.

Say nothing. Just smile ☺

Rivelli happened to be near the front entrance of the tent when Will arrived. He looked at Will, smiled and whispered something into the ear of his blonde companion.

'Ah, Signor Rivelli,' said Will, marching straight over with his hand outstretched. 'In for the kill, are you? Jolly good.'

Rivelli did not return the greeting.

'We might be a bit late starting this evening,' said Will. 'We've had a few technical hitches. I'm sure you understand.'

'Ah. What a shame. I had heard something of the sort.'

'I thought you'd understand. You've had a few hitches of your own, haven't you? Well, that's the fashion world. We have to make the best of what we've got. Let's just hope everyone has a short memory, eh, Massimo?'

Rivelli did not like being called 'Massimo' by men, especially homosexuals.

'Because we had a bit of a shock a few days ago, you see,' continued Will, acting for all the world as if they were the best of friends, even touching Rivelli's girlfriend on the arm in an over-familiar gay sort of way. 'Our whole spring/summer collection was stolen! Yes! Right out of the studio! I mean, who would have believed that? So we've been in a hell of a state as you can imagine, chasing around town trying to put something together.'

'Unfortunate,' was all Rivelli said.

'Yes, terribly unfortunate. Still, the police have been fantastic. It's absolutely amazing how seriously they took it all. I believe they're very close to making an arrest.'

'Indeed. Very good.'

'Isn't it? Anyway, Massi old chap, I must dash. Lovely to meet your latest slut girlfriend. You're even cheaper than the last one, darling.'

Rivelli reached out to grab him, but Will slipped between the bystanders too fast.

The catwalk was nearly forty feet long, lined on either side by twenty tiered rows of seating, thrusting down the tent under a massive lighting rig that looked as if it could pull the whole edifice down, or set it alight, or just drop on someone's head. At one end there was a plain white diorama, on to which various designers had projected experimental films, or hung logos, or, if the budgets were small, simply shone a few coloured lights. For the Cissé show, a huge piece of flame-coloured silk had been dropped from the roof, covering the diorama, concealing a battery of wind machines which made it move like flame.

The guests took their place in the front rows – journalists, fellow designers, top stylists and, in the most visible seats, the celebrities, the actors and singers and supermodels and sport stars by whom the success of a show was measured. Cissé was a hit before a single stitch had been shown.

Victoria made do with a fourth-row seat, stage left.

Christine and Andy were front row, stage right, but far too near the stage to be really important. Victoria looked down on them in every sense of the word, and watched Christine waving and blowing kisses towards the DJ booth.

Rivelli escorted his scraggy new girlfriend to their front-row seats, and whispered in her ear. She smiled. She had terrible teeth.

How he must miss me, in his heart of hearts, thought Victoria.

Ben finished his set, the house lights went down, and massively amplified cello music boomed through the tent.

Just before the tent went dark, both Victoria and Christine had the distinct impression that they had seen Joel slipping out from the back-stage area and disappearing into the shadows.

But there was no time to think about it. The show had begun. Rivelli found his companion's hand, and squeezed. He was going to enjoy this.

The cello spun out a long, slow melody, a sad, plaintive line that unfurled through the tent like a black ribbon. The lights on the catwalk faded until all that could be seen was a dim, throbbing pulse of light on the wall of flaming silk. A vague drum sound, like a heartbeat, and then the tiniest of pinlights on the silk, bright white, a floating full stop of light, and the silk split open, and through the slash there came a shoe. A beautiful, simple, white leather shoe with a four-inch heel, and then a foot, a beautiful, coffee-coloured foot, followed by an ankle, a shin, a very shapely calf, a delicate knee.

The foot planted itself on the floor in the growing circle of light. The audience held its breath. Rivelli squeezed tighter.

A hand came through the slit – an elegant, coffee-coloured hand with clear nail varnish, followed by another hand, and then the thigh that was connected to the knee, and then the arms up to the elbows, and then the cello swelled and was joined by other strings up and down the register, the circle of light grew, the drumbeat became faster and more complex and then, smash, through the slash in the curtain came a female figure, naked but for those blinding white shoes, her hair a huge afro glistening with gold dust, dabs of gold on her breasts and what looked like the tiniest of see-through sparkly gold G-strings concealing her groin . . . The model shook her hair, shook her shoulders and shimmied down the catwalk, to all intents and purposes naked, stopping halfway down where she posed, hand on hip, turned, threw her arms above her head and then bent over, her head facing stage right, her arse, lightly flossed by a sparkling thread of G-string, towards Rivelli.

Rivelli gripped so hard that his girlfriend cried out.

She held the pose for a second . . . two seconds . . . three seconds . . .

Long enough for everyone to get the point.

And then she ran to the far end of the catwalk where she remained, dancing, her hands thrown above her head, her little feet stomping in their white shoes, her hips shaking.

The silk parted again, and another model appeared, swathed head to foot in black fake fur, a ridiculous parody of a movie-star coat, her hair pulled back from her face, a long switch falling straight down her back.

Would she, too, be naked underneath?

She stormed ten paces along the catwalk, stopped, turned, scowled, and dropped the fur.

Underneath was the most spectacular black dress that Isabelle had ever been able to imagine, the dress she had dreamed of making since first she started dressing up her dolls in bits of old cloth from her mother's sewing box. The most expensive silk, cut in a simple circle around the neck, long fitted sleeves that sat right on the wrist, the bodice slashed from the collar bone to the navel, where a single satin button held the whole thing together. And from there it flared out madly, a huge episcopal cape of a skirt, completely open at the front, revealing not only the legs but the hips too, covered now by a tight black silk undergarment. A pair of black strappy heels. No jewellery.

She stalked the catwalk, stopped in front of Rivelli, crossed her ankles and spun on the balls of her feet, the skirt rising up around her like Superwoman's cape.

The audience stood and cheered.

Dress after dress came down the catwalk, twenty in all, the last of them tiny mini-dresses in heavily sequinned satin, bird of paradise colours, each piece getting louder applause than the last, cameras working overtime to record the collection that would, within six months, have been imitated in every corner of the fashion-conscious world.

And then the final gesture, the moment they had all been waiting for, the model who, more than anyone, had come to represent the Cissé style, Amelie Watts, with her blonde hair and her porcelain skin . . .

She slinked through the silk in a blood-red shift dress, a heart-breaking piece of couture that made every woman in the place sigh with envy. She walked flawlessly to the end of the runway, each perfectly shod foot landing exactly in front of the other, stopped, turned, returned, came halfway back and then, as the music hit its last few chords, ba-ba-ba-baam, and the lights came up to a blinding golden glare, she reached behind herself, wriggled her shoulders and her hips and wham! The dress flew off her body, was tossed into the air and fell, showering glitter over Amelie Watts's naked skin.

Blackout.

Then they all came on, all twenty of them, all in huge black fake fur coats, moving down the catwalk like enormous fledglings, all in step, left right left right left right left, until they were evenly spaced out and dropped the coats and stood with their hands on their hips, face front, face left, face right, showing off their Cissé gowns for one last hurrah, and then they faced back, applauding as Isabelle came blinking into the light to take her bow, acknowledging the standing ovation with a shy smile and an awkard curtsey.

Rivelli and his companion sat stony-faced throughout the whole thing, slipping out of their seats during the blackout. They headed for the exit just at the same time as a dark figure detached itself from the shadows ahead of them.

It was Joel.

'Oh, shit,' he muttered, and hurried away.

Rivelli ran after him, grabbed him by the shoulder, yanking him harshly round. Joel stumbled for a moment, righted himself and stood panting, eyeball to eyeball with Rivelli. Sweat stood out on his upper lip.

'You fool,' whispered Rivelli. 'What happened?'

'I don't know, I swear,' said Joel, his voice breaking. 'Please, Mr Rivelli, sir . . . it's not my fault.'

Joel backed away from the tent, towards a stand of plane trees, into the gathering darkness, where the sound of applause was muffled, distant.

'You told me everything was arranged.'

'It was. I promise you, Mr Rivelli, I did exactly what you said.'

'You lie.' Rivelli smacked Joel around the face with the back of his hand. 'You fucking try to mess with me, boy, I told you what happens.'

'Please, Mr Rivelli, sir . . .'

Rivelli struck him again; this time Joel ducked, and Rivelli's fist slammed into the trunk of the tree. As he was swearing and shaking his hand and getting ready to plough into Joel once again, something moved in the shadows and another figure stepped towards them.

'Hello again, Massimo.'

Will stepped up beside Joel, and put a hand on his shoulder.

'You okay?'

'Yeah . . .' Joel rubbed his jaw. 'Nothing too serious.'

'So, Massi darling,' said Will, 'do go on.' He waved his phone in Rivelli's face; a little red 'record' button winking in the gloom. 'I'm all ears.'

Isabelle witnessed the show and its aftermath as a series of images, like a PowerPoint slideshow operated by a lunatic. First of all the dresses arrived, bundled up in black bin bags with just an hour to go before the show . . . and then there was the frenzy of unpacking and untangling which she could only watch through an unbelieving Valium haze . . . clouds of steam as the stylists ironed out the worst of the creases, sponged off the dust and dirt, hung them on rails and inspected them for damage . . . But there was none. Somehow the dresses had survived, somehow they were here, she did not know how, and somehow they were going over the models' heads or being stepped into and zipped up and smoothed down. And as Ben played the last few numbers of his pre-show set, the director gave the models their final instructions, and they stood in a huddle and tapped their knuckles together and made tiny little jumps in the air until the first solemn notes of the cello called them to themselves and they wiped their faces clear of expression and prepared to walk the runway.

It seemed, to Isabelle, to last approximately ten seconds, perhaps less, and then she was on, blinded by the light, being pulled by bony hands, wanting to run but her feet sliding forward as if she was in water, remembering to bow, to behave, as Will was always telling her, 'like the star you are', not some nervous drugged-up college-leaver.

She curtseyed to left and right and could not be sure of what she saw but she thought that it was her mother and her father and that they were sitting in the same row, and then she was pulled away, floating off to the other side, smiling and bobbing and trying not to lose her balance.

And then there was someone very tall with a French accent and a black suit telling her that she was being taken for lunch tomorrow and they were going to discuss 'the deal', and when she said 'what deal?' he laughed in a peculiar French way and said 'You know, you are going to do a collection for Givenchy . . .'

And then there was her father putting his arms around her waist and squeezing her, lifting her up in the air, spinning her around, and every time she turned she saw her mother laughing and clapping. 'We're so proud of you, darling,' said her father, 'we're so proud,' and his arm was round Christine's waist, and Isabelle felt happy and angry at the same time.

Where was Will? She looked around for him, she wanted his arm to lean on, but he was not there.

He was never there when she needed him.

She needed a drink.

She needed a line of coke.

She needed someone to explain what had happened and how the clothes had got there and why everyone was clapping and smiling and kissing her and wanting a photograph.

She saw Ben in the DJ booth, bopping around in time to the music, the headphones clamped over his hair, a big smile on his face, waving – maybe to her, maybe just to the crowd – far out of reach.

Someone put a glass of champagne in her hand, and she downed it in one.

'Hey, that was fantastic' – a familiar voice in her left ear, she turned and there was a face she'd seen on a thousand magazines and album covers, handsome and groomed. Mike Christian, the platinum-selling British rock star with his angelic good looks and his devilish romantic reputation, who alternated massive stadium shows with philanthropic works for every good cause under the sun. *He* thought *she* was fantastic. Cameras exploded around them.

'There are some people I'd like you to meet,' said Mike, taking her arm.

They seemed to pick up more famous people as they walked through the tent, like scraps of metal attracted to a magnet, and by the time they reached the VIP enclosure, they were quite a party.

'I'd have dressed up a bit more if I'd known I was coming here,' said Isabelle to no one in particular. When she walked in on Mike's arm, there was a round of applause. At least three of the women were wearing Cissé.

Fiona Walker was not one of them. She was looking rather severe, in a high street sort of way.

'Well, you had us all fooled there,' she said, standing straight in front of Isabelle, blocking her way.

'Oh . . . Yes . . .' How much did people know?

'We thought you were just going to be a one-trick pony.' She raised a glass of champagne. 'I have to hand it to you, Isabelle Cissé. Dan was right. You do have talent.'

Dan! Where was he? Isabelle looked right and left, but could not see him in the sea of famous faces.

'He's outside, love,' said Fiona, suddenly matey. 'They didn't have enough VIP passes for everyone, I'm afraid, and, well . . .' She gestured around her. 'Dan doesn't really fit in here, does he? Mr Marks and Sparks.'

'Neither do I,' said Isabelle, but she was already being whisked away from Fiona who, when it came right down to it, was only a sales agent.

She disappeared into a crowd, where she had the not unpleasant sensation of being eaten alive.

Victoria knew everyone, but very few people seemed to know her – even people who had kissed her arse in the good old days. If she couldn't get to Rivelli, at least she could hurt Christine, by seducing her son. She had to do something.

She made her way towards the DJ booth as Ben was packing up.

'Great set,' said Victoria, as Ben stepped down, a big grin on his wide, handsome face.

'Thanks. I saw you dancing.'

'Did you really? I bet you say that to all the girls.'

'No.'

He wasn't exactly a great conversationalist, thought Victoria, but she persevered.

'Well, your big sister is the star of the show.'

'You know her?'

'Oh yes, we go way back. I got her her first big break, you know.'

'Right.' Ben was looking over her head, searching for his family.

'So, do you have a deal?'

'What?'

'A record deal. I mean, I assume you're a recording artist. The way you mix . . . You can always tell.'

Ben stopped looking around. 'Yeah, I am as a matter of fact.'

'I knew it. What sort of stuff?'

His eyes lit up. 'All sorts. Electro. Kind of mash-ups. Putting stuff together that sounds fresh . . .'

Victoria felt someone looking at her, caught the flash of a familiar pair of eyes in her peripheral vision. Adjusting her hair gave an excuse to glance to one side – and there was Rivelli, not so much watching her as glaring at her, an expression on his face like a ravenous wolf. Ah, he had got rid of his date. At last. She nodded, lowered her eyelids, and turned back to Ben, who was still talking in musical terms that meant nothing to her.

She gave him another forty-five seconds, then 'You see, I'm going on to a party tonight that's going to be full of A&R people, if you fancied coming along. I mean, they're always looking for new talent. I think you should come.'

'For real?'

'Do I look as if I'm joking?'

'No.'

'Listen,' said Victoria, consulting her watch, glancing aside again to make sure Rivelli was still there, 'I've got to do a bit of networking, won't take me more than half an hour. Does that give you time?'

'I've got all my stuff.'

'Don't worry about that. We'll take a cab. Where do you live?'

'I'm staying with my mum . . .'

'Oh . . .' She tried to sound surprised. 'Well, I'm in Notting Hill.' She looked directly into his eyes. He was young – very young – but not inexperienced, she imagined.

'It's a deal. Half an hour.'

'I'm Victoria, by the way.'

'Safe,' he said, and she tried not to wince. 'Ben.' They shook hands on the deal.

He went one way, she went another.

* * *

'It doesn't look as if we're going to see her.'

'I know. Well, that's the price of fame, I suppose. I had no idea she was so . . .'

'What? Talented?'

Andy looked at Christine, Christine looked at Andy.

'Is that awful?' she said. 'I've always been proud of her, supported her to the best of my ability, but I suppose in the back of my mind I never thought that this fashion thing was going to take off.'

'Looks like we underestimated her, then.'

'Doesn't it just.'

'It would have been nice to speak to one of our children, at least,' said Christine, taking Andy's arm and strolling out into the evening air. After the heat and noise of the tent, it was a blissful relief. 'But I can't see Ben either. I suppose he's been whisked off somewhere.'

'In that case,' said Andy, 'let me whisk you off too.'

'Where to?'

'The night is young. Let's go for dinner.'

'You play your cards right, I might let you see me home.'

Rivelli was not in the mood for conversation. He grabbed Victoria by the arm, pulled her behind a curtain and kissed her hard on the neck. She knew his moods; he was angry, he needed the kind of executive stress relief that only the seasoned mistress could provide.

The tent did not offer many opportunities for rough-but-discreet sex, but instinct led her backstage. They were not asked for passes. Rivelli's face was pass enough.

Cissé's models were changing into their own clothes, nipping in and out of the toilets. Victoria saw an unoccupied cubicle, barged past a girl who was about to nip in ahead of her, and pulled Rivelli in after her. The walls were only fibreglass, and far from soundproof, and they might well knock the whole thing down, but there was a lock on the door and that was all that mattered.

Rivelli did not speak. His face was dark, his eyes glowing with fury. Victoria bent over the sink, lifted her skirt and braced herself against the wall, one hand on either side of the mirror. She could see Rivelli's reflection as he unzipped, brought himself to full erection with a few brisk tugs and slaps, spat into his hand and then, kicking her feet a yard apart, entered her from behind.

Isabelle escaped from the celebrity scrum and went in search of her parents who, by that time, were poring over the menu in a restaurant in Charlotte Street. She couldn't find them, she couldn't find Ben, and she couldn't find Will. The next show was about to start, and people were taking their seats.

She ran into Dan Parker coming out of the gents as she was about to go into the ladies.

'Congratulations,' he said, looking rather morose. 'Great show.'

'Thanks.' She felt tongue-tied.

'All those celebs,' he said, waving towards the VIP area. 'Good for business.'

'Yes . . .' She wanted to say that she felt awkward with them, at a loss for conversation, that she would much rather go for pizza with him than . . .

'Well, it's good to see you,' he said, moving away.

'Are you . . .' She was going to say 'with anyone?', but instead she said 'staying for the next show?'

'I suppose I should. It's kind of expected.'

'Oh.' Perhaps he was shy, she thought, and expects me to make the first move. 'Well, we could go for a . . .'

'Isabelle!' Will, at last, shoving his way through the crowd. 'Fucking hell! You're not going to believe this when I tell you!'

Dan backed away, and was lost in the crowd.

'Is it Givenchy?'

'Oh, that. No. I was going to save that for tomorrow. Good, isn't it?'

'I suppose so . . .'

'That's one of Dan Parker's little deals. Clever lad, that Dan.'

'He was just here . . .'

'No, this isn't about that. It's about Rivelli. Guess what?'

Isabelle followed a blond head through the crowd; it might be him, it might not. The superstar DJ cranked the volume up, the lights went down, and she lost him.

'Go on,' shouted Will, 'guess!'

'Huh?'

'It was Rivelli who stole the collection.'

But she did not seem to have heard him.

Victoria had to think on her feet. She'd seduced Ben with one thought in mind – to hurt Christine, lashing out blindly because she saw the means to do so. It would be no great hardship to have him in her bed, randy, uncomplicated in comparison to Joel, a welcome return to men after her lesbian interlude with Leanne. She hadn't thought much beyond that – walking out with Ben on her arm, under Christine's nose, flaunting it, making a scene, making them talk. That would have been a good night's work.

And then along came Rivelli, all anger and urgency, his face dark in the mirror as he watched himself going into her, then wiping himself, slapping her on the arse and leaving without saying goodbye. There was no condom to dispose of; there never was with Rivelli. And it had been some time since Victoria had been on the pill; given the current state of her love life, that was one thing she didn't need to worry about. It would do her good to have a break.

In fact, she thought, as she went back to the party to find Ben, it had done her good in more ways than one. Rivelli might very well have got her pregnant. Okay, it had never happened before, even when she'd 'accidentally' slipped up on the birth control, but that didn't mean it couldn't. He was fertile; he had a son to prove it. Why shouldn't she conceive from that one furtive Fashion Week fuck? And then she had him. He could ignore a mistress. He could not ignore a mother.

But supposing it hadn't worked, and his sperm had not reached their destination? Supposing Rivelli, the great Italian Stallion, was firing blanks after all? That would be a joke. Maybe his own son was not really his. If so, he would never admit it. That, to Rivelli, would be worse than ruin. His manhood called into question? Never. He must remain as he believed himself to be, a potent male.

And that was where Ben came in so handy. Twenty years old, fit and healthy, high on his success, and, with a couple of drinks inside him, staring at her tits like a hungry baby. She had only to get him into a cab before he got too pissed to perform, up the stairs to the master bedroom – Leanne would never know – and let nature take its course.

They fucked for hours. Experience was all very well, but at times like this, when you really needed to get the job done, there was nothing like the stamina of youth.

'Right, Joel. I need some answers.'

Will couldn't really get angry with him, not yet: Joel had saved the day, after all, and been extravagantly demonstrative when they got home after the show, as if, by having sex, he could put off indefinitely the time for explanations.

'I suppose you'll have to tell the police.'

'I've told the police already. And they're as keen as I am to hear what really happened.'

'I told you. Rivelli got me to hold the clothes to ransom. It was never meant to get this serious. It was never meant to involve the law.'

'Do you know what they think of me?' asked Will. 'They think I had some silly spat with my boyfriend and that you ran off with the collection as a way of getting back at me. Either that, or they thought I set the whole thing up as a way of getting money out of Isabelle. So either I'm a hysterical queen, or I've got the fashion equivalent of Munchausen syndrome, kidnapping my own collection.'

Joel laughed, but stifled it quickly.

'It's not funny.'

'It is.'

'It won't be, when I get done for wasting police time.'

'Seriously?'

'Seriously.'

They lay together for a while, sharing body heat.

'Then we'd better tell them it was a row. A misunderstanding.'

'Okay. I'm prepared to do that. I must be bloody mad, but if it keeps you out of trouble . . .'

'I'll make it up to you.'

'Damn right you will.' Joel started caressing him again. 'Stop that. We can lie to the police, but on one condition. You tell me what really happened.'

'Fair enough. Where do I start?'

'How did you meet Rivelli?'

'I went to see him.'

'Why?'

'I'd heard a lot about him.'

'Who from?'

'You. People. He's famous.'

'And you thought you'd just swan in and . . . what, exactly?'

'I thought he might give me a job.'

'Right. Just like that.'

'Why not? I didn't want you to think I was just sponging off you. I thought he might be able to . . . use me in some way.'

'And did he?'

Joel grinned. 'No way. Not like that. He's not . . . you know.'

'He's straight. Like you, right?'

'Anyway, he gave me a bit of courier work. Delivering stuff.'

'You never mentioned it.'

'It was cash in hand. He told me to keep it quiet.'

'And then – what? He just sprung the big one on you? "Hey, Joel, steal the entire Cissé collection for me, there's a good lad, here's twenty quid".'

'Something like that, yeah.'

'And you didn't think that was a bit odd.'

'He said it was like . . . a joke.'

'Did you notice me laughing?'

'No. But he told me he was going to give it back. It was just a business thing, he said.'

Just how thick is he?

'Do you swear to me, Joel, that you really did not know that he was trying to put us out of business? That you honestly believed this was some kind of elaborate business strategy?'

'I swear.'

'And that when you realised things were not as they seemed . . .'

'I told you, didn't I? I confessed. I took you to where the clothes were.'

'You did.'

'See? I did the right thing.' He sounded as if he really believed he had.

'So what are we going to do now, Joel? What am I going to tell the police?'

'You can't tell them about me and Rivelli.'

'Then he gets away with it.'

'But if you tell them . . . then I'll be in trouble.'

'You are in trouble.'

'Please . . .' Joel snuggled against him. 'I'll never lie to you again.'

'Do you promise?'

'On my mother's life.'

Will lay in silence for a while, stroking Joel's thick black hair.

This is probably a mistake.

'Okay. I'll believe you – this time. We'll tell the police it was just a lovers' tiff. They think we're all fucking mad anyway. Let's just hope they're too busy to take it any further. Rivelli's off the hook – but so are you.'

'Thanks, Will. You won't regret it.' His hands moved south again.

'I'd better not.' This time, Will did not push him away. 'But you must promise me, Joel, that if Rivelli ever gets in touch with you again, about anything, you tell me immediately. Right?'

Joel made a noise that probably meant 'yes', but his mouth was full.

Part Three

London, Los Angeles, Tokyo, Milan

Chapter 22

It was a bitter January morning, the plane trees in Lincoln's Inn Fields bare and brown. The lawns, which in summer were crowded with the younger members of the legal profession eating sandwiches and loosening ties, flirting and gossiping and soaking up the sun, were empty but for a few hungry blackbirds pecking hopefully at worm casts. Christine sat on a bench, warming her hands round a takeaway coffee. She was shivering, and not just from the cold.

The phone call came when she was on her way to chambers, bracing herself for another day of putting on a brave face. It was months since the collapse of the Rivelli divorce, but the profession had not forgotten. Nobody was briefing her.

Keep your head down. It will blow over. This time next year . . .

'Chris, it's Linda.' Her voice was slurred. Christine checked her watch; it was nine o'clock in the morning. Surely to God the old fool wasn't still pissed from last night . . .

'Oh hi, Linda. Look, I'm just on my way into . . .'

'I'm in hospital.'

'What?' She's fallen down stairs again, perhaps broken something this time.

'Guy's Hospital. I wondered if you could . . .' She broke off to cough. Christine held the phone away from her ear, and swore under her breath. 'Sorry, Chris. I wondered if you could come in and visit me.'

'Of course,' said Christine brightly. 'I'm a bit tied up today, but tomorrow . . . Well, I'll have a look at my diary when I get to chambers. It's a busy week, but . . .'

'I've got cancer, you see.'

Christine stopped in her tracks. A man walked into her.

'You've . . . got . . .'

'Cancer. Of the bowel.'

'Oh, Linda.' So that's why she hadn't called over Christmas.

'So I wondered if you could . . .'

'Of course. Of course. I'll come today.'

'Thanks, love. I hate to be a nuisance. It's a bit of a shock.'

'Are you . . . are they going to operate?'

Linda laughed, and started coughing again. 'Sorry, Chris.' One more big hack, and in a wheezing voice she said 'It's a bit late for that, I'm afraid. Look, come and see me, right?'

Christine walked back into Lincoln's Inn Fields, sat down before her knees gave way, and stared at the dead leaves, feeling the cold creeping into her bones.

Linda is dying. I must phone Andy.

But Andy was away again, and there was no one else she could talk to.

'Christine?'

'Oh!' She jumped. 'God!'

'Sorry, I didn't mean to scare you.' It was John Ferguson, bending slightly at the waist to peer down at her, briefcase in one hand, neatly rolled umbrella in the other, one of hundreds of identical men on their way to work. 'Are you okay?'

'John.' She couldn't think of anything to say. He had found her sitting on a park bench nursing a cardboard cup of coffee, looking as if she'd lost her mind.

He probably thinks I'm not going into chambers any more . . . That I've turned into one of those people who sit on park benches all day . . .

'Sorry.' She pulled herself together, forced a smile. 'I've just had some bad news and . . . Well, it's rather upset me.'

'Ah.' He sat down beside her, apparently in no hurry.

'It's Linda.'

'Oh dear. What now?'

'She's . . .' Christine felt her chest go hollow, felt pressure building in her head, demanding release. 'She's got cancer.'

'Ah.' John folded his gloved hands in his lap, stared down at his shoes.

Of course . . . His wife . . .

'Sorry, John. This is the last thing you need. It's hit me rather hard for some reason.'

'Yes. It does.'

She blew her nose, took a sip of coffee, stood up. He remained seated, looking across the park to the bare trees. 'How is Sue?'

John looked up at her. With a shock, she realised that his eyes were full of tears.

'She died last week.'

Victoria dragged herself out of bed, feeling as if she had been run over by a bus. Every limb ached, and her stomach was doing cartwheels. It felt exactly like a hangover, but she'd hardly touched a drop for weeks, telling everyone she was on detox. She crept to the bathroom, taking care not to wake Leanne, knelt by the toilet and vomited as quietly as possible.

Nearly four months gone, and I'm still getting morning sickness. It's not fair . . .

She stood up, rinsed her mouth at the sink and spat. It was cold in the bathroom, and she pulled her dressing gown around her.

How long before I start to show?

She still looked slim – thank God for Pilates and good posture – but she knew it was there, bigger every day, and soon she would have to take special care over her dress. Nothing tight . . .

On the day she found out, after staring in awe at the unambiguous blue line in the little window, she phoned Adele. She had to talk to somebody, and she didn't think Leanne would be sympathetic. Of the three people she'd had sex with at the relevant time, Leanne was the only one who could definitely not be the fater.

'What do you mean, it might not be Massimo's?' asked Adele, over *bruschetta* in the Harvey Nichols café. 'How many others are there?'

'Only one.'

'Who?'

'Oh, he's nobody,' said Victoria, remembering Ben's broad back, his skin like warm caramel, the sweetness of his kisses as he made love to her for the fourth time in a night. 'Just a DJ that I met at a party.'

'Just a DJ? You mean you picked up some kid and you . . .' Adele lowered her voice. 'You were not . . . careful?'

'It wasn't planned, darling.'

'Then of course you will do the sensible thing.'

'Will I?'

Adele dabbed her mouth, put down her napkin. 'Let us think about this for a moment. You do not have a home.'

'I could, if . . .'

'You do not have a partner.'

'But when Rivelli finds out that he's going to be a . . .'

'You have no money.'

'No, but I can . . .'

'The only way that you're going to get any of those things, darling, is by finding yourself a new friend. And nobody, I repeat, nobody is going to look at you with a baby hanging off your titty.'

'It worked for you.'

'Oh!' Adele threw her head back and laughed. 'Darling, that was different.'

'It's always different for you, isn't it?' said Victoria, cursing Adele for her effortless elegance, the casual way in which she wore clothes she had bought for herself, jewellery she had bought for herself.

'But Victoria, surely you don't think . . . Oh, no, *vraiment* . . .'

'What?'

'That he will take you back. Rivelli.'

'Why not?'

'Have you learned nothing?'

'I know him, Adele. I've loved him for a long time, and he has loved me.'

'My poor girl.' Adele reached out; Victoria withdrew her hand. 'You are making a very big mistake.'

'I know what I'm doing, thank you.'

'But you do not. Now, shall we have a pleasant lunch? I have said what I have to say. I do not expect you to take my advice, because you never have. But we can be friends, can't we? Come on. It will be my treat. Choose the wine.'

'No, thanks,' said Victoria, picking up her handbag. 'It's bad for the baby.'

'It seems weird to be leaving,' said Will, looking around the empty studio. The last crate had been taken away; everything going into storage, or being shipped to Los Angeles.

'We've outgrown it,' said Isabelle, picking her way through stuffed black bin bags full of rubbish, eighteen months' worth of detritus, poly-styrene cups, empty water bottles, old magazines, offcuts, phone numbers scribbled on Post-It notes, never called.

'I know . . .' Will unplugged his laptop from the phone socket for the last time, closed it up, put it in its case. 'But I'll really miss it. So much has happened here.'

Isabelle turned her mouth down, as if she was tasting something nasty. 'Yeah. Burglaries. Drugs. Freezing to death on a dirty mattress on Christmas Day.' *Watching you fuck some boy.* 'Time to move on. When Chelsea's ready it'll be much better. More space. More light. More convenient for everything.'

'More expensive.'

'I can afford it.' She put her coat on – a long black wool coat that had been sent over by Jasper Conran – and brushed off a few specks of dust. 'Anyway, the lease is up. They're knocking this place down. I don't suppose even you can screw your way out of that one.'

Will didn't respond. At one time he'd have pinched her bum or poked her in the ribs, and they'd have tickled and giggled their way out of trouble. It wasn't worth it these days. She always meant exactly what she said. She had changed fast.

'Anyway, Chelsea's going to be great,' she said, fiddling with her phone, not looking at Will. 'It's what I always wanted. A great big Victorian house with a huge studio space. All mine.' Her phone rang. 'All mine . . .'

Will picked up a couple of rubbish sacks and carried them out into the street. They'd be taking it all away this afternoon. He'd lock up for the last time, take the keys round to the estate agents, and that would be the end of that. No more studio. No more sandwiches on the green. No more late-night takeaways or impromptu discos or parties-for-two . . .

Isabelle pushed past him, still talking on her phone, leaving the studio without looking back.

'Of course, Mike,' she was saying, 'I'll be there. Just send the car. Okay. Love you too.' And then she was gone.

Instead of shaking her hand and wishing her well and saying that he really had to get to work, as he had every right to do, John put Christine's arm through his and walked her around Lincoln's Inn Fields until she stopped crying.

'This is ridiculous,' she kept saying. 'I mean, it's Linda. It's not as if it's even unexpected. She's always been so . . .' And then she'd start crying again.

John was not embarrassed. 'You've known her for a long time,' he said. 'Since before the children were born. Before you married Andy, even.'

'Was there ever a time before I married Andy? It's hard to remember,' said Christine, blowing her nose for the hundredth time; it must be bright red by now. 'Time has a way of accelerating at our age,' said John. Christine glanced up at his profile. His hair was greyer, the lines around his eyes a little deeper than before.

'I'm sorry I didn't know about the funeral,' she said. 'I would have come. Or at least sent flowers. I was very fond of Sue.'

'It was just family. Sorry, but I couldn't face crowds.'

Is that what I am? Just one of a crowd?

'And we didn't have flowers.'

'Right.' He obviously didn't want to talk about it. 'I see.' But if he didn't want to talk, why was he walking round and round, arm in arm, neither of them sure of what to say, whether they were still friends or even colleagues any more. Time to take the bull by the horns.

'John.' She swallowed hard. 'I never had a chance to apologise for what happened . . .'

'It's okay. Mr Rivelli is no longer my responsibility.'

'I know what everyone's saying about me.'

'You don't listen to that rubbish, do you?'

'The thing is, they're right. I broke the biggest rule in the book. I'm a laughing stock. I don't need to hear the jokes, because I've heard them all before.'

'Don't punish yourself, Christine.'

'I don't need to, do I? The profession will do that far more efficiently than I ever could. It's started already. First of all they turn me down for silk . . .'

'Everyone's turned down first time.'

'Bless you, John. Then the jobs start drying up.'

'I know I've not been instructing you. It's been a bad time. But you mustn't worry. We'll soon find something.'

'I don't want you to find something for me. I know the score. I'm going the same way as Linda. Chambers can't actually get rid of me, as long as I keep paying my rent. But I'll slip down the ladder rung by rung till I'm back in the magistrates' again, doing hearings for parking tickets. That's Christine Fairbrother, they'll say. She used to lecture us about personal conduct. Now look at her.'

'Feeling a bit sorry for yourself, Christine?'

It was like a slap in the face.

'What?'

'This *mea culpa* routine. Don't you think you're taking it a little far?'

She disengaged her arm from his. 'Is that how it seems to you?'

He smiled. 'A little.'

'Hmmm . . .' They walked on, more distance between them.

'And you think it's the end, do you?' He raised his hands. 'The big tragedy.'

'You tell me.'

'Worse things happen at sea.'

Okay, you've lost your wife. Your tragedy trumps mine.

'That's what Andy keeps telling me.'

'Ah,' said John, that half-smile still on his face, 'how is Andy?'

'Fine.' Should she tell him? They'd known each other for long enough, surely. 'We're sort of making another go of it. Or trying to, at least.'

'Ah.' Three paces, four, five, in silence. 'Well, that's good news.'

'I hope so.'

'The kids must be pleased.'

'Yes,' said Christine, who didn't have a clue how either Ben or Isabelle felt about it. 'They are. We are.'

'Good,' said John. They had reached the gate. 'Well, Happy New Year, then.'

'Oh, John . . .'

'Don't worry so much, Christine,' he said, putting a hand on her shoulder. 'Things have a way of working themselves out.' The hand was still there, the kind, crinkled eyes full of amusement and sadness.

'Thank you.' She kissed him on the cheek. 'Goodbye, John.'

They turned away from each other, she towards her office, he towards his.

* * *

If Rivelli would not return her calls, she had no choice but to speak to him directly. And if that meant hanging around outside the office in the freezing cold, then so be it. As long as she wrapped up warm, Victoria could wait.

Marylebone High Street was busy with shoppers, tourists and ladies who lunch. Sooner or later, someone would recognise her; one could only lurk around outside Conran for so long without attracting attention. And whatever lie she thought up – 'Oh, I'm just looking for a new bedroom suite!' – they would be sure to jump to the right conclusion. But she had to see him, and if necessary, she would come back tomorrow. And the next day. And the next day.

She had one card left to play – and it was an ace.

What was she hoping for, now, at the end of the game? She could hardly expect Massimo to enfold her in his arms, call her his little Mamma, and whisk her off to live happily ever after in France/Italy/Sardinia. She could barely hope to be reinstated as a kept woman. If the rumours were true, Rivelli might be out in the cold himself before too long. There was talk of bankrupcy, even criminal proceedings. She had better stake her claim now, salvage what she could from the wreckage.

'Massimo!'

His head swivelled, and he nearly missed a step. He saw her across the street, signalled 'Stay!', as you would to a well-trained dog, and dodged through the cars, agile on his feet.

'Victoria!' He sounded pleased. She nestled into her rabbit-fur collar.

'I'm sorry, I had to see you.'

'Not here.' There was a time when they'd have jumped in a cab to Kensington without a second thought. Now, however, there was no more Kensington. 'The office. Come.'

Nobody looked up as they stepped from the lift. The place hadn't changed much since last she was there. It was quiet. No one around. Must have been a big party last night, she thought. They'll roll in at about midday, thinking that's an early start . . . She could almost pretend that things were just as they had always been: that they were on their way to a lunch or a party, or taking a company car to the airport to catch the an evening flight to Nice, New York . . .

'Come in. Sit down.' He took her coat, hung it up carefully. 'It's been a while.' He perched on the edge of the desk, smiling down at her as if nothing had happened. Well, thought Victoria, two can play at that game.

'You look well, Massimo.' He did too, damn him: no bags under the eyes, no dramatic weight loss, no balding or crow's feet. Nothing to indicate imminent ruin. Perhaps the rumours were just that.

'*Grazie.*'

He did not pay her a compliment in return. His phone rang, he grabbed it, gabbled something angry in Italian and slammed it down. He turned back to her, his lips parted in a carnivorous smile.

'So, Victoria.' He was looking at her legs; thank God it was far too early for them to be ruined by varicose veins and water retention. She recrossed them. 'What do you want?'

'You know what I want, Massimo.'

'Ha! Always the same Victoria.' He prodded her thigh with the tip of one highly polished black shoe. She shuddered.

'I wasn't talking about that. Or, at least, not only that.' It wouldn't do to let him think that she was anything other than majorly hot. 'I need to talk about . . .'

'Please do not say "us", Victoria.'

'Why not?'

'There is no "us" any more.'

'Ah.' She felt a shiver in her shoulders, but controlled it. 'At least you didn't say there never was.'

'No, of course . . .' He waved his hand, brushing away the past like cobwebs. 'But, as you know, things have changed.'

'You are no longer married.'

He stood up, walked to the window and looked out, his back to her.

'You must know . . .'

'Massimo,' she said, 'I'm pregnant.'

He carried on looking out of the window. The phone rang once, the shortest of rings, and stopped. She could hear people outside the office talking, moving around. Traffic hummed past the window; in the distance, a siren.

'Did you hear me?'

'I heard you.'

'Well?'

'You must do as you see fit.'

Turn round, you bastard. Turn round.

'It's yours, of course. There's nobody else.'

'Ah.'

'And I'm keeping it.'

For a man who believed that condoms were instruments of Satan, and who frequently insinuated that women who used birth control were little better than whores, he could hardly start arguing in favour of abortion.

'I see.'

'Massimo, I'm telling you that I'm carrying your child.'

At last, he turned. His face told her nothing.

'Yes, I understand. It is a surprise.'

'I hope it's a nice surprise.'

He smiled – those teeth again.

'Yes . . . Of course.' He picked up the phone. 'You must allow me to arrange a car for you.'

'It's all right, you know,' she laughed. 'I can still get around. I'm not even showing yet.'

'How long?'

'Nearly four months.'

'Fashion Week?'

'Yes.'

'You have not told anyone.'

'No.' She had told Adele, and that was as good as taking out a full-page ad in *The Times*. 'Of course not.'

'Please, I must think. I will . . . Yes. I must . . .'

She stood; the desk was between them. 'Massimo, I hope that you trust me, after all our years together.'

He smiled, cracked his knuckles. 'Of course. If not you, then who can I trust?' He looked straight into her eyes; his expression was unreadable. She wanted to kiss him, to kneel, to throw her arms round his legs and beg him to take her back, to take care of her.

'Call me, Massimo. Just call me.'

She walked out to the lift, hearing the office door closing softly behind her.

* * *

The flat in Bethnal Green never felt like home, so it wouldn't be hard to say goodbye. The studio – well, the studio was full of ghosts. London was full of ghosts. It wasn't home any more. Home was where she'd grown up with a mother and a father and a brother, and all that was over and done with and in the past.

The future was Los Angeles and Mike Christian.

Mike, who picked Isabelle up at the Fashion Week show, who squired her around town and got her into the papers every day, and who promised to carry on where they left off when she got to LA for the Oscar nominations. They would be the new Power Couple – the singer and the designer, music and fashion, established and cutting-edge, irresistible. Okay, he had a bad relationship record, and, as Will was quick to point out, he'd shagged his way through most of Hollywood. But that was just jealousy talking. Will didn't want her to go to LA without him.

Isabelle was going out for a week of meet-and-greet before the nominations – and, more importantly, for a week in the media spotlight as Mike Christian's girlfriend, a new star in the firmament, young, gifted and black. When the time came to get one of her dresses up the red carpet outside the Kodak Theatre, she did not want anyone to say 'Isabelle Who?'

A week – but, if things worked out, she intended to stay for a while. There was nothing to keep her in London. Solicitors and estate agents were sorting out the house in Chelsea – four floors of light and space and exposed brick and sanded oak, an absurd extravagance, but, now that the business with Rivelli was sorted out, an affordable one. An army of builders and decorators would take over, under Will's guidance. He would project manage. He would 'run the London office', whatever that meant. And when Cissé moved to Los Angeles, the London office would close. The house could be rented or resold. Will would . . . well, Will would never be out of work.

Only one thing remained before Isabelle left for Los Angeles. She had to see her mother. Tempting as it was to slip away, she forced herself to pick up the phone and arrange lunch – one last time. Let's see if we can spend a couple of hours together without screaming. Let's see if she can force herself to be pleased for me. I won't talk about Mike, and she can keep quiet about whoever she's seeing now.

She won't go on about the abortion, and I won't mention Rivelli. We can be mother and daughter, chatting about clothes and recipes and whatever else normal people find to fill in the silences when they're not shouting at each other. One more go.

Joel disappeared a few weeks before Christmas, in theory to visit his family. Since then, there had been no word. Will sat at home restlessly clicking his mouse, but there was nothing in his email apart from work stuff, house stuff, begging letters from former St Martins students and the thrilling news that he'd won four hundred thousand pounds on the Kenyan State Lottery. Nothing on Facebook, or Messenger, or MySpace. No calls, no texts, not even a Christmas card. Of the dozens of ways Joel could have got in touch, he had availed himself of none.

So that was over, then. He'd left Joel off the hook about the theft, and as soon as the coast was clear, Joel had done a bunk. So much for falling in love.

He'd let Rivelli off the hook as well. The confession that he'd been so clever to record was useless. If he used it, he incriminated Joel – and, now that he'd lied to the police to keep Joel out of trouble, he'd incriminate himself as well. The police were satisfied – well, perhaps 'satisfied' wasn't quite the right word – that the whole business was a storm in a teacup, and let them off with a few stern words about wasting police time. Will had nothing on Rivelli at all. The money that he owed Cissé was further from their reach than ever.

Of course, as soon as the new collection went into production, they would appoint a new manufacturer; Will had the sole satisfaction of taking his business elsewhere, and letting everyone know that Rivelli was a swindler. Further than that he dared not go. He simply had to hope that, somehow, Cissé could survive without the money from their first year in business, most of which was still sitting in Rivelli's bank account somewhere in Milan. Well, the orders were coming in all right. Walker Parker were happy on that account. Isabelle's stock was high – she was famous now, a celebrity on both sides of the Atlantic. Surely that had to count for something. The paltry six-figure sum that Rivelli owed them was just a drop in the ocean – wasn't it? They could chalk the whole thing up to experience, and move on. If only Isabelle wasn't so hell bent on this bloody great white elephant in Chelsea. But even that was possible – if they got to the Oscars. That would solve everything.

And if not? Goodbye Cissé, goodbye to a future in fashion, hello again to his father's haulage company and a lifetime of regret. All because of Joel.

The first shock came when Andy opened the door. Andy, not Christine. Isabelle saw her father as if for the first time – saw how handsome he was, how well put-together, how his clothes fitted where they touched. Christine was right behind him, wearing an apron, wiping her hands on a tea towel, grinning like the Cheshire cat.

'Well!' Christine came towards her, put her hands on her shoulders, kissed her on both cheeks. 'Here we all are, together at last.'

Isabelle walked straight through to the kitchen. 'Is Ben here?'

'He's upstairs. Fooling around on a guitar, I expect.'

Isabelle took the stairs two by two.

'Do you want a drink, darling?' shouted Andy, but she did not reply. 'What the fuck is going on?'

Ben was sprawled on the bed, a guitar lying across his groin, headphones on, eyes closed.

'Oi!'

She kicked him on the leg, and he sat up.

'Hi sister. What's up?' He half pulled the headphones off; she could hear tinny little twiddles as he fooled around on the fretboard.

'You tell me. What's he doing here?'

'Dad? I dunno. Come for lunch, I suppose.'

'Come for lunch? Don't be so bloody ridiculous. They're divorced. Or were you too stoned to notice that?'

'I think it's nice that they're friends again.' Ben scowled, which was a rare occurrence. 'Now you're here, I'm having a drink.'

'I'm not going down there until I know what's going on.'

She was fifteen again, taking refuge upstairs until everyone was so worn out by the bad atmosphere that she got what she wanted.

'Okay.' Ben unplugged the headphones, switched off his guitar. 'See you later, then.' He slouched out of the room.

She could just leave. Walk out of the front door and never see any of them again. It was so tempting. She looked out of Ben's bedroom window; there was the gate, the red brick wall, a row of dark conifers and beyond them the street. Jump in a taxi and then away, away to Los Angeles and Mike and the future.

'Isabelle!' Her father's voice; she didn't answer.

'There's a drink for you down here. It's going flat.'

Going flat? Champagne, then? What was the occasion? What were they about to spring on her?

'Are you coming?' His voice nearer now, halfway up the stairs. 'Are you in the loo?'

She burst out of Ben's room. 'No I'm not.'

'Ah.' He saw her expression, and the smile vanished from his face. 'There you are.'

'What's going on, Dad?'

'What do you mean?'

'You here. Ben here. Champagne.'

He didn't deny the champagne. 'Just seeing you off in style. Any objections to that? We're very proud of you.'

'Huh.'

'What?'

'I said "Huh."'

'Meaning what, precisely?'

He leaned against a cupboard door, folded his arms, crossed his legs, waiting for an explanation. There was a time when this would have led to an argument and threats, an explosion of temper, then reconciliation and hugging. Not now.

She walked past him and down the stairs.

Christine was making gravy. *Gravy!* When did she last make gravy? It wasn't Christmas, for God's sake.

'This mine?' Isabelle took the fullest glass of champagne, and without saying cheers drank half of it at a gulp. She intercepted a look between Christine and Andy.

'So,' she said. 'Happy families.'

Christine stirred the gravy a little more vigorously. 'It's lovely to be all together.'

'Is it?'

Ben drifted into the living room, picked up a magazine and threw himself on to the sofa.

'When are you off to LA, then?' asked Christine.

'Day after tomorrow.'

'How exciting!'

Isabelle said nothing, swirled the last mouthful of champagne around the bottom of her glass and drained it.

'Make sure you check out the new Rice–Brotherson building,' said Andy. 'I did a lot of the interiors on that.'

'I'm going to be busy.'

'More champagne?' Christine signalled to Andy, who refilled Isabelle's glass.

'Must be hard for you to believe that you've come such a long way in such short time,' said Christine.

'Not really.'

'We're so proud of you.'

'Are we?'

'Right,' said Christine, turning away and pouring the gravy out of the pan, into a bowl. 'I think we're just about ready. Darling, will you carve?'

Darling? She never called him *darling* when they were married.

Isabelle went to the conservatory, and looked out over the garden. It had been a wet morning, but now the sun was shining, reflecting off sodden leaves and shiny berries. She remembered when the conservatory had been built – to Andy's design, of course – when she was in her teens, thirteen or fourteen. She remembered sitting in there on hot summer days when she'd played truant, curled up on soft cushions, smoking cigarettes, naked, the wicker chairs printing into her arms and thighs. She remembered the arguments with her mother when she'd smelt the smoke. She remembered entertaining her first boyfriend in there, well on the way to losing her virginity. That had happened upstairs.

A light touch on her shoulder. She span round.

'Is everything all right, darling?' Christine, in that ridiculous pinny.

'Yes.'

'You seem a little tense.'

'Do I? Well, I wonder why that might be.'

Her mother looked pained. 'Isabelle, I don't understand. You wanted to come round and say goodbye.'

'To you. Not to have the whole family thing thrust down my throat.'

'Excuse me?'

'What is he doing here?'

'Your father?'

'No, Mickey Mouse.'

'I thought you'd be pleased.'

'What's going on, Mum? I mean, what is it that you're trying to do, exactly? I'd just about got used to the idea of the toyboy . . .'

'Isabelle, for God's sake.'

'Then you sprang Massimo Rivelli on me.'

'That was . . .'

'And we all know what happened there, don't we?'

Christine was looking out of the window; a gust of wind brought huge sycamore leaves flapping through the garden like strange yellow birds.

'And now, what do you know, Daddy's home.'

Christine folded her arms, kept her back turned.

'What's your next trick? I mean, what's left? Lesbianism? A career in porn? You're running out of ways to shock me.'

'Do you really think . . .'

'I thought men were the ones that had midlife crises, not women. Is it a menopause thing?'

Christine rushed out of the conservatory, tears streaming down her face. 'You've become a cruel little bitch,' she said, and headed for the stairs.

'Maybe I always was,' said Isabelle.

And those were the last words they exchanged for a long time.

Chapter 23

It took Rivelli a week to get over the shock, as he put it, of the baby
– but, given time, the Italian heritage kicked in and he started thinking
there was nothing quite as important as being a Pappa. He called one
evening and told Victoria that he would take care of everything, that
he had plans for her and the child – plans that she must keep to herself.
He was still under investigation by the Revenue, he said, beset by
creditors, and must be very careful about how he was seen to be spending
his money, but when it had all blown over and he was really free, they
would be together. There was plenty of time. The baby wasn't due for
months – it would be spring again, and they would be together at Le
Mûrier, this time for good. Could she bear to leave London? What
did she think about being a Sainte-Maxime housewife? She would
have all the help she needed. She wouldn't have to lift a finger.

She was leaving in three days. Take such-and-such a flight from
Gatwick to Nice. Someone will be there to meet you. The staff will
have everything ready. All you have to do is take it easy, enjoy yourself, go shopping, rest, wait for me. I'll be there as soon as I can. Stay
quiet, tell no one where you are or you'll arouse the lawyers' suspicions
and we'll be back at square one. The quieter you keep it, the sooner
we'll be together . . .

Victoria packed few possessions, leaving as much as she could behind.
She was attentive to Leanne, tolerant of intimacy, showing interest in her
projects and business. But Leanne was sulky and brusque, always ready
to pick a fight, accusing Victoria of seeing men behind her back. Well,
she would be out of there on Monday, leaving London a long way behind,
ready to begin again in the one place where she had always felt at home.
She hoped Massimo would hurry – but if she had to be alone anywhere,
it might as well be Le Mûrier. She could relax and recover, and think
about what might yet turn out to be the one big spanner in the works.

If the baby was Ben's.

If the baby was black.

But how black could it be? Ben was half-and-half, lighter skinned than his sister, almost the same colour as Rivelli when Rivelli had been slapping on the olive oil and roasting himself in the Provençal sun. The baby would be even lighter, Ben's genes mixed with hers – and she, as Rivelli often reminded her, was whiter than white. Unless the baby was some kind of throwback, and emerged from her womb as black as coal, there was little reason for anyone to suspect a thing. Besides, Rivelli got there first. His sperm had a good five hours' lead on Ben's. It had to be his. Please God, it had to be his. Let it be his.

Linda was sleeping a lot, and when she wasn't sleeping she was high on morphine, but that didn't really matter: Christine was used to seeing her under the influence. Instead of sitting in chambers waiting for briefs that never came, Christine sat by Linda's bed in Guy's Hospital. If the clerks needed her, they could call her; she could be back in the Temple in fifteen minutes. Up here, at least, she was doing something useful, even if Linda didn't know she was there for much of the time. She wasn't bored. She caught up on reading, she busied herself on her laptop, and in between times she looked out of the sixteenth-floor window over a vast panorama of London, the river and the City and far beyond on every side, as if Linda and the other patients and the nurses and doctors and visitors were already being airlifted to heaven.

'Chris . . .' Linda sounded amazed to find her old pupil by her bedside every time she woke.

'How are you feeling?'

'Bit groggy. Water?'

Christine poured from the plastic jug into the plastic glass, held it up to Linda's lips. She had lost a lot of weight. Her hair, which had always been a frizzy mop, was thin and sparse, revealing her scalp. How fast it took you. How cruel.

'Thanks, babe.' She folded her hands above the sheet; an old woman's hands, thin, clawlike, picking at the bedclothes.

'It's a beautiful day. Amazing views you've got from up here.' What does one say to the dying? What's left that won't hurt them or remind them of how little time they have?

'Can you see the Old Bailey?'

'Yes, clear as a bell.'

'Which way?'

'Over there.' Christine pointed. Linda extended her neck a little, like a tortoise.

'I like to know where it is. Scene of former glories, and all that.' She patted the bed. 'Come and sit with me for a minute.'

'Okay.' Christine took Linda's hand, stroked the bony knuckles, the papery skin. She was covered in bruises from canulas.

'I'm very proud of you, you know.'

'Oh, come on, Linda.'

'I am.' Linda coughed a little, dribbled out of the side of her mouth. Christine passed her a tissue. 'I know I've been a pain in the arse sometimes.'

'You haven't . . .'

'But it was always good to know that you were there. I could tell people that I'd had some part in your success.'

'Come on, you didn't do so badly yourself.'

'You were the lucky one, Chris. The star. Biggest star of your generation.'

'Don't. You'll make me . . .'

'You had the success and the husband and the family . . .'

Where is this going? Is she going to throw it all in my face?

'And one day, you'll take silk.'

'I don't think there's much hope of that now, Linda.'

'Rubbish,' said Linda, laughing weakly. 'Everyone knows you'll be a QC one day. I bet you – within a year. Eighteen months at the most.'

'You seem to have forgotten a certain awkward business . . .'

Linda's eyes were huge and wet. 'Rivelli!' She barked the word.

'Rivelli,' said Christine.

'They'll forget that soon enough.'

'I don't think so. Stories like that don't just go away.'

'Oh, we have ways of shortening people's memories,' said Linda. 'You know there were photographs, don't you?'

'Photographs? Christ.'

'Yes. Someone was watching you.'

'I suppose everyone has seen them.'

Linda pursed up her mouth and raised her eyebrows. Her cheeks were sunken, her face a skull. 'No, I don't think so. I made sure of that.'

'What do you mean?'

'You know Gerry. Pennington and Blythe.'

'Of course.'

'He got hold of the evidence. Showed it to Janet Rivelli.'

'I thought something like that . . .'

'You know where he got it from?'

'No.'

'Rivelli's former mistress.'

'Victoria Crabtree?'

Linda wagged a finger. 'That's the one. Who in turn had got it from her boyfriend. Who, a little bird tells me, might not have been absolutely unknown to you.'

'I don't . . .' The penny dropped. 'Oh my God. Joel.'

'If you say so. You must have made a very good impression.' Linda chuckled. 'So he takes the photograph, shows it to Victoria . . .'

'Victoria and Joel? You mean they were . . . together?'

'So it seems. You and she have rather a lot in common, don't you?'

'Linda, really, I don't think that's any of your business.'

'Sit down, Christine, and listen to what I have to say. Victoria bides her time, waits for her opportunity, and then, at the perfect moment, sends the photograph to Gerry at Pennington and Blythe.'

'Of course. She was in court.'

'Gerry thinks he's struck gold, and shows it to Janet . . .'

'Who then discloses all the details of Rivelli's hidden assets . . .'

'Your case is shot down in flames . . .'

'And I'm the laughing stock of the bar.'

'Yes.' Linda coughed, swallowed. 'For now.'

'And the photograph . . . What did it show, exactly?'

'I don't know, darling.'

'You didn't . . .'

'No. I didn't. And I made bloody sure that nobody else did either.'

'What do you mean?'

'Gerry is a horrible man, but like most men, he'll listen to reason if you really spell it out to him. So I told Gerry that if he showed that photograph to a single person, if I even suspected that he'd showed it to anyone, then the world would find out about him and the grand-daughter of a certain senior partner at Pennington and Blythe.'

'My God.'

'You see? Being a disgusting old gossip has its uses.'

'What did he do?'

'He deleted it, Chris. Right in front of my very eyes.'

'You did that for me?'

'Of course, darling. That's what friends are for.'

'I never know where you're going to turn up next, Isabelle. Every time I look around, you seem to be there.'

'Hello Maya.'

'Welcome to LA, darling. I suppose it's your first time.'

'Yes, it is, actually. But I don't suppose it's yours. Daddy would have brought you.'

'Of course. When I was in my teens, I lived out here with him for a while. Went to high school in Bel Air.'

'How lovely for you. Which wife was he on then? Oh, look, here's Mike. I'm sure you know Mike Christian. You know everyone. Mike, look, it's Maya Rodean.'

'Yeah.' Mike barely looked at her. 'Listen, sweets, we're going over to the Chateau. You coming?'

'Sure. Be with you in just a second. Old friend from London, you know. Catching up on all the gossip.'

'Okay. Car's waiting.' Mike kissed the top of her head and walked away to join his famous friends.

'You're quite the rock star wife, aren't you?' said Maya.

'I don't know. You're more familiar with the breed.'

'Didn't take you long, did it? First sniff of success and you're out of London like a . . .'

'What? Rat up a drainpipe?'

'I was going to say a dog out of a trap, actually.'

'You're too sweet, Maya. So, how's the new collection coming along? Any interest?'

'Oh, didn't you know? I'm doing an exclusive line for H&M.'

'Congratulations, darling, that's wonderful. All the great designers have done lines for H&M. Madonna. Kate Moss.'

'And what about you, Isabelle? What have you got up your sleeve this time to amaze and delight us?'

'I don't know, really. I seem to have run out of ideas . . .'

'That's what I heard . . .'

'Since I sold the entire spring/summer collection to Neiman–Marcus. Now I've got to come up with something new.'

Maya's mouth was hanging open.

'Well, it looks good on the CV. I suppose these little things help. Bye for now, Maya. Sorry to dash off like this. My boyfriend, the singer with the biggest selling British band of the last five years, is holding the limo for me. Can we give you a lift anywhere? H&M?'

'Sweet of you to ask, darling,' said Maya, 'but no thank you.'

Everything fitted into one small suitcase. That was it – all she'd got to show for a lifetime. A few pieces of couture, some jewellery, diaries, laptop, phone, shoes – no point in taking the really high heels, she wouldn't be able to walk in them soon – and the essential toiletries. It was practically hand luggage.

Leanne was away for a few days. The timing was perfect. When she came home, there would be no Victoria. It would take her a while to realise that anything was wrong. Perhaps she was just out with Adele, or doing the rounds of the shows, a spot of shopping. And then night would fall, and the house would be quiet, and Leanne would start to worry, to look around, to realise that Victoria had gone. And she would never be able to find her. Victoria would make quite certain of that. She booked the cab, and began counting down the hours until she reached Le Mûrier, and life could begin again.

Linda died in her sleep, alone. The nurse told Christine that there had been no pain. A brother, whom Christine had never met, was arranging the funeral. There was nothing for her to do.

Nowhere for her to go.

She told the clerks she had flu, and sat at home for three days, not reading the papers, not answering the phone – not that the phone rang much. Andy was away again in Dubai, with no immediate prospect of his return. Ben was back at college. Isabelle – well, wherever Isabelle was, she was not speaking to her mother. And Linda, whose drunken late-night phonecalls had irritated her so much, Linda who had salvaged her reputation with one final act of kindness – Linda was dead.

John Ferguson sent a card.

Sorry to hear you're under the weather. Get well soon. John F.

Perhaps he had a job for her – but she was in no mood for pity or charity. The Rodean divorce, she knew, would go elsewhere. Greenbaum was bound to get Rocky Rodean. He'd got everything else. He'd got silk.

Nobody was talking about anything except the Oscar nominations. Any day now, the world would know who would be walking down the red carpet in February. Journalists, photographers, magazine editors and agents sat in clusters in the bars and restaurants of Hollywood, scribbling names on pieces of paper, crossing them off, poring over *Variety*, conversing in whispers, behind hands.

Isabelle was only interested in one category: Best Actress.

The minute the announcement was made, she'd call Will and get him to courier over whatever was necessary. Dresses of every colour, shape and length with which to tempt the nominees. The competition was fierce. Paris had rolled out the big guns, and they would be there with their million-dollar dresses, their jewellery and accessories, their chequebooks open. Cissé was young, new, almost unknown, British, a designer David battling the Goliaths of couture.

It might work.

It must work.

The nominations were days away. Isabelle could think of nothing else.

A ring at the doorbell. Probably a religious lunatic asking if she wanted to meet Lord Jesus Christ, or someone to read the meter, perhaps. Unless it was . . . No, John would never come round unannounced, would he?

A silhouette through the frosted glass of the front door – a man. Christine experienced a moment of fear, but she could not exactly say why.

'Who is it?'

Surely not Joel . . .

'It's Will.'

Will? It took a few moments, and then she opened the door just as he was saying 'Isabelle's partner'.

Oh God. Something is wrong.

'Will! Come in. Are you alone?'

'What? Oh, yes. She's still in LA.'

'Yes, of course. Are you all right? Is Isabelle all right?'

'She's fine.' He stood in the hall, wiping his feet repeatedly on the mat, clutching a bottle of wine. 'I'm sorry to disturb you.'

'Is that for me?'

'What? Oh, yes.' He handed the bottle over. 'You must think it's very strange, me coming around like this.'

'Well, I suppose it is, rather.'

'The thing is, I need some advice.'

'If you want advice about my daughter, you've come to the wrong place.'

'It's not that.'

'Has she sent you around to tap me for more money?'

Will laughed. 'No. But it is about money, all the same.'

They sat in the kitchen and opened the wine.

'You know Isabelle and I did not part on the best of terms when she went to LA,' said Christine.

'She's . . . difficult, at the moment.'

'You're telling me. So what's the problem.'

'She's buying this house in Chelsea. We can't afford it.'

'I thought things were going so well.'

'They are. But we're owed a lot of money.'

'Don't tell me. Rivelli.'

'How did you know?'

'Call it a lawyer's instinct. How much?'

'Hundreds of thousands of pounds.'

'Ouch. And Isabelle doesn't know this?'

'I've tried to tell her.'

'But she won't listen. Yes, that sounds like my daughter.'

'And the trouble is, there's nothing I can do about it. I've . . . well, I've done something rather stupid.'

He told her about Joel, and the kidnapping of the collection.

'Hmmm,' said Christine. 'Theft to order. Nasty little crime. Nasty little man.'

'Who? Rivelli?'

'I meant Joel. You know that he and I have history, I suppose.'

'You?'

'There's no need to sound quite so surprised. If anyone should be surprised, it's me. He seemed so . . . well, heterosexual, to put it bluntly.'

'You know what models are like.'

'Models? He's not a model.'

'What?'

'He's a fitness instructor.' Will looked blank. 'I see there's a few things he hasn't told you about. I bet you didn't know about Victoria Crabtree either.'

'Victoria Crabtree? What's she got to . . . Oh no. Say it isn't so.'

'Yes,' said Christine. 'Isn't that nice. We've all got something in common.'

'And he told me that he just went to see Rivelli on a whim.'

'Some whim.'

They opened a second bottle.

'So let me get this straight,' said Will. 'You had Joel. I had Joel. Victoria had Joel. Victoria had Rivelli. You had Rivelli.'

'You know that, then.'

'I'm afraid Isabelle mentioned it.'

'Well, it's true. I'm not particularly proud of it. God, I've got rotten taste in boyfriends, haven't I?'

'Me too.'

'My daughter hasn't had an affair with Joel as well, by any chance, has she? I mean, he wasn't the father of that child that she . . . you know? I don't think I could stand that.'

'No, of that you can be certain. His name was Marco, he was a dancer.'

'Right. What a lot I'm learning today.'

'And now she's with Mike Christian.'

'So I read in the papers.'

'And she's out in LA being a celebrity and expecting to come home to a great big house in Chelsea and a big pot of money in the bank and I can't tell her that the whole thing has gone belly up.' Will put his head in his hands. 'I don't know what to do.'

Christine was frowning. 'Something's very wrong here.'

'You're telling me. I've screwed up. My stupid bloody feelings for Joel . . .'

'Yes,' said Christine, 'you've screwed up, but that's not it. We've both made mistakes in that department. But there's something else.' She paced around the kitchen, wine glass in hand. 'Everywhere I turn, every time something happens in this family, it always seems to have something to do with Victoria Crabtree. Isabelle's drug problems. My . . . little spot of bother in the high court. Finding out about Isabelle's pregnancy. Joel and the photographs. Everywhere I look, she's there. And behind her, there's Massimo Rivelli. What else is she going to do?'

'You don't know the half of it,' said Will, and told her about the dragon dress.

'A pattern emerges, as we say in the legal profession. So – what are we going to do?'

'I don't know,' said Will. 'It all seems hopeless. Without the money, we'll go broke.'

'Then we must see what we can do,' said Christine. 'Leave it with me.'

Victoria was sick on the plane, but it didn't matter; she could feel the child inside her, and a little nausea was a small price to pay. She was leaving England for a new life in the sunshine. The last two years were like a dream – a self-destructive nightmare. Now she had what she wanted: a home, a future, Rivelli. A child. It was all so simple. The child solved everything.

As long as it was his. Not Ben's. It must not be Ben's.

She collected her bags, and breezed through customs, already sure that she could smell the pine trees and the rosemary, still green in the middle of winter.

The driver would be there to meet her.

She walked through arrivals and scanned the crowd for her name.

There it was, VICTORIA CRABTREE on a clipboard.

'Hello, Dave.'

A familiar face, thank God – Dave the driver, Rivelli's fixer in the south of France.

'You're looking well, Miss Crabtree. Come for long this time?'

'I hope so, Dave,' she said, letting him take her case. 'A very long time indeed.'

Chapter 24

Isabelle stayed up all night to hear the nominations announced at dawn – in time for the morning news on the east coast. It was not unusual for her to be up at first light; life with Mike was largely nocturnal. They'd done the rounds of the pre-announcement parties, but ducked out of the ceremony itself; Mike could get invited to anything, but Isabelle preferred to hear the news alone. Then she could start planning, undisturbed by shrieking.

'See you at the after-party,' said Maya, as Isabelle left the pre-party.

'I'm afraid I'll be working,' said Isabelle.

Maya swished past with her nose in the air, and was absorbed by her retinue.

Of the five nominees for best actress in a leading role, only two interested Isabelle; the others, besides being insipid beanpoles with no tits, already had deals with major Paris couture houses. Isabelle had done her homework. There was no point pitching to someone who was already being paid millions to wear Versace.

This made Isabelle's job a lot easier, and she was confident that one, if not both of the remaining actresses would wear Cissé on the night.

There was Tilly Ostergard, the young redheaded star of *Our Little Secret*, the controversial box-office smash about a woman's triumph over child sexual abuse.

And there was Mercy Williams, already being hailed as the greatest comeback of the century, who had hauled herself out of well-publicised crack addiction not only to record a Grammy-winning album but also to star in *Moanin' Low*, a biopic of Libby Holman.

One was twenty-four, the other officially fifty-five. One was white, the other black. One was a US size six, the other, thanks to a strenuous exercise regime (available on DVD), had got down to a size eight. Both would look sensational in Cissé, and there was just time to fly back to London, create unique custom dresses for one or both, and return in time for the ceremony. She had five weeks. A lot could happen in five weeks.

While Maya Rodean and the rest of LA's fashion celebs set about getting themselves into the papers/Perez Hilton/rehab, Isabelle was on the phone to agents, publicists and managers. If anyone could manage a lunchtime meeting she would be ready, press book in one hand, samples in the other.

John Ferguson had called again, and this time Christine went to see him.

'Got any work for me, guv?'

'Nothing yet.'

'Then what? Just the pleasure of my company? I'd have thought you'd had enough of that.'

'I wanted to talk to you about Massimo Rivelli.'

'Oh.' She sat down. 'I see.'

'Don't worry, Christine. I'm not about to read you the riot act. I was just wondering about . . . well, about Isabelle, really.'

'Isabelle?'

'Does she still have dealings with the company?'

'Yes, worse luck. They owe her a lot of money. Why?'

'It's just that after the case went down the plughole, I made a few enquiries about our friend Signor Rivelli. And what I found out was not very nice.'

'That sounds familiar. Go on.'

'The stuff that came up in court about the overseas companies was just the tip of the iceberg. That's just what Janet knew about. Then there's this.' He pulled a suspension file out of a drawer; it was fat to bursting with paper.

'And what is this?'

'Let's just say that a good friend of mine in Companies House did me a little favour and ran a check on Massimo Rivelli.'

Christine opened the file, took a quick look through.

'International, isn't he?'

'Oh yes. Most of it's harmless enough on the surface. But you know me, Christine – suspicious mind. I think what we have here is one gigantic money-laundering operation.'

She picked up the file, felt the weight. 'That's one hell of a lot of laundry.'

'Well, there's money in drugs.'

Christine swallowed. 'Are you absolutely sure about this, John? I mean, he's a garment manufacturer. Isn't it all just a bit James Bond?'

'Maybe, maybe not. I'm not suggesting the Rivelli is the one who organises the traffic, or even makes the deals. I'm sure he keeps his hands clean enough. But look at where the companies are based. All of the most notorious tax havens in the world. And why the interest in Burma? Not exactly a fashion centre, Burma.'

'Sweatshops?'

'I'm sure Mr Rivelli has interests in all your major areas of organised crime. Child slavery, drug smuggling, arms dealing, people trafficking, you name it.'

'But he's such a public figure.'

'So was General Noriega.'

'Come on, John.' Christine shivered. 'You're frightening me.'

'That,' said John, 'was the general idea.'

Victoria spent a lot of time in the pool, lying on her back watching the swallows whizz over the house, or resting her arms on the edge, looking over the trees and villas towards Saint-Tropez. Oh, the peace was heaven, and the expectation that Rivelli would be there any day now. That's what Dave kept saying: *any day now.* He was just tying things up in London, sorting out a few loose ends before he took a good long holiday, just the two of them at Le Mûrier.

Could it be that it had all worked out just as she had planned? Janet had sued for divorce, got her settlement – more than Victoria had hoped, but Rivelli would manage, he always did. Rivelli was free, and he believed he was going to be a father. Yes, she could follow the way his mind would work. He was angry with her at first – he'd cut off her credit card, even booted her out of the penthouse, tried to cut her out of his life. But now, thanks to some clever moves and a few frantic minutes in a toilet, the unplanned masterstroke that completed the picture, he was coming back, and he was grateful. She'd freed him from Janet, she would give him a child to replace the dud back home, and she had proved that she could be trusted to keep her mouth shut.

Because there was more, much more, that Victoria could tell about Massimo Rivelli if she chose to open her mouth. She hadn't been his mistress for ten years for nothing. She'd overheard late-night phonecalls, she'd been present at business meetings in nightclubs with unsavoury-looking characters who really didn't look as if they had much to do with the garment industry. Why, even Dave, good old Dave who drove them around and tended to odd jobs around Le Mûrier, had other uses about which Victoria was quite able to guess. There were reasons why Dave and his wife no longer lived in London, why it was more convenient for them to live in comparative obscurity in the south of France.

She knew what she was getting herself into, all those years ago when she first met Massimo at Adele's place. His reputation preceded him – enhanced him, even, with a sort of criminal glamour. There were rumours of business associates who had suddenly disappeared, of rivals who were, one day, rivals no longer . . . God help anyone who crossed Massimo Rivelli. God help Christine Fairbrother and Janet Rivelli and Will Francis and the rest of the fools in London. Victoria turned in the water, felt the Provençal sun warming her belly, slightly swollen now, and let the water support her, floating, floating effortlessly . . .

Mike was doing a concert in New York, and Isabelle was left rattling around the house in Laurel Canyon, making calls, sending emails, trying to keep on top of which samples had gone where, commanding an army of couriers and florists, cursing the time difference that made it so bloody difficult to talk to London. There was nothing for it: she'd have to go back and sort things out herself – as soon as she knew who was going to be wearing Cissé . . .

'Darling, such a shame, but never mind, there's always next year and the year after that and the year after that,' said Maya when they met at a trade event at the Fashion Institute of Design and Merchandising. 'If you're still in business, of course.'

'Oh, I will be, don't you worry about that.'

'Mmmmh,' said Maya, sticking her tongue into her cheek. 'Let's hope so.'

'And you, Maya. How's H&M coming along? I'm sure I saw your stuff in Santee Alley last week. What's next? A line for Wal-Mart?'

Maya laughed super-loud. 'Oh darling, didn't you know? I've bust a new deal with Laruche. Isn't that a hoot? Paris here I come.'

Isabelle hadn't heard, and wasn't at all sure that she believed.

'So there's a very real chance that we'll meet on the red carpet, as it were,' said Maya. 'How *are* you getting on? It must be so hard as an *independent*.'

'Very well,' lied Isabelle.

Maya saw someone she knew, looked at Isabelle with that special look of pity that most people reserve for crippled puppies, and swanned off.

Laruche? One of the big five Paris couture houses? Could it be true, after her famous flop with Versace? Had this news spread to London? Would they all be kissing her arse again, all those failed designers and St Martins staff who were so quick to bury her before? Would Cherry Lucas be featuring 'Maya for Laruche' in *Vogue* before the end of the year? Had the wheel of fortune turned so quickly?

It was tempting to think it had – because Isabelle, for all her glowing press cuttings, her Fashion Award, her celebrity endorsement and rock star boyfriend, was getting nowhere fast with Tilly Ostergard and Mercy Williams. Their people didn't get back to her; Christ, even her people's people were beyond her reach. LA, for whatever reason, had a downer on London. Edgy was out, classic was in, Cissé was nowhere. Back to London, and lower your sights. There's always the Baftas, she thought, with a sinking feeling.

'Surprised to see me?'

Surprised? Fucking furious, more like.

'Leanne! How on earth did you find me?'

'It wasn't difficult, Victoria. You're not as careful as you think you are. Besides, where else would you go?'

'You'd better come in,' said Victoria, but Leanne already had, dumping a hold-all in the hall. At least she hadn't packed for a long stay.

'Nice.' Leanne whistled. 'Very nice. I can see the attraction. So – when were you planning on telling me?'

'Telling you what?'

She can't know – can she?

'About your little disappearing act. What was I, Victoria? A handy place to stay? A bit of sexual tourism? A meal ticket?'

They sat down in the reception room, on sofas that faced each other across the wide, quarry-tiled floor. Victoria buried her toes in the fur rug. She felt cold.

'I'm sorry. I feel awful. I was so . . . confused.'

'Oh, tell that to the marines, sweetheart. You're the least confused woman I ever met. Don't try all that Baby Doll crap with me. You knew exactly what you were doing.'

'Okay. I thought you were bored of me. I wanted to leave before you threw me out. I couldn't face that again.'

Why has she come?

'I wasn't going to throw you out.'

'You would have done. Sooner or later.'

'I was actually hoping that you would stay.'

Oh shit.

'In fact, Victoria . . .' Leanne crossed the room and sat next to her on the sofa, 'there something I've been meaning to tell you.'

Victoria got up, without really meaning to.

'Before you go any further, there's something I need to tell you.'

'What? You're back with Rivelli? I'd sort of figured that out for myself, thanks.'

'No.' Victoria looked out over the terrace towards the glint of the pool. 'I'm pregnant.'

Silence fell.

'Say something.'

'Is it his?'

'Of course it's his.'

'I don't see any "of course" about it.' Leanne was frowning.

'You're angry, I know. That's why I had to leave. I couldn't face you. It was such a shock, finding out . . . and I panicked. I just ran. I didn't know where else to come.'

'And he took you in with open arms, is that it?'

'What else was I supposed to do?'

'It never occurred to you to tell me, then. You didn't think for one moment that I might understand and actually help you? That I might actually care for you?'

No, that never occurred to me.

'I'm sorry.'

Leanne got up and joined her at the window, slipping an arm round her waist, feeling her stomach. They stared across the garden, not speaking.

'A baby,' said Leanne, finally.

'Yes.'

'And you're . . .'

'Keeping it. Yes.'

'Wow.' Leanne walked back to the sofa, sat down and hugged her knees. 'When you're really big – you know, just before it's born – can I paint you?'

Dan summoned Will for a meeting in a pub near the Walker Parker office. Cissé's payments were seriously overdue, and if money didn't come through soon Dan could no longer hide the fact from Fiona.

'The thing is, Dan,' said Will, staring miserably into his Diet Coke, 'we've got a bit of a cashflow problem.'

'I know,' said Dan. 'I'm afraid that sort of news travels rather fast.'

'And I don't think Rivelli is intending to pay up.'

'But he must.'

'I can't make him.'

'You can. He's under contract.'

'It's . . . complicated.'

'Does Isabelle know?'

The same old question. 'She knows what she needs to know.'

'I see.' Dan's brows knotted. 'So what are we going to do?'

'I don't know,' said Will. 'I was rather hoping you might have some suggestions.'

'I can move things around between accounts, I suppose,' said Dan. 'Fiona won't notice. That buys you some time.'

'Great . . .'

'So that when the next lot of orders are fulfilled, you can pay us from that.'

'Once we've found a new manufacturer.'

'What?'

'Well I'm not going on with Rivelli. How can I?'

'Has he released you?'

'No, but . . .'

'Then how can you sign with anyone else?'

'He's in breach of contract, isn't he?'

'Yes, technically. But you'd have to take it to court to get out of it. And that would cost a lot of money that you don't have.'

'But he can't just expect us to carry on giving him orders and letting him pocket the money and . . .' Will suddenly stopped. 'Why are you looking at me like that, Dan?'

'He's done it before.'

'What?'

'There was another company, just like you, two or three years ago. Lot of promise, lot of hype, signed with Rivelli, thought they had a golden future.'

'I don't like the sound of this.'

'He bled them dry, kept them under exclusive licence, and every time someone else tried to sign them, for some reason they mysteriously backed off at the last minute.'

'You mean he threatened them?'

'I don't know for sure.'

'But why? What's in it for him?'

'Money. I don't know. Power.'

'Shit.' Will finished his Coke. 'Why didn't anybody warn us?'

'I tried,' said Dan.

Not hard enough.

'Well, he's not going to do the same to us. Fuck him. I won't let it happen. I'm going to take him to court and get that money out of him if it fucking well kills me. Joel will just have to face the music. I can't let Isabelle down.'

Now Dan drained his drink. 'How's she getting on?'

'Fine.'

'I saw her in the papers with that . . . singer.'

'Mike Christian. Yeah.'

'Is it serious?' Dan looked far more worried by this than the prospect of Cissé being ruined by a ruthless maniac.

'Don't know. She doesn't tell me much any more.'

They sat in gloomy silence for a while.

'Fancy a pint?' said Dan, and mooched off to the bar.

They spent a surprisingly pleasant few days together at Le Mûrier, walking on the beach, having lunch in Sainte-Maxime or Saint-Tropez, occasionally running into people that Victoria knew, or people who recognised Leanne, but mostly unmolested. They slept together, but chastely; Leanne had not initiated sex since discovering that Victoria was pregnant. They cooked, slept, and went for long, companionable drives through the countryside, or along the coast, or up into the Massif des Maures, the beautiful mountains to the north of the gulf. Dave left them with a little Renault runaround, full of petrol. Victoria was still on the boss's insurance, he said. And the boss would be coming out next week.

Next week. She had to get rid of Leanne by next week.

'Surely you have things you should be doing,' said Victoria, as they drove along the looping, switchback mountain road towards Fréjus. 'Paintings to work on, deals to make, all the stuff that kept you busy when we were in London.'

'You trying to get rid of me, babe?' said Leanne, her arm resting on the open window. 'It's quiet this time of year. Besides, I could do with a holiday. It's nice here. I might take a house myself, do some painting. Bit of landscape. Maybe bring a class out here.' She chuckled. 'They'd pay a bloody fortune for this. Beautiful country-side, good wine, good food, and Leanne fucking Miller. Five grand a head, easy.'

'Good idea,' said Victoria, nervous about the idea of Leanne and Rivelli coming face to face.

'Don't worry, babe, If Loverboy takes care of you, I'll fade into the background as your good, devoted friend. I'm not the stalking type.'

Victoria laughed, but wondered.

She flew to Nice . . .

'Oh, how beautiful,' said Leanne, as they crested a ridge, struck by a sudden view of tree-cloaked slopes, Aleppo pines, holly, cork oaks, chestnuts. 'Stop the car for a moment.' Victoria slowed while Leanne rummaged for her camera. 'Wow. Pull over here.'

Victoria stopped at the side of the road in a rough patch of gravel,

a low line of scrubby bushes marking the beginning of the rocky slide
down into the wooded valley.

'Hang on a sec, babe.' Leanne got out of the car, stretched her legs,
looked at the drop and whistled.

'Be careful!'

'Don't worry about me.' She scampered ahead, devouring the landscape, shooting it with her camera, standing with her hands on her
hips, lost in admiration.

I could drive away now . . . never see her again . . .

Then Leanne turned, her face pale, and started walking briskly back
to the car, saying something, gesturing with her hands, breaking into
a run.

Victoria heard the lorry before she saw it in the mirror, a horrible
dead drone from its engine, a jittering squeal from its multiple wheels.

Leanne ran forward, froze and screamed.

The lorry struck the Renault at the back – she'd parked at an untidy
angle, just as she did in London – and spun it around in a clockwise
direction, sending the left front wheel over the edge first. The car
teetered for a moment, and Victoria felt certain she was safe, that she
could climb out of the passenger side without too much difficulty. She
undid her safety belt, leaned across, and then the world tipped at an
angle, and she saw the sky where the earth should be.

Chapter 25

American Airlines departed LAX just after seven o'clock in the evening. Given the vagaries of time zones and flight duration, it would be lunchtime the next day when Isabelle arrived at Heathrow. This simple fact was too much for her to process. As soon as her luggage was checked, she placed herself in the hands of fate, or at least AA's first-class service. First-class travel, especially over such a distance, was a necessity – but, thought Isabelle, an affordable one. Thank God for success.

The days of first class may soon be over, however, if she did not secure one of her actresses for the Academy Awards. She'd done everything right – she'd lunched the right people, kept her profile high, attended the parties and fundraisers for charities that she knew Tilly Ostergard and Mercy Williams supported. She'd shamelessly used Mike's famous friends to drop a friendly word in the right ears. Short of rugby tackling the actresses outside the Kodak Theatre, ripping off their clothes and forcing them at gunpoint to model Cissé, there was little she could do. But for all that effort, nothing was happening. Apart from the vaguest expressions of interest, she might as well have saved her breath. As Los Angeles gave itself over to Oscar fever, Isabelle seemed further than ever from the red carpet.

And now, Tilly Ostergard was on location somewhere in eastern Europe, shooting a period drama about Lucy Hobbs Taylor, America's first female dentist, entitled *Smiling Through*. Mercy Williams was flying to London to shoot a music video and do a show at the O2 – not bad for a woman who, only a year ago, was lucky to get lipsynching gigs in gay clubs. And so Isabelle was following her. She didn't know what else to do.

She'd booked herself into the Soho Hotel for three nights; another luxury, but Cissé could stand it. Besides, where else could she stay? She'd let the flat go, and the house in Chelsea wasn't even hers yet, the solicitors were dragging their feet so much. She'd have to put a rocket under Will for that. He should be out there every day, cracking the whip. What else did he have to do?

She slept for a few hours, and woke up as the plane hit turbulence over the east coast. Nothing to worry about, said the captain, but Isabelle felt her stomach plummeting down into the ocean, the air in the cabin suddenly several degrees hotter.

She wanted a hand to hold, someone to laugh at her, to take the piss out of her fears, but she was travelling alone. There was so much space in first class that her nearest neighbour wasn't even in grabbing distance. A stewardess smiled at her; that would have to do. There would be plenty of people in London. She wouldn't be alone. All the old faces, all the old places . . . Will . . . Dan . . . Her stomach lurched again. *Bloody turbulence*, she muttered, and closed her eyes.

Victoria lay in a hospital bed, her left arm and shoulder in a cast, bandages on her head, her eyes swollen shut. A drip went into her right arm. She was still unconscious; apart from a brief moment of lucidity just after they got her on to the ward, she had been out cold.

Victoria was lucky. Leanne Miller was dead.

The press went mad. An internationally famous artist, a known lesbian, struck down by a hit-and-run driver on a remote road in the south of France, where she was holidaying with her girlfriend. Her pregnant girlfriend. Her pregnant girlfriend who was hovering between life and death, the fate of her baby hanging in the balance.

But Victoria was a sentimental sideshow to the main event – the murder, for so it seemed, of a famous person. The police were still looking for the vehicle that had struck them, tipping the Renault over the cliff edge, striking Leanne a glancing blow that sent her soaring through the air to crack her skull on the rocks at the roadside. When a passing motorist found her, the puddle of sticky black blood was already thick with flies.

The story was on the front cover of every newspaper in England. Ben, who was visiting Christine for the weekend, read the report and went very pale indeed.

'Oh shit.'

'What?'

'I knew her.'

'Leanne Miller?'

'No.' He pointed to the fourth paragraph. 'The woman she was with.'

Christine felt cold fingers around her throat as she read the name 'Victoria Crabtree'.

'How . . . How did you . . .'

'I met her at a couple of Isabelle's things. We . . . you know. Got off.'

It's happening again. Victoria Crabtree and my family.

'You mean you had sex with her?'

'Yeah.'

'It says she's pregnant.'

'Yeah.'

'Did you use . . .'

'No. She said she was . . . Oh Christ.'

Rivelli had ways of finding people who didn't want to be found. And Joel made it so easy – the stupid kid hadn't even changed his mobile phone number. All it took was a couple of calls, an offer of ridiculous money for a job that didn't exist, and he was delivered to Rivelli's office in the back of a company car.

'Don't stand there looking as if you're going to piss your pants,' said Rivelli. 'I'm not going to hurt you.'

Joel was sweating, even though it was a cold February evening. The thin white shirt was sticking to his back.

'What do you want, Mr Rivelli?'

'I have a proposition for you, Joel.'

'I . . . I can't go back . . . Not after the last time.'

'You owe me, Joel. I don't like people who break contracts. I gave you a very easy job to do, and I paid you very well. You fucked it up.'

'It wasn't my fault . . .'

'You told him. Will.' Rivelli pushed Joel gently into a chair, stood before him. 'Your boyfriend.'

'He's not my boyfriend.'

'Oh, but he is.' Rivelli looked down, remained standing. 'Most definitely he is your boyfriend.'

'Okay.'

'Does he love you, Joel? Hmmm? Are you that good?'

'Well, I think he might . . .'

'Little lover boy . . .' Rivelli smiled. 'Everyone has had a taste. Will. Christine. Victoria. You are very popular. You must be very good.'

'I suppose.'

'And now I want you.'

'You?'

'But not for that. This is something different. And the reward is very high.'

This sounded more like it. 'How much?' asked Joel.

'Your life.'

Christine called Will.

'About our friend Rivelli. Have you seen him recently?'

'No.'

'Where is Isabelle?'

'Still in LA, as far as I know.'

'She's not returning my calls.'

'Is that unusual, Christine?'

'No. Have you spoken to her?'

'She sends me orders by email from time to time.'

'When was the last time?'

'You're worried about something, aren't you?'

'Yes. Have you heard about Victoria Crabtree?'

'My God, you don't think Rivelli had anything to do with that, do you?'

'I don't know what I think any more.'

'But why would he want to kill Leanne Miller?'

'I don't think he did. I imagine she just happened to be in the wrong place at the right time. It was Victoria he was after.'

'Why?'

'She was pregnant.'

'With his child?'

'Maybe that's what she told him. But it could easily be . . . someone else's.'

'That's ridiculous, Christine. I know he's bad, but surely he's not that bad.'

'He owes you money, right? And he owes Revenue and Customs

money. He owes his ex-wife money. I've been doing a bit of digging around, Will – all those dodgy companies that came up in the divorce case. Rivelli is up to his eyeballs in debt on all sides, and anyone who tries to get money off him now is putting themselves in danger. And then, on top of all of it, along comes Victoria Crabtree claiming she's carrying his child. He sees child maintenance payments stretching out into the future.'

'And so he tries to kill her? Come on.'

'He's cornered. He's lashing out.'

'But if that's the case, then we're all in danger. Including me, because I'm trying to recover the money.'

'Don't!'

'Too late. I've already started legal proceedings. If I don't, Cissé goes under. I have no choice.'

'You must withdraw.'

'Are you serious? I mean, he's just as likely to go for you. He blames you for losing the divorce case.'

'Indeed. And he blames Joel for bungling the burglary.'

'It looks like he's planning to wipe out everyone in my address book. Is there anyone else I should know about?'

My unborn grandchild.

'You may joke about it, Will, but I'm serious. Take care. And for God's sake, tell my bloody daughter to take care too.'

'You know what I want,' said Rivelli.

'Another job like the last one?'

'Not quite. I want him dead. Will Francis.'

Joel sat back in his chair, as if winded. 'Oh.' He felt sick. 'I can't . . .'

'You don't have to do anything,' said Rivelli. 'You can't even steal a few lousy dresses; you don't think I'm going to trust you with anything more complicated?'

'No.'

'I want him where I can see him. I want you to stick to him. Keep him happy. Deliver him to certain places at certain times.'

'But . . .'

'No buts, Joel, please. Do this for me, and maybe you have a nice future, plenty of money, plenty of friends, plenty of pussy. Maybe.'

'And if I refuse?' asked Joel.

Rivelli just smiled.

Isabelle sat in her room at the Soho Hotel, flicking through the TV channels, wondering who she should call.

Will.

Dan.

Ben.

Mum.

Dad.

EastEnders.

Police Camera Action.

Extreme Makeovers.

Dog Borstal.

Friends.

Buttons on the remote, buttons on her phone, all those messages left unanswered.

She spoke to nobody, watched nothing, ate an airport sandwich.

Welcome home . . .

It was hard to know just how scared she should be. Isabelle, wherever she was, would not speak to her – but if anything really had happened to Isabelle, surely Christine would be the first to know? The news from the hospital was ambiguous; Mademoiselle Crabtree was stable, that was all they would say, and there was nothing to suggest that it really had been anything other than a horrible hit-and-run. The papers were starting to refer to it as a 'tragic accident' rather than a murder. Leanne Miller's prices had gone through the roof. Nobody cared much about Victoria Crabtree and her unborn child.

Christine sat at home waiting. The jobs were still not coming through. Andy was still not back. Ben was gone. She felt as if her life was on hold. Just this sense of dread . . .

The doorbell rang, and she jumped to her feet, grateful for any company.

'Miss Fair*brother*.'

Rivelli.

She put her hand to her mouth. 'Oh.'

He tried to get a foot in the door; she moved out on to the porch, closed the door behind her.

'I'm afraid I can't invite you in, Massimo. The place is a mess.'

'I don't mind.'

'Whatever you have to say to me, you can say out here.'

'Oh, come now.' He produced something from behind his back; Christine almost flinched. 'I brought you a bottle of Prosecco. Let's say *buon anno*.'

'It's a little late for that.'

'I insist.'

'No, really,' said Christine. 'I insist.'

Rivelli held the bottle by its neck, like a weapon. If Christine screamed very loud, someone would surely hear her. 'You are angry with me, of course. I understand.'

It would not do to expose her suspicions. 'Angry? No. You win some, you lose some. That's how the legal profession works.'

'Yes. You lose some.' Rivelli frowned. 'You will not let me in?'

'I will not.'

'I wish I could persuade you.'

'Your powers of persuasion have done quite enough damage, thank you very much.'

He leaned against the wall. 'Good. Then I will cut out the pleasantries.'

'Please do.'

'I know what you are doing.'

'That doesn't surprise me. I'm sure you know all sorts of things.'

'I do not like being spied on, Christine. I know you have been sniffing around, looking into my private affairs.'

'Thank you. If that's all . . .'

'I am not one of your English gentlemen, you know. I am not like John Ferguson, or your husband, or your son. I am not afraid of hurting a woman.'

'Ah, I wondered how soon it would be before you threatened me. Are you aware of section four of the Public Order Act, nineteen eighty-six?'

'Your laws do not . . .'

'Relating to intentional harassment, alarm or distress?'

'Call off your dogs, Christine. I will not stand for it.'

'I'd have to check the exact wording, but it's something like threatening, abusive or insulting behaviour.'

Rivelli raised his voice, tightened his grip on the bottle. 'I am warning you, Christine . . .'

'Up to six months in prison, I believe. I can get back to you on that.'

He stepped towards her, the vein in his forehead bulging, the security light casting deep shadows under his eyebrows. They were very close. She recognised the smell of his aftershave, the smell of his sweat. Ridiculous memories of sexual pleasure danced around in some wrongly wired part of her brain.

He breathed hard.

'Goodbye, Mr Rivelli.'

Seconds passed, and then he left.

Her hands were shaking so much it took her nearly half a minute to open the door, expecting at every moment to hear the swish and feel the shattering crunch of a bottle smashing on to the back of her head.

Chapter 26

When Isabelle finally picked up her messages, it felt as if her world had shattered into a thousand pieces. Her mother was hysterical about Massimo Rivelli – mad, menopausal woman, thought Isabelle, screwed up with guilt now she's back together with Dad. Trying to make out that it was all somehow Rivelli's fault. Will was hysterical about money, saying that the house had fallen through, again trying to blame Rivelli when quite clearly it was his own incompetence that had got them into this mess. She was a star in LA – how could she possibly be on the brink of ruin in London? Will would have to go. There were plenty of people eager to take his place. Even Dan, sensible, phlegmatic Dan, was warmly concerned about her welfare, urging her to come in for a meeting – but that was just his cowardly way of getting her out on another date, for another stammered confession of his feelings. She deleted them all.

But she had to see Will, because she needed some money, and the cupboard seemed to be bare. It didn't take him long to persuade her that Cissé's problems were far from imaginary.

'I've only been out of the country for a few weeks,' she said, 'and everything seems to have fallen to pieces.'

Will tried not to lash out in retaliation. 'I've done my best.'

'Well it obviously isn't good enough. I mean, out there they lay out the red carpet for me.'

'And why would that be, I wonder? Because of the excellence of your couture, do you think, or because you're shagging Mr Bloody Perfect?'

Isabelle opened her mouth to reply, but thought better of it.

'I'm sorry, Princess,' said Will, 'but you can't just run away to La-La Land and pretend that this isn't happening.'

'So what do I need to do?'

'Get in the Oscars.'

'Oh, is that all?'

'Come on,' said Will. 'Surely they're all crawling on their hands and knees up the red carpet behind you, begging to wear your stuff. Oooh! Get your hands off me, Scarlett! No means no, Angelina, now back off!'

'Well what am I supposed to do? Every time I think I'm getting somewhere, it all falls through.'

'Who have you been talking to?'

'All the right people. The PRs. The agents.'

'That sounds like all the wrong people to me.'

'Oh, I see. And you know Hollywood so well, I suppose.'

'I can tell you one thing, even from my lowly position. You never get anywhere in this business by going through the right channels. You need some inside track. Who's dressing Tilly Ostergard?'

'Don't know.' Isabelle was sulky, not meeting his eyes.

'I heard it was Laruche.'

'Yeah?' She positively snarled. 'Well it must be true then, if you heard it.'

'And how do you imagine Maya got her? Not, I assure you, by sitting around waiting for agents to return her calls. Now, what about Mercy Williams?'

'I don't bloody know. She's impossible to pin down. I've sent them everything, they've received it, she's looked at it apparently, and then . . . nothing. It's like trying to hit a moving target.'

'You know she's in London.'

'Of course I bloody know she's in London! Why else do you think I'm here?'

'Obviously not the for the pleasure of my company.'

Isabelle's eye's flashed. 'How's the house coming along?'

Shit, thought Will, *here we go.* He took a deep breath.

'If you want this to be the parting of the ways, Isabelle, just say so. I wouldn't want to be a millstone round your neck.'

'Right.'

I could walk out now and never see him again. I could fly back to Los Angeles without seeing my mother, without seeing Dan, and leave it all behind . . .

'Well?'

Isabelle stood up fast, almost knocked her chair over. 'For Christ's sake, what am I supposed to do? I'm a designer. I make pretty dresses.

I'm not a fucking accountant or a private detective. You and my mother between you make it sound like a Quentin Tarantino movie.'

Will looked at her coolly. 'Pulp Fashion, anyone?' Isabelle sat down. 'Let's face facts, Princess. The house is not going to happen. You don't have the money. Better to pull out now while you still can. Rivelli is a crook and a bastard who's already tried to ruin us once and won't forgive us easily for calling his bluff. Your mother has reasons for thinking what she thinks. You want to know what you can do? You can design the most beautiful dress the world has ever seen for Mercy Williams to wear at the Oscars, and you can trust me with everything else. Or you can walk out of that door now, and go down in history as that cute black girl that Mike Christian dated for a couple of months. It's make your mind up time.'

Isabelle sat in silence for a while, picking her nails. Then she said 'Bias-cut silver satin, I think.'

'Right.' Will pressed a few buttons on his mobile. 'You're on.'

'Who are you calling?'

'Remember Ricky? That little redhead I . . . er . . . You know, last year?'

'Oh yes. The sponsorhip deal.'

'The very same. Well, he's been pestering me for a return match. I thought I'd give him a go. He did have a very nice arse.'

Isabelle held out her hands in frustration.

'Oh, sorry,' said Will, 'did I forget to mention? He works for the promoter who's putting on her London gigs this week. Perhaps, if you're very nice to me, I might have a word.'

Victoria could sit up in bed, eat, drink and talk. She couldn't read; her head ached too much for that. She tried the TV, but the headphones got on her nerves, and her French was not up to the gabbling dialogue of daytime soaps and current affairs. The nurses were useful for fetching and carrying, but they didn't want to talk. Nobody would tell her what had happened – and she didn't much care, thanks to the painkillers. She was dimly aware that she was pregnant – that would explain the monitors taped to her belly – but beyond that, everything else was a comfortable blur. She kept waking up believing she was back on the couch in her old flat, a copy of *Vogue* in one hand, a cup of cold coffee and a burnt-out cigarette reminding her that she'd just nodded off, waiting for Massimo to call . . .

Massimo. Why wasn't he there? Surely he had heard by now? A faint fluttering of anxiety began in her stomach, worked up to her heart. He should be here beside me, taking care of everything, paying for everything. Because without him . . . who? She could not go through it alone. Where were her friends? Where was . . . she searched through the soft grey corridors of her memory, looking for a name and a face she could not find. Who was it? Someone . . . a woman . . . Leanne . . .

And then the nurses were back, checking the drips, monitoring the fetal heartbeat, and Victoria swam back into the deep, cool waters of oblivion.

Christine called John. If anyone could throw the cold water of reason on her increasingly heated suspicions, it was him. They met for coffee in a chain café just outside the walls of the Inns. It wasn't busy. No clerks or colleagues to eavesdrop, just enough piped music to make sure they weren't overheard.

Christine went through it all as coldly and concisely as she could. Rivelli's visit to the house, her suspicions regarding the death of Leanne Miller, the paternity of Victoria's unborn child, her concerns for the safety of Isabelle and Will.

'What you're saying, in effect, is that Massimo Rivelli has a vendetta against you and pretty much everyone connected with you.'

'It sounds ridiculous, I know.'

They stared in silence at a piece of A4 covered in names and arrows that Christine had drawn. Everything led back to RIVELLI and VICTORIA.

'It does sound ridiculous,' said John, sipping the last of his coffee, 'but that doesn't mean it isn't true.'

Christine let out her breath; she didn't realise until then that she'd been holding it. 'Oh, John. I don't know whether I ought to be relieved or frightened. But at least I'm not going mad.'

'People like you and me don't go mad.'

'So the only alternative is that I'm right.'

'Yes,' said John, rubbing his chin. 'It does rather begin to look that way.'

'Then what the hell am I supposed to do?'

'Have you discussed this with anyone?'

'No.'

'Andy?'

She caught John's eye for a while, then looked away. 'No. Not even Andy. He's out of the country for a while . . .'

'Ah.'

'And besides, I'm not sure that I'd discuss it with him anyway.'

'Right.' John looked at the diagram again. 'Well, that's what friends are for,' he said, then cleared his throat. 'It's a long time since I did any criminal stuff.'

'Me too.'

'But I remember one piece of advice that my first boss told me. If you want to understand a criminal, you have to think like a criminal.'

'Go on.'

'Let's start from the assumption that Rivelli is as bad as you think he is. I don't have any reason to disagree. He lied through his teeth during the divorce, and we know that he's involved in organised crime. That's good enough for me, or perhaps I should say bad enough. So: he blames you for screwing up the divorce case, and he thinks you're after revenge.'

'Which I'm not . . .'

John held up his hand. 'He hates his ex-wife because she's bleeding him dry. He hates Will because he stood up to him and is taking him to court. The money doesn't matter so much, but the negative publicity does. That could be the final nail in the coffin.'

'And Victoria?'

'He believes she is carrying his child. And perhaps she knows things, or suspects things, that could damage him.'

'But do you really think he'd try to kill someone?'

'I don't know,' said John, 'but it's always better to be safe than sorry, don't you think?'

'How can we stop him?' said Christine.

'That's easy,' said John. 'We use the law.'

'People like him are beyond the law.'

'Christine, really,' said John, 'you disappoint me. Since when has anyone been beyond the law? It's simply a question of stretching the law to suit the circumstances. The question in my mind is not how we can stop Rivelli, but which of the many ways of stopping him would be the most effective.'

'Go on.'

'At present, we suspect him of a lot but can prove very little. What we need is evidence. We need someone to talk.'

'Janet?'

'Never. She hates you – even if you did inadvertently win her case for her.'

'Will? Joel?'

'Wouldn't stand up in court. Will's withdrawn the original charge.'

'Then that leaves . . . oh God.'

'Exactly. Victoria.'

'But she's in hospital. In France. I don't even know if she's still carrying the child. And I don't for one instant think she'll speak to me, after all that's passed between us.'

'But we know something that she may not even suspect,' said John. 'Her beloved Massimo Rivelli tried to murder her. If you can persuade her of that, she might just come up with what we need.'

'Are you suggesting . . .'

'I certainly am,' said John. 'Bon voyage.'

We can't be broke, thought Isabelle – but nonetheless she checked out of the Soho Hotel sharpish, and texted her father. He was in Dubai, but that suited Isabelle just fine. She had no desire to see him, particularly not to see him cosying up to her mother. She only wanted to use his flat.

There were spare keys with the concierge, and within a couple of hours Isabelle was standing at the window of the Docklands flat, looking down on the very same view that her mother had admired under somewhat different circumstances.

It was nice, the flat. Clean and neat, big enough not to be cluttered, small enough to be cosy. Handy for transport. Great views, good light, and not noisy. If Chelsea fell through, she wouldn't mind a place like this. And if Andy was really getting back together with Christine, wouldn't it make sense to hang on to the flat as an investment, and let her stay there?

She'd be alone, of course, but there would always be trips to LA to see Mike . . . To do shows . . . Wouldn't there? Maybe. If she could only get to the Oscars . . . If the business didn't go bust . . .

She stepped away from the window; it was too high, the view too great, just too much space. She drew the curtains.

She was hungry, having stormed out of Will's place without eating, and so she rummaged through the kitchen for food.

The cupboard was bare.

Well, she'd have to go out. She didn't mind eating alone. But eating alone in fashionable Los Angeles restaurants was rather different from sitting in an east London tandoori, being chatted up by waiters and stared at by other customers. If only there was someone she could call and go out with, just a friendly, spur-of-the-moment type thing . . .

But there was no one. She'd let them all go, and willingly. All her old friends, all the kids from Saint Martins, all the people she'd chatted and gossiped to in Hoxton Square that summer – when was it, a hundred years ago? And what was she left with? A few agents and publicists and stylists who might think it was worth spending an evening with her, unless, of course, they knew that Cissé was going down the pan. They'd all be chasing Maya now. Maya meant Laruche. And Laruche meant Tilly Ostergard. And Tilly Ostergard was the favourite for the Best Actress Oscar.

There had always been Will before . . .

Ben was at college. Dad was in Dubai. Mum . . . well, she wasn't speaking to Mum.

And then she suddenly remembered Dan Parker, and pizzas by the river, and talking about childhood pets, dancing along the Embankment, one kiss that should have led to others but never did . . .

How long ago?

How long ago . . .

Dispirited and giddy, she let herself out of the flat. A trip to town, somewhere there was life, just to stop this horrible feeling of vertigo.

A woman was walking along the corridor, feet noiseless on the heavy carpet. She was tall, good looking, a bit older than Isabelle but no more than thirty, unless she had the best Botox in town. She was wearing a long belted suede coat, dark tan boots – they looked like Salvatore Ferragamos to Isabelle – and she was carrying a very desirable YSL handbag in blue leather. Posh neighbours Dad has, thought Isabelle, as the woman stopped and rummaged in her bag for a key.

And then she looked up, and saw Isabelle coming out of the flat. Her mouth fell open. The key, held forward, jabbed forward like a weapon.

'Excuse me,' she said, 'but who the hell are you?'

'I'm Isabelle.'

The woman frowned. 'You've got a key?'

'So have you.'

The woman stepped to the right; Isabelle mirrored her.

'He's not here, you know.'

'Of course I know,' said the woman. 'I've just come to pick something up.'

'I see.' Isabelle felt prickles of excitement at the back of her neck. 'Well, be my guest.' She stepped aside.

The woman fumbled with the lock, clearly upset, and said 'I'm sorry, but you still haven't told me who you are?'

Isabelle walked down the corridor, not looking back, trying to hold in her laughter until she was safely in the lift.

'Oh, poor Mummy,' she said, when she was finally alone. The lift was mirrored, reflecting the biggest smile she'd worn for ages.

'About bloody time!'

The sharp-suited young redhead grabbed Will by the back of the neck, rubbed his skull with his knuckles and gave him an open-mouthed kiss.

'Hi, Ricky. Sorry – I've been so busy . . .'

'You can say that again. All I ever hear about is Cissé this, Cissé that. Well, what do you want? Apart from me, obviously, and you can have that later.'

'Really? I didn't realise I'd made such a good impression.'

'A lasting impression,' said Ricky, rubbing his bum. 'Anyway, enough of this dirty talk. Cut to the chase. You haven't called me after a year just to hear what a good shag you are.'

'No. You're right.' *Does this mean I'm going to be unfaithful to Joel?*

'Come on, then. Ask away. Chances are you'll get what you want.'

'You're still in music, right?'

'Yes. Oh God, tell me this isn't just because you want tickets for Mercy Williams.'

'Well . . .'

'Okay. Two. That's the best I can do.'

'Thanks, Ricky. But that's not really what I wanted to ask you. There's something else . . .'

When the doctors thought she was ready, Victoria met the police. It was all very carefully handled; she was in a single ward, with an interpreter, and there were only two of *them*, a man and a woman. The woman did most of the talking, in good English. The interpreter only had to say 'Are you sure you understand?' from time to time.

It took them nearly five minutes to get round to telling her that Leanne Miller was dead. And then it took a further minute for the fact to find its way to Victoria's consciousness.

'Are you sure you understand?' said the interpreter, as Victoria went as white as her bedsheets.

'Leanne . . .'

'I am so sorry,' said the policewoman, in a tone she'd use for a bereaved spouse. 'I realise this is a terrible shock.'

Victoria was shaking, but not because of grief.

'What happened?'

They told her – the car parked by the side of the mountain road, the lorry, Leanne's broken body, the rescue services' heroic efforts to remove Victoria from the wreckage.

'And have they . . . do you know who . . .'

'We have launched the fullest possible investigation. We will find the person who did this.'

'You will?'

Victoria's eyes were wide, the pupils dilated.

'Are you sure you understand?'

She understood – too well. The truth was thundering along a road in her mind, headlights blazing, horn blaring, ready to crush her with the full force of realisation. It was coming. It was coming. She gestured frantically with her hands, and the nurse just managed to slip a papier-mâché bowl under her chin as she started vomiting.

* * *

'Damn it, Isabelle, you didn't even tell me you were coming to London and now that you're here, you're won't even return my calls. Am I really such a monster?'

'I'm sorry, Mum, it's not that. I've just got a lot of business stuff to take care of an then I'm flying back to America.'

'But I have to see you.'

Why? Something you have to tell me? Something about Dad? I already know . . .

'I'm sorry. I'll be back soon enough. After the Oscars. That's really all I can think about at the moment.'

'I'm worried, darling. There's something I have to discuss with you.'

'Fire away.'

'In person.'

'Look, I have to go. But for what it's worth no, I'm not on drugs, I haven't touched the stuff in months and I don't intend to ever again. Yes, I'm eating properly. Yes, I'm very happy, I'm going out with a man called Mike, he's in a band that you won't have heard of.'

'Isabelle, I really need to . . .'

'Yes, we're having sexual relations, and yes, I'm being very careful, I'm on the pill and he uses condoms, we know what we're doing, so I'm not going to get pregnant or catch AIDS or doing anything else to disgrace you.'

It sounded as if Christine was crying. 'Oh, Isabelle . . .'

'Gotta go, Mum.' She'd gone too far, but it was her mother's fault. 'I'll see you soon, I promise. Wish me luck.'

She put the phone down before Christine could say another word.

'Look, Joel, don't wait up for me. I'm going to be very very late. I've got to go to a gig and then to the after-party. I'm really sorry.'

'Ah, don't worry, mate. I could do with a night off, to be honest. I'll tidy the place up a bit, get an early night. Who are you going to see?'

'Mercy Williams.'

'Wow. Lucky you. Where is she playing?'

'The O2. Sorry I can't take you, Joel, but it's one of these work things – you know, they only give you one ticket.'

Joel frowned. 'I really ought to come with you.'

'Come on. You don't like this sort of thing, you've told me so a thousand times. Too gay for you.'

'Where are you sitting?'

'What? I don't know. I'm a guest.'

'Who's guest?'

'Ah, that's what this is all about. He's called Ricky, he's a music promoter, yes we had a little fling about a year ago, no I'm not going to do it again.'

'That's not what I meant. I just want to know . . . where you are.'

'I'm touched. Look, I'll try to come straight home. Be patient.' He caressed Joel's backside. 'I'll make it worth your while.'

Joel pushed his hand aside and stormed out of the room.

That's just what I need, thought Will. *A suspicious boyfriend.*

It didn't help that Joel's suspicions were justified. Will had every intention of doing whatever it took to gain access to Mercy Williams. He didn't go after Joel, just shouted 'I love you' before leaving the flat.

The words seemed to echo as Joel picked up his phone and called Rivelli.

Dave visited her on the fourth day after she regained consciousness.

'Is there anything you need, Miss Crabtree?'

'Where's Massimo? I need to see him.'

'He's on his way.'

'Does he know where I am?'

'Of course he does.'

I haven't told him.

'Then . . .' She felt sick again, and retched.

'Is it the baby?' asked Dave. 'My Sue was sick a lot in the first few months.'

Victoria smiled weakly, and dabbed at her mouth with a tissue. 'I think I need to sleep now,' she said.

Isabelle was awoken by banging at the door.

Christ, not his fancy woman again . . .

She put on a dressing gown. It was just getting light outside.

'What do you want?'

'It's me.'

She looked at the spyhole – and saw Will, dishevelled, drunk perhaps, his hair a mess, his shirt wrongly buttoned. She opened the door.

'The old git downstairs was asleep so I thought I'd give you a lovely surprise.'

'Lovely,' said Isabelle, slip-slopping into the kitchen and filling the kettle. 'Do you know what time it is?'

'It's never too early for good news, Princess.'

Will was bouncing around on the balls of his feet, like a boxer.

'Sit down, please. You're making me feel sick.'

'Sorry about that, darling,' said Will, in a voice thick with overdone concern. 'Wouldn't want to do that for the world. Well!' He threw himself on to the couch, kicked off his shoes and buried his feet in the cushions. 'Guess where I was tonight?'

'Don't play games, Will. It's very early in the morning.'

'I went out with Ricky, he of the lovely red hair and the pneumatic bum, remember? And Ricky just happens to be working with a little-known American artist, you may not have heard of her, she's barely known, more a cult than anything else . . .'

'Mercy Williams.'

'Gosh! You *have* heard of her.'

'You've . . . you've seen her?'

'Seen her, honey?' He imitated Mercy's West Indian-inflected accent. 'You're looking at her New Best Friend.'

'So is she . . . ?'

'Listen, and I'll tell you. Ricky got me a ticket for the show – which was amazing, by the way, if you're interested. And he got me into the after-party, which we didn't stay at for very long because by that time I thought he really deserved a bit of the old Will's Wonder.'

'Please.'

'Yes, that's what he said. But more important than all that, he got me into the studio where they were shooting the video for her new single.'

'You mean you actually . . .'

'Hung out with her, yes. Gave her a few fashion tips, you know the sort of thing.'

Isabelle was speechless.

'You see, the new song is . . . well, how best to describe it?' He made arcs in the air with his hands. 'An urban ballad, I suppose you might say. It's elegant, but with an edge. Modern, but classic at the same time. In fact,' he said, as if the thought had only just occurred to him, 'a bit like a Cissé evening dress.'

'Ah.'

'Ah indeed. And you see, poor Mercy just didn't like the clothes that the stylist had brought along. A right load of old tat with designer labels in. Didn't look good on her. Made her look – I don't know. A bit muttony, really.'

'Poor Mercy.'

'So we got talking, somehow or other, and I sympathised with her wardrobe crisis, and made a few suggestions.'

'Such as?'

'Well as luck would have it, I happened to have a couple of your little numbers about my person – and what do you know, they were in her size.'

'What a surprise!'

'I know! Isn't it? There was a rather lovely plum coloured thing that you had in *Vogue*, and that silver dress with the gathering at the chest and the pleated shoulders.'

'Oh, that.'

'Well, for want of anything better to do, she nipped behind a screen and tried them on, and what do you know?'

'They were the best dresses she'd ever worn.'

'Funny! That's exactly what she said.'

'And she wore them in the video.'

'Yes, my dear. Both of them.'

'And she's going to . . .'

'Hush, Princess.' Will reached over and touched his fingertips to her lips. 'Let me ask you something first. Did it ever occur to you why you weren't getting anywhere with Tilly Ostergard and Mercy Williams?'

'I don't know. Because I'm not very good at all that side of things.'

'True, true,' said Will, with a smirk. 'But more than that.'

'Because I need you to work with me, and I've treated you despicably.'

'There is that, yes. But something else. Come on. Guess again.'

'I don't know. Because I'm not as famous as the others. Because I'm British. Because I'm black.'

'Mercy Williams isn't exactly white, is she? No – there's another reason that you're far too nice to guess. Why do you think all these stylists and agents and PRs and so on are overlooking you, when you've got such a fabulous pressbook and all those awards?'

'Bad luck?'

'Yes, you could call it that. I prefer to call it Maya Rodean.'

Isabelle gasped. 'What do you mean? You can't be serious.'

'Well, as I was saying to dear Mercy, my New Best Friend, it's such a shame that she'd never got a chance to try on a Cissé dress before, because obviously they were made for her, and she was made for them. She agreed, she said she loved your stuff and had asked her people to get it for her, but she'd been told that Cissé was going out of business and that you were in trouble with the police, or something.'

'What?'

'So I said, well, that's news to me, and even though Isabelle can be an ungrateful little bitch and has long since stopped confiding in me, I think I'd know if either of those things were true.'

'It's a fair cop.'

'But she said no, that's absolutely what everyone in Hollywood was saying, and when I asked her who exactly everyone was, can you guess what she said?'

'Maya Fucking Rodean.'

'Well those weren't her exact words, but two out of three ain't bad. Yes, our dear old friend Maya Rodean. She's been going round town telling everyone that Cissé is done for. Considering that she's just signed with Laruche, the timing was rather good, wasn't it?'

'She wanted to get into the Oscars.'

'And you, my dear, are the competition.'

'The bitch. What are we going to do?'

'I'll tell you what we're going to do, Princess. You're going to design the most beautiful dress of your entire career for Miss Mercy Williams to wear on the red carpet. Then we're going to fly out to Los Angeles and we are going to make sure that nothing, I repeat nothing, stands between us and the Academy Awards. Is it a deal?'

He held out his hand; she shook it.

'It's a deal. Hollywood, watch out. The British are coming.'

Chapter 27

Everyone was going to the airport.

Christine decided that if her daughter would not come to see her, she would go and see her daughter, and if necessary give her a lift to Heathrow. Isabelle was on a lunchtime flight to Los Angeles (Will had divulged the information), Christine was flying at six o'clock to Nice; plenty of time, then, to kidnap her own daughter and tell her what was on her mind while they were both in the car.

Will was on the same flight as Isabelle – economy rather than first class, so they wouldn't be sitting together, which was something of a relief. He didn't suggest that Christine might like to pick him up as well; he'd had enough Cissé family psychodrama to last him a lifetime, and wanted to conserve his energy for Mercy Williams and the Oscars.

Unknown to Will, Joel was also on a flight to Los Angeles, from another airport with another carrier, his ticket paid for not by Cissé but by Rivelli Srl.

And Rivelli himself was flying out of London, under an assumed name – he had several passports – to spend some time with his mother in the family home in Milan.

'You'd better come in, now you're here.'

Christine wasn't expecting a warm welcome, and had come determined not to get into a fight, whatever Isabelle said.

'I thought you might like a lift.'

'I see.' Isabelle did not say *thank you*. 'I suppose you've been here before?'

She's snooping around for information about Dad.

'Dad's flat? Of course.'

'Yes.' Isabelle looked hard at her. 'I thought you must have done.'

'Nice, isn't it?' Christine walked to the window.

'Not bad.'

Isabelle carried on packing.

'I'm going to France myself.'

'Right.'

Oh really Mum? That's nice. Is it a holiday? You deserve one, you work so hard. Are you meeting Dad? I'm so pleased your back together again, sorry I was such a little cow about it.

As none of that dialogue was forthcoming, Christine just replied 'Yes, right.' No point in telling Isabelle why she was going. *I suspect that my ex-lover, your manufacturer, is trying to kill all of us, and I'm just after a bit of evidence from his ex-mistress – you know, the one that got you into coke.*

'You don't have to do this, you know,' said Isabelle. 'I can still afford a taxi.'

'Is that why you think I'm here? Just to save your cab fare?'

'Well? Isn't it?'

'As a matter of fact,' said Christine, keeping her cool, 'it was the only way I could think of to see you.'

'And why the great hurry to see me all of a sudden? I'm sort of busy at the moment. Can't it wait till I get back from LA?'

'Not really, darling, no.'

'Okay.' Isabelle picked up her suitcase. 'I'm ready.'

They didn't speak until they'd been on the road for five minutes.

'Are you sure you know where you're going?' said Isabelle.

'You may find this hard to believe, darling, but in the thirty or so years that I've been driving around London, I have gone to Heathrow once or twice.'

'Okay. Keep your hair on. Now what's the big emergency?'

'Have you spoken to your father recently?'

Ah. Here it comes. The third degree.

'No. He's in Dubai. Why?'

'When's he coming back?'

'Mum, what's all this about? Are you spying on Dad?'

'No. I'm concerned for you, actually. I want you to call him.'

'Look, Mum. I'm on my way to Los Angeles for what might very well be the make or break of my career. I'm trying to get one of my dresses on the back of an actress who has a very good chance of winning the Oscar. It may sound terribly trivial and stupid to you, but it matters to me. I don't have time for this stuff about Dad.'

'Darling, I . . .'

'Also, I have a boyfriend out in Los Angeles, and I'm very much looking forward to seeing him again. I have a life, Mum. I have things to do. I know that comes as a bit of a shock to you . . .'

'God almighty, Isabelle,' said Christine, abandoning the legal tone, 'you should just listen to yourself! I'm trying to tell you something important and all you can do is give me the spoilt brat act. Okay, I'm impressed. You're going out to the Oscars. Hurrah. I hope you win. Is that what you want me to say?'

'Yes.' Isabelle folded her arms and stared out of the window. They plunged into the Rotherhithe Tunnel, the lights beating rhythmically against her tired, itchy eyes.

Christine took a few deep breaths and tried again. She wanted to talk to Isabelle about Rivelli, to warn her to take care in Los Angeles, to check in with her father while Christine was in France on the trail of . . . what? A murder mystery?

'Has Ben said anything?'

'Ben? Don't try and involve him as well.'

'Why not? It concerns him as much as any of us.' *Especially*, thought Christine, *if he's the child's father.*

'I don't see why,' said Isabelle. 'Dad doesn't discuss his private life with Ben any more than he does with me.'

'I'm not talking about . . .'

Clunk.

Isabelle stared out of the passenger side.

'Sorry, Isabelle, but what has your father's private life got to do with anything?'

'Nothing.'

'Something's happened, hasn't it? I can tell.'

'No.'

'What is it, then? You're obviously dying to tell me.'

'God, Mum, don't start having a go at me!'

'I'm not. I mean, you're Daddy's girl, after all. I'm sure he tells you all about it. I'm sure you have a good laugh behind my back.' Christine's good intentions evaporated; her cheeks were burning, her eyes wet.

'I don't know what you're talking about.'

'Your bloody father.' Christine slapped the wheel. 'He's still doing it, isn't he? Screwing around behind my back. My God, why did I think he'd ever change?' There was a catch in her voice, and she shut up.

Isabelle had never seen her mother like this before – upset, vulnerable, not in control. The reality of the divorce came into sudden, unwelcome focus. Christine had sailed through it untouched, Isabelle always believed, cold as ice, not a hair out of place. And now she was blinking back tears, her hands shaking on the wheel.

'I'm sorry.'

'Don't worry about me, Isabelle. Just don't say anything to him.'

'I won't.'

They were approaching Heathrow.

'There are some tissues in the glove compartment. Could you get me one, please?'

They drove the rest of the way in silence.

'I won't see you off, if you don't mind,' said Christine, after parking.

'Okay.' Isabelle hauled her suitcase off the back seat, stuck her head back through the passenger window to say goodbye. Her mother did not lean across to kiss her.

'Thanks for the lift, then,' she said, with a stabbing sensation around her heart. Christine looked stricken, deadly pale.

'My pleasure,' she said, a deep furrow between her eyebrows. 'Have a good trip.' She might have been seeing her off on a school outing.

Isabelle walked away, glancing back to see her mother still sitting at the wheel, staring at the blank concrete wall ahead of her.

Will always got to airports ridiculously early because he hated being rushed, but on this occasion he was happier than usual to be sitting on his own in departures with hours to spare. He'd checked in his luggage – a small case of his own clothes, a large case jam-packed with Cissé gowns – and was enjoying a full English breakfast. Heart attacks be damned, he thought, tucking into a shiny brown sausage skewered on a piece of white toast. If we don't get to the Oscars, my life's not going to be worth living anyway. In any case, he was hungry. His farewell to Joel, which had lasted most of the night, had burned up a lot of calories.

Back at Will's flat, Joel was collecting his few belongings – tooth-brush, underwear, trainers, and a few items of clothing that he now regarded as his – and shoving them into a hold-all. A car was on its way.

The house on Corso Magenta was gated and grilled, the walls several metres thick, the roof a solid and impenetrable structure of slate. Even helicopters couldn't see what, or who, was inside.

Rivelli arrived in Milan in time for lunch with his mother, the octogenarian Contessa Luisella Mirabelli delle Chiaie, a cobwebby aristocrat with fond memories of Il Duce and very little interest in the world beyond those ancient four walls. She adored her son in a formal sort of way, but found his actual physical presence unsettling, and flinched when he went to kiss her. If there were callers, she would receive them. Rivelli's office was at the top of the house, where he was connected to the world through every communications device known to modern man. He could command his empire without ever leaving Palazzo Rivelli.

Victoria was jittery, her mind wandering, partly from fever, partly from fear. They were still pumping her full of painkillers and antibiotics, monitoring the fetal heartbeat every few hours, insisting that the temperature was nothing out of the ordinary, just an infection, under control. Whenever she asked if she would lose the baby, they suddenly seemed to have lost their command of English.

Dave visited every day with another story of unavoidable delays. The boss would be here soon, he said. In the meantime, there was nothing to worry about. She must simply sit tight and let the doctors do their job. Rivelli would take care of everything.

The police came back a couple of times, but when they were satisfied that Victoria remembered nothing about the vehicle that had hit her – nothing about the driver, the make, even the colour – they lost interest. The enquiry had moved on. The police told her to concentrate on getting better. They all said the same thing – the doctors, the nurses, the police, Dave. Sit tight, relax, get better, everything is under control.

Then they gave her more painkillers, and she slept for hours.

She awoke in the middle of the night, sweating and in pain, convinced that she was losing the baby. She wanted to tell someone.

Rivelli?

Ben?

Someone must care.

She called for the nurse, and asked for her phone, but the nurse just checked the baby's heartbeat, murmured words of comfort and adjusted her drip.

She slept again.

Christine landed at Nice airport after a nightmare of delays, misinformation and, to add insult to injury, turbulence. It didn't matter. It all seemed to match her state of mind. So, her ex-husband was cheating on her again, was he? And it had taken the vindictive tongue of her spiteful daughter to make clear to her what she should have suspected all along. What, after all, had really changed for Andy? They'd spent some time living apart, and during that time he'd presumably cheated on his girlfriend of the day, then he'd taken up with her again and gone straight back to his old ways. The only difference was that she didn't do his laundry or cook his dinners any more, and there were a few minor matters financial and domestic to consider, but apart from that, it was business as usual. How could she ever think it would be otherwise?

She made her way through the crowds to the taxi rank, clutching in her hand a piece of paper bearing the name of the hospital where, the papers said, Leanne Miller's pregnant friend was recovering. She might have gone, of course; she might even be dead. All Ben's attempts to reach her had failed, the phone permanently switched off. But how many English women of Victoria's description could there be recovering from road traffic accidents in the Nice area? She climbed into a cab, made herself understood, and was whisked away.

After some initial awkwardness, Isabelle and Will got on rather well in Los Angeles. Things seemed more organised when Will was around. Calls got returned, appointments were kept and there was no need to eat alone. Mike was back, of course, but Mike was busy – he'd be there on the night, but now he was in the studio, not coming home till late, if at all. It was nice to have Will around – and it saved on hotels. Mercy Williams was behaving like a trusted family pet, referring to

Will as 'my stylist' and inviting them over to her house for fittings. The silver dress, the few ounces of shiny satin on which the whole future of Cissé was staked, was taking shape. Will and Mercy laughed and joked their way through the fittings, and when Mercy had some last-minute fears that she would look like an oven-ready turkey, Will started calling her Turkey Lurkey, and she called him Chicken Licken. Isabelle she more or less ignored, treating her as little more than a glorified dresser. Isabelle did not care. The dress looked good. The dress looked *great*.

Two days passed in a whirl of press calls and interviews, fittings and meetings, and suddenly there were only twenty-four hours to go until the Academy Awards. Isabelle, nervous to the last, began to calm down when she saw a press release from Mercy Williams's management announcing that she would be wearing Cissé on the red carpet. 'I dare those bitches to do their worst,' said Mercy to Will. 'I'm flameproof.'

The night before, the whole of Los Angeles was one big party. Mike whisked Isabelle off to a gig at the Hollywood Bowl, where he had a box and a hell of a lot of hospitality, then out to a club. He was not the most attentive of boyfriends, and restricted his conversation to asking her repeatedly what her chances were of 'winning the Oscar' tomorrow. At first she tried to explain that she wasn't actually nominated, then she tried to explain what it meant just to have a dress on the red carpet, but by that time he'd lost interest, perhaps assuming that she was already making excuses for losing, and that he would soon be finding reasons to dump her.

Nobody would sleep in town tonight. Plenty of time to go home, get dressed, get to the theatre on time . . .

Will worked late, setting up interviews, talking to all the important bloggers, preparing different versions of emails that would be sent off as soon as the awards were over and then, exhausted, jumped in a cab and gave the driver an address in West Hollywood. He had been invited to a 'bachelor pool party' by a friend of a friend in the adult industry, who had told him, very matter-of-factly, that there would be 'a lot of hot men there', and so Will, who would not sleep anyway, gladly accepted.

The water in the pool was Hockney blue, the light artificially sunny, the bodies the colour of expensive veneer, shiny and smooth, as if someone had just gone over them with a duster and a squirt of Mr Sheen. Will accepted a Martini from a waiter in a small apron and nothing else, and made his way towards a larger-than-life drag queen who was got up as Mercy Williams in *Moanin' Low*. Well, if that wasn't an ice-breaker, nothing was.

He was intercepted by a firm hand on his bicep.

Wow, he thought, I know they're all queer for Englishmen, but I've only been here for thirty seconds . . .

'Will.'

'Joel! What the hell . . .'

Joel kissed him on the lips. 'Couldn't keep away, could I.' He put an arm round his shoulders. 'Welcome to LA.'

'*D'accord*,' said the driver, casting his eyes over the address.

Christine sat back and relaxed. After the hell of the journey, she had nothing more to worry about. She surrendered to *la circulation* and let the driver do his job.

They'd come here once on holiday, when the kids were quite small, staying in a villa that belonged to a client of Andy's, a lovely place up in the hills with a pool. The children adored it, splashing around all day, playing with some French kids from the villa next door, ending up brown as berries and bilingual. Christine and Andy spent the days sleeping, reading, shopping and eating. It all seemed wonderful at the time. She knew now, of course, that he'd been unfaithful to her even then – possibly, almost certainly, with someone connected to that very job. His client's wife, perhaps? His daughter? Or another architect? Someone from the surveyor's department? Who knew? Where there were women, there was danger.

And he hadn't changed, apparently. If what Isabelle had oh-so-casually let slip was true, Andy was still making a fool of her, even now, after the divorce. All that bullshit about trying again, putting the past behind them – which she had been stupid enough to fall for, duped yet again by the fact that there was a man in her bed making love to her – it had all been lies. Of course it was lies. They always lie, all of them. Andy, Joel, Rivelli, they all used her, lied to her, kept her quiet with flattery and sex and then, once they'd lulled her into a false sense of security, wham! Out went the rug from under her feet, down came the hammer on the same old bruise, smash went the delicate crystal fantasy that she'd been constructing in her head.

Perhaps this whole crazy pilgrimage to France was some weird act of revenge. But if that was true, it wasn't just revenge on Rivelli that interested her. It was revenge on the whole bloody pack of them. She would put Rivelli behind bars, she would put Andy behind her, she'd do her time in Siberia and then, when the briefs started coming in again, she would dedicate the rest of her life to bringing down vengeance on every erring bastard of a husband who thought he could get away with taking his wife for a ride. So what if they weren't the high-profile, highly paid cases that would buy a luxury lifestyle and get her silk before she was fifty? She wasn't interested in all that any more.

She was a woman with a mission, and this was just the beginning. Now there was no stopping her.

Except, that is, for the traffic around Nice, which showed no sign of moving.

'Surprised to see me?'

'Why didn't you tell me you were coming out?" I wanted to show you that I wasn't just sitting on my arse all day while you were at work. I was going to auditions, and I got a job.' He held out his hands. 'And here I am.'

'Yeah – but porn . . . Are you sure?'

'It's not porn, Will.' Joel rolled his eyes and tutted. 'It's erotica.'

'Oh, right. That's okay then.'

'I reckon I'll be pretty good. He's going to try me out in one scene, and then if that goes okay, he's going to build me up to star level.'

'Great. My boyfriend the porn star. Sorry, the erotica star.'

'Is that a touch of jealousy I detect?

God, when did he become such a queen?

'No, really. I'm happy for you. I'm . . . well, Joel, I'm proud of you. I think you've found your true vocation at last.'

Sarcasm was wasted. 'Yeah. It's going to be excellent. I mean, they have the best parties.'

Will looked around at the herds of meat on the hoof, the well-dressed predators.

'And some of the birds in this industry are fucking awesome.'

'Birds? Forgive me, Joel, but this is gay porn that you're doing, isn't it?'

'Gay, bi, whatever. We don't make those distinctions.'

'Don't we? I do.'

'I mean in the industry. Hey, come on, there's someone I want you to meet.' He grabbed Will's arm and dragged him over to the poolhouse, where a young man – although not so young, once you got close – was holding court, reclining on a sun lounger, a cocktail in one hand.

'Hey, Ivan!'

A plucked eyebrow was raised; the forehead did not move.

'Joel. Come.' He patted the lounger. 'Sit with me.' The accent was hard to place – possibly, beneath a thick Californian overlay, there were eastern European origins.

Joel did as he was bidden. 'Ivan, I want you to meet my . . . very good friend, Will Francis. He's over here for the Oscars.'

Ivan pouted a little, as if exhaling hot air, and looked up at Will.

'What category?'

'Best Actress.'

'Very funny. Now, Joel, how about you freshen this up for me?' He swirled the watery dregs of his cocktail around the glass, which he held at groin level.

'Sure, Ivan.'

Joel allowed his fingers to brush Ivan's crotch, then disappeared to the bar. Ivan beckoned Will down to his level.

'You're not going to be a bore, are you?'

'I beg your pardon?'

'You're not one of these jealous boyfriends, are you? That's followed him out here to try and keep an eye on him?'

Will stood up. 'I wouldn't dream of holding him back,' he said. 'Working with you is a dream come true. I mean, this is the big time, right?'

Ivan did the blowing thing again, as if he was just so damn hot that it was the only way he could cool himself.

'Come on,' said Joel, when the party was breaking up, 'everyone's going on to Circus.'

'I've got to get some sleep,' said Will. 'It's a big day tomorrow.' Joel hadn't asked a single thing about the Oscars. 'I need my beauty sleep.'

'Sleep? Don't be stupid. Nobody sleeps in this town.'

'But the Awards ceremony starts in . . . Christ! Six hours!'

'See? No point in going to bed now. Let's go out dancing. It'll be fun. Everyone will be there.'

'Everyone in the adult industry? Whoopee.'

'Fuck this,' said Joel, pushing out his lips in a passable imitation of Ivan. 'I don't think you're even pleased to see me.'

'I am, you know I am. It's fantastic that you're here. It's fantastic that you've landed such a . . . plum part. We'll go to the club. I can't work all the time. I've done everything. We're ready. We just have to sit back and watch. What could possibly go wrong?'

Joel wasn't listening. 'Fabulous.'

When did you ever say 'fabulous'?

'Ivan will take us. He always has the best drugs.'

'*Non, madame, elle n'est pas içi.*'

'Are you sure? *Etes-vous sûre?* Victoria Crabtree. English woman. *Anglaise. Je crois qu'elle est enceinte.*'

'*Désolée, madame.* We can not say this. *Mademoiselle* Crabtree is no longer here.'

'But she was? *Elle était?* When . . . Oh God. *Quand est-elle quittée . . .*'

The nurse–receptionist shrugged, raised her eyebrows, signalled to a young man in a suit with a name badge.

'Madame, I regret, one can not pass on confidential details.' He sounded as if he was reading from a card. 'We can only say that we do not have this lady here. That is all.'

'But this is an emergency.'

'You do not have her phone number?'

'Yes. But she doesn't answer.'

'Then perhaps she does not wish to speak to you, *madame.*'

'Don't be ridiculous, she doesn't know what I . . . Oh this is absurd. I'm a lawyer. *Un avocat.* This is important.'

'Excuse me, *madame.* This is the rule. I am sorry.'

'You will be,' said Christine, wondering if she could get any more sense out of the local police.

* * *

Isabelle got home at two o'clock in the morning. Her body clock was all over the place, and she didn't feel at all tired. She was sober – unlike Mike, who tumbled into bed drunk as a skunk, and immediately fell asleep. Isabelle took a shower, wrapped herself in a satin kimono and went to see if Will was awake. If he wasn't, he soon would be. It was time to start getting ready.

She tapped on his door, which was standing ajar – well, at least that meant he didn't have company.

'Will? Are you awake?' The room was dark. 'Come on,' she said, making her way to the window and drawing back the blinds. 'It's time to get up.'

A little of the city's light pollution filtered in from outside.

'Wake up, sleepy head.'

She turned round. The bed was empty, made up, exactly as the maid had left it yesterday morning.

Chapter 28

It was nearly three a.m. and Will was still not home. Isabelle was annoyed. She had to dress, and how could she possibly dress without Will to advise her? And she had to eat something – she couldn't go through the whole thing on an empty stomach. She left a message on his mobile.

Look, Will, I don't know where you are or what you're doing, but please could you tear yourself away and get your arse back here so we can get ready? You're cutting it a bit bloody fine.

And then she'd started worrying, knowing perfectly well that this was not in Will's nature. He should have been the one pacing the marble floors, wondering where in hell she'd got to and what she thought she was doing, partying on the night before the Oscars, not telling him where she was and who she was with, nagging her like her mother would nag her.

She went back to her room. Mike was still out for the count, snoring, one arm hanging over the edge of the bed. There was no point waking him. He'd still be pissed. He'd tell her not to worry, then grunt and fart and pull the sheets over his head. He didn't care. When she went back to London with Will, she'd chuck him, and tell Will he was right all along.

Where the hell was he?

'I'm sorry, *madame*,' said the desk sergeant, 'but if you do not know the date of the accident, it is very difficult for us to trace.'

'It was this month.'

'There are many accidents in this region. Do you know the exact location?'

'No, I don't . . . But the woman's name. Victoria Crabtree. You must have some record. It was in all the papers.'

'*Madame*,' said the *femme-agent*, 'we will do our best to search our files for you. At present, we are very busy. If you could come back again in two days.'

'Now listen,' said Christine, who had been rather good at crushing police officers in the criminal courts, 'I am not someone to be dismissed in this way. I have come here to report an attempted murder.'

'Murder? *Oh, ça . . .*'

'And if you are not qualified to help me, I will speak to your senior officer.'

The woman glared at her, but she was outclassed. Sometimes, thought Christine, it was good to be English.

'Now, *madame*,' said the *Capitaine*, a handsome man in his fifties, who could not take his eyes off Christine's legs, 'what appears to be the problem?'

'As I explained to your colleague out there, I have reason to believe that someone is attempting to kill my friend. Her name is Victoria Crabtree. She checked into a hospital in Nice but now she has disappeared. She is pregnant and vulnerable.' He stared at her. 'Do you understand?'

'Yes, *madame*, I understand very well. It is a serious accusation. Perhaps you have mistaken yourself?'

'I do not think so, *monsieur*. I am a lawyer.'

He sighed, clicked out his ballpoint pen, prepared to write.

'And what is the name of your . . . *comment dire . . .* your prime suspect?'

'Massimo Rivelli.'

The pen stopped suddenly, a few millimetres above the paper.

'Ah.'

'You have heard of him?'

'*Oui, madame.* Monsieur Rivelli is *bien connu.*'

He has the police in his pocket.

'Then perhaps you will understand . . .'

'A moment, please.'

He left the room, no doubt to make a call.

She couldn't wait any longer. Will was missing – and Isabelle would have to go to the Oscars alone. Mike was in no fit state to escort her, however great the publicity coup; turning up for the Academy Awards with a stinking, drunken unshaven megastar was really not going to help. She dressed – it didn't take long, just a shower and half an hour in front of the make-up mirror, then stepping into one of her own dresses, a simple plum-coloured calf-length number, and a trusted pair of Manolo Blahniks, a final frizz of the hair and, as an afterthought, a gardenia from an arrangement in the hall behind her right ear.

The car was ready.

She called Will's number one more time, and, when he didn't answer, called the police.

'I know this sounds ridiculous,' she said, 'but I want to report a missing person.'

Twenty minutes later, she arrived at the Kodak Theatre.

Isabelle knew how to get out of a car – both feet first, knees together, slide forward and then sort of unfold into a standing position, being careful not to lean over too much – one didn't want to give the photographers a tit shot. Not accidentally, at least.

She was looking good, she knew, and a few of the photographers dutifully snapped her just in case she was *somebody*. But they didn't seem to recognise her without Mike – and most of them were still focused on the last couple to walk up the red carpet, a tiny little woman with a huge head accompanied by a slouching giant of a man, both of them covered in tattoos and piercings. The fact that they were alive at all, both out of prison and *together*, was headline news. The rest of the photographers were looking over Isabelle's shoulder for whoever might come next. Gorgeous and talented she may be, but that was really not enough. She'd need something really salacious to get their interest.

She kept smiling until she was inside, feeling as if she'd just turned up to a school disco without a date. Without Mike, she was just a little black girl from England, Europe, and why would anyone want to talk to her?

There was a commotion behind her, a blitzkrieg of flashguns, and suddenly a phalanx of security men in tight tuxedos barged into the lobby, clearing a path. Some of them, Isabelle noticed with horror, were armed. They formed two lines, feet planted firmly apart, arms folded. Isabelle, near the door, had a perfect view down the red carpet.

The red carpet up which Mercy Williams was walking, stopping, posing, turning, running a few steps, blowing kisses, throwing her head back, laughing. At this rate it would take her twenty minutes to get into the theatre.

Mercy Williams – as of the last news bulletin, the bookies' favourite for the Best Actress award.

Mercy Williams – wearing a Cissé dress.

A man pushed in front of Isabelle, blocking her view just as Mercy stepped through the doors and into the lobby. She wanted to scream, to get Mercy's attention, to let her know that she was here and that she was so grateful, so proud, that this was the biggest moment in her life . . . But a pair of broad, gym-built shoulders was pressing back into her face. She crouched down, stuck her head through the forest of legs, dislodging the gardenia, which was quickly trampled to compost. And so she saw the hem of her gown, close enough to admire the stitchwork in the silver satin, a pair of sturdy black calves tapering to elegant ankles and a pair of life-threatening Patrick Cox jewelled sandals that seemed to float half an inch off the floor.

So that was it. Everything they had worked towards, accomplished.

She withdrew her head from the scrum, but not before getting her nose squashed into an arse.

The security guards dematerialised, and she was swept by the tide towards the main room.

Ticket check after ticket check after ticket check.

The interior of the Kodak Theatre was bigger than some towns in England.

Isabelle found her place, and placed her bag on the empty seat beside her. He might yet arrive, out of breath, grinning, some ridiculous story at the ready.

Huge video screens relayed the arrivals, the red carpet highlights.

They were all here – somewhere among those tiny shiny dots down there, each arrayed in tens of thousands of dollars' worth of borrowed finery, were the most famous people in the world. Among them Mercy Williams.

Mercy Williams in a Cissé dress.

She came up on the screen – an oven-ready turkey dancing and posing her way up the red carpet, her face almost bare of make-up, just a touch of silver around the eyes, a dark purple lipstick high-lighting her mouth, her hair brushed out in a natural afro.

'She could be your mom,' said someone behind Isabelle, tapping her on the shoulder.

She could be your mom . . . She couldn't wait to tell Will that one. *Why isn't he here? He should be here. He got us here.*

'Mrs Fairbrother.'

'Miss, actually, but . . . Yes.'

They all spoke such good English, she felt quite ashamed of her mangled attempts at French.

'You say something about Massimo Rivelli.'

She was prepared for a fight. If the *Capitaine* looked like one of Rivelli's cronies, his superior, a *Commandant*, looked like Rivelli himself.

'That's right. I have reason to believe that he was responsible for an accident involving a friend of mine.'

'You have some proof, of course.'

'No.'

The two men looked at each other.

'*Monsieur* Rivelli is not unknown to us.'

Here we go. The old pals act.

'I believe he has property in this area.'

'Yes.'

'And perhaps you are aware . . .'

'*Madame . . . pardonnez-moi, mademoiselle*, I must ask you why you suspect this.'

This was no time for beating about the bush. 'Because Mr Rivelli is a crook. A . . . oh God, what . . . *un criminel.*'

'Crook I understand. And you believe that he has . . .' The *Commandant* gestured in the air like a magician. 'Somehow he has arranged for a little accident.'

'Yes, that's exactly what I believe.'

'*Bien.*'

Don't you dare throw me out.

'You will excuse us for a moment, *mademoiselle.*' The two officers stood. 'We need to make a call.'

She stopped worrying about Will, and started concentrating on the awards. There was all the usual song and dance, a hundred miles away on the stage, as if she was looking down the wrong end of a telescope,

much easier to see on the screens. She had crossed oceans and continents just to watch the Oscars on TV.

She tried not to fidget during the writing awards, the visual effects,
the sound mixing, editing, art direction and cinematography, and started
thinking about Will again. She perked up a bit for make-up, and took
a good deal of interest in costume design, and made a mental note to
win that at some point in the not-too-distant future. Another goal to
focus on.

And then it was the supporting roles.

Mercy Williams's co-star didn't win. But that was probably a good
thing. They would never give Oscars to two black actors in one year.
That just wouldn't happen. The field was still clear. Mercy could still win.

Not that it mattered. That's what Will would tell her: the job was
done, they'd been on the red carpet, they had arrived. They had achieved
the impossible – from graduation to the Oscars in less than two years.
They had done what no other British designer had done before them.
The next few years were going to be Mercy, legendary, the stuff of dreams.

That's what he would tell her when she saw him, later, after the
show, after laughing off whatever disaster had befallen him, good old
Will, always some adventure to recount.

'And the nominees are . . .'

She had a sensation of abrupt sideways motion, and thought that
there was an earthquake, but the foundations of the Kodak Theatre
remained firm. It was just the feeling of slipping into unreality, of living
real life through the medium of fiction. This could not be happening
to her, as she had seen it happen so often before to others . . .

'Tilly Ostergard, for *Our Little Secret.*'

Cheers and whistles.

'Roberta Ralston, for *Thin Ice.*'

Whoops and hollers.

'Shirley-Anne Prentice, for *Gerald and Company.*'

Sighs and aaaaahs for an actress so near the grave.

'Helena Moorcastle for *The Architect's Secret.*'

Grave applause, which always greeted English actresses.

'And Mercy Williams, for *Moanin' Low.*'

Mayhem. Cheers, whistles, whoops, hollers, a kind of frenzy. Mercy's
face lurched into giant close-up on the screen.

Security men appeared in the aisles. God, surely they weren't anticipating a riot? Crowds hurling themselves from the balcony to devour
the stars, *Day of the Locust*-style?

The announcer fumbled cutely with the envelope. 'Oh, I'm so
excited . . .'

A uniformed guard made his way along the row.

'Sit down, buddy!'

'Get out of my way, asshole!'

'And the winner is . . .'

And hand tapped Isabelle's shoulder. She looked up. Will?

'Oh my gosh . . .'

'Miss Cissé?' He pronounced it *Cissy*. She saw his badge. LAPD.
'Yes?'

'The winner is Mercy Williams!'

Hysteria, over which the police officer shouted 'Please come with
me, ma'am. There's been an accident.'

This time there were three of them: *le Capitaine, le Commandant et le
Commissaire.*

'*Bonjour, madame.*'

She couldn't be bothered to correct him. This one had a very full
head of white hair, a deep tan and blue eyes. He looked like George
Peppard, Christine thought.

'You have, I understand, a complaint to make of Massimo Rivelli.'

Is he about to tell me that they play golf together?

'Yes. I do.'

'Please.' They all sat down, three men on one side, Christine on the
other.

'I believe that he may have been responsible for an attack on a friend
of mine.'

'A Miss Crabtree, yes?'

'That is correct.'

'And you believe this Miss Crabtree to be in hospital here.'

'I understood that she was.'

'Yes.'

'And I believe she is in further danger.'

'From Mr Rivelli?'

'Yes. And please don't tell me that you're going to make a further phonecall, and then come back with yet another officer. Are you going to help me, or not?'

The *Commissaire* stroked his chin. '*Non, madame*, the telephone calls have been made. We have found your friend.'

'You . . . you've found her?'

'Yes. She is in a private nursing home near Antibes.'

'She was moved?'

'Two days ago. Under a different name.'

'Oh my God. Is she all right? Is the baby . . .'

'We will take you, madame. There is a car outside.'

'Is he dead?'

'No. But he's very badly injured. He's unconscious.'

'Oh my God. Please take me to him.'

'All in good time, Miss.'

They stepped out of the lobby into the not-so-fresh air.

'Oh shit . . .' She suddenly started shaking, and tears poured down her face. She fumbled in her clutch bag and found a tissue. Inside the theatre, they were still cheering Mercy Williams, who was making a lengthy victory speech. The world was watching a Cissé gown.

The officer put his jacket round Isabelle's shoulders. It wasn't how she'd planned her outfit, but she was glad of the warmth.

'We're taking you to the station. We'll get a coffee there.'

'I must see him.'

'Not much to see at the moment. They're taking good care of him at the hospital. But we need to ask you a few questions.'

The private nursing home was very private indeed. To the casual observer, it was indistinguishable from the dozens of other modern villas that dotted the hills around Antibes, complete with gated entry, security cameras and a lot of thick, thorny hedges. Christine's police escort treated their arrival more like a raid than a visit to a sick friend. She noticed with a mixture of alarm and relief that two of the four officers who accompanied her were armed. Obviously a gun was considered more appropriate than a bunch of grapes.

The *Commandant* announced himself at the entryphone, and flashed a badge at the camera eye. There was a long pause before the gates squeaked open. Christine was ushered through, the *Commissaire* at her side, an armed officer behind them. One remained at the gate, the other, she assumed, nipped round the back.

There was nothing inside to suggest that this was a medical establishment. There was a lobby, and off the lobby, an open door from beyond which came the sound of low voices. The armed officer ran noiselessly up the stairs.

A man and a woman came into the hallway. The *Commandant* addressed them in French. They looked blank and shifty and did not respond.

'My name is Christine Fairbrother. I'm looking for a friend of mine. Is she here?'

The man and the woman looked at each other.

'Her name is Victoria Crabtree.'

A voice from above shouted '*Elle est içi!*', and suddenly boots were thundering across the floor from the front and rear of the house. The man and the woman huddled together, their faces pale. He muttered 'Oh, fuck,' confirming Christine's suspicion that they were English.

The *Commandant* reeled off the French form of the caution, and very politely ushered them back into the room whence they had come.

'Can you think of anyone who would want to hurt Mr Francis?'

'No . . . I mean, here in LA? No. Absolutely not.'

'But elsewhere?'

'I suppose at home . . . I mean, in this business you make enemies.'

'But nobody that had a grudge against him, that you can think of.'

'No. Will's the nicest person in the world. Everyone loves him.'

'Miss Cissé, were you aware that your friend is gay?'

Isabelle laughed. 'Oh for God's sake.'

But the police officer wasn't laughing. 'Miss Cissé?'

'Of course I was. I mean, he's my best friend. He's like a brother to me. He's closer than a brother . . . He's . . . like . . .' She started crying again.

'This is difficult for you, I know. But did you have any reason to believe that Will was involved in anything at all . . . kinky?'

'Like what?'

'Do you know what S&M is?'

'Of course I do.'

'Well?'

'Well what? Are you asking me if Will was into that stuff? No. Not as far as I'm aware.'

'Not as far as you're aware . . .'

'For heaven's sake, he might have gone in for a bit of spanking or whatever . . . No, don't write that down! I'm only guessing! I mean, we all have our . . . moments.'

'You never noticed marks on his body.'

'I wasn't in the habit of examining his body.'

'He never turned up to work with a black eye.'

'No. Absolutely not. If anyone had hit Will, I'd have . . .'

'Okay, okay. Now, Miss Cissé, I need you to think very carefully. Do you know the names of any of Will's boyfriends?'

'He didn't have any boyfriends in LA. Doesn't have, I mean. He doesn't know anyone here, apart from me and . . . well, Mercy Williams.'

'That's not quite true, I'm afraid. We've traced him to a party in West Hollywood last night. He seems to have been quite well known there.'

'What do you mean? Of course he went to parties. He was networking. But he didn't have any particular friends.'

'It was a gay party.'

'What are you implying? That he picked up some nutter who beat him into a coma? Because if that's what you think, why aren't you out there looking for this bastard instead of sitting here hinting to me that he somehow asked for it?'

'We're doing nothing of the kind, Miss.'

'I'm sorry. I'm just . . .'

'Please, think carefully. We need to know the names of any boyfriends that you think he might have been seeing. Anywhere. Don't try to cover anything up. Here, or in London, or anywhere else.'

'I don't know his boyfriends. There was someone called Ricky . . .'

'His surname?'

'I don't know. He works for a music company of some sort.'

'Who else?'

'There was no one else. Well, unless you count Joel, of course.'

'Who?'

'Joel. He's a sort of hanger-on. I think they might have been having a bit of a thing.'

'His surname?'

'I don't know.'

'Can you describe him?'

'Tall, dark hair, good looking. I think he's Australian.' She didn't mention that he'd also had an affair with her mother.

One of the police officers walked out of the room, looking very serious.

Dave only just had time to put a call through to Milan before the police burst into the house and arrested him and his wife. Rivelli himself answered the phone, nodded a few times and said nothing.

Downstairs in the reception room, the Contessa Luisella Mirabelli delle Chiaie was entertaining an old admirer with *biscotti* and *vin santo*, getting gently stewed while reminiscing about the good old days when people knew their place, law and order reigned throughout the land and the trains ran on time, not that she ever had cause to take one. Her gentleman friend, who remained unmarried in his sixties and rather specialised in aristocratic ladies with not much longer to go, refilled her tiny crystal glass and admired her collection of rings. How lovely, he thought, they will look on my fingers . . .

Neither of them heard Rivelli's footsteps as he stomped from office to bedroom, hastily packing a bag.

Joel was picked up wandering around Hollywood Boulevard, his clothes torn and stained with blood. The officer who took him in for questioning said that he was in a confused state of mind, and that he became unconscious in the car. During the subsequent interview, he nodded out frequently, and he could give no coherent account of his actions or whereabout in the last twelve hours.

He was picked up just five blocks away from where Will was found, lying unconscious in a locked garage. The police had been alerted by a man walking his dog, who had become alarmed when little pooch started licking at a pool of blood seeping from under the garage door. He dialled 911, the police arrived quickly on the scene – which, given it was Oscars night, was little short of a miracle – and found the badly battered but still living body of a male in his twenties, the contents of whose wallet identified him as Will Francis, a British citizen.

While Will was treated for serious head wounds in the Cedars-Sinai emergency room on Beverly Boulevard, Joel was in an interrogation room at West Hollywood Station. He didn't seem to know who he was, and was carrying no form of identification.

They asked him repeatedly where the blood had come from, as it was clearly not his own – there were no cuts on his body. His face was bruised, and he was walking awkwardly, as if his feet or legs had been hurt, but he could give no account of this and there were no outward signs of injury.

Most of the time, he made wordless slurring noises, slumping over the desk or slipping down in his chair until he was almost on the floor. The police recognised the signs of a GHB overdose; they saw it in West Hollywood all the time. A doctor was on standby if he became unconscious.

They gave him water and coffee and made him walk around the room. Swabs were taken from the blood on his clothes and hands, and sent off to the lab for analysis.

When he finally sobered up enough to speak – and this took some hours – he seemed to believe that he was in a gym or health club environment; an immediate call went out to see if there had been any incidents reported in West Hollywood's bodybuilding community. He could still not answer direct questions about his name or his actions – but the officers detected an accent that was not local.

'Is he Scottish?' asked one.

'I don't know,' said another. 'He sounds kind of like, I don't know, maybe from New England.'

'No,' said a third, with some certainty – he was a film fan, and had seen a few Baz Luhrmann movies – 'he's Australian.'

Victoria was unconscious when they found her. An ambulance, under police escort, took her to hospital, where she was immediately put back on drips and monitors. The doctor who attended her said she had been heavily sedated, possibly with morphine. She would be fine, but he could not vouch for the baby. Its heartbeat was fine, but beyond that he would not commit himself.

Christine set up camp at Victoria's bedside, waiting for her recovery, and while she was waiting, she phoned John Ferguson.

'Beyond reasonable doubt?' he said.

'No. But give them time. The police here seem to know what they're doing. They only have to establish a connection between the English couple at the so-called nursing home, and our friend Massimo Rivelli, and we're in business. Wait till the newspapers get hold of this one. They'll go mad.'

'They certainly will,' said John. 'And what about you? Are you doing all right? Anything you need?'

You, thought Christine, but banished the thought.

'No, I'm fine. I just wish we knew about the baby.'

'Is there anything at all that I can do?'

'Besides what you're doing already? I don't think so.'

'I didn't mean as a lawyer. I meant as a friend.'

'Oh.' That wasn't quite what she'd been hoping for, but it would do. 'No, I'm fine. I'll see you when I get back.'

'Okay.' He sounded crestfallen. 'I . . . hope things work out.'

'They will,' said Christine, trying to sound bright. What, after all, was she expecting?

While the rest of Los Angeles was going to work or going to Oscars parties, Isabelle was going to hospital. Will was out of the ER and on the ward, where he remained on the critical list. He had not regained consciousness, and there was every possibility that he was in a coma. They would not be able to assess the extent of brain damage, if any, until they had stabilised his condition.

Isabelle, still wearing an evening gown of her own design, had forgotten all about Mercy Williams and the fame and fortune that awaited her as the woman behind what was now the most talked-about dress in the world. Her phone was so full of voice messages and texts that the SIM card was in danger of meltdown – but she had not even thought to turn it on.

A police officer accompanied her on to the ward. 'You better prepare yourself, honey,' she said. 'He don't look so hot.'

Will looked like the Mummy, wrapped in bandages, a tube stuck in his mouth, held in place by sticky plaster. What little of his face was visible – a bit around the eyes and lips – was so swollen and discoloured that she was hard pressed to recognise him. But his hands were resting above the blankets – those hands that had so often held hers, or goosed her, handed her a coffee, helped her with a roll of silk or a fiddly pattern. She recognised the hands.

'Can I touch him?'

'If you're very careful,' said the nurse. 'He's kind of delicate.'

Isabelle took Will's hand so gently, as gently as she'd touch a newborn baby. She dared not squeeze.

'Is he going to . . . be okay?'

'We're doing our best for him.'

'Please do.' Tears were rolling down her face, collecting at the end of her nose, dropping on to her dress. 'Please. Please don't let him . . .'

The nurse put a hand on Isabelle's shoulder. 'It's okay, darling. He's going to be okay.'

Isabelle looked for reassurance in the nurse's eyes, and saw only trouble.

Chapter 29

'We've never really met, have we? Not properly, I mean.'

'No. I suppose not.'

Victoria looked tired and, without make-up, older than Christine remembered. Her hair was pulled back in a loose ponytail, and needed washing. There were scabs on her forehead, the remains of the cuts and grazes she'd sustained in the accident.

'And yet,' said Christine, 'we always seem to be under each other's feet.'

'Do we . . .' Oh God, thought Victoria, please don't let her start with the accusations. I can't take it.

'But first things first. How's the baby?'

'Ah.' Victoria closed her eyes, waiting for the onslaught. 'You know about that, then?'

'Of course. He told me.'

'Who?'

'Ben, of course.'

'I thought you might mean . . .'

The name hung in the air between them, unspoken. Plenty of time for that later, thought Christine. 'He's frantic with worry. As am I, I might add.'

'I didn't want anyone to know. It was an accident.'

'And what were you planning to do, exactly?'

'I don't know.'

Yes you do. You were going to pass it off as Rivelli's and live on his hand-outs for the rest of your life even though it's going to be my grandchild . . .

'Well, it looks as if circumstances rather overtook you.'

'Yes.' Victoria was staring towards the door of the ward, hoping that someone might come in and interrupt this awkward interview. Why was Christine here? After all Victoria had done to her, or tried to do, what did she want?

'Have you spoken to the police?'

'Yes. I told them. I didn't see anything.'

'And did they ask you who might want to do a thing like that?'

'They asked me a lot of questions about Leanne Miller.'

'That's not what I mean.'

'No . . .'

'Because she wasn't the intended victim, was she, Victoria?'

'I don't know . . .'

'I think you do.' Christine's voice was soft, persuasive. 'I think we both know what this is about, don't we? And the police know too.'

'Oh God.'

'The only question is, are you willing to make a statement?'

'No . . .'

'You must, Victoria. He tried to kill you and your baby. Does that mean nothing to you?'

'It was an accident.'

'And the kidnap? Was that an accident too?'

'What?'

'The house where they were keeping you. Dave and Sue, the English couple. Ah. I see that you don't know all this.'

Victoria would not look her in the eye. Christine did not want to distress her – but on the other hand, she had the safety and well-being of her daughter to consider. With Rivelli at large, and Isabelle in Los Angeles, Christine was uneasy.

The nurse came in, took Victoria's temperature and blood pressure, refilled her water jug and left a sheaf of newspapers and magazines on the bed – *Vogue*, of course, plus *Voiçi*, *Paris Match* and a copy of *Le Monde*.

Victoria was grateful for the distraction, and rallied somewhat. 'Look, if you don't mind, I'm really not feeling up to this at the moment. Can we talk about it later? When I get back to London, perhaps?'

'We need to talk now.'

'Christine,' said Victoria, 'why exactly are you here? We're not friends, are we? You don't like me, and God knows I have plenty of reasons not to like you either. So shall we drop the Good Samaritan act and get down to business?'

'As you wish,' said Christine. 'I want to put him behind bars.'

'Who?'

'Who do you think? Massimo Rivelli.'

'Why?'

'Because he is dangerous.'

'To women like you, perhaps. He must have left a lasting impression.'

'This isn't about revenge, Victoria.'

'You could have fooled me.'

'This is about justice. The man is a criminal. He's threatened me and my daughter, he's involved in just about every racket going, and now this.' She waved her hand behind her, indicating the hospital ward. 'It's not a coincidence, is it?'

'Right. And you're some crusading superhero who just wants to do the right thing.'

'That's about it, yes.'

'And who has my best interests at heart.'

'Yes.'

'Because you believe,' said Victoria, patting her belly, 'that this is your grandchild, I suppose.'

'Is it?'

'Who knows.'

'Look, Victoria . . .'

'How old are you, Christine? If you don't mind my asking.'

'Forty-eight.'

'Not quite old enough to be my mother, then.'

'No, I suppose not,' said Christine. 'But old enough to be your mother-in-law.'

'Don't be ridiculous.'

Silence fell. Victoria flicked angrily through *Voici*.

'You've dreamed this whole thing up,' she said at last, with a croak in her voice. 'Massimo isn't some kind of murderer. He's . . . he said he was going to look after me.'

Christine said nothing; her eyes were fixed on the front page of *Le Monde*, lying upside down on the bed.

'I don't believe he intended any harm. He was looking after me. Dave and Sue are old friends. I've known them for years. They look after the house. I mean, Dave picked me up at the airport, for God's sake . . .'

'Oh my God.' Christine grabbed the newspaper, turned it up the right way.

'Rivelli's not a murderer. He wouldn't. Not me.'

'Oh no. Oh please God no.'

'What?'

Christine handed her the paper, pointing with a trembling figure at a downpage story under the headline OSCARS: HOMME DANS LE COMAS APRÈS L'ATTAQUE, HOLLYWOOD, LOS ANGELES.

'Will . . . Oh my God. I must call Isabelle.'

Christine rushed to the door, and then stopped in her tracks. She looked back at Victoria, who was leaning round in bed, straining her neck.

They read the name in each other's eyes.

Rivelli.

In another ward, in another hospital, in another country, on another continent, Will had not regained consciousness.

Isabelle went home to change, pack a hold-all and tell Mike what had happened. There were reporters outside the house, shouting questions about Mercy Williams – their only point of interest in the story, let alone the fact that her best friend lay dying in a hospital bed – but she pushed through them with a look on her face that could even scare her mother into silence.

Mike was not there.

There was a bottle of champagne on the dining room table, and a note that read 'Congratulations! See you later.'

Nothing about Will. He didn't know. Why should he know? The reporters outside the house – well, they were nothing new. They'd been there before – not so many of them, admittedly, but then it wasn't every day that one of you got a dress to the Oscars, was it? Perhaps Mike was sulking. Perhaps he didn't like being upstaged. Perhaps he'd served his purpose.

Then again, not yet. Will needed care, and care cost money. Mike had money. Isabelle – for all her success – had none.

She turned her phone on to call Mike, to ask him for advice about lawyers and money and healthcare insurance. She didn't have a clue about these things. What had Will said? She had the business sense of a small furry animal. How right he was.

No sooner did she have a signal than the phone started beeping and pinging and flashing. 'You have four hundred and fifty-two voice messages' it told her. 'You have seven hundred and forty-eight text messages.' Then it went dark, flashed again a few times, and came up with something that looked like a late Piet Mondrian. She tossed it impatiently on a table in the hall, went out the back of the house and picked up a cab.

The police were waiting when she got back to Cedars-Sinai.

He's dead.

'Miss Cissé? Could you come with me please?' The officer took her firmly by the arm, and led her to a small office near reception.

'We need to ask you a few questions.'

They think I did it.

'What?' She sounded guilty to herself. 'What's happened to Will?'

'Nothing's happened to Will. He's still doing . . . fine.'

'You're lying to me. Something's happened.'

'We've made an arrest, Miss Cissé.'

'Oh my God. Oh thank God. Who? Who did this?'

'His name is Joel Warner.'

'That's impossible. Joel lives in London. Joel's got nothing to do with this.'

'We need you to confirm his identity.'

'Why me?'

'Because he's not making a lot of sense right now, honey.' The officer wiggled a finger around his temple. 'He's been taking too many funny pills.'

'But I hardly know him.'

'You'd recognise him?'

'I suppose so.'

'We're going to the station. It won't take long. Don't worry – he won't know you're there, if that's what you're worried about.'

'No . . . It's fine . . . Of course I'll come. But why . . . I mean it can't be . . .'

'By the way, Miss,' said the officer, when they were driving up to the station, 'does the name Rivoli mean anything to you?'

'What? Rivoli?'

'Something like that. Rivoli. Ravioli. He keeps saying it, over and over again, but he won't say what it means. I just wondered if . . .'

'Ravioli?'

'I guess he just likes Italian food,' said the driver.

Isabelle saw Mercy Williams's face on a newsstand – a special edition of the *LA Times* with a wraparound cover. Head and shoulders. Silver straps. Golden statuette.

'Rivelli,' she said, almost to herself.

'That's it, honey. Rivelli. Who he?'

She could not get hold of Isabelle, she could not get hold of Andy or Ben, and in a panic she called John.

He didn't have anything very comforting to tell her. The English newspapers had also reported a mysterious fire at a house in Surrey, the home of Janet Radcliffe, former wife of the Italian garment manu-facturing giant, Massimo Rivelli. Ms Radcliffe, who was unhurt, said that her son had been trying to cook chips in the kitchen in the middle of the night, and the pan had burst into flames. Both mother and son had been discharged from hospital and were recovering with friends. The fire had caused hundreds of thousands of pounds' worth of damage.

'Where is he?' asked Christine. 'Surely they've got to arrest him now.'

'Don't worry,' said John. 'They'll find him. Just . . . look after your-self, Christine, and hurry home.'

'I didn't know you cared,' said Christine.

'Ah, but I do.'

Isabelle looked through the one-way mirror. Joel was sitting in a bucket chair, wearing what looked like a surgical dressing gown. His face was bruised, but it was recognisably him.

'That's Joel.'

'You're sure?'

'As sure as I can be. I don't know him that well, but . . .' She thought back to the first time she'd seen him, in her mother's kitchen. 'Yeah. That's him.

'Thank you, Miss Cissé. Now we can get this show on the road.'

'Would you be willing to testify against him?'

'Don't be ridiculous. I can't prove anything.'

'You would be an invaluable witness.'

'I'm sorry, Christine. I can't.'

'You must.'

Victoria was sitting in a chair now, and could walk again; the baby seemed to be fine.

'Tell me about Joel Warner.'

'You know as much about him as I do,' said Victoria. 'You got there first, after all.'

'Well then, we're equal. We both had each other's cast-offs.'

'Massimo was not a cast-off.'

'How did Rivelli meet Joel? Did you introduce them?'

'No I did not.'

'Did you talk about him?'

'No. Not really.'

'Did you know that he was working for him?'

'No. I told you no. We had a brief affair. He was a very popular boy. I'm sure you know why. After I finished with him, he took up with Will. That's all I know.'

'Victoria,' said Christine, 'we've got three crimes in three countries. Three different jurisdictions. It's going to be very difficult to get Rivelli in the dock unless someone is prepared to stand up in court and testify. Janet won't do it; she says the fire was an accident.'

'Perhaps it was.'

'And the police in LA are treating the attack on Will as some kind of kinky sex game that went wrong.'

'Perhaps it was.'

'And I suppose you still think that lorry just happened to be speeding along that particular stretch of road just after you and Leanne were taking a jolly little spin out to Fréjus.'

'Why not?'

'Why are you trying to protect him, Victoria? You can't still love him.'

'Love?' said Victoria, spitting the word at Christine. 'What could you possibly know about love?' She folded her arms across her stomach and looked out of the window. 'Please go now.'

'Victoria . . .'

'Go.'

* * *

Police attention was focused on the house in Corso Magenta. Rivelli had been seen coming and going – he was a prominent local figure, and hard to miss. But when officers arrived at the *palazzo* to question Signor Rivelli about allegations being made about him in Los Angeles, he was not at home. Contessa Luisella Mirabelli delle Chiaie received the officers wearing what looked like court dress, a white fur stole around her shoulders, jewels in her fine white hair. 'My son is away on business,' she said, and would say no more. They made a perfunctory search of the premises, but Rivelli was not there. Their commanding officer, who was a good friend of the Rivelli family, eventually called his counterpart in LA and told him that he was unable to question Signor Rivelli at this time.

And in the interim, Rivelli slipped quietly out of Malpensa airport on a flight for Tokyo. He flew economy, under false papers, and was admitted through immigration as a Saudi citizen visiting Japan on business. It was a busy day at Narita Airport, and nobody gave the well dressed, highly westernised businessman a second look. Mr Abdulaziz took a taxi into town.

Chapter 30

Three crimes, three jurisdictions. Christine flew home as uncertain as when she flew out, visions of Rivelli and Victoria and the unborn child dancing ahead of her, just out of reach.

There were messages from John as soon as she turned her phone on. Instead of driving home, she went straight to chambers, parked the car and walked smartly round to Ferguson McCreath's offices.

'The driver has turned state's evidence,' he said, before she had even sat down. 'He's singing like a canary, as they say in the movies.'

'Dave?'

'The very same. He's not unknown to Scotland Yard, and he faces extradition for a string of charges as long as your arm. He's done a deal with the French police. He'll give them enough to put Rivelli away for life if they'll put him into a witness protection programme.'

'Seriously? He's that scared?'

'So it appears. He moved Victoria on Rivelli's orders.'

'Good. But about the accident?'

'He knows nothing.'

'Then it's not good enough.'

'That's exactly what the French police said. And so Dave had to dig a bit further back into his memory. Dig being the operative word.'

'And what did he find?'

'A very interesting story from long, long ago. Once upon a time, there was a construction firm run by a man called Stefano Cassano who, as the name suggests, was Italian. Now, Signor Cassano was a very good friend of a young man by the name of Massimo Rivelli – in fact, he was married to a cousin on Rivelli's father's side. So Rivelli, being a good family man, put a lot of work Cassano's way, and he did very well indeed. When Rivelli was starting up as a manufacturer, Cassano built his factories. When Rivelli wanted a new house, Cassano got the job. Planning permissions just rained out of the sky, and by the mid eighties Cassano was a very rich man indeed, and Rivelli's cousin was a very happy woman. And so, when Rivelli hits the big time and decides to reward himself with a nice holiday home in the south of France, who do you think gets the contract?'

'Cassano.'

'Correct. Well, it's going to be a beautiful house, according to Dave. Nothing but the best. Marble floors, big windows, a land-scaped garden, lovely old tiles in the roof and the cherry on the cake – a clifftop pool, with views over the bay to Saint-Tropez. Sounds lovely, doesn't it?'

'Lovely.'

'But Cassano got greedy. Rivelli was busy, and while the cat was away, the mouse decided to cut corners in order to maximise his profits. He started using cheap materials and cheaper labour, and he pockets the difference without mentioning it to Rivelli. But Rivelli is not stupid. He's keeping an eye on his investment. And one day, he makes a little site visit on a Sunday when the builders are not there and he sees the the lining of the pool is already cracked and the tiles are falling off the roof. So he has a chat with the foreman of the works and finds out things that Cassano doesn't want him to know. So Rivelli is very grateful to that foreman.'

'Was that by any chance . . .'

'Dave the Driver. Very clever, Miss Fairbrother. Anyway, Rivelli makes sure that from that point on the work is done according to his exacting specification. They fix the roof and they clean up the inside of the house and they rip out the pool and completely rebuild it.'

'Ah.'

'And you know, they do a very good job of that pool. Best quality materials. Good thick lining, made of concrete in a steel shell, the whole thing sunk into the hillside maybe five, six metres depth. Beautiful finish – blue and gold tiles, marble surround. Nothing but the best. It's like something from the ancient world. It will last for ever.'

Christine's eyes met John's.

'But you know, if in a thousand years they come along and they dig that pool up, they're going to get one hell of a big surprise, those archaeologists. Because what they're going to find, sunk in the concrete liner of the pool, encased in steel and finished off in blue and gold tiles, is the body of Signor Stefano Cassano.'

Isabelle had to come home. She didn't want to; she'd have stayed at Will's bedside until he woke, given the choice, but there are such things as responsibilities for the designer of a globally famous dress, and Will would want her to face up to them. So it was with a heavy heart that she disembarked at Heathrow.

Andy was at arrivals to meet her.

'Your mum told me you were coming home today. She would have been here herself, but you know her. I suppose she's got a big case on. Didn't really have time for me. Everything else has to take second place, as usual.'

He sounded uncommonly bitter.

'Have you and Mum been talking, then?'

'Yes.'

He knows that she knows.

'Right. Good.'

'And that's something I need to discuss with you, Isabelle.'

'Mmm. I kind of thought you might. But right now . . .'

'When you were staying at my flat . . .'

'Yes?'

'Did you by any chance . . .'

'I didn't catch her name. Good taste in shoes though. Salvatore Ferragamo. Very expensive, Ferragamos.'

'Ah.'

The traffic was bad getting out of the airport, and Andy said very little that was not directed at other drivers.

'The thing with your mother,' he said, when they were finally on the M4, 'is that she's a very black and white type of woman.'

'Hence Ben and me.'

'I don't mean in that way.'

'No. I didn't think you did.'

A long pause while they glided along the motorway.

'I mean, you know that she and I had sort of . . . well, we were going to give it another go . . .'

'You got back together, you mean.'

'That's just it.' Andy went to slap the wheel, but moderated the force of his blow at the last moment, and tapped it peevishly. 'Your mother thought we had. As usual, she jumped to conclusions.'

'Could that have anything to do with the fact that you were sleeping with her again?'

'It's not as simple as that.'

'Is it ever?'

'What do you mean?'

'I don't know, Dad. You tell me. What did it mean to you?'

'I'm very fond of your mother.'

'And what about Ferragamo Lady? Are you very fond of her?'

'Yes I am, as a matter of fact. If it's any of your business.'

'Oh come on, Dad. You let me stay in your flat. Presumably you knew that she'd come calling sooner or later.'

'She wasn't supposed to.'

'Right. So perhaps this was just the poor woman's way of asserting herself. She thought that I was some sort of rival, and she came to see me off.'

'What did you tell her?'

'Nothing. Funnily enough, Dad, we didn't exactly get chatting.'

'And then you ran to tell your mother. Well thanks a lot.'

'Hold on a second. You're trying to make *me* the bad guy here?'

'I'm not trying to do anything. I just want you to understand that things aren't always as clear cut as they seem.'

'Right. So are you and Mum back together again or not?'

'She doesn't seem to think so.'

'And you? What do you think?'

'I don't know, Isabelle.'

They reached Acton. The situation seemed hopeless. Isabelle thought about Will lying in hospital, about Joel in prison, about the mass and mess of work that awaited her, the failure of her dreams about Chelsea and the bills that had not been paid and the agents clamouring for new designs to sell into the stores on the back of the Oscars. She thought about her mother, how confused and how hurt she must be.

How lonely.

'You know what, Dad,' she said, 'if you don't mind, I think it would be a good idea if you dropped me off at Mum's.'

Andy grunted. They drove on.

'Probably just as well,' he said, at length. 'My flat's a bit . . . well, a bit of a mess at the moment.'

Victoria made a statement to the French police before she flew home, to the effect that she had been Massimo Rivelli's mistress, that she was carrying a child he believed to be his, and at the time of the accident she was waiting for her lover to join her at Le Mûrier where they would discuss their plans for the future and the baby. No, Rivelli had never threatened her. He seemed pleased about the baby, and had even hinted that, now he was divorced from his wife, they might be together on a more permanent basis.

Had she been to Le Mûrier before? Yes, many times, she loved it there and regarded it as a second home.

Had Rivelli ever told her anything about when he had it built? Not that she could recall.

Did she have any reason to believe that Massimo Rivelli was a violent man? No, he had always been tender and affectionate with her.

Did she know Joel Warner? Yes, they had been lovers in London. Was she aware that he was gay? Well, she'd had her suspicions.

They let her go, satisfied that she knew nothing. She had not mentioned the rumours that abounded about Rivelli from long before she knew him, the hints that Adele had dropped, the strange, half-boastful remarks that Rivelli made about how he would crush the competition.

She flew back to London and disappeared. Her parents in Hertfordshire were not particularly loving, but at least they would shelter and feed her and keep the outside world at bay. After all, like it or not, they were going to be grandparents too.

Holed up in the bedroom she had barely spent a dozen nights in since leaving home at the age of eighteen, dozing in a single bed, cuddling the same toys she'd cuddled as a child, Victoria weighed up her options.

She knew, of course, that Rivelli had tried to kill her, and, when that failed, had sought to dispose of her in other ways. She had no doubt whatsoever that Christine and the French police had rescued her and her unborn child from certain death. She felt strangely calm about the whole thing. After all, she was not alone. He had tried to kill Will, and burnt down his ex-wife's house; it was only reasonable to assume that she was not going to get off lightly either.

And yet she could not bring herself to turn him in. That would have meant that the last ten years had all been for nothing – that the dream for which she'd sacrificed everything, career, home life, her entire future, had turned out to be a nightmare. She could never have Rivelli now – they would get him for something, with or without her help, and even Victoria would not stoop so low as to run after a man who had tried to murder her. She'd hardened herself to rejection on a small, mundane scale; that was something all mistresses had to do. But attempted homicide was not the sort of thing you could forget for a pair of diamond earrings and a Cavalli evening dress. Murder was hard to forgive.

But if not Rivelli, then who? She could hardly throw herself on her parents' mercy; they were already nervously watching the net curtains, dreading the arrival of unexpected callers to whom they would have to explain Victoria's sudden presence and the increasingly obvious reason for it. Adele? Even if she would take her in for the short term, just to get the lowdown and enjoy another opportunity to gloat, Adele was too closely associated with Rivelli and his world. It was too late for the abortion Adele advised – and, after all, the baby had survived car crashes and morphine injections. She owed it a fighting chance.

Leanne was dead.

And who did that leave? Ben? What if, after all, he was the baby's father? It was just a one-night stand. He was a kid – what, nineteen? twenty? He could hardly provide for her. Of course, his parents were wealthy, and his sister, if she managed to pull herself out of her current difficulties, would be the richest of the lot.

But could Victoria really expect help from a family that she had tried so hard to destroy?

Andy dropped Isabelle at the house, got her case out of the boot, and said 'No, I won't come in, thanks.'

They didn't hug, and he drove away. It was like the last time she'd seen her mother. Had she orphaned herself?

The lights were on; Christine was in.

Isabelle walked up to the door, took a deep breath, and rang the bell.

'Oh.' Christine blinked and rubbed her eyes, which were red and tired. 'It's you.'

'Hi, Mum.'

'You'd better come in.'

'Thanks.'

Christine ducked into the living room, and Isabelle heard her blow her nose. She emerged looking a lot brighter.

'Congratulations!' She kissed Isabelle on both cheeks, lightly resting one hand on her shoulder. She did not hug her.

'Thanks. I came straight here from the airport.'

'So I see.'

'Is that okay?'

'Of course, darling. It's still your home. I've not changed the locks or anything dramatic like that.'

'Good.'

'Cup of tea?'

'Mmmm . . . Is it okay if I . . .'

Shit. I don't want to cry. If she can keep it together, so can I.

'What?'

'If I stay for a few . . .'

No. Deep breath. I've got nothing to reproach myself with.

'Stay for as long as you like. I'll put the kettle on.'

Christine went through to the kitchen. Was this how it would be, then? Coldness, politeness, cups of tea? Too much water under the bridge. Too far out at sea. No way back.

'Mum, I . . .' The tap was running, and Christine couldn't possibly hear. 'I'm so sorry. Sorry for everything.'

She dragged her case upstairs, one bumping step at a time, and by the time she reached the landing she'd worked herself into a right temper. 'I bet Maya Rodean has people to do this sort of thing for her,' she said, quite loud, 'and she hasn't just won a fucking Oscar.'

She sat on her bed for five minutes, and tried to collect her thoughts. When she came down, Christine was sitting at the kitchen table, poring over papers. Two cups of tea were steaming on the granite work surface.

'Sit down.'

'Thanks.'

They sipped tea for a while.

'Are you staying?'

'Can I? I'm sort of rather homeless at the moment.'

'I thought you'd stay with Dad.'

'Not this time.'

More tea.

'Congratulations, by the way. On the Oscars.'

'Oh. Thank you. That's the furthest thing from my mind at the moment.'

'Right.'

She thinks I'm pushing her away again. Why is it always like this?

Isabelle was frowning, her dark eyebrows coming together at a deep vertical line. How soon before she had to resort to Botox?

'How's Will?' You could hear the effort in Christine's voice.

'Not too great actually.'

'No. That's rather what I feared.'

He's dying and I don't know what to do . . .

'I'm so sorry, Isabelle.'

'So am I.'

'I mean, about Will.'

'Oh.'

Now or never.

'I meant about everything.'

The kitchen clock ticked. The phone rang. Christine reached out for it – it might be John with some update. Isabelle drew breath to let out one of her highly articulate sighs – but Christine switched off the telephone and put it in a drawer, buried under tea towels.

Isabelle exhaled.

'Go on. You were saying.'

The moment had rather passed for the big blubbering confession that Isabelle had been on the verge of making. 'Oh, you know. I've been such a pain in the arse recently.'

'Recently?'

Don't do this, Mum . . .

'Well I've been so busy with work, I haven't always had time to be . . . as nice as I might be.'

Who would have thought that this would be so difficult? 'Now you know what it's like, then,' said Christine, looking her daughter straight in the eyes. 'Sometimes, without meaning to, we let work get in the way of the things that really matter.'

'Yes.'

'You see? We have more in common than either of us likes to admit.'

Isabelle held her mother's gaze. 'So it seems.'

Isabelle's phone rang in her pocket. She took it out, saw the name 'Dan Parker', and switched it off.

'I need to talk to you about Dad.'

'Ah.'

'He picked me up at the airport, you know. Gave me a lift.'

'That was thoughtful of him.'

'At your suggestion, I presume.'

'Well, I may have mentioned that it would be a nice gesture.'

'You're still speaking to him, then?'

'I'm not sure that "speaking" is quite the word, but yes, we communicate after a fashion.'

'I don't know why you bother.'

'Because he's the father of my children.'

'Is that the only reason?'

'I thought not. But you were kind enough to set me right on that score.'

'Mum, I didn't mean to . . .'

Christine held her hand up. 'You don't have to say anything. I'd rather not be made a fool of a second time. I should thank you.'

'I didn't want you to be hurt.'

'Really?' Christine fiddled with her mug, running her finger around the handle. 'Do you actually mean that?'

'Yes.'

'Right.'

'I do now, anyway. Mum, I know I've been a bitch.'

'Nobody calls my daughter a bitch.'

'I've wanted to hurt you.'

'Darling, you've succeeded.'

'But sometimes, it seemed like . . . It was the only way I could . . .'

'Isabelle, please don't say it was the only way you could get my attention. I've heard that one in court too many times. Why did you take all those drugs, Mr Bloggs? Why did you feel the need to burn down the house? Why did you beat your wife up? "Because I wanted attention." That doesn't really wash after you're about six years old.'

'Oh, what, then? You think from the age of seven we should just be able to stand on our own two feet? That we don't need you any more?'

'Darling, I don't think you can say that you were in any way neglected. You've always had everything you wanted.'

'But I never had you. You had your work. That came first.'

'And now you know how that feels, Isabelle. And if one day God willing you ever have children then you will know how bloody hard it is. How you can never do the right thing. How you're pulled in ten different directions every hour of every day – your husband, your children, your job, let alone yourself. And what do you get in the end, for all that compromise and self-sacrifice?' She wanted to say 'loneliness and ingratitude', but that sounded too harsh, too final.

'Self-sacrifice? Mum, come on. What have you ever sacrificed?'

'My marriage.'

There didn't seem to be much answer to that, and for once Isabelle had the good sense to keep her mouth shut.

'So,' said Isabelle, after a long, painful silence. 'Looks like you've got a big gig coming up.' She indicated the pile of papers on the kitchen table, covered in highlighter pen and festooned with index tags.

'Yes, I have, actually,' said Christine, shuffling the papers around. It was all to do with Rivelli, but Isabelle didn't need to know that. 'Just in the nick of time, really. The coffers were getting rather empty.'

'Yeah, but you're all right, aren't you? Big fat salary and all that.'

Christine smiled. She was used to explaining this at parties, but had always assumed that her own family would know better. 'Barristers are self employed, darling. No work, no pay.'

'Oh, well . . .'

Really?

'And I haven't really worked for six months.'

'Since . . .'

'Rivelli. Exactly. I rather blotted my copybook with that one.'

'But you're okay now, aren't you?' Isabelle actually sounded worried.

'It seems so. I've done my time in the wilderness. Since then, plenty of other barristers have done even more stupid things. One of my learned friends was recently found to be keeping a large stash of cocaine in his desk drawer. In chambers. The sort of amount that couldn't possibly be for personal use. The type of thing that would land a civilian in jail for quite some time.'

'Wow.'

'You didn't think drug abuse was confined to the fashion world, did you? God, it's like a snowstorm in the Inns sometimes. And then of course we've had the Christmas party season. That usually throws up a few indiscretions. No – I'm old news now. Everyone's forgotten about my little indiscretion.'

'Huh. I wish.'

'Actually, darling, I rather need to talk to you about him.'

'No need. You were right. I should have listened.'

'What do you mean?'

'He's behind what happened to Will. I'm almost certain of it.'

'That's quite an accusation,' said Christine, trying to keep the excitement out of her voice. This was exactly what she'd been hoping for – the final piece of the jigsaw. She didn't want Isabelle to think she was glad – that might sound heartless. 'Do you have any evidence?'

'Not evidence, exactly. But it's Joel.'

'Joel? What, *my* Joel?'

'Everyone's Joel, I'm afraid.' I'd have enjoyed saying that to her once, thought Isabelle. Not now.

'What's he got to do with anything?'

'He's been arrested for the attack on Will.'

'Oh my God. In Los Angeles?'

'He was picked up wandering around the streets covered in blood.'

'Will's blood?'

'Well, I suppose so.'

'And the police think he did it? Joel?'

'Yes.'

'No.' Christine almost shouted. 'He wouldn't. It doesn't fit. He didn't do it.'

'Well, that's exactly what he's saying.'

'And who does he think is behind it?'

'Who do you think?'

'Rivelli.'

'Got it in one.'

'Darling, would you think it awfully rude of me if I made a call? Please don't have a go at me. I want to talk to you. But on this occasion . . .'

Isabelle opened the drawer and retrieved the phone from its nest of tea towels.

'Be my guest.'

In a ward of the Cedars-Sinai Medical Center in Los Angeles, a nurse suddenly looked up from the notes she was reading and rushed to the bedside of a young male patient who had been unconscious for several days. An electronic beeping noise told her that he was going into cardiac arrest.

Chapter 31

A doctor crouched over Will's bed, a stethoscope pressed against his chest. The heartbeat was there, irregular and shallow, and then – boom, boom, boom, it thudded like a horse kicking against stable walls.

It was bad – very bad indeed. It looked like a result of the trauma – a sudden drop in blood volume, possibly due to internal bleeding. The heartbeat stabilised, but it was weak, and Will was getting cold. If his brain wasn't getting enough oxygen, he could suffer permanent damage. They connected him to a ventilator, and watched the monitor like hawks. One more episode like this was likely to be fatal.

'Oh no . . .'

Isabelle's wailing voice carried down the stairs. Christine sprang to her feet; her child was in pain, and she must help her.

'What is it?' She bounded up the stairs two at a time. Isabelle was standing on the landing, the phone at her ear, her face as white as a sheet.

'Okay . . . Okay, I understand . . . Yes . . .'

Christine reached out to her; Isabelle put up a hand, turned away.

'Thanks. Okay. Thanks a lot. I will. Goodbye.'

'What's the matter? What is it?'

'It's Will.'

'Oh no.'

'He's . . . he's had a massive heart attack and . . .'

'Oh darling.'

'They think he's going to die.'

Isabelle went to her mother's arms, rested her head on her shoulder and gave great dry, shaking sobs.

Will arrested again first thing in the morning, and again the doctors brought him back to life.

'He's tough, this one,' said a doctor to a nurse. 'He might just make it.'

But what he'd make it as – a man, a child or a vegetable – was anyone's guess. This was LA, not Vegas, and nobody felt like gambling.

'Darling, you can't let everything go to rack and ruin just because Will is ill.'

'He's a bit more than ill, Mum. He's dying.'

'Don't say that. Come on, you've got to think positive thoughts.'

'Oh, and what what would you suggest?' Isabelle couldn't help lashing out. 'Shall we all get down on our knees and say a prayer?'

'That might not be such a bad idea,' said Christine. It was usually at this point that she withdrew, and left Isabelle to stew in her own bitter juices, but on this occasion she stayed.

'I'm so frightened, Mum,' said Isabelle, after a while. 'I'm supposed to be going to Tokyo next week. Tokyo! I can't face it, not without Will . . . If he . . . I can't manage on my own.'

'You're not on your own, Isabelle,' said Christine, relishing the warmth of her daughter's body in her arms. Horrible as the situation was, and however much she hoped that Will would recover, she could hardly suppress a feeling of euphoria that her child had been delivered back to her.

Victoria's father didn't seem surprised when the police came looking for his daughter. He simply showed the two officers into the front room, where his wife offered them tea, and went upstairs.

'The police are here,' he said, as if he'd been expecting it ever since she darkened his door. 'They want to talk to you about something.'

That something turned out to be the mummified remains of a man that had recently been unearthed beneath the swimming pool of Le Mûrier, Sainte-Maxime, in the south of France. A house belonging to a Mr Massimo Rivelli. Did she know anything about this? Did she have anything to add to statements that she had made to the French police?

She played her cards close to her chest even then, evading their questions, feigning ignorance. Finally, the officers asked her parents to leave the room.

'Were you aware that Massimo Rivelli ordered your removal from the hospital?'

'Yes. He said he was going to look after me.'

'Do you know a man known as David Smith? It's not his real name.'

'Could be anyone.'

'He was the caretaker at Le Mûrier.'

'Oh, that Dave. Yes, of course. I know him well.'

'Did you know what he and his wife were planning to do to you in that private nursing home?'

'No.'

'They were going to kill you.'

Victoria could always think quickly when she was in a tight spot, and so it didn't take her very long to decide what she was going to do.

'I think I'm beginning to remember something about the accident,' she said.

Isabelle got dressed and dabbed some concealer under her eyes. It felt like the first day back at school after the summer holidays – a sense of unreality, as if one world was overlapping with another. Surely she could not work at a time like this? With Will hovering between life and death on the other side of the planet, with her family life turned upside down, her mother alternately hugging her and running to the phone for long, hushed conversations with unknown callers, frantically scribbling notes and lists, scratching around on the internet, producing hot meals and clean clothes out of thin air, like a magician . . . And on top of all this, there was Tokyo Fashion Week to deal with, four days of shows and parties in the Far East, alone and friendless.

She had to pull herself together for a meeting with Walker Parker. She'd ignored their messages for as long as she could, but when she finally heard the words 'meltdown' and 'foreclose' she decided that she owed it to Will to show her face.

She had not been to Hoxton since walking out of the studio in January, never looking back. Not so many weeks ago, really – and yet it seemed as if she was revisiting her remote past, like an old woman returning to the scene of a distant childhood. The buildings looked the same, more or less – something had been knocked down, surely, and that scaffolding never used to be there – and there were the same trees, the same patches of grass, the same grey London skies above it all. But the feeling was different, the people strange, as if the old inhabitants had been swept away, replaced. She looked around for reassurance, for the faces she had known in the past, the hellos and how are yous of those early days of sandwiches in the square. But there was nothing.

'Hello!' Dan appeared at the door as soon as she put her finger on the buzzer, almost as if he'd been looking out for her. 'How are you? You look great.'

'I feel terrible,' said Isabelle, 'but thank you anyway.' He stood a yard away from her, hands hanging awkwardly by his side, wearing a nice crisply ironed blue and white striped shirt, a pair of grey wool trousers, polished black oxfords. His blond hair was neatly cut, his face clean shaven, and he exuded health. 'It's nice to see you, Dan.' It was, too. He was like a breath of fresh air in a sickroom.

'Thanks.' He beamed.

'Come on then,' she said, taking a step towards him, 'give us a kiss.'

They pecked each other on the cheek, and he blushed like a schoolboy.

'Right, let's face the music,' said Isabelle, knowing that Fiona Walker was waiting for her, like a dragon curled round a hoard of bad news.

'It won't be that bad,' said Dan, seeing the look on her face. 'Nothing that can't be sorted.'

'Quite honestly,' said Isabelle, as he opened the door to Fiona's lair, 'I couldn't care less.'

'Ah, Isabelle.' Fiona looked up over her glasses, her metallic red bob swinging on either side of her jaw like curtains. 'Good of you to come in.' She gestured towards chairs. Dan held one out for Isabelle, got her seated. Fiona looked down at the papers on her desk, a headmistress reading over a report card.

'We've been very worried about you, Isabelle,' she said, taking off her glasses.

'Thanks. Things are pretty rough at the moment. Will is . . .'

'In fact, we're pretty much reaching the end of our tether.'

'Ah.'

'We're very seriously out of pocket on the Cissé account.'

'You're not the only one,' said Isabelle, with a touch of levity that she instantly regretted.

I can't do it alone . . .

'And I wondered if you could tell us when we might expect to be paid?'

'The thing is, we're still waiting for money from Rivelli.'

'That's not our problem,' said Fiona, and Dan shifted uneasily in his seat. 'I warned you about Rivelli, but you wouldn't listen. He's done this to so many people. He's put better people than you out of business.'

This was getting personal, and Isabelle did not trust herself to speak.

'That money is being pursued through the courts, I believe,' said Dan. 'We can hardly expect them to pay us while that's going on.'

Isabelle glanced up, and saw Fiona's gorgon gaze turning on her business partner. 'Dan,' she said, 'could you get the Cissé file for me, please?'

'I've got it right here,' said Dan, not budging.

Fiona breathed deeply, but did not blush. Isabelle imagined that, if she did, it would be a greenish colour.

'We are in a very awkward position,' said Fiona. 'We have a relationship with our key retail clients, and if we can't fulfil our obligations to them then we have to take steps to repair that situation.'

'I know that, but the thing is, Will . . .'

'Just this morning, I've had Debenhams on the phone, asking where the new Cissé stuff is. I didn't know what to tell them. Do you have any suggestions?'

'No, I'm sorry, but while . . .'

Dan interrupted. 'How about reminding them that a Cissé dress just featured at the Oscars and they should be rethinking their pricing structure for next season?'

Fiona took a long, slow drink of water. Isabelle watched the rim of the glass in case ice crystals started forming.

'And you've put me in a very awkward position with Browns. They've paid for stock that has not arrived. They're asking us for their money back.'

Isabelle looked from Fiona to Dan, and shrugged. She picked up her handbag. 'I don't know what to say.'

'I need some answers, Isabelle.'

'And I don't have any for you.' Her voice wavered, and she swallowed. 'I'm sorry. You'll have to wait.'

'I can't wait.'

'Then I don't bloody care.' She could feel snot pooling at the back of her nose, and had to swallow. 'I'd better go.' She stood up, but Dan put a hand on her shoulder.

'No. Don't go. I've got some answers, Fiona. For Debenhams, for Browns, for anyone else who asks, and for you, for that matter.'

Isabelle sat down. Fiona stood up. Isabelle wanted to giggle.

Fiona said 'Dan.'

'I think you should get right back on the phone and tell those clients just how bloody lucky they are to have a deal with the most important young designer of her generation. A woman who got a dress at the Oscars within two years of leaving college. A woman who is about to headline at Tokyo Fashion Week and has been offered a job at Givenchy. And you should tell them that if they're not happy to wait a little while until these financial difficulties are sorted out, we'd be quite happy to take the Cissé account elsewhere.'

Fiona folded her arms, as if she was waiting for a naughty subordinate to finish having his say. 'Oh would we, indeed?'

'Yes, Fiona,' said Dan. 'And I would remind you that this company is called Walker Parker. Not just Walker. If you ever feel the need to threaten our clients in the future, I'd be grateful if you'd consult me first.'

Isabelle realised that her mouth was hanging open, and shut it.

'Right,' said Fiona. 'Well, I don't think there's any point in continuing this discussion at present.'

'No,' said Dan. 'You're damn right there.' He held the door open, then followed Isabelle through it. 'Lunch?' he said, still sounding angry.

'It's only just gone eleven o'clock.'

'All right. Call it brunch. Come on.' He grabbed his coat. 'As long as they serve alcohol.'

She stopped him before he left the building, and laid a hand on his arm.

'Why did you do that, Dan?'

'Because she drives me round the bloody bend.'

'Right.'

'And because I happen to believe that you're the best designer in the business and we should be bending over backwards to keep you sweet.'

'Well . . . thanks. But I don't want you to . . .'

'And of course there's one other reason, but you don't want to hear about that.' He laughed noiselessly, shrugged, settling his coat over his broad shoulders.

'Come on,' she said. 'They're supposed to do a bloody good Bloody Mary at the Hoxton Grille. My treat.'

'No, I . . .'

'After that performance, it's the least I can do.' She marched on to the street, and beckoned him along. He followed her at a brisk trot, like an eager Labrador puppy.

Rocky Rodean had been the nation's darling for nearly forty years. The fans had followed him through disappointing albums, flop musicals and a string of failed marriages, and still they adored him. They tutted over his messy love life, his failed marriages, but they turned up for his concerts. There was even enough residual affection for him to sustain his daughter's fashion career, and to steer her to the safe haven of a job with one of the big Paris couture houses. But all these things were peripheral to the basic fact that Rocky Rodean had been a presence in people's lives for so long that, like Cliff Richard and the Queen, it was impossible to imagine life without him. To hate Rocky Rodean would be like hating your own childhood.

Representing Rocky's wives in the divorce courts was not an easy gig, as several barristers knew to their cost. Even if you won, and got the wife *du jour* what she wanted, you'd be jeered and booed outside the courts by armies of fans. On one occasion, eggs had been thrown. Christine did not want to be pelted with eggs, but beyond that she didn't really care if the nation hated her or loved her. When John Ferguson asked her, over lunch, if she felt ready to get back to work and offered her the Jessica Rodean brief, she did not hesitate to say yes.

After a couple of Bloody Marys, Isabelle threw caution to the winds and started doing Fiona Walker impersonations. Dan nearly expelled tomato juice through his nose, and started coughing violently instead, until his eyes watered and the veins stood out in his neck and forehead. Isabelle patted him on the back. When he'd finished coughing, she continued patting.

'Thanks,' he said, wiping his eyes and blowing his nose.

'My pleasure.'

Food arrived – two full fry-ups. Isabelle needed both hands for that.

'I'm starving,' she said. 'It feels awful to be sitting here drinking and eating and having a lovely time while Will's lying in hospital.' Her knife and fork hovered above her plate. 'But I need to eat.'

'What's wrong with him?'

She told him.

'You're very fond of Will, aren't you?'

'Yes,' said Isabelle, mouth full of bacon. 'I don't think I can do this without him.'

'Right.'

Dan sipped his drink.

'You should be with him.'

'I know. But . . .' She gestured helplessly with her cutlery. 'What can I do?'

'Get on the first plane to LA and stay there until he's better.'

'He might never get better.'

'He needs you, Isabelle, and you need to be there. You're not doing yourself any favours by being here.'

'Cheers.'

'I don't mean it like that. Don't worry about Fiona, I can take care of her. And if she doesn't like it, she can lump it. We've outgrown each other. It's about time we . . . well, you know. I need to do a lot of thinking.'

'Not because of this. Not because of me.'

'Not just that, no.' Dan thoughtfully stabbed his egg yolk with a bit of sausage. 'But I don't want to talk about Fiona. I want to talk about you.'

'Okay,' said Isabelle, suddenly afraid he was going to make a declaration. Well, let's get it over, she thought, like a woman at the dentist's.

'Go to LA. Look after Will.'

'But Tokyo . . .'

'Don't worry about Tokyo. I'm going anyway. If you can make it, there are plenty of flights from LA. If not, I'll take care of business for you.'

Isabelle said nothing.

'Don't you trust me?'

'Of course I trust you, Dan. You're about the only person in the world I do trust. But I just don't understand why you would do all this. You're risking your job, you're pissing off your clients, you're staking everything on Cissé when you know perfectly well that in six months' time there might not even be a Cissé. Why would you do that?'

I know why.

He put down his knife and fork.

'Because I love you,' he said, very simply. 'I always have, from the very first time I met you.'

Isabelle's hand flew to her mouth; she couldn't help it.

'Sorry,' said Dan. 'I didn't mean to say that. But now you know.'

Massimo Rivelli saw himself as a horse – a magnificent Arab stallion, in fact – upon which a host of parasites was feeding. There were fleas and flies and mosquitoes, worms and ticks and burrowing larvae, there were little birds pecking at his skin and his ears, and there were beetles crawling in his wake to eat his shit. Every so often he would whisk his tail or toss his mane, stamp his hooves or kick with his hind legs, to drive them away. If necessary, he could bite. But whatever he did, the army of parasites got bigger, fattening on his resources, inviting their friends to the feast. How soon before it would be dogs and jackals and vultures that were feeding on him? How much longer could he keep going?

Massimo Rivelli also saw himself as a hero, one of the ancient sons of Gods who fought against monsters and won. He was Jason battling the Hydra – and every time he chopped off one head, another grew to take its place. He was Perseus slaying Medusa, he was Theseus in the labyrinth, he was Hercules cleaning the Augean stable. What he lacked in formal education, Rivelli made up for with an exaggerated sense of self-importance.

He would make a fresh start in the East – like Alexander the Great, another of his personal favourites. There were opportunities in the East. Offers had been made – not quite as respectable as the work he had been doing in Europe, but just as lucrative. Dropping the fashion front would be a relief. He could focus on the core business: drug smuggling, people trafficking and, when necessary, a spot of contract killing.

But making a fresh start in a new town cost money, and money was the one thing Rivelli did not have. His assets were frozen, pending tiresome legal processes in three countries, and his trusted lieutenants had turned against him. They would regret that. What Rivelli needed right now was a lump sum, and quickly.

What Rivelli needed was a desperate multi-millionaire.

What Rivelli needed was Rocky Rodean.

And what better way of getting to Rocky Rodean than through his daughter, Maya – who, conveniently, was just about to arrive in town for Tokyo Fashion Week.

Rodean v Rodean was a gift to the press, who unanimously sided with Rocky and deployed their vast investigative power to dig up old photographs of Jessica doing something suggestive with a baguette at a party in 1994. This proved she was a slut and should be burnt at the stake.

It was a gift to Maya Rodean, who surfed a fresh wave of publicity just as she was launching her new collection for Laruche. She made herself available for quotes and photo opps, and always insisted that she was credited as 'designer daughter Maya'. She travelled to Tokyo on a tsunami of publicity, determined to make the most of her father's personal unhappiness.

It was even a gift to Jessica who, though far from confident that she'd get the ridiculously high sum that she was asking for, had already secured an extremely lucrative book deal and was lining up celeb reality shows over the next four or five years.

In a quieter way, it was a gift to Christine and John. Of course, they were both pleased on a professional level to be working on the biggest divorce case of the year, even if they were on the 'wrong' side, the wife's side. But it was just the sort of challenge they both relished – and, as Christine reflected, it was her opportunity to wipe out all memories of the Rivelli fiasco and get back on course for silk. But it was welcome in another way too; it gave Christine and John yet another excuse to spend a great deal of time together without having to analyse too closely the reasons why. He was freshly widowed, she was divorced but not disentangled from Andy – of course neither of them was looking for any new romantic entanglement. This was just two old friends and colleagues working together in the way they knew best, the old team back together, with something to prove this time – yes, that was what put the fire in their bellies and the colour in their cheeks every time they met. It was like being young and hungry again. It was exciting.

They both kept an eye on developments in the Rivelli case, but now it was out of their hands. Police authorities in America, France and the UK were making their investigations, and Rivelli had gone to ground, leaving a trail of devastation in his wake. Will was out for the count in Los Angeles, hovering on the brink of death. Janet was camping out in the parts of her house that had not been damaged by fire, still claiming that it was an accident, presumably so scared of her ex-husband that she did not dare to mention the most obvious explanation. Victoria, who had somehow survived the crash that killed Leanne Miller, was out of Christine's reach – and her due date was approaching. Isabelle's future hung in the balance, seemingly ready to topple like a house of cards.

So why did Christine feel so positive about the future?

Victoria sat in her bedroom, her ears ringing, her eyes staring blindly at cracks in the ceiling.

Rivelli had tried to kill her.

The police had evidence.

Nothing she could say or do would change that, no amount of plotting or scheming would alter the fact that the hopes and fears of the last ten years had amounted to this, a botched attempt on her life by a man who cared for nothing and no one other than himself.

Well, two can play at that game. And so she'd talked – told them everything she knew or suspected, and when that wasn't enough to satisfy her, she invented some more. By the time the police left, they had enough on Massimo Rivelli for several life sentences.

She felt the baby kicking inside her womb. Rivelli's child? A part of him, still living inside her, when everything else had died? It could not be. She would not let it be. If it's his, she thought, I will use it against him. I will do whatever I can to hurt him, through the part of himself that he has left in me. I will make him sorry that he ever came near me with that goddamned pepper grinder.

And then suddenly she remembered the warmth of the Provençal sun, the taste of *aïoli* and *bourride*, the tang of salt water on her skin, the feeling of Massimo moving inside her, and all that had sparkled and shone in her life for so long, everything that gave her pleasure and status and self respect, poured out of her in a torrent of tears and cries and bitter, empty retching.

Her parents, sitting downstairs reading their newspapers, heard their daughter's agony, looked to the ceiling, sighed, and looked back at their papers.

'Don't say anything now,' said Dan. 'Ignore me. Go to LA, look after Will, and maybe I'll see you in Japan. Sorry. I didn't mean to blurt it out like that. This is the last thing you need.'

'No,' said Isabelle, 'I'm glad you did. And I'm flattered, I really am.'

'Oh God,' said Dan, smiling joylessly. 'The brush-off.'

'I don't know what to say. I can't think straight. Must be the Bloody Marys.'

'Yeah,' said Dan, 'must be. Fancy another? I think I do.'

'No, better not.'

The mood had deflated like a burst balloon. They looked at their empty plates.

Isabelle's phone rang. She jumped up and ran from the restaurant. Dan watched her through the window, pacing up and down on the other side of the thick plate glass. He played with a bit of bacon rind, drawing aimless tracks in the egg yolk on his plate, wondering why he kept on coming back for more from a woman who would surely never care for him in the way that she cared for Will.

She ran back in, her face glowing.

I wish I could make her look like that.

'It's Will,' she said, her voice higher than usual. 'He's awake. He's come round.' She sat down and buried her face in her hands. 'He's going to be okay.'

* * *

The police were ready to talk to Will as soon as the doctors were content that he was in no immediate danger of arresting again.

'Do you remember anything, Mr Francis? Anything at all?'

Will stared at his hands, counting his fingers as if he had never seen them before. His face was still badly bruised. It was hard to tell what, if anything, was going through his mind.

The doctors had told the police that he might not remember much. He might have short-term amnesia. It might be worse than that. He might have brain damage.

'Will? Can you hear me?'

Will turned his head, very slowly, his mouth hanging slightly open, his lips dry. The police officer watched him working his jaw, like an old woman chewing on nothing. It was hopeless. The guy was a vegetable.

Will's hand fluttered on the covers, gesturing to the side of the bed.

'Hey, nurse,' said the policeman. 'He wants something.'

The fingers came up to the mouth.

'Water,' said the nurse. 'He wants water. He's asking for it.'

Christ, thought the cop, he's like an infant. This is horrible.

The nurse held the water to Will's lips, and he drank, his throat jumping, water running down his chin. He sighed, and licked his lips.

'As a matter of fact,' he said, in a voice woozier and fainter than normal, 'it's all starting to come back to me.'

Chapter 32

Andy had not seen Christine since he got back to England. He knew that she knew, that his daughter had grassed on him — why else was Christine not calling? When they said farewell, she'd been keen, affectionate, demonstrative, much more so than she had been during their marriage. Well, if she wanted him back that much, why not? It was ridiculous, this charade of a divorce, with separate establishments to maintain, seeing the kids on his own. Christine was so much better at all that stuff than he was. Andy wanted nothing more than to get back to normal with Christine, to come home, to pick up where they left off.

But now, the phone wasn't ringing, and there could only be one explanation for that. Isabelle — whom Andy always assumed was on his side — had let the cat out of the bag. And she was quite a cat, his Rosa, whom he'd been seeing for about six months and hoped to get at least another year out of. It was so much easier conducting these affairs without needing to lie. No more 'I'm going to leave my wife', no more sneaking around in hotels and empty flats. But it was also a lot less fun. Women tended to be more demanding if they knew you were actually single. They put up with all sorts of crap if you were unhappily married; single men, however, were expected to toe the line. And without the frisson of concealment, affairs became relationships. Andy wasn't too sure he wanted relationships. He had Christine for that.

Easter came and went, and still no call. If Ben had been home, he hadn't bothered to contact his father; presumably Christine had poisoned his mind against him. Isabelle was back in Los Angeles — out of harm's way, at least. Best place for her. Reluctant as Andy was to face the music, he had to have one more crack at Christine, and if the children were out of the way, so much the better. He hoped she was still in the professional doldrums, as she had been during their recent reunion; she'd be more likely to welcome his return, particularly as he'd just pulled off another huge deal in Dubai for a large leisure complex on what was once a piece of unique natural habitat. He'd cover the place with green balconies and terraces, plant trees on the roof – that would make up for it. He was flush with money. Christine would be a fool to turn him down. So what if he'd taken a lover while they were living apart? She'd done the same. He could throw that in her face. They could hurl accusations, then decide to put the past behind them, make a new start, officially this time. Tell the kids properly. Daddy's home.

If Will had died, the police would have constructed a neat case against Joel Warner who, at the time of his arrest, was covered in Will's blood, off his head on crystal meth and in possession of enough drugs to supply most of the West Hollywood area for an entire weekend. He had burn marks and bruises on his body – it looked like a routine gay murder, an open and shut case. It wouldn't take much to blow Joel's ridiculous babblings about some guy called Ravioli right out of the pool.

But now Will had come round, and the picture had changed. Sadly for the LAPD's conviction record, it wasn't kinky sex games gone too far that Will started to remember. It was a fragmented narrative, coming out in small vivid unconnected pieces, about leaving a pool party, going on to a club and being picked up by a group of men who took them back to a chill-out at an apartment up in Laurel Canyon. And that's where things had started to go badly wrong.

The baby was due in June – three months to go. Victoria couldn't stay with her parents a moment longer; their silent disapproval was becoming toxic. As a last resort, she threw herself on Adele's mercy. She had nowhere left to run.

Adele treated Victoria like a piece of fragile porcelain, forcing her to rest as much as possible, discouraging her from doing anything for herself, let alone going out of the house. 'You nearly lost it once in France, again in London,' she said. 'You may not be so lucky a third time.' It was not in Adele's nature to be broody, although she had a son herself – but she was great believer in the value of children as investments. Adele, who had counselled Victoria for years to dump Rivelli and find herself a richer, older, easier-to-manage boyfriend, was now staking everything on this child's magical ability to transform its supposed father from commitment-avoiding cad to conscientious provider. And if Rivelli needed a little legal persuasion, the baby was the best leverage money could buy.

'But he's not going to be much use to me if he's behind bars, darling,' said Victoria. 'He's a wanted man in at least three countries. I can't really see myself dragging a child along on prison visits.'

'Rivelli has been in trouble before,' said Adele. 'He always comes up smelling of roses.'

'Not this time.'

'What happened, Victoria? I thought you loved him. Now it seems you are determined to betray him.'

'Attempted murder has a way of taking the bloom off the romance,' said Victoria. 'Besides, I'm not at all sure that I need him any more.'

'Darling,' chortled Adele in a particularly dismissive way, 'don't think for one moment that you can make it on your own. A child needs a father.'

'Hugo did all right without one.'

'Hugo's father took care of us very nicely. And he still does.'

'Yes. Because you gave him no choice.'

'Well? He understands responsibility. So will Rivelli.'

'Quite apart from the fact that I'm not at all sure that it is Rivelli's child . . . No, don't interrupt. I don't want that man to have anything to do with it. He's a crook, Adele. A murderer.'

'You always knew he was a rogue.'

'A rogue? I think he's a little more than that. He tried to kill me.'

'So – he will pay all the more.'

'Your reasoning is insane, Adele.'

'Darling.' Adele waved her hands around as if Victoria had just farted. 'It is all part of the game.'

'I don't want to play any more,' said Victoria. 'I want things to be normal.'

'You, Victoria? You will never be normal. A little mother at home, with a daddy and a baby? Who's the lucky man? Not your little stud from the party. Oh, that is good.' Adele laughed, throwing her head back, showing expensive dentistry.

Victoria said nothing. Adele was right: the idea of involving Ben was ridiculous. Besides, she was living on Adele's generosity. She couldn't afford to piss her off. Where else would she go?

So she just laughed along with Adele, put her feet up on the sofa and settled herself to sleep.

Adele left her to it.

Victoria closed her eyes, and tried to picture herself and Ben – whose face she could barely remember – living together, bringing up baby, celebrating birthdays and Christmas. It was hard to make out, like figures seen in a mist.

And then she saw Rivelli, close up, in sharp focus, his brown body, his grey hair and blue eyes, his huge square strangler's hands. She shuddered, and the baby stirred.

'Don't worry, my darling,' she said, smoothing her stomach with circular motions of her hands, 'he can't get us.'

When Isabelle arrived at Cedars-Sinai after a long flight and a nightmare of misplaced reservations at the hotel (Mike was out of town – and she wasn't so sure about Mike any more), she found Will sitting up in bed flanked by two police officers, one in uniform, the other plainclothes, who looked as if they had just stepped off the set of a glossy daytime soap.

'Well, you've got everything you need, I see,' she said, kissing him on the forehead. The last time she'd seen him he was as good as dead. Now he was Will again – still bruised, still scarred, but alive, wonderfully, undeniably alive. She wanted to hold him, to squeeze him, to bury her face in his armpit and scream out all the rage and fear and sadness that she'd been through in the last weeks. But he didn't look quite up to that.

'Yes, they're treating me quite well,' said Will, his voice slightly slurred. A tooth at the front was broken. 'At the moment I'm being interrogated. I rather like it. Care to join us?'

'Sir,' said the uniform – dark hair, immaculate sideburns, square jaw – 'you sure about that?'

'Oh God, yes,' said Will. 'She knows the worst, and what she doesn't know she's guessed. She's not my wife or anything.'

Isabelle sat at the foot of the bed. 'Don't mind me,' she said. 'I'll just sit and look at him.'

'Do something useful, like designing some new uniforms for the poor nurses,' said Will. 'They look terribly dowdy. Internationally known award-winning designer, you know,' he said to the cops. 'Now, where were we?'

'At a party in Laurel Canyon,' said plainclothes, a blond edition of his uniformed colleague. 'You had just taken something in the bathroom.'

'Oh Will.'

'No interruptions from the stalls, please. Yes. That's right. We were with this bloke that Joel had picked up with – what the hell was his name? He's a film director. Porn. A foreign accent. Swarthy looking guy, plucked eyebrows, shiny Botox face, and those ridiculous jaw muscles you get from taking steroids. What the hell was his name?'

'Carry on, Will. It'll come to you.'

'Anyway, him, I want to say the Russian. That's it. Ivan. I remember thinking how suitable it was, because darling, he was *terrible*. He was all over Joel, treating him like a possession, then constantly asking me if I minded.'

'And did you? Were you jealous?'

'Yes. A bit. But I was more . . . how can I put it? Repulsed.'

'Did you fight?'

'No, no. Not in my nature, is it, Princess? I'm more the put-up-and-shut-up type, then I slag them off behind their backs. Anyway, we all ended up in the loo – sorry, the bathroom – me and Joel and Ivan the Terrible, and these two big hunky guys who seemed to know Ivan, I assumed they were, you know, actors. They looked the type.'

'Had you seen them before?'

'Possibly on an adult website.'

'Were they at the pool party?'

'Difficult to say,' said Will. 'They all look the same. Bald heads, big muscles, thick necks, tribal tattoos. I mean, they're ten a penny out here, aren't they?'

'And what happened?'

'Well, we took something.'

'What?'

'I think he said it was coke.'

'You inhaled it?'

'Yes. I don't do anything else. Oh dear, that probably makes me sound like a habitual drug user. What I mean is I never drink funny liquids in bottles and I never inject or smoke.'

'How did it make you feel?'

' A bit like pre-med. I don't remember much. I have a vague impression that we all started having sex.'

'Where? In the bathroom?'

'Well we can't have done, can we? There wouldn't have been room. I have an image of being in a bed somewhere, with those two . . .'

'The bald guys?'

'Yes. It all seemed terribly exciting at the time, rather like watching a movie. I wasn't sure if I was really there or not. Sorry.'

'What about Joel and the other one, Ivan? Were they there?'

'I just don't know.'

'Okay. You were having sex with two tattooed hunks,' said the blond plain-clothes man.

'Yes. Lucky me.'

'What next?'

'That's it. Fade to black.'

'What about Joel?'

'I don't think he was . . . I don't know. I have a very vague recollection of him bending over me, but it's more like a dream.'

'What was he doing?'

'Crying.'

'Crying?'

'Look, this could all be bullshit, but I have this image of his face with tears running down the cheeks. And there was light behind him – a very dim grey sort of light. It was very peaceful, and I remember thinking how beautiful he was. I mean, he is. He's very beautiful. Well, I think so, anyway.'

'Did he say anything?'

'I'm not sure. He might have said "Sorry," I suppose.'

'Sorry?'

'Yes. I'm almost sure he said sorry. And I reached up to touch his face, and I wanted to tell him how beautiful he was, but my fingers seemed to go right through him, as if he wasn't there at all, just like a hologram or something. And that's the end of that. The next thing I remember was waking up in here.'

'Thank you, Will,' said the blond cop. 'That's enough for now.'

'What's going to happen?' asked Isabelle.

'We're going to have another little chat with Joel.'

'Send him my best,' said Will. 'I do hope he didn't try to murder me. I'm really quite fond of him.'

They had just finished dinner, and were about to do a spot of Rodean casework, when Andy turned up unannounced. John answered the door; Christine was in the kitchen clearing up.

'Hi Andy. Long time no see.'

'Hello, John.' They shook.

'I'm just leaving, actually. We've been burning the midnight oil.'

'So I see,' said Andy, surveying the empty wine bottle, the remains of the meal. 'Well, good to see you.'

'Don't rush off,' said Christine, stabbing the corkscrew into another cork. 'Have another drink.'

'No, really, I don't think I'd better. Busy day tomorrow. Can't have a hangover.'

'Okay. Well, thanks for everything, John.'

'My pleasure.' He put his coat on. 'We'll get there in the end, Christine.'

'I do hope so.'

They kissed in the hallway, and he was gone.

'Get where, exactly?' asked Andy, when she was pouring the wine. 'You and John. What's all that about?'

'Big case, you know,' said Christine. 'All very messy and complicated.'

'It looks it.'

'So,' said Christine, handing him a glass. 'To what do I owe the pleasure?'

'Well, if Mohammed won't come to the mountain . . . Cheers.'

'Cheers.'

'I was beginning to wonder if you ever wanted to see me again.' He had a wounded note in his voice, hoping this would arouse her pity.

'Funny that,' said Christine. 'I was beginning to wonder exactly the same thing.'

'I'll always care about you, Chris. You know that.'

'That's not what I meant, really.' She took a big swig of wine. 'It was more a question of whether I ever wanted to see you again.'

'Well, here I am. How does it feel?' He leaned towards her, took her hand. She withdrew it.

'It's funny,' said Christine, gently withdrawing. 'Now that it comes to it, I don't have anything to say.'

'Good. We've talked enough. How about you and me . . .'

'Although I suppose there is just one thing.'

'Yeah?' His voice was deep and thick. 'Say it.'

'Get out.'

His face froze for a moment in that expression of lustful charm she knew so well, and then the brows contracted.

'I beg your pardon?'

'I think that pretty much sums up what I want to say to you at this particular point in time.' She scanned the ceiling, as if she might find something to add. 'No. That says it all.'

'What's going on, Chris? Are you and John . . .'

'It's a bit late in the day to act the jealous husband, Andy.'

'I thought you and I were . . . you know. Back on.'

'So did I.'

He brooded into his wine. 'Look, I don't know what Isabelle's told you, but . . .'

'It's okay, darling.' She patted his arm. 'You don't have to say anything. Let's just call it a day, eh? No hard feelings. Time to move on. It's been fun.'

'Is that all you've got to say? It's been fun? Is that all this means to you?' He stood up and turned his back to her.

'No, Andy. That's not all. You meant everything to me – everything in the world, more than the children, more than my job, more than all of this.' She gestured around the kitchen, the house, the garden, the world beyond.

'So why can't we be like we were? Come on, Chris. I want it. You want it.'

'Because you killed it, Andy.' The mask slipped, and her voice was harsh and ragged. 'You stole my past. I'm not giving you my future.'

He turned to face her, seeing in a flash the next forty years of their lives together, all that could have been, growing old and watching the children and the grandchildren grow up, taking care of each other and loving each other more with every new year of memories between them. And then the vision disappeared like smoke, and there was Christine's agonised face and two half-drunk glasses of wine glowing like little suns under the halogen spotlights.

He could think of nothing to say, and left without finishing his drink.

Maya was never alone. She went nowhere without an entourage, and while most of them looked as if they could be knocked down by a gust of wind, they were potential witnesses, and thus a nuisance. Rivelli wasted no time in making useful acquaintances in Tokyo – drivers, warehouse owners, bribable cops – and had the plan perfectly in place when Miss Rodean's fashionably shod foot touched the tarmac at Narita International. He would kidnap her, call Rocky Rodean's people with a ransom demand, and if the money was not instantly forthcoming he would release online video of Maya's fingers being chopped off. She would never sew again.

All he needed now was the opportunity, and he spent several hours going over the Tokyo Fashion Week schedule, looking for a moment when Maya might be vulnerable. At last, he found what he needed.

The Los Angeles police picked up Ivan without much trouble; he was a well known man about town. They had enough on him to put him away for five, maybe ten years – but there were worse crimes in LA than small-time drug dealing and brothel keeping. Why bust him? He was a popular and successful adult movie star-turned-producer. His face was on billboards in some of the less family-oriented districts. He paid his taxes, contributed to AIDS charities and appeared on cable TV. In his own small way, Ivan was a celebrity, and celebrities could get away with more than civilians.

But not murder.

It didn't take long to persuade Ivan that it would be in his interests to tell the police who had arranged for Will to be brought to a certain club at a certain time, to be given certain drugs and introduced to certain people with secluded apartments in Laurel Canyon. They spelt out the consequences if Ivan chose to keep this information to himself: arrest, ruin and probable incarceration. Prison, they said, was not quite how he had portrayed it in his movies.

And so he told them about how one of his investors had made him an offer he could not refuse – enough money to open his own studio, maybe his own store, in return for certain services, which he had provided.

No, the money had still not been forthcoming.

And the name of this welcher?

Massimo Rivelli.

'You don't think that you might be going a bit too far on this one, Jessica? It's not that I don't believe you. It's just that I'm not sure that that judge will.'

'I'm telling you, he hit me.'

'Just once,' said Christine, 'or regularly?'

'A few times.'

'In anger?'

'Yes, of course in anger.'

'When you were arguing?'

'Yes. I mean, he didn't just walk in one day and start beating me up.'

'What were you fighting about?'

'That's none of your business.'

Christine took off her glasses and sighed. Here we are again, she thought. Another vindictive spouse spewing bile all over the court-room. Jessica maintained that Rocky Rodean, the nation's favourite uncle, was a wife-beating thug.

'If we're going to win this case,' said Christine, 'we have to give the overwhelming impression that you are in the right. Do you understand me? If the judge thinks that Rocky raised a hand against you with good reason . . .'

'What? How dare you? How could there ever be a good reason to hit me?'

I can think of several.

'Then he's not going to be swayed by some unsubstantiated allegation of domestic violence.'

'What do you mean, unsubstantiated? I took photographs.'

'Which is good, well done,' said Christine, thinking what a disgusting life Jessica and Rocky must have had together. 'But I still need to know why he did it. What was the argument about?'

'I'd rather not say.'

'Okay,' said Christine. 'Let's take a look at the newspapers, shall we? Mr Rodean alleges that you had been having an affair behind his back . . .'

'That's a lie!'

'That this wasn't the first time . . .'

'It's not true.'

'And that he lost his temper and slapped your face. Is that what happened?'

'No it's not. I'll tell you what we were really arguing about. His bitch of a daughter.'

'Maya?'

'Yes. She's hated me from the moment I married Rocky. She's done everything possible to poison his mind against me. And this time, she went too far. She told him I'd been screwing around behind his back. I swear to God I wasn't. I may be a dumb blonde, but I'm not stupid. I know which side my bread's buttered on. I flirt with people, who doesn't? But I was never unfaithful to Rocky. Not once.'

'Right.'

'Unlike him.'

'What?'

'I said, unlike him. Rocky can't keep it in his pants. Never could. Ask his ex-wife – the one before me, I mean. Nobody turns him down, from sixteen to sixty.'

'Sixteen? Did he really . . . I mean, are you just saying that, or were there . . . younger girlfriends?'

'You bet there were.'

'And you're prepared to tell the court that?'

'Why not? I've got nothing to lose.'

'And do you happen to know who any of them are?'

'Well, there was one little tart who appeared in one of his videos. She can't have been much over sixteen.'

'Find her,' said Christine. 'Let's see what she remembers. That might turn out to be a very expensive mistake on Mr Rodean's part.'

* * *

'So what are you going to do, Princess? Are you going to take the Givenchy job?'

'I don't know. It's a lot to think about.'

'I think you should do it.'

'But . . . Everything we built up . . .'

'Got you to this stage. Job done. Onwards and upwards.'

'But Will . . . what about you?'

Will was sitting up in an armchair, looking out the window across the LA twilight. Hundreds, thousands, millions of lights twinkled down there, brighter and sharper as the sky turned from blue to pink to grey to black.

'Oh, I'll be all right. As soon as I'm up and about again, I'll get on the phone and see what's on offer. People were always trying to poach me off you before. Maya Rodean, for instance.'

'Oh Christ Will, you wouldn't?'

'I don't know. Might be fun. You take the job at Givenchy and I'll get a job with Maya at Laruche, both of us in Paris. We could share an apartment in St Germain des Près and have bitchy lunches at Pierre Gagnaire. Lovely.'

'Don't be silly. If you're moving to Paris, you'll come and work with me.'

'Or I might go and work for Mercy Williams. She loves me.' He gestured towards a huge construction of white orchids. 'She sends me flowers. You don't.' He stuck his bottom lip out; it was still cut and discoloured, and it obviously hurt. He swore, touched it with his fingertips.

'I haven't said yes yet.'

'Oh come on, darling, the money they're offering . . .'

'I'm scared. That's the bottom line. Scared of going to Tokyo tomorrow, scared of the press and the agents and the journalists. I need you, Will. I want to stay here.'

'Not on your Nelly. You bugger off to Tokyo and knock 'em dead. I'm fine, or at least I will be.'

'It feels like the end, Will.'

'It's the end of one story, Princess, and the beginning of another. Even more fabulous, and even more exciting.'

'And we all live happily ever after?'

'I'd settle for living, period, thanks very much.'

'We never did find our Prince Charmings, did we?'

'Oh, I don't know. Tomorrow is another day. And you know what? I think if you were to call a certain person in London, he might just be ready with the glass slipper.'

'I don't know what you're talking about,' said Isabelle. But she did.

Chapter 33

'So where is he?'

'Your guess is as good as mine,' said John. 'He could be anywhere. There are plenty of places in the world where a man like Rivelli can just disappear.'

Christine shuddered. 'I'd feel a lot happier and safer if I knew where he was. Every time the doorbell rings, I jump out of my skin. Every time the phone rings I think it's going to be the police telling me that Isabelle's had an accident, or Victoria saying that she's lost the baby.'

They were walking along the Strand, on their way to another conference with Jessica Rodean. Christine was nervous and distracted. John put an arm round her shoulder and squeezed her close. 'Calm down. You can be sure of one thing – he won't show his face in this country, or in America. He's made things too hot for himself. My money's on some nasty little rathole in Asia.'

Christine felt comforted. John was tall, his arms were strong, and he knew her better than almost anyone. He knew all her mistakes – and he still believed in her enough to brief her in *Rodean v Rodean*.

'The last year has been so stormy,' she said, blowing her nose before they entered the lobby of Ferguson McCreath. 'I do hope we're in for some rather more settled weather.'

'Spring is just around the corner. Come on. Let's see what madam has dredged up for us today. Some of this mud has got to stick.'

Christine looked into John's kind blue eyes, straightened her skirt and focused on demolishing Rocky Rodean.

Dan Parker was by nature a cautious man. It took a lot for him to speak his mind; he always thought of the consequences of every word and action, and often, as a result, let life pass him by. That moment of spontaneous emotion in the Hoxton Grille had plagued him with remorse and embarrassment all the way from London to Tokyo; he blushed when he thought about it, even when there was no one around, even when he was alone in bed at night, high above the city in his single hotel room. Being cautious could be a curse; any chance he may have had with Isabelle had surely long since evaporated, now that she was an international design star with a rock 'n' roll boyfriend.

But being cautious had its advantages as well. He made sure that every single piece of Cissé business for Tokyo Fashion Week was properly organised, whether Isabelle herself turned up or not. Then he made double sure. He made two itineraries – one for if she arrived, one for if she didn't. If, by some miracle, she got on to a plane from LA to Tokyo, he would be there in person to hand it to her. She would have nothing to worry about; she only had to shine. If, by his agency, she could be relieved of one moment of stress or discomfort, then he would sacrifice anything to achieve that end, whether she knew it or not. Dan knew, of course, that he was desperately in love with Isabelle, but for the time being, disguising it as professional efficiency made it that much easier to deal with.

Officially, Dan was in Tokyo to represent the interests of Walker Parker and their various clients on both sides of the shop counter. But he could do that in his sleep, not that he was getting much of that; he spent every available hour planning how to make Tokyo Fashion Week into the happiest experience of Isabelle's life. She would want for nothing – she would be cushioned from the rough and tumble of life in a strange city, and just to be on the safe side – that Dan Parker caution again – he engaged the services of a driver and a limousine who would be at her disposal twenty-four hours a day. He hired a translator who would accompany her to meetings and shoots. He even bought a little personal GPS tracker, in case she got lost in a strange city – she could simply leave it in her bag, and wherever she was, he could find her. Yes, Dan Parker really had thought of everything.

Joel wasn't out of the woods just yet – there was a lot of explaining to be done before he was allowed to leave the state of California, and even though he was out on bail, the police were far from satisfied that he was not guilty of something or other. This wasn't enough to keep him in the state pen, however, and so, at last, he was free to visit Will, who was convalescing beside the pool at Mike Christian's house. Isabelle may have left, and Will certainly wouldn't put money on her coming back, but there had to be some advantages to having a best friend shagging a rock star, and at times like this a comfortable bed, a pool and a retinue of staff were very welcome.

Will had lost a lot of weight after the attack; he'd been in hospital for nearly a month, and had only just started eating again. He slept a lot, and spent most of his waking hours trying hard not to cough, sneeze or laugh, it hurt his broken ribs so much. But there were no signs of brain damage, his heart was behaving itself, and the other major internal organs had escaped unscathed. The doctors told him it was little short of a miracle that he'd survived, and Will felt rather smug about that.

The housekeeper showed Joel out to the pool, where Will was lying on a recliner in the shade of a canvas awning, an open book face down on this stomach, his eyes hidden behind a huge pair of shades. It was impossible to tell if he was awake. Joel's heart jumped, and he felt a sudden urge to turn and run, never to see Will again, to return to whatever life he had left behind in Australia and dismiss the last year as a nightmare.

He stood frozen in the doorway, the light of the afternoon sun dazzling him.

'Come to say sorry?'

He wasn't asleep, then.

'Yeah,' Joel mumbled.

'Didn't quite hear that. Speak up.'

'Yes. I'm sorry.'

'Right.' Will pulled his legs up one at a time, slowly, painfully, to make space for Joel beside him. He patted the recliner. 'Come on, then. Say what you've got to say.'

Joel sat, his hands pressed between his knees, his toes turned in, staring into the hazy middle distance.

'He told me he wanted to kill you.'

Will didn't need to ask who. 'And you didn't think to mention this to me?'

'I didn't know what to do. He told me I'd go to prison if I said anything.'

'I see.' Will took off his sunglasses; his eyes were still bruised, one of them badly bloodshot. 'And that was worse than me dying.'

'I thought he was bluffing.'

'People like Rivelli don't bluff.'

'I know that now. I'm sorry.'

Will sighed. 'Come on, then. Let's have the whole story. I promise I won't shout at you.'

'Thanks.'

'But only because it hurts too much. Right. You have five minutes. Make it count.'

'Rivelli told me that he wanted to know where you were at all times. He wanted me to stick by you so that when the time came he could . . . get you.'

'I see. So you were just a minder.'

'I called him to tell you where you were, what you were doing.'

'And the porn movie?'

'That was real. He got me that job. The money was good.'

'Did you actually get round to filming anything? I'm curious. It would be something nice to remember you by.'

'Oh Will.'

'Don't start sobbing. Come on. I'm eager to hear the rest of your story.'

'Then he told me that he wanted me to deliver you to a certain club at a certain time.'

'Well, you did that all right. Like a good little doggie, dropping the prize at the master's feet.'

'But I didn't think . . . honest to God, Will, I didn't believe that they'd . . .'

'Well they did. And you stood by and let them.'

'I didn't. I swear, I tried to stop them. We were all having sex in the bathroom in Laurel Canyon – do you remember?'

'Vaguely.'

'And when they started to hurt you, I fought them. Honestly I did, Will. I did everything I could. But there were so many of them.'

'Hmmm.'

'And then they forced me to take drugs . . .'

'That must have been hard.'

'And they covered me in your blood and then drove me out and dumped me in the street with my pockets full of gear. And that's when the police found me.'

'I don't suppose the police believe you any more than I do.'

'I don't care what they think,' said Joel. 'They can lock me up and throw away the key. But I can't stand thinking that you might . . . that you might blame me for . . . what happened. Oh God, I thought you were going to die.'

'Yes,' said Will, brightly, 'we all thought that. And I very nearly did.'

'They wouldn't let me see you.'

'Under the circumstances, I'm not surprised.'

'I shouldn't even be here.'

'You're not by any chance here to finish the job, are you? I mean, for all I know, Rivelli could still have you on the payroll.'

'No!' Joel's face was white, his eyes wet.

'Well that sounded genuine enough. Now, darling, if you'll excuse me, I need to have a little rest. Much as I have enjoyed your visit, I find company quite exhausting just at present. The maid will show you out.'

'Can I see you again?'

'Why would you want to do that?'

'Because . . . I thought we might . . .'

'Get back together again? Oh Joel,' said Will, putting his shades back on, 'don't let's ask for the moon, and so on. At the moment, I'm getting used to the idea of being alive. I don't think I'm quite ready to talk about "us".'

The Rodean trial opened on a Monday, with crowds outside the Royal Courts of Justice, some simply to gawk and take photos, others angrily chanting, holding placards with such peculiar slogans as JUSTICE FOR ROCKY. When Jessica arrived, accompanied by John Ferguson and her brother, the crowd howled and spat as a forest of raised arms holding mobile phones sprouted above their heads. When Christine arrived, sober in her black wool gown, one hysterical sixty-year-old, who had been in love with Rocky Rodean since first she saw him on *Ready, Steady, Go!*, screamed 'How can you sleep at night, you bitch?'. Christine remained calm. She had heard it all a thousand times before.

The entrance hall to the RCJ opened above her and around her. She had clicked across those marble floors a thousand times, and never given it a second thought. Today she felt as she'd felt when she and

Andy first visited St Peter's in Rome, as if the whole weight of the building was pressing down upon her, dwarfing her, ready to collapse and bury her beneath the weight of authority and tradition. It was her first appearance since *Rivelli v Rivelli*, when she'd skulked out the back way and beaten a hasty retreat to John Ferguson's office; she felt as if she'd been in hiding ever since. This was her comeback, no less significant, if less spectacular, than Elvis in black leather in 1968, or Ali's rumble in the jungle. It was with those two apparently inappropriate images in her mind that Christine Fairbrother took a deep breath and pushed open the courtroom doors to face the judge.

When Isabelle saw Dan waiting for her at arrivals at Tokyo Narita International, there was no point in pretending that she wasn't pleased. Her heart fluttered, and the blood rushed to her head, and instead of hiding it all in a display of fashionably detached cool as she would once have done, she let her luggage trolley roll along unguarded and threw her arms around his neck. Dan managed to catch the trolley, catch Isabelle by the waist and receive a big kiss on the lips without falling over or bursting into tears, which he rather felt like doing. He busied himself with the luggage and getting her to the car, while she prattled happily about funny things that had happened on the flight, and they both felt quite extraordinarily happy.

'Right,' he said, as the driver took them smoothly out of the airport, 'here's your schedule.'

'My goodness,' she said, flicking through the pages, 'you have been busy.'

'Well, someone's got to take care of you.'

'That's what Will always said.'

'I'm really glad that he's on the mend.'

'Me too. My God. I just realised. I'm in Japan!'

They watched Tokyo approaching, a huge gleaming sculpture of steel and glass.

'So, what's first?'

'Get you to the hotel, get some food inside you, then get you to the *Elle Japon* shoot.'

'Oh my God. Is that really going ahead? I look bloody awful.'

'They'll have stylists.'

'You're supposed to say "No, Isabelle, you look perfect."'

'Sorry,' said Dan, blushing. 'Not very good at that stuff.'

She took his hand. 'That's why I like you, stupid.' Then she caught sight of a giant animatronic Hello Kitty, and further conversation was impossible.

Victoria was flatsitting in Hackney for a few months, as a favour to a friend of a friend who was working in New York for a while; it was rent free, and while it didn't exactly measure up to the Kensington penthouse, it was clean and comfortable and secure. There was a security guard in the entrance hall, locked doors on every landing, and bolts on every window frame. Once you were inside, you were alone – and that suited Victoria fine. It was a place to rest and to nest. By the time the friend of a friend came back, the baby would be six months old. Plenty of time then to consider her next move.

The flat didn't have a phone, and if she kept her mobile switched off Victoria didn't need to talk to anyone. Not to Adele, who had driven her away with her constant, smothering concern. Not to her parents, who, she thought, were quite capable of phoning just to send a frosty silence down the line. Not to Ben, nor to his mother, who were circling around the unborn child, ready to claim it as their own. Nobody else would want to find her. She'd told the police everything she knew, and until such time as they found Rivelli – if ever – they were finished with her. The press, who had shown some interest in her as lesbian Leanne's pregnant mystery blonde, had moved on to other, juicier stories. Victoria was alone.

And so, when the stomach cramps that had been niggling away in recent weeks suddenly got very much worse in the middle of the night and felt very much like contractions, and her waters suddenly broke, soaking the mattress, Victoria had nobody to help her except the security guard and the paramedics who came to take her into the maternity unit at Homerton Hospital.

As Victoria went into labour in Hackney, and Isabelle stepped out of the shower high above Tokyo, Christine lay awake in bed in Highgate, reflecting on the first day of *Rodean v Rodean*. It had gone well, even better than she'd dared to hope. Jessica had behaved herself, answered yes and no when required to, and done nothing remotely attention seeking. Rocky turned up late, unshaven, wearing a crumpled jacket with the sleeves rolled up – exactly how Christine herself would have styled him for the role of the errant husband. Jessica, by contrast, looked demure and dignified in a navy blue suit that they had selected themselves in Selfridges. The press could print all the baguette-swallowing photographs they liked; this was a woman who had grown up, tried to be a good wife and had it all thrown in her face by a repulsive old philanderer who was old enough to be her father. And when the court heard, later today, about some of Rocky's younger playmates – young enough to be his granddaughters – the job was as good as done.

Christine felt a warm glow around her heart, something she had not felt for a very long time. She lay on her back, folded her arms neatly across her chest and, much to her surprise, managed to go back to sleep. She dreamed of her children as they were a long time ago, when Ben was a baby and Isabelle a demanding toddler, and somehow Andy was there, and the children were crying, and Andy was taking them away in a car, and she could not stop him.

The *Elle Japon* shoot was in a studio in Shinagawa that took up the whole top storey of a skyscraper with views right over the Tokyo waterfront area. The car dropped Isabelle off, and she was ushered into a lift that rose at alarming speed straight into outer space. When the doors opened, she was surrounded by stylists and assistants and journalists and interpreters who carried her into make-up and sat her in a chair in front of a mirror. The first thing she noticed, reflected beside her, was Maya Rodean, her face covered in pale green sludge, with teabags on her eyes. She was surprisingly easy to recognise.

'Hello, Maya,' said Isabelle. 'Fancy meeting you here.'

'I can't talk,' said Maya, her lips barely moving, 'or I'll crack. This stuff costs a fortune. Still, Laruche want me to look my best.'

Isabelle resisted the temptation to tell Maya that she looked better than she'd ever looked before, and settled back into the chair. *Elle Japon* were featuring them as, it seemed, they were always destined to be featured – as the new wave of young British designers, momentarily putting the UK back on the fashion map before the spotlight moved on to Paris, New York or Milan. The fact that both of them were about to shake the dust of England from their Jimmy Choos for lucrative contracts with French couture houses did not dim this moment of Anglophilia. Maya had already crossed the Channel, and was comfortably ensconced in Laruche with a massive salary and minimal workload, most of which was farmed out to her eager minions. Isabelle, while she had not yet officially decided to say '*oui*' to Givenchy, knew in her heart that she would.

Isabelle was in make-up for thirty minutes – twenty-five minutes longer than she would have taken at home. Maya did not emerge for another hour and a half.

'That fucking seaweed has brought me out in lumps!' she screamed. 'You can't photograph me. You'll have to reschedule the shoot!' Minions rushed from every side – Maya never rolled less than six deep – and moved towards the lift. Photographers screamed at assistants who screamed at translators who said, very quietly, 'We beg you to re-consider, Miss Rodean,' but by then it was too late, Maya was in the lift and the doors were about to close.

'Great,' said Isabelle, looking up from a copy of the magazine, 'they can just feature me on my own. Suits me.'

The lift doors moved together, and would have closed completely had not Maya stuck her foot in the gap, risking irreparable damage to nearly two thousand pounds' worth of shoe.

'On second thoughts,' said Maya, marching right back in again, 'my schedule is packed, and who knows when I'll find the time to get back to Tokyo.' She snapped her fingers. 'Mirror.'

A mirror was produced, and she observed her face like a man who suspects he's cut himself shaving.

'You'd better damn well Photoshop me to death, darling,' she said to a young man with huge blue-framed spectacles and a gold lurex scarf, whom Isabelle took to be the art director, 'or I will have your guts for garters. Translate that!'

'I'm sure someone has a paper bag,' said Isabelle, as they took their places on two thrones that had been set up in the middle of the studio. She half expected to see Union Jack bunting and corgis.

There was some predictable wrangling over which throne Maya would take; as the established Paris couturier with the celebrity father,

she naturally felt that she should be in the larger one, but then that
was behind the smaller one, and she naturally felt that she should be
in front, and would have threatened once again to walk out had one
of her minions pointed out that the smaller throne in the front would
make her look proportionately large.

Maya sat rigid, staring straight into the camera in order to express
her hard, punky, Vivienne Westwood-ish edge. Isabelle relaxed, hitched
her legs over the arm of the chair and smiled.

'Oh for God's sake,' said Maya, 'you're ruining the composition.'

'Let's leave it to the photographer, shall we?'

'No! This is my shoot, and they've only got you along to make me
look good.'

'Really?' said Isabelle. 'Thanks for telling me.'

'Listen, sweetheart,' said Maya, barely moving her lips as the camera
clicked away, 'if you didn't play the urban card so effectively, nobody
would pay you the slightest bit of attention.'

'I beg your pardon?'

'You and Mercy Williams. That's the only possible reason why she
wore that awful tinfoil dress to the Oscars. Because you're black.'

'Oh, and I thought it was because of all the kind words you'd been
putting in for me with her people,' said Isabelle, who had not forgotten
Maya's attempts to keep her away from the Academy Awards.

Maya was sweating, and kept being dabbed. She swatted the make-
up artists away like flies.

'God,' said Maya, 'I don't have time to think about people like you.
I mean, I'm the one with the career.'

Isabelle laughed out loud when Maya said this, and the photographer chose just that moment to press the shutter. Maya, sweating,
frowning and bug-eyed; Isabelle relaxed, laughing, head thrown back.

'That's it!' said the photographer, through the medium of the translator. 'We're done here.' He also made a few other remarks about the
relative merits of his two sitters, which the translator thought better
to leave in the original Japanese.

Maya and Isabelle were still sniping at each other on the way down
in the lift. Isabelle, who had bitten her tongue so much it resembled
lacework, finally blurted out the fact that, without her famous surname,
Maya would never have even got into St Martins. Maya retaliated by

dredging up Isabelle's overdose, her mother's affair with Rivelli – and, when they stepped out of the building, was sharing her opinion that it might have been better for Will to die in Cedars-Sinai. God, thought, Isabelle, do I really have to put up with this for four days? They had been booked everywhere together, the assumption being that two English girls would naturally be best friends, and were due to be taken straight from the studio to a gala reception at the National Art Centre. Isabelle's driver would take them both; tightfist Maya had been only too quick to agree to that one . . .

Isabelle was so preoccupied with thinking up a snappy comeback that she didn't even look at the man who was holding a car door open for her. She simply got in at one door while Maya got in the other, and they put as much cream leather between them as was possible for two women in the back of the same limousine. The car glided off as Maya barked orders into her phone and Isabelle stared out of the window at the alien city beyond the smoked glass.

She didn't even begin to suspect that anything was wrong until they turned up a narrow side street that seemed to lead straight into the water, then made a sharp left and bounced over potholes towards what looked like a light industrial estate.

'For Christ's sake!' shrieked Maya. 'Tell your bloody driver to watch where he's going!'

Isabelle looked at the back of the driver's head – same black hair, same charcoal jacket as before – and tried to catch his eye in the rearview mirror.

She tapped on the glass partition.

'Where are we going?'

The driver made no response.

She tried to slide the glass open; it was locked. She tapped again, a little harder. 'Excuse me! Where are we going? Where is this?'

Still no response. The car drew up outside a new-looking warehouse, where an odd assortment of vehicles were parked. The driver said a couple of words into his phone, and the warehouse doors slid open.

'Maya,' said Isabelle, 'I think something's wrong.'

'What?' Maya looked around, waved a dismissive hand. 'No, this is fine. Warehouse party or something. Sorry, darling,' she said to whoever she was speaking to, 'I was interrupted.'

'I don't think this is . . .'

The car doors were opened, and two men handed them out. Like the driver, they were inconspicuously dressed in grey suits. Maya thrust her bag at one of them and led the way, hobbling across the broken road surface in her enormous fetish-inspired shoes. Isabelle stood for a moment, uncertain whether or not to follow, but a strong hand on her arm steered her from the car and into the warehouse.

Once inside, the doors rolled shut behind them.

'Where's my fucking PA?' said Maya. 'There's supposed to be someone to meet me at every place we go to.'

'I don't think this is a scheduled stop,' said Isabelle.

'What do you mean?'

'Well, Maya,' said Isabelle, clutching her handbag close to her chest, 'I rather think we've been kidnapped.'

Rocky Rodean sat in the Royal Courts of Justice with what the newspapers would describe as 'a dignified expression' on his face, as Jessica Rodean spilled out a long account of his infidelities with women a quarter of his age. She spoke of girls being brought to hotel rooms by well-paid minders, she spoke of drink-and-drug-fuelled parties that often ended in fights – in fact, by the time she'd finished giving evidence-in-chief, Rocky was starting to make Gary Glitter look like a wholesome family entertainer.

The press was not quite ready to start believing her – yet. For the next day or so, they would stick to the party line that had got them through all of Rocky's previous divorces – that he was a good, decent bloke, one of us, and that his wives were gold-digging whores. Even so, nobody was setting up the VICTORY FOR ROCKY headlines just yet. Jessica's counsel seemed to have rather a lot of witnesses to present. And in newspaper offices across the capital, reporters were dusting off scurrilous old stories about the nation's favourite old rocker, stories that, for a long time now, had been suppressed and disbelieved. Was it possible that they were sitting on the scoop of the century – that Holy Grail of popular journalism, the fall from grace of a major public figure? Rocky Rodean had always been impervious to criticism – but nobody could sustain a scandal of these proportions, if Jessica's allegations turned out to be true. Even Rocky, with all his money, couldn't buy his way out of that one. If Jessica won the amount that she was asking for, and Rocky's professional fortunes took a nosedive, he'd be broke within a year.

The court rose for lunch, and a gaggle of panicky-looking personal assistants surrounded Rocky in the main hall.

'It's Maya,' they gabbled. Rocky was not really concentrating; Maya always wanted something, even at the most inopportune moments.

'Yeah, yeah,' he said. 'Just deal with her. It's not a good time.'

'She's been . . .'

'Look, mate, I'm busy.'

'Kidnapped.'

'What?'

'In Tokyo. Kidnapped.'

'You're taking the piss.'

'There's a ransom demand.'

'Oh for Christ's sake. This is just some nutter. Deal with it.'

'Of five million pounds.'

'What the . . .'

'Or they're going to post video footage on the internet of her fingers being chopped off.'

'Call the fucking police, then.'

'And they say if we do that, you'll find her head in the left luggage lockers at Tokyo Station.'

'Five million quid?'

'That's right.'

Rocky thought for a moment, and then said 'The way things are going, I ain't got it.'

Chapter 34

That night, after a labour that lasted for nearly seventy-two hours, Victoria gave birth to a baby boy, nearly three months premature. He was immediately taken away from her into the neonatal intensive care unit where he was put in an incubator and pumped full of antibiotics. He was suffering from jaundice and respiratory distress syndrome but, said the doctors, had a pretty good chance of survival. The next twenty-four hours would tell. Was there anyone Victoria wanted to call, before they gave her a sedative and allowed her to get some much-needed rest? Victoria thought for a while, and then said no.

Isabelle and Maya were in a room that looked very much like one of the tutors' rooms at Saint Martins, about ten feet square with some battered office furniture, dirty industrial carpet on the walls and malfunctioning fluorescent tubes let into the ceiling. A poster on the wall reminded them that they were in Tokyo, with a blue-and-black photo of the city skyline.

The door was locked, and no matter how much Maya shouted, nobody came. There was a jug of water on the table, and a metal bin in the corner, which would have to make do as a lavatory. Their handbags had been taken from them, as had their shoes, which, rightly in Maya's case, their captors thought could be used as offensive weapons. They didn't get a good look at the men who brought them there. They were all Japanese, well-dressed, in their thirties or forties, it was hard to tell.

It was very quiet in the room, at least when Maya stopped screaming. She'd gone through all the major stages of grief in the first half hour: denial ('I can't believe this is happening to me!'), anger ('How dare they do this to me!'), bargaining ('Let me go and I'll make it worth your while'), depression ('Oh God I'm not dealing with this at all') and finally acceptance ('Go on, then, kill me and get it over with'), without once mentioning the fact that Isabelle had been kidnapped as well. Finally, she cried hysterically, had to wee in the bucket, turned to

Isabelle and said 'What are we going to do?' It was the first time she'd used the first person plural pronoun, and Isabelle found herself warming to her. Was this some weird new variant on Stockholm Syndrome? Would she actually end up liking Maya Rodean? 'We have to keep calm, Maya. Whatever this is about . . .'

'It's about me! Someone wants to stop me!'

Isabelle found herself cooling again. It felt much more natural. 'Maya, you don't really think this is something to do with fashion, do you?'

'What else could it possibly be?'

Isabelle thought about trying to explain, but saved her breath. To Maya, there was nothing else in the world that mattered. Oh well, she thought, at least she can't possibly suspect me of having arranged the whole thing, can she?

'This isn't by any chance your doing, is it?' said Maya.

That was when Isabelle decided to wait it out in silence.

When Isabelle didn't turn up to the gala reception at the National Art Centre, Dan texted her – the shoot was probably overrunning. He didn't like to disturb her while she was working, and although he'd booked a table for dinner after the party, that could always be re-scheduled. A shoot for *Elle Japon* was important, and if they couldn't keep to their timetable, he'd just have to adjust his.

When the reception was winding down, and neither Isabelle nor Maya had turned up, to the consternation of the English language contingent, Dan tried to call Isabelle's mobile. It was switched off. He called the photographer's studio and learned that Maya and Isabelle had left on schedule at five p. m. That was three hours ago. Even in Tokyo traffic, it couldn't take three hours to travel a couple of dozen city blocks.

He called the limousine company, who told him that the car and driver had been stood down on his orders earlier that afternoon, did Mr Parker not remember? Miss Cissé would be making her own travel arrangements from now on.

That was when Dan called the police.

Day two of *Rodean v Rodean* was Christine Fairbrother's finest hour, the pinnacle of her career, her redemption in the eyes of the legal profession and almost guaranteed to elevate her to Queen's Counsel before the year was out.

Christine walked through the hordes of furious fans outside the RCJ with Jessica by her side, their heads held high, ignoring the screams of abuse, not seeing the obscenities on placards waved above the sea of angry heads. They disappeared into the building just as Rocky arrived, scribbling a few desultory autographs, scowling when he usually smiled, eventually telling a particularly insistent fan who had followed him faithfully for forty years to 'fuck off and get a life'. This did not go down well, and for the rest of the morning the crowd melted away like slush in a thaw.

Observers in the court found the next few hours painful in the extreme. Christine brought witnesses to attest to Rocky's regular infidelities and dangerous taste for young flesh. She cited instances of his violent treatment of women, establishing a pattern through his three previous marriages. When it came to the vexed question of money, and how much Jessica deserved as a settlement, Christine traced Rocky's downward career path through the eighties and early nineties, then read out press coverage of his shocking affair with the then Jessica Winters, ex-girl-band singer, occasional TV presenter and celeb mag fixture, who was then twenty-five years old. She demonstrated how Rocky's media profile had shot up in the wake of the affair, how he released a single that went straight to number one – his first top ten hit for twelve years – and how he enjoyed massive back catalogue sales for the next three years, as he divorced Wife Number Three and married Jessica, Wife Number Four. Since that reversal of fortune, for which, Christine argued, Jessica was entirely responsible, Rocky had toured all over the world, appeared on chatshows, written a book and even tried out cars for *Top Gear*. And what did Jessica get in return? Heartbreak, black eyes and her nose rubbed in her husband's borderline paedophile affairs.

Jessica, well trained by her counsel, kept her remarks short and factual. She remained calm under cross-examination. Every time she felt the urge to open her big mouth and have a pop at Rocky, she thought of the line of zeros on the settlement cheque, and kept her mouth shut. This was a technique that Christine had used before on vengeful wives; it never failed.

At the end of the second day, in defiance of the odds, in defiance of the press and of 'the people', whose favourite Rocky had so long been, the judge found in favour of Jessica Rodean – or, as she would henceforth be known, particularly on the cover of her tell-all auto-biography, Jessica Winters.

Rocky Rodean left the Royal Courts of Justice considerably poorer than he had arrived. He retreated to his gated estate in Buckinghamshire and gave strict instructions that he was not, under any circumstances, to be disturbed.

Christine returned to chambers and sent off her application to become a QC.

Second time lucky.

Two men came into the room and very quietly closed the door behind them. Isabelle and Maya huddled in the corner. 'What do you want?' bellowed Maya, in the voice that had made her the scourge of the Bedales hockey fields, and then clammed up with a little whimper when one of the men produced what looked like a designer Stanley knife from his trouser pocket.

He stepped towards them, the knife extended. Maya grabbed Isabelle's arm, and pushed her forward. It was hard to know whether, in her terror, Maya was simply trying to hide behind her, or whether she was offering Isabelle as a substitute. The man with the knife advanced. He had been told not to leave the room without one of Maya Rodean's fingers in a plastic ziplock bag.

The baby was tiny, a little yellow fledgling that had fallen too soon from the nest, its skin dusty with what looked like flour, its eyes puffed closed as if it had been beaten up. Pipes fed in and out of its body, sensors monitored every inch of its chest. Such a small scrap of life, so insignificant, and yet, it seemed, so tenacious. It had been bounced over the edge of a cliff, poisoned with morphine, ejected into the world long before it was ready, prey to every infection a London hospital could chuck at it – and yet, somehow, it was still breathing, fighting off the jaundice, its heart pumping those few precious drops of blood around its body, determined to live.

When Victoria first saw it through the plastic walls of the incubator, she felt ashamed. She, who had given up on life so many times, who had let people and circumstances trample all over her, pushing her this way and that, forcing her from one disastrous compromise to another, was put to shame by this tiny collection of bastard cells, a mistake whichever way you looked at it, that was so doggedly determined to keep breathing and growing and to cling on to life as the only thing that mattered.

'I think I'll call him Felix,' she said to the nurse. 'It means lucky, doesn't it?'

'Yes,' said the nurse, wondering whether Victoria wasn't rather counting her chickens.

'Is he going to live, do you think?'

'We certainly hope so.'

'But he might not.'

'Well, it's too early to say . . .'

'Thanks,' said Victoria. 'You see, I'm just wondering if I should tell his dad.'

'Oh,' said the nurse, to whom this kind of thing was all in a day's work. 'Well, it might be an idea.'

If she knows who it is.

Victoria stared through the perspex walls of the incubator and looked for clues. Was it Rivelli's? Was it Ben's?

Who would she call?

John had reserved a table for three at Tom Aikens to celebrate the verdict; usually, there was an endless waiting list, but the words 'Jessica Rodean' had a way of freeing up space. Jessica joined them for an aperitif but declined to order food; she had people to see and places to go, and lasted just long enough in Tom Aikens to be photographed before putting herself entirely in the hands of her publicist.

'I'm not sure if I actually heard the words "thank you" in all that,' said Christine, when Jessica had gone, leaving her alone with John.

'What she lacks in manners she more than makes up for in money,' said John. 'I'll make sure that my invoice reflects any deficit in the gratitude column.'

'So,' said Christine, as John poured out the rest of the champagne, 'we did it.'

'Short and sweet,' he said, raising his glass. 'Just the way I like it. Here's to you, Christine Fairbrother. The best in the business.'

'We make a good team, John,' said Christine. 'In and out of court.'

'Thank you,' said John, looking straight into her eyes. 'I wonder . . .'

'Yes?'

'I wonder if I'm about to make a very big mistake.'

'Hmmm?' She looked at him through her glass, the bubbles rising in wavering columns through the golden wine. 'What might that be?'

'I'm going to ask you if you think that we could . . . I mean, given that we have this professional relationship, I know it might not seem appropriate, but if we don't . . .' He paused, then put his drink down on the table and sat up straight. 'Christine,' he said, 'would you like to go out with me?'

'I thought you'd never ask,' she said, and for once neither of them had anything further to say on the matter, as John leaned across the table and kissed Christine on the lips.

Everything has fallen into place, she thought, as she closed her eyes and let the feeling of rightness sweep through her. Her career was back on course, she would take silk in the next six months or sooner, she had a new man in her life who had the great advantage of being an old friend, and she had given her heel of a husband his marching orders. If only she could tell the children. If only Isabelle and Ben were here to share the moment with her . . .

'Keep away,' said Isabelle, trying to sound brave but not feeling it. Maya was crouching behind her, holding on so tight to Isabelle's waistband that she was in danger of pulling her skirt down. From a sudden sharp smell, Isabelle guessed that Maya no longer needed the metal waste paper basket.

The man with the knife advanced, while his accomplice pointed and waved and said something in Japanese that Isabelle could not understand. It sounded angry.

'Look,' said Isabelle, her voice rather gruff but otherwise quite controlled, 'I don't know what you think you are doing but you have got the wrong people. We are fashion designers, do you understand?' As long as she kept talking, the man seemed disinclined to act. 'English fashion designers. We have nothing for you. We don't have any money. Please just let us go and we won't say anything more about it.'

Everyone shut up for a moment, then the man at the door started rattling away in Japanese again.

'Say something else,' said Maya. 'You're good with them.'

'Please put the knife away,' said Isabelle, who did not like the tone of exasperation in the other man's voice. 'You don't want to hurt us. You'll be in very serious trouble if you do. If you just let us go, then nothing will happen.'

The man with the knife took a big step forward, and Maya screamed.

'That's enough,' said a new voice – English, accented. The door was open, and there stood Massimo Rivelli, neatly groomed, immaculately dressed as ever.

'Massimo, thank God,' said Maya, standing up, her legs dripping. 'There's been a hideous bloody mistake. Would you tell these – these Japanese people that they are in shit right up to their bloody necks?'

'Yes, Maya,' said Rivelli, stepping into the room, 'there has been a horrible mistake. A serious, costly mistake. By your father.'

'You . . . My father? What are you talking about?'

'And,' said Rivelli, turning towards Isabelle, 'by your mother. Why is she always in my way? Everywhere I turn, your mother. Your mother!'

He was starting to sound hysterical.

'I don't know what you mean.'

'But as luck would have it, I have two little birds for the price of one. Let's see what we can do with our two little birds, shall we? Let's see if we can make them sing.' He clicked his fingers, gestured to the man at the door, who barked orders. The man with the knife stepped forward and made a grab at Isabelle, catching her by the wrist. She stumbled forward, fell against him and saw the blade of the knife flashing above her head then turning, arcing downwards towards her hand.

Felix made it through the first night, and started to look a bit pinker the next morning; the antibiotics were working, the jaundice was receding and he was starting to breathe under his own steam. He was starting to look like a human being. He was starting to look like Ben Cissé.

A child needs a father . . .

In a moment of panic, seeing herself cruising the aisles of Lidl for the cheapest disposable nappies, Victoria dug deep into her SIM card and found a number that she had taken in a moment of post-coital sentiment and never thought to call.

'Is that Ben?'

'Yeah.' The voice was guarded.

'It's Victoria here.' Pause. It sounded as if he was in a bar, even though it was nine o'clock in the morning. Typical bloody student. 'I don't know if you remember me. Victoria Crabtree. We met . . .'

'I remember you.'

'How are you, Ben?'

'All right. You?'

It would have been so easy to hang up, to slip out of his life forever, to deny him the knowledge of his child . . . to deny Christine the knowledge of her grandchild.

'There's something I need to tell you, Ben,' said Victoria, staring out of the window over Hackney. It was not a view she would ever get used to.

'Yeah? What?'

'You're a father.'

Christine lay in bed, wondering why it had taken her and John Ferguson so long to find their way to each other. Yes, there was the small matter of their marriages, their children, the fact that they were colleagues in a profession where any breath of gossip was enough to kill careers – but all of that seemed irrelevant when compared to the way that they had fitted together in bed, when they took off their clothes, both shy, both comfortable with the fact that they were, neither of them, in the first flush of elastic-skinned youth, both wanting the same thing. Suddenly she was no longer a barrister, he was no longer a lawyer. They were not picking over the corpse of another dying marriage, arguing tactics, discussing fees and contracts. They were that rarest of things, two old and loving friends who had become, through some miracle of circumstance, lovers. And who both felt, when they awoke the morning after, that they would stay that way for the rest of their lives.

They finally got up at about half past eight, both of them feeling like truant schoolchildren, and it wasn't until nearly an hour later that Christine, showered and dressed and enjoying an excellent cup of coffee, turned on her phone. It had been switched off since she'd entered the Royal Courts of Justice yesterday morning.

There were several messages, nearly all of them from her children – congratulating her, she supposed, and smiled as she set about reading and listening.

Five minutes later, she was in a cab from John's house in Battersea speeding, as much as that is possible in London, to Homerton Hospital in Hackney. John, meanwhile, was on the telephone to the police in Tokyo.

The knife missed – Isabelle pulled her hand back just in time, kneed her assailant savagely in the balls then fell back and sat heavily on Maya, winding her. She hit her head against the wall, but scrabbled to her feet and stood her ground, looking around for something with which to protect herself. All she could see was the chair, which was just about within reach, and a trashcan full of urine. She grabbed the chair just as Rivelli was saying something about 'that's not a very good idea, Miss Cissé, not a very good idea at all,' sounding exactly like a villain in a movie, and not a very good movie at that, she thought, wondering at the irrelevance of her thought processes. She held it by its plastic back, legs sticking outwards, as if she was a lion tamer. If anyone came near her with a knife, she would do her best to inflict as much damage as possible. Maya, curled up on the floor, fought for breath.

There was a dull bang from somewhere far away, and she saw Rivelli flinch for a second, looking over his shoulder, raising his eyebrows in signal to the man by the door, who slipped out of the room, and then slipped back in very quickly, pushing Rivelli out of the way, trying to slam the door shut, but it was too late, boots were kicking it open and in no time at all two fully armed Tokyo police officers were pointing guns at Massimo Rivelli's head.

'Can I hold him?'

'No. I'd rather . . . The nurses said . . .' Victoria was reluctant to surrender the baby, now that she'd finally been allowed to hold him in her arms. She felt an unexpected surge of possessiveness. Christine's hands were reaching out as if she would take the child away.

'He's beautiful,' said Christine, crouching as near as she could get to the child. His eyes were still slits, the skin around them red and puffy, the fists clenched up in tight little balls. A sleek lick of black hair went from crown to forehead.

'What will you call him?'

'Felix, I think, because he's bloody lucky to be alive, all things considered.'

'Felix . . .' Christine felt a rush of emotion, and had to sit down in the plastic bedside chair.

I know he is Ben's. I can feel it.

'And what will you put on the birth certificate?'

'Father unknown,' said Victoria, firmly.

'I see.' Christine swallowed hard. The child, so small, might never know her. Victoria could disappear if she wanted. There were no ties between them; she had no claim on their future.

I cannot lose him.

'He looks just like Ben did at his age, you know.'

'Really? He looks like all the other babies on the ward, if you ask me.'

Silence fell between them. Other babies cried, other new parents talked and laughed and kissed.

I must keep talking.

'What are you going to do, Victoria?'

'I'll manage.'

'I mean what about money?'

She wants to buy him.

'Oh, I expect I'll manage. I've got a place that I can stay for a while.'

'A place . . .'

'Yes.'

Silence again.

'I know what you're thinking,' said Victoria.

'I'm not thinking anything.'

'I know I don't have much to offer the child. I didn't really want it. You probably want it more than I do. I've had a pretty pointless life, going from one man to the next. You think I'm not fit to look after him.'

'I didn't say anything of the kind.'

'And you're wondering why I don't just accept the fact that Ben's the father and let you help me.'

'Well . . .'

'The thing is,' said Victoria, 'I don't want to spend the rest of my life being dependent on other people's good will. I want to make something for myself.'

'Is this really the right time?'

'It's now or never.'

'But Victoria,' said Christine, 'that means starting at the very bottom. It means child benefits and council housing, and counting every penny that passes through your hands.'

'I know.'

'And what will you do when he needs clothes, or medical attention, or toys? What will you do when he's hungry and you can't feed him?'

Victoria stared into the child's sleeping face. It held no answers. 'I don't know,' said Victoria. 'Something will turn up. I'm lucky that way.'

Massimo Rivelli, who was already wanted on two continents for charges ranging from murder downwards, was now in prison in Tokyo, charged with kidnap and wrongful imprisonment. And that was just for starters. Maya Rodean was on a plane, halfway across the Pacific Ocean, bound for Paris, swearing that she would never go east of the Bois de Vincennes for the rest of her life. Isabelle Cissé and Dan Parker, after they had been released by the police, were sitting in a suite in the Tokyo Park Hyatt, marvelling at the fact that, had it not been for a cheap personal GPS device that Dan had bought at the airport and slipped into Isabelle's handbag when he met her at the airport, they might all have been in very different places indeed.

Isabelle was badly shaken. The last thing she needs, thought Dan, is another unwelcome declaration of love – but he knew, from the first moment she went missing, that if he did not do something about this pain that stirred him up every time he thought of Isabelle, saw her, read her name, he must cut her out of his life forever. And that would mean . . . what? Giving up his job, leaving London, perhaps, putting it all behind him and starting all over again. One day, maybe, he would forget her, meet someone else, move on. But for now he knew that he must give it one more shot, whatever the pain of rejection.

But it would have to wait. He couldn't do it while they were in Japan. This was not a good place for them – and he didn't want to risk his last chance by rushing into things. London would be better. He saw her off on a first-class flight home, and returned to his hotel to tie up a few loose ends, the sensation of her final farewell hug clinging to him like a phantom. Was it just gratitude? Was it more? If so, was it enough to make her change her mind . . . For three more days, he must torture himself with those odds, losing sleep, waiting until circumstances reunited them and he told her everything.

Felix turned out to be a highly appropriate name for Victoria Crabtree's son. He shook off jaundice, and within forty-eight hours of birth was proving what a fine pair of lungs he had by yelling the neonatal intensive care unit down. He was discharged to the ward following day, and on the fourth day of his life he and his mother were allowed to go home.

'Home', at this point, was only a borrowed flat in Hackney, an area of London of which Victoria was already heartily sick, as it was deficient in Michelin-starred restaurants, poorly served by cabs – and as for clothes shops, it was saris or nothing. Victoria's noble stand against the clutching hands of Christine Fairbrother and her family did not last; the moment she brought Felix home and closed the door behind her, looking around the blank white walls, listening to the constant hum of traffic, the wail of sirens, the dull thud of someone else's music, she knew that she would have to get out of here fast. Christine was right, damn her – it all came down to money. And as Victoria's earning power at present was precisely zero, and she could hardly expect to attract a new protector with – how had Adele put it? – 'a baby hanging off her tit', she would be obliged to throw herself on the mercy of the state. She had been on the dole once, as a student, for precisely the duration of one summer vacation, and if that was anything to go by, she'd rather hand Felix straight over to the authorities and put herself on the game while there was still time. She had a stomach-turning vision of DSS waiting rooms, of carpet tiles and stretch covers, underwatered potted plants and posters about child benefits translated into Urdu and Turkish, and suddenly Christine's unspoken offer of help, however humiliating, however compromising to the New Improved Independent Victoria Crabtree, began to seem quite attractive.

Anything was better than this, wasn't it? Four walls for six months, and then moving again, starting again, applying for benefits again in a new borough, watching the baby grow up in nit-infested schools, watching herself sagging into leggings and jumbo t-shirts and jowls and eyebags, her hair tied back in a scrunchie, no trace of the woman who had once almost been Signora Massimo Rivelli in the pine-and-rosemary-scented heaven of Sainte-Maxime, the woman who had inspired the great, doomed English artist Leanne Miller, paintings of whose naked body, rendered in savage, swirling oils, now hung on the walls of museums and private collections all over the world . . .

It would not do.

She texted Ben, wondering if he'd like to come round for a crash course in nappy changing. Let him love the child, she thought. Let him love it enough to make it part of the family . . .

Moving to Paris meant leaving everything, and everyone, behind. It meant a final severance from family, a parting of the ways with Will, goodbye to London, the city she'd grown up in, her inspiration, her home. True, as Will and others pointed out, it was only a short hop under the Channel on Eurostar, but Isabelle knew that if she made the move to Givenchy and the upper echelons of the fashion world, her life would not be her own. She would spend the next twenty years walking the highwire, in the spotlight, without a safety net. It would be exciting, glamorous, and rewarding on every material level – and then she would be in her forties, no kids, too thin, hard as nails, her neck sore from always looking over her shoulder at the latest pretender to her crown.

Now she'd got it, she wasn't sure if she wanted it.

Will said he'd never speak to her again if she didn't go. He wanted to be able to say 'my friend Isabelle at Givenchy', to get tickets to all the best shows and to have a very nice place to stay whenever he fancied a long weekend in Paris. Ben thought it would be 'cool', and everyone else just asked her outright how much she'd be earning.

Her parents told her to do whatever she thought was right. Her publicists thought it was the best news since the Angels appeared to the Shepherds. Everyone was keen, except Isabelle, who was afraid.

She set up a make or break meeting with Walker Parker. If they could come up with a persuasive argument for keeping Cissé based in London, expanding the brand and selling not just at home and the US but in major retailers all over the world, she would stay. If not – if they only wanted to keep her for their own financial gain – she would leave.

Fiona Walker was not there.

'She's ill,' said Dan with a smile, as if he might have poisoned her. 'I'm afraid you'll have to put up with me.'

They sat on either side of Dan's desk. The walls of his office were bare, the shelves empty. There was nothing to suggest a working life, let alone a career in fashion. Dan was wearing a crisp white shirt, the top button undone, brown pinstriped trousers, brown brogues. He's looking good, thought Isabelle, and wondered whether his dress sense had improved, or whether it was just one of those freaks that badly dressed people sometimes pull off, like a stopped clock being right every twelve hours.

The windows were open. It was the first really nice spring day, when grey skies and drizzle and cold gritty winds were impossible to imagine.

'So,' he said, 'have you come to settle your account?'

'I don't think I can ever do that. You saved my life. If you hadn't come along . . . Well, I don't like to think what might have happened.'

'Don't thank me. Thank that clever little GPS tracker. Handy things.' He blushed, and looked away.

'Don't be silly,' said Isabelle. 'My mother thinks you're some kind of superhero, flying in at just the right time to save the helpless heroine from a fate worse than death. I'm inclined to agree with her.'

'Oh well, if you're mother thinks so . . .' Dan smiled, played with a loose button hanging by a thread from his shirt front, then looked up at her. They had not seen each other since she left Japan. Less than a week – but back here in Hoxton, so far from the high drama and higher buildings of Tokyo, all that peril and passion and determination seemed very distant indeed.

'Well, I would say that you've never been in a better financial position in your life. All your debts are paid. Orders are being fulfilled, and more are coming in every day. Since the Oscars, you're the one they all want. And they're selling all they can get.'

'Thanks to you,' said Isabelle.

'Just doing my job, lady,' said Dan, in a terrible American cop voice. 'Garment manufacturers are ten a penny. Now that Rivelli's gone down, they're all jockeying for position. The Cissé account is a hell of a big prize. I could name my own terms.'

'You're brilliant.'

'Not really.' He blushed. 'Still, it worked out well, I'll say that much.'

'Is Fiona pleased?'

'No, I wouldn't say Fiona's pleased. In fact, Fiona isn't really talking to me much at the moment.'

'Oh? Why? Not because of what happened last time.'

'That, and a lot of other things. You may have noticed that the cupboard is a bit bare.' He gestured around the office.

'I thought that was just the way you liked it.'

'Minimalism? Not really me. No – I'm leaving.'

'You're . . .'

'I should have done it last year, year before even, but I'm glad I didn't. Wouldn't have had a chance to work with you.' He sounded rather gruff.

'What will you do?'

'Set up on my own. It's high time.'

'Oh, well . . . That's great. Good for you.'

'I know what you're thinking,' he said. 'I'm not cut out for fashion. Good as a lieutenant, someone to take care of the numbers and the business plans, but front-of-house? Dan Parker? No.'

'I didn't mean that.'

'But you know what? I've learned a valuable lesson, working with Fiona Walker, which is that bullshit can get you a long way, but results can get you even further. You've been very good for me, Isabelle.'

'What do you mean?'

'You handed your business over to me, whether you meant to or not, and you gave me the chance to show the fashion world what I could do. I brought Cissé back. I was Mr Fix-It. You know, there's a lot of designers out there, far more famous and well established than you, whose business affairs are hopelessly messed up. They need me, and now, thanks to you, they know they need me. I'm somewhat in demand.'

'Well. I'm pleased.'

'So I'm going to rent some office space across the square, and see if I can put Fiona Walker out of business in a year.'

'Great . . .'

'But you don't want to hear about my plans.'

Yes I do.

'You came here to ask for advice. Presumably about Givenchy.'

'You've heard, then.'

'Of course. I probably knew before you did. So? What's the plan?'

'I don't know whether to take it or not.'

'That's easy. You should take it. No question about it at all.'

'But leaving London . . .'

'London's over, as far as fashion's concerned. The bubble's burst. Look around you – all those rising stars turning out the same tired streetwear they've been doing for the last five years.'

'I didn't know you noticed such things.'

'I notice what sells.' He unbuttoned his cuffs and turned them back. His forearms were thick, covered in golden hair. 'Cissé will do well for a couple of years, then you'll start to struggle. Someone else will take your place. No reflection on your work – but it's not about the quality of the design any more. Not in England. It's about whether your face fits. At the moment, yours does. You're new, you're young, you're beautiful, you've got Mercy Williams and you've got a rock-star boyfriend.'

'Had. Had a rock-star boyfriend.'

'Well,' said Dan, after the shortest of pauses, 'the point is that you're . . . well, you're the . . . you know, you're the . . .' He stopped, looked up at her with a frown, looked down again. 'Really?' he said. 'It's over?'

'With Mike? It never really began.'

'Oh. Right.'

'Right.'

Birds were singing in the square, ridiculously loud.

'What was I saying?'

'Givenchy. Paris.'

'Yes. Absolutely. It's the chance of a lifetime. They won't ask you again. You should definitely go.'

'Mmm.'

'And, you know, maybe if things go well for me over here, I might be looking after some of your stuff in years to come. How about that? That would be weird, wouldn't it? If I got the Givenchy account.'

'Yeah,' said Isabelle, who wanted to cry. 'Weird.'

Dan felt as if his heart had relocated to his throat. He was finding it very hard to form words. He unscrewed the cap of a bottle of water; it was empty, but it gave him something to do. He held it to his mouth, took the last drops. It did the trick.

'Of course, there is an alternative scenario,' he said.

'Yes?' said Isabelle. 'What would that be?'

He looked at her for the longest time, blue eyes gazing directly into brown, and said 'I come with you.'

It was Christine who arrived first, not Ben.

'There's something I need to tell you,' she said, placing her brief-case against the hall wall. She had come straight from court, dressed in a grey suit.

'Come through,' said Victoria. 'He's just got off to sleep. Look.'

They bent over the Moses basket (only five quid from Nobby's Bargains on Mare Street) where Felix was dozing peacefully, his fists raised in a gesture of blessing, or surrender. Christine sighed and cooed. Maybe Adele had been right all along – a baby was money in the bank.

'He's beautiful.'

'Yes,' said Victoria, who hadn't had much time to think about it. 'He really is.'

'Sleeping all right?'

'Not bad.'

'Feeding?'

'So far so good.' And he was; he knew exactly what Victoria's breasts were for. 'Would you like a coffee? It's only instant, I'm afraid.'

'That's okay,' said Christine. 'You sit down. I'll make some when Ben gets here.' She looked at her watch. 'In about twenty minutes. I hope you don't mind me crashing the party like this.'

'Not at all.'

I presume you have your reasons.

'It's about Massimo Rivelli.'

'Ah.' That wasn't what she was expecting. Victoria picked up a baby blanket, folded it and smoothed it. 'What about him?'

'He's in prison.'

'Oh.'

'In Japan.'

'Japan? Oh. Right.'

Victoria carried on stroking. The baby snored quietly.

'You didn't know, then?'

'About what?'

'He kidnapped Isabelle.'

'He . . . kidnapped Isabelle?'

'And Maya Rodean.'

Victoria put the blanket down on the arm of the sofa, and went to the window, with her back to Christine.

'It's all right. They're both fine. In case you were . . . wondering.'

'Of course.' Victoria put a hand to her brow. 'I'm sorry. You must have been worried.'

'Fortunately, I didn't know about it. Please, Victoria. Sit down.'

Victoria drifted over to an armchair and ran her fingers over the worn velvet cover.

'He was holding Maya to ransom, threatening to cut off her fingers if her father didn't pay up. Isabelle just got . . . Are you listening to me?'

'How awful.'

'He tried to kill you and Felix. He very nearly killed Will. He threatened me, and set fire to his ex-wife's house. Now this.'

'Why exactly are you telling me this, Christine? Are you trying to tell me that you were right all along?'

'I don't think right and wrong really come into it any more. I just thought you ought to know. In case you were . . . interested.'

Victoria snapped back into focus. 'In case I was thinking of looking Massimo up and telling him that he had a new little bambino back in good old London, is that it? In case I was so desperate for his money that I would take him back no matter what. Is that what you really think of me?'

Yes.

'No. But I know you and Massimo were . . . well, for a long time you were . . .'

'You know nothing about it whatsoever.'

The baby started to cry. Victoria stared at Christine.

'Nothing at all.'

'He's crying, Victoria.'

'I know!' screamed Victoria, all her frustration boiling up as she brought two fists smashing down on to her knees. Thank God you're here, she thought. If I was alone, I might hurt the baby.

It was at this point that Ben, the new father, the twenty-year-old music student, rang the doorbell. Ignoring an atmosphere that would have sent more sensitive souls running for a biohazard suit, he marched into the living room, knelt by the Moses basket, picked up his crying son and soothed him back to sleep.

Dan lived in a two-bedroom flat in Kennington – not one of the fashionable squares, but a pleasant-enough side street off the main road – with cream walls and grey carpet and a few Ikea prints here and there.

Isabelle barely noticed any of this. She waited while he paid the cab, shivering a little in her coat – the night had turned suddenly cold – and then he took her by the arm and led her through the hall, up the stairs and into his living room. The blinds were up, orange light flooding in from the sodium streetlamps, casting shadows of two figures against the wall – two figures that gradually merged into one.

They kissed, standing, for what seemed like hours, the warmth from Dan's hands and lips soaking into Isabelle's body, into her bones, right through her, like brandy.

'I love you, Isabelle,' he said when he came up for air. 'I've always loved you.'

She did not know what to say in reply – she wasn't yet sure if she loved him too – and so she kissed him again, and this time, when she opened her eyes to see his face, the smooth planes of his cheeks, the strong jawline, blond hair sticking out from his forehead, eyelids closed as if in a dream, she knew what her answer must be.

She stood back, took both his hands in hers, and said 'Let's go to bed.'

Isabelle had not had a particularly glorious sexual career. There had been boys at school, seduced at home, all over in a flash. There were affairs at college, most of them conducted under the influence of too much drink and drugs, often secretive, always messy, never fulfilling. There was the long frustration of her love for Will, and the dark energy that compelled her through New York . . . And all that had happened as a result of that. Pregnancy, abortion, the fear that she would never be able to be touched again, the closing down of that part of her that longed for warmth and intimacy.

And there was Dan, his hands unfastening her dress, pulling his shirt over his head, lying down on the bed, pausing to catch his breath, laughing, kissing her again, and finally both of them naked, legs between legs, arms encircling, mouths joined. When he entered her, she felt none of the pain, or rage, or frustration that had propelled her through so much of her life, but only the here and now and the joy and gratitude that had brought her to this place at this time with this man.

When she woke up in the morning, she knew that they would stay together.

'Paris or London?' she said, kissing him awake.

'Don't care.'

'Paris is nice. Trees. Parks. Shopping.'

'Yeah,' said Dan. 'So's London.'

Isabelle turned her mouth down. 'Bendy buses. Knife crime. The bloody Olympics.'

Dan poured two glasses of orange juice. 'Well – smelly drains, rude waiters, no decent restaurants.' He ripped open a plastic packet. 'Croissant, madame?'

'Let's heat them up, at least.'

'I'm hungry.' He bit into his, flakes of pastry falling on to his chest, getting caught in the surprisingly thick dark hair that covered it, darker than the hair on his head. He was only wearing a pair of green-and-white striped boxers; she was wearing a bright red Arsenal t-shirt. The kitchen was at the back of the house, and got the morning sun.

'Oh for goodness' sake.' She switched the oven on and arranged the croissants on a tray. The interior of the oven was suspiciously clean.

'Don't do a lot of cooking, do you?'

'Not a lot.'

'Can you make a decent cup of coffee?'

'Ah,' said Dan, jumping to his feet, 'that I can do.' He put his arms round her waist, kissed her. 'I'm not dreaming, am I? Not this time.'

'No,' she said, 'this is reality.'

'Good,' he said, and ground the beans.

'That smells good.'

'You'll have fresh-ground coffee every morning when we're married,' said Dan. 'You did say yes at some point last night, didn't you?'

Isabelle put her face over her hands and nodded her head.

'Good. Just wanted to get that straight.'

It was all happening too fast – like everything in the last two years of her life. Leaving college, setting up in business, the struggle to get the first show, all the deals, the trips to New York and Paris and Los Angeles, the features in *Vogue*, the awards, the Oscars . . . Everything piling up on top of everything else, like a spoilt child with too many toys at Christmas, throwing one aside to open another. Her mother, her father, Will, Maya, Joel, Ben, Victoria . . .

And now Dan.

It should have been so hard to make the choice, to throw her life into a new and unexpected direction, changing all her plans, all her options, for a man that she barely knew.

But it was easy. So easy. As easy as coffee and croissants and a kiss on the neck, as easy as spending the rest of the day in bed.

Epilogue

It seemed strange to be drinking champagne at eleven o'clock in the morning, but then, as Christine thought as the first cork popped, it's not every day that you go to the House of Lords to be appointed as Queen's Counsel. Sun was shining through the open French windows, birds were singing, daffodils nodding in the garden. It was the first really warm day of spring – a perfect day to change a heavy gown of wool for something lighter and cooler in silk.

A little smoke appeared at the mouth of the bottle, a few bubbles, but they died back; John Ferguson knew how to open champagne properly, just as he knew how to do everything else, with efficiency and grace. Their eyes met, and she gave him a little round of applause. He looked younger now than at any time in the last five years, the face fuller, the eyes less tired. Love could do that to you.

He handed her the first glass, and kept pouring; there was just enough in one bottle for everyone. When they were all served, he proposed the toast.

'Ladies and gentlemen, we all know why we're here. So please join me in raising your glasses to Miss Christine Fairbrother, QC.'

Seven glasses were raised and clinked in every possible combination.

'Congratulations, Mum,' said Ben, who was standing as close as possible to Victoria without actually pressing himself against her.

'Well done, Christine,' said Victoria, who never took her eyes off her son, now a robust one-year-old, sitting on the floor under the kitchen table playing with a wooden spoon.

'Bottoms up, Miss F,' said Will, who had finally got rid of that awful scrappy little beard, and now sported a rather fetching scar that broke the line of his left eyebrow. Apart from that, he was unscathed.

'Mum,' said Isabelle, who had been up since six helping her mother to dress – in a Cissé gown, of course – 'I'm so proud of you.'

'And I'm proud of you too, darling,' said Christine, who still found it hard to believe that the teenage tantrum queen had a job, and a nice, proper boyfriend, in Paris. She hated to admit it, but having a couple of near-death experiences seemed to have improved her daughter. After watching Will almost die, and then facing her own mortality at the hands of Rivelli's henchmen in Tokyo, Isabelle had emerged a calmer, brighter person, much easier for a mother to love. Thanks, in no small part, to that superhero boyfriend of hers who, today, was looking more Clark Kent than Superman.

'Cheers, Christine.' Dan was here at Isabelle's side, in a navy blue suit that went rather well with his girlfriend's outfit. He had the look of a man who had been rather successfully taken in hand.

John said nothing, just kissed her on the lips, and went off to take some canapés out of the oven. While Isabelle and Christine had been dressing, he'd been cooking. He was just as good in the kitchen, thought Christine, as he was in the bedroom.

And so the day had come – the day so long dreamed of and longed for, the day she thought she might not live to see, when Christine Fairbrother would take silk. It was not how she thought it would be. The cast of characters was different. Andy was absent, long since relocated *sine die* to Dubai, where he could amass a tax-free fortune and salve his disappointments with ex-pat women and overpriced liquor. Christine wondered if he was still using the old 'my ex-wife doesn't understand me' line. She wondered if he was looking after himself, or running to fat. She didn't much care one way or the other; what feelings she still had for Andy amounted to little more than a benign curiosity. And gratitude, of course, for fathering her children. Beyond that she could not in conscience go.

And she had a grandson under the kitchen table, emitting occasional squeals and yelps and almost-words, who, every day and in every way, grew more obviously the fruit of Ben's loins, from the curly hair to the ready smile and the chubby arms and legs. Ben had been a bonnie baby – that was the accepted euphemism for 'fat' in those days – and so was Felix. His limbs looked like strings of sausages, his face was wider than it was high, and his bottom positively wobbled. Like Ben, he would doubtless grow into a lean six-year-old and a gangly fourteen-year-old and strapping great man by the age of eighteen. And a father by twenty . . . She hadn't seen that one coming. And for all that Victoria kept her distance, dodging Ben's attempts to touch her, ducking any compliments or courtesies he showed her, she could see them drawn together through the child whose love for his father shone out of every smile, every chuckle, every twinkle of those wide eyes, a bluish-grey at birth, now almost an exact match for Ben's brown. How much longer could Victoria keep him at arm's length? It hurt Christine to see her son pushed away, frustrated – but they were here, weren't they, all of them together when it really mattered? And if things could work out for Christine and John, for Isabelle and Dan, if she could get silk after all that had happened, after the strange nightmare of a year ago, when their lives had descended into some kind of surreal crime caper, then surely things would come right for Ben . . .

So this was the end. All the battles fought, the mistakes made, the lessons learned. She'd got away with it. She'd done what the big boys did – screwed up, been caught out and knocked down, picked herself up, dusted herself off, waited until the robing-room gossip had died down and the story of the Family Barrister Who Fucked Her Gangster Client had passed into Inns lore. And then she'd come back, at first pushed unwillingly by John and then, when the fully glory of *l'affaire* Rodean had blazed forth, dragged into the limelight by celebrity after celebrity, until she'd almost eclipsed them. 'Who's next?' the papers asked, speculating wildly about everyone from the most recently married reality stars to long-wed members of the Royal Family who were supposed to have sought Miss Fairbrother's advice. With a profile like that, the Lord Chancellor could hardly turn her down.

And the cherry on the cake? Massimo Rivelli was in prison in France, after some frantic international bargaining, and would stand trial in May for the murder of Stefano Cassano. It was the worst of all the crimes they could charge him with. The outcome was certain.

Guilty.

After all her years in the legal profession, Christine was not a woman to count her chickens until they were hatched, fledged and pecking around the farmyard – but, in this case, she felt a reasonable degree of confidence that, barring disasters and prison breaks, she and her family could look forward to a peaceful, prosperous and Rivelli-free future.

If he cosies up to me one more time I am going to scream...

It was weird being here, playing happy families, everyone so welcoming and accepting when not so long ago Victoria would have done anything in her power to drag Christine and her family into the gutter. But now they were all friends, just because she had the baby, who only had to wave his fat hands and gurgle in order to secure a roof over his head, food in his belly and the promise of a prosperous future. Of course she couldn't turn any of it down – and they had been kind, all of them, without ever deliberately humiliating her. Putting up with Ben's over-familiarity was a small price to pay. She wasn't stupid; she'd tolerated worse things in order to keep herself housed, fed and decently shod. But this – gathering in a sunny Highgate kitchen with champange, daffodils and birdsong to toast the success of a woman who, only a little over a year ago, she had regarded as her most deadly enemy was... *creepy.*

A woman with whom she had shared not one but two lovers...

A woman who had given birth to the man who had fathered her child...

A woman in whose ex-husband's Docklands flat she and Felix were now living...

It had been managed so tactfully. John Ferguson made all the proposals, in the most discreet way imaginable, over lunch, you understand, not in his office – this was a friendly arrangement, not a business deal, nothing *legal* about it. Victoria had been glad of the free meal – glad to get Felix out of the damp, noisy flat in Hackney, the nightmare of benefits, the banging of feet on the stairs, the mysterious rings on the doorbell in the middle of the night.

'The thing is,' said John, 'there's an empty flat in Docklands, the owner has gone abroad, the mortgage is paid off and the bills and service charges and so on are all taken care of...'

All taken care of...

The words made Victoria feel as if she was slipping into a hot, scented bath.

'And it would just make so much more sense if you moved in there, at least until you've got yourself sorted out.'

Which will be never.

She didn't ask many questions. She knew it was Andy's place, that Andy had gone away and that Christine had, somehow, guilt-tripped him into putting the flat at her disposal. It had Christine's fingerprints all over it – everything falling into place so neatly, everything ordered and clean and functional, like this kitchen, like John Ferguson, so deftly turned from colleague to lover, and they looked so *right* together, damn them, just as Isabelle looked right with Dan, and Ben looked right crawling around on the floor to play with Felix, so clearly his son and not . . . anyone else's.

But for Victoria – nothing fitted. The flat was fine, of course, luxurious, as good in its way as the penthouse in Kensington, if a little less convenient for shopping and lunching, but at least it was warm and secure, the lifts always worked, there was a concierge to help with the buggy, room for the Tesco van to park when they delivered the groceries – groceries nominally paid for by Ben, who was taking his responsibilities very seriously, but Victoria wasn't a fool. She knew that a music student and part-time DJ could not afford to pay that amount into her bank account by monthly standing order. Christine had bought her lock, stock and barrel.

But once she was up there in the clouds, overlooking the docks and the city beyond, there was nobody home for Victoria, just the baby . . . And, for all that she'd thanked God when he was delivered safe and sound, she could still not put her hand on her heart and say that she was glad to be a mother. Oh, he had his moments; he was beautiful, everyone told her so, but her heart did not leap when he smiled, she had not felt the need to phone anyone when he started to crawl or when his lips formed a sound that might have been 'Mama'. She supposed that love would come. It might make sense of things at last. But every morning was the same – just another round of feeding and washing, cleaning and cooking, sleeping when she was able, getting out when she could be bothered, discouraging visitors, dwelling on the past.

'And here's to Victoria!'

She hadn't listened as everyone toasted everyone else, yukking it up in the sort of lovefest that now, more than ever before, made her feel sick and excluded.

It was Christine's voice.

'Welcome to the family, Victoria. I really mean that.'

Victoria smiled weakly and raised her glass; she could barely taste alcohol these days without wanting to be sick. She wanted to throw it back in the woman's face – all her success and her money, her family and her obscenely satisfying sex life – but she was not that stupid. She needed the money, the flat, the endless offers of babysitting. One day, perhaps, when Felix was older, at school, when she had found her own happy ending, she could free herself from the chains of their affection and gratitude and start all over again, but for now . . .

'Thanks, Christine, I appreciate it. All of it.'

The words tasted bitter, and she washed them down with champagne. 'Excuse me a moment.'

The upstairs bathroom was quiet and cool. She rested her forehead against the mirror, waiting for the hammering in her chest to pass, and then pulled her knickers down and sat on the loo. She felt alone – awfully, terminally alone. They wouldn't miss her downstairs. They had what they wanted – Felix, playing happily with his father, the illusion of one big happy family in which she was just a bit player. And for now, as long as Felix needed a mother, she was safe. But for how much longer? What would happen when he went to school – a school that Christine would doubtless pay for? When he wanted toys and holidays that Victoria could never afford? They'd take him away from her, and she'd be left with nothing. Of no further use. Nothing to bargain with. She'd be forty, then fifty, alone, too late to start again.

The past was like a dream to her now. She'd been sleepwalking for ten years through an unreal world of lovers and luxury, vaguely aware of alarm bells that were ringing somewhere far away, but refusing to wake . . . Well, now she was awake all right. This was reality – this tenuous grasp on a lifeline that was slipping through her fingers, this play-acting, the smiles and cheers and thanks that allowed them to believe that they had found their happy ending.

A fat teardrop gathered at the end of Victoria's nose, and fell with a plop on to the bathroom floor, just between her feet. It was followed by another, and another. Victoria put her hands over her face and sat, knickers round her ankles, skirt lifted round her waist, and cried until she had no more tears left.

Nobody came looking for her.

'My two favourite men in the whole world.'

The champagne had gone straight to Isabelle's head, and she grabbed Will on one side, Dan on the other, and pulled them into a clumsy group hug.

'You always did have good taste, Princess.'

Dan manoeuvred her on to a chair before they all toppled over, and placed a selection of canapés in front of her.

'Come on, Isabelle. Eat something, before you get completely plastered.'

'He's very attentive, your boyfriend,' said Will, after Dan had been commandeered by John to serve more drinks.

'All a question of training, darling,' said Isabelle, tucking into puff pastry, mushrooms and truffle oil.

'I don't need to ask if you're happy. You're sickeningly radiant.'

'Thank you, my dear. I can't complain.'

'Paris living up to expectations?'

'Far exceeding them, thanks. I miss London, though.'

'Yeah . . . your family.'

'Oh, them.' Isabelle licked her fingers; one piece of flaky pastry clung to her chin, but Will didn't feel the need to tell her about it just yet. 'Actually, I get on better with my family the less I see of them. Mum and I are best of friends now. She loves Dan.'

'Well,' said Will, 'she always did have a taste for younger men.' He nodded towards where Dan was filling Christine's glass, chatting and smiling. 'You want to watch that, you know. One reads of these things in the popular press.'

'Fuck off,' said Isabelle, tossing a canapé at Will's head. He swatted it away, sending Parmesan-flecked asparagus skidding across the table top. Isabelle picked it up and popped it in her mouth. 'Waste not want not.'

'You're quite the canny businesswoman now, aren't you?'

'Not really. I leave that sort of thing up to Dan. I just muck about with fabrics and make pretty dresses.'

'He hasn't got you dangerously involved with any homicidal gangsters, by any chance, has he?'

'Not yet.'

'How dull for you.'

'Yes . . . One does miss the frisson of imminent attack. But he has ways of making up for it.'

'I imagine he does. It's always the quiet ones.'

'You have no idea.'

'Spare me the details of your sickeningly happy married life, thank you very much. What about Givenchy? Any dirt to dish?'

'Not much. It's very businesslike. They let me do pretty much whatever I want to do, and I deliver the best collections of the season. It's a fairly comfortable arrangement.'

'No more false modesty for you, then.'

'*Absolument*. And what about you, Will? How's business?'

'Oh, not too bad. Shopping for a living. It's not as much fun as it might seem, you know.'

'No, but then again being the fashion buyer for one of the biggest stores in London must have some compensations.'

'Well, the salary eases the pain somewhat.'

'And what about . . . You know.' She gestured to his head. 'Everything all right?'

'Not bad. Headaches sometimes. Weird panic attacks. Might be a form of epilepsy . . .'

'Oh, Will.'

'But then again might not be. Too early to tell at this stage. The general consensus of the medical establishment is that I'm bloody lucky to be alive, so who am I to argue?'

'You sound like Maya, in one of her endless magazine interviews.'

'Don't say that!' Will gasped in mock horror. 'Honestly, that woman. Only Maya Rodean could turn a kidnap ordeal into a marketing strategy. If I see one more *OK!* cover with her mug staring out of it, I'll scream. Honestly, couldn't Dan have just rescued you and left Maya to her doom?'

'And Joel? Any news?'

'Oh, Jolene. Well, he's still in LA, still making porn movies, still insists that he's going to break into the big time. We keep in touch.'

Christine sailed past with a drink in her hand. 'All right, children?'

'Just talking about your ex-boyfriend, the porn star,' said Isabelle.

'Oh well, here's to him,' said Christine. 'I suppose he's found his niche. He was certainly good at it.'

'As several of us here can attest,' said Will. 'Speaking of which, where is Victoria?'

'Not sure,' said Christine. 'Look, Isabelle, it's almost time to get going. You might want to tidy yourself up a bit.' She gestured to her chin; Isabelle found the flake of pastry, and glared at Will, who looked wide-eyed and innocent. 'Taxi will be here in a minute. Ben? You ready?' She clapped her hands, just as she had when they were children, late for school. 'Come on. Let's get going.'

Two women in a black cab on their way to Westminster, both wearing Cissé gowns. The older of the two, her dark hair cut in a smart bob, a very few grey strands highlighting the brown, wears a dark magenta satin sheath, a catwalk sensation at the recent Cissé-for-Givenchy show, not yet for sale in the UK, and when it was it would stretch the budget even of a super-successful family barrister. The younger is in fuchsia pink, bias cut, sleeveless, with a plunging neckline, a gathered waist and an uneven, scalloped hem – something she's playing with, not quite the finished product, whipped off the back of a dummy, the last bit of sewing finished by hand as the Eurostar sped under the sea. Her hair is combed out into an almost perfect sphere, held back at the front with a pair of her boyfriend's sunglasses. Their shoes are by Louboutin, both pairs.

'Oh that bloody woman,' says Christine, checking her lipstick in a small hand mirror. 'How does she always manage to ruin everything?'

'Now now,' says Isabelle. 'I'm sure she didn't have a nervous break-down on purpose, just to spoil your day.'

'Huh. You could have fooled me.'

'Anyway, I think you should be very proud of Ben. He took control of everything quite wonderfully. He's a natural father.'

'He's a better father than she is a mother, that's for sure.' She clicks the compact shut, throws it into her tiny black handbag.

'Oh give her a chance, Mum. It can't be easy.'

'I just wish she'd let him in.'

'What, you mean do the decent thing and get married for the sake of the children? I'd have thought you'd seen enough of that sort of thing in your working life.'

Christine sighs. 'You're right. I just don't want Ben to be hurt. And I want the best for Felix.'

'I expect they'll muddle through somehow. We all do, don't we?'

Christine takes her daughter's hand. 'We do.'

The taxi is stuck behind a bus at Camden Town.

'So,' says Christine, 'will I do?'

'You'll do very nicely indeed. You look fantastic. I'm very proud of you, Mum.'

Christine opens her mouth to say something, stops, does a double take. In the end, all she can say is 'Well.'

'Well what?'

'Nothing.' She doesn't want to antagonise her daughter, not now they're getting on so well. 'I'm just . . . Pleased. Thank you.'

'I suppose this is where I should say that I'm sorry, isn't it?'

'We've all had our moments,' says Christine. 'Let's not dwell on it. Now is not the time for tearful scenes. I've just got my make-up right.'

The cab breaks through the traffic and hits a run of green lights through Bloomsbury and Holborn and down to the river. Big Ben is glinting in the spring sunshine.

'This is it, then,' says Christine, as the taxi pulls up outside the Palace of Westminster. 'Wish me luck.'

'You don't need it, Mum. You're fantastic.'

They are standing on the pavement, surrounded by the crowds in their suits and dresses, the hustle and bustle of kissing and embracing, cameras beeping and clicking, cars coming and going.

'Well, you're the best-dressed one here, that's for sure.'

'Thanks, darling, but look at the competition.' Christine picks a thread off the bodice of the gown, smooths the satin over her hips. 'What a shame I have to go and hide it all under a black gown and a dirty great horsehair wig.'

She unzips the long plastic carrier and slips the black silk off its hanger. It rustles softly. Isabelle catches it in her hands, feels the familiar slither of the fabric over her fingers.

'Oh, I don't know. I think it's quite a look. Forensic chic. Leave it to me, Mum. In a year's time, they'll all be wearing it.'

But it is time for Christine and Isabelle to go their separate ways, one to the gallery, the other to secret places known only to initiates. They grasp each other quickly in a hectic hug, and then Christine is gone. Isabelle watches as her mother disappears into the crowd, one black gown among the many.